DEAD
EVEN

Books by Annelise Ryan

The Helping Hands Mystery Series:

Needled to Death
Night Shift

The Mattie Winston Mystery Series:

Working Stiff
Scared Stiff
Frozen Stiff
Lucky Stiff
Board Stiff
Stiff Penalty
Stiff Competition
Dead in the Water
Dead Calm
Dead of Winter
Dead Ringer
Dead Even

The Mack's Bar Mystery Series by Allyson K. Abbott
(who also writes as Annelise Ryan):

Murder on the Rocks
Murder with a Twist
In the Drink
Shots in the Dark
A Toast to Murder
Last Call

DEAD
EVEN

ANNELISE RYAN

www.kensingtonbooks.com

KENSINGTON BOOKS are published by

Kensington Publishing Corp.
119 West 40th Street
New York, NY 10018

All Kensington Titles, Imprints, and Distributed Lines are available at special quantity discounts for bulk purchases for sales promotions, premiums, fund-raising, and educational or institutional use. Special book excerpts or customized printings can also be created to fit specific needs. For details, write or phone the office of the Kensington special sales manager: Kensington Publishing Corp., 119 West 40th Street, New York, NY 10018, attn: Special Sales Department, Phone: 1-800-221-2647.

Library of Congress Card Catalogue Number: 2020945428

ISBN-13: 978-1-4967-2257-7
ISBN-10: 1-4967-2257-4
First Kensington Hardcover Edition: April 2021

ISBN-13: 978-1-4967-2258-4 (ebook)
ISBN-10: 1-4967-2258-2 (ebook)

10 9 8 7 6 5 4 3 2 1

Printed in the United States of America

For Chrissy, Ja'neane & Billy

CHAPTER 1

Death is an unwelcome and relentless stalker in everyone's life. It comes when it wants, sometimes with warning, sometimes with stealth, disrupting all around it, stealing happiness, contentment . . . one's very breath. And sometimes, like today, it comes in a bizarre fashion so unpredictable and tragic as to seem completely random. Yet there is little natural randomness here. Based on what I was told when the call came in, this death was clearly planned, aided, and abetted by at least one of us mortals, though I suspect the planning portion lasted about as long as the hot-dog morsel my toddler son dropped on the floor for our dog, Hoover, at dinner a few hours ago.

Death is what I do. My name is Mattie Winston and I'm a medicolegal death investigator in the Wisconsin town of Sorenson. My job used to be forestalling death to the best of my ability. I worked as a nurse in the local hospital for the first thirteen years of my career, six in the ER and seven in the OR. But these days my job is to stalk death much the same way it stalks the denizens of the county I live in. I help determine how death arrived, whether it had any human or other help along the way, and if it did, who or what that might have been.

Apparently, death is a busy stalker tonight, because it's supposed to be my night off. But Christopher Malone, the person I job-share with, called and begged for help because he already has two other deaths to tend to out in the county. At least the call I'm on is relatively close, a home just beyond the outskirts of town and only a few miles from my own house. It's a large, sprawling ranch on several acres of land and set back from the road, accessed via a long driveway that splits off and circles around a fountain in front of the house on one side and leads to a three-car garage on the other. It's an isolated setting, the nearest neighbors on either side being a half mile or so away.

The façade on the house is stone and stained-wood siding, the windows are tall and arched, and outdoor lighting has been strategically placed to highlight an immaculate lawn, tasteful landscaping, and a utility shed that's bigger than the cottage I called home a few years ago. As I climb the stairs to the front porch, I'm serenaded by a chorus of crickets and cicadas. The smell of lilacs in bloom permeates the air and I know this will cause some pain for Hurley. He hates the smell of lilacs because they were his mother's favorite flower and there were tons of them at her funeral. He associates the smell of them with her death.

Inside the house, a uniformed officer points the way and says, "Room at the end of the hall." I follow his directions, taking in the open living room and kitchen as I walk through. Judging from the high-end finishes and state-of-the-art kitchen, the people who live here clearly have money. I walk down a hallway and pass another uniformed officer, Brenda Joiner, and a woman who is leaning against the wall, her head hung down, long black hair obscuring her face.

"I'll be with you in a minute," I say, and Brenda nods. The

woman with her doesn't move. I open the door to the room at the end of the hall and go inside, closing the door behind me.

When I reach the dead man, slumped onto the floor, back against a wall, feet splayed out in front of him, I can't help but think that life is the one thing money can't buy. I recognize the victim, not because I know him, per se, but because I know of him. His name is Montgomery Dixon and he's a well-known, highly successful real estate agent here in Sorenson. I've seen his FOR SALE signs all around town for years, all of them featuring his picture in one corner. He also advertises in the local rag all the time, again with his picture plastered on every ad.

My recognition of him won't serve as an official identification—that will require family identification, a comparison to his DMV photo, and, if they are on file, a comparison of his fingerprints, or perhaps dental records. But all of that will be mere routine because anyone living in or near Sorenson will know the man when they see him, even with his face altered by the flaccid, almost plastic mask of death he wears now. He's a handsome man, even in death, with a full head of brown hair, brown eyes, and cherubic cheeks. Though they aren't visible now, I know he has dimples in each of his cheeks. I'm not sure of his age at this point, but I'd guess somewhere in his mid-to-late forties.

In some ways, this scenario resembles other unexpected deaths I've seen. There is an odd look of surprise on the man's face, something I've witnessed many times before in sudden death victims. If not for two things, I might think his death was from something like a major heart attack or the rupture of an artery inside his brain, causes that have left that look of surprise on the faces of other victims. One telltale sign that this is not the case is the darkening pool of blood spreading out around him. Trails of it have run down his T-shirt, pooled in the lap of his sweatpants, oozed over his hips, and seeped down into the cracks of the hardwood floor.

The other clue that this was not a natural death is the broken shaft of a pool cue protruding from the man's chest near the area of his heart. I've seen people die a lot of different ways, but death by cue stick is a new one.

I set down my scene kit, open it, and remove a small video camera. A cursory exam of the victim is enough to tell me that there is no need for the EMTs, though I wonder if they were here already and left, or if they were never called.

"Devo," I say to the uniformed officer standing guard near the door to the room. "Was EMS called?"

Devo, better known as Officer Patrick Devonshire, is busy looking at something on his phone. His distraction annoys me—we've become a society of downward-looking, phone-obsessed people—but in his case, it's a necessary evil. Devo doesn't do well with blood, guts, decay, or any of the other fun things my job may entail. If he sees or smells any of these for any length of time, the odds of him barfing on my crime scene are better than good. The phone is his way of keeping his mind otherwise occupied and his stomach contents where they belong. He barely looked at me when I entered the room a few moments ago, and now he answers my question without taking his eyes from his phone.

"They were called. A guy came in and checked the vic for a pulse, shined a light in his eyes, and then said he was fixed, dilated, and already cold. Then he stated the time and left. That was at ten twenty-eight."

"Only one EMT?"

"There were two of them, but only one touched the guy."

"You got their names?"

"Of course," Devo says with a hint of indignation.

"Where did the EMT touch him to check for a pulse?"

"On his neck," Devo says. "Right side," he adds, anticipating my next question and making me smile.

"And did he have to lift the victim's eyelids?"

"Nope. Poor guy's been staring wide-eyed like that the whole time."

I make a mental note of all of this because it's possible the EMTs might have left trace evidence behind, and then I shoot a quick video of the body where it is. The narrow end of the cue stick, about three feet of it, is on the floor beside the victim's left foot. Where it was broken from the rest of the shaft, there are sharp, jagged shards of wood. The broken end of the remaining, thicker portion of the stick—the weapon of choice—is embedded in the man's chest.

A scan of the rest of the room reveals two beer bottles on a side console table—one empty, one with a small amount left in the bottom—a second cue stick atop the red-felted pool table, five pool balls on the table's surface, including the cue ball, and the remaining balls in a tray at one end of the table. I get all of this on camera thinking that between the balls, the cue sticks, and the beer bottles, there should be a wealth of fingerprint and DNA evidence.

Three walls of the room are covered with framed photos, the fourth wall holds a cue stick rack next to the door with four sticks in it and two empty slots. I walk around and study the pictures, all of which have been taken here in this room with the pool table in the background. They all feature Montgomery Dixon and one or two other people, most of whom are also recognizable because they are members of the rich-and-famous elite. There are pictures of Montgomery with governors—current and past—and other politicians, including a high-ranking and well-known senator. There are pictures of him with a famous hotel magnate; with a B-level movie star, who owns a vacation home not far from here; with a well-respected movie producer; and with some less famous, more local dignitaries, such as the mayor of Sorenson, a couple of doctors I know, and a local artist, who recently earned national acclaim with his unique sculptures. Clearly,

Montgomery Dixon rubbed elbows with some very powerful, wealthy, and important people.

I set my camera aside, pull on a pair of gloves, and then do a cursory exam of my victim. His skin is cold to the touch and the flesh on his jaw and neck is stiffening, indicating he's been dead for a couple of hours. I glance at my watch and a quick mental calculation gives me a rough estimate of his actual time of death being between eight and nine p.m., as opposed to the one declared by the EMTs. I note a shiny substance on the left side of Montgomery's neck, which puzzles me, and I get a swab sample of it. Next I set out a thermometer to get an ambient room temperature and then I carefully lift the lower right hem of Monty's shirt and insert a second thermometer through his skin and into his liver. While the thermometers do their thing, I examine the hands and secure paper bags around them. By then, my temperature readings are ready and I record them in my notebook, noting that they also support a time of death that is around two hours before the time the EMT noted.

With that done, I abandon my victim for the moment, shuck my gloves and bag them, grab both my still and video cameras, and venture back out into the hallway, leaving Devo in the room. Brenda and the woman are still standing in the hallway, though now the woman is looking at me, allowing me a better look at her. She has a slender build, shoulder-length black hair, large green eyes, and a near-perfect manicure, though judging from the way she's gnawing away at the side of her thumbnail, it won't be perfect for long. I see resignation on her face and something else . . . fear perhaps?

"Hello again," I say, standing before the woman and smiling. "You are Mrs. Dixon, correct?"

She nods. Her eyes are red-rimmed, but currently dry. "Please call me Summer," she says, a statement that strikes me as oddly social for the occasion.

"And that is your husband, Montgomery, in there?" I say, nodding toward the room I just left.

"Monty," she says in a dull voice. "Everyone calls him Monty. He hates the name Montgomery." She pauses and lets out a nervous titter. "Though I don't suppose it will bother him much now, will it?"

I give her a wan smile. "I'm very sorry for your loss," I say. "I'm sure this must be quite a shock to you."

She says nothing, looking away from me and down the hallway as if she's planning her imminent escape.

"My name is Mattie Winston. I'm a medicolegal death investigator here in Sorenson. I work with the police and my boss, Dr. Izzy Rybarceski, the medical examiner. Our job is to figure out what happened to Monty."

"That's rather obvious, isn't it?" Summer tuts impatiently. She rolls her eyes, looks longingly at the cigarettes and lighter she is clutching in one hand, and then shows them to me. "Do you mind?" she asks in a pleading tone.

I do mind, but it's her house and, technically, I don't have the right to tell her no. But I do have a plan to forestall her. "I don't want to do anything here in the house that might potentially compromise evidence," I tell her. I turn to Officer Joiner. "Brenda, would you run out to my car and grab an evidence pack and a scrub suit from the back? They're stored in the right wheel-well area."

Brenda nods and disappears. I turn my attention back to Summer Dixon.

"There will be a detective arriving here soon who will need to talk with you. But before that happens, I need to gather some items from you as part of our investigation."

"What items?"

"Well, the clothes you're wearing, for one. I know it's a bit awkward, but it's very routine in cases like this. There might be evidence on the clothing of anyone who has had contact with the crime scene or the victim."

Summer looks righteously offended. "Are you suggesting that I killed Monty?"

"No, I'm not. But your presence here has exposed you to the crime scene. Evidence can be easily transferred at times, and you'd be surprised what we can pick up from the clothing of people who are present. We had one case where a cat hair transferred to the clothing of a family member, even though there were no cats in the house. Turned out that cat hair was left behind by the killer and got attached to the family member's clothing. It helped us solve the case, but if all we'd focused on was the evidence immediately on and around the victim, that bit of evidence might have been overlooked and a killer would have gotten away with it."

This story isn't totally true. It did happen, just not to me. It's something I saw on a true-crime show I watched on TV, but Summer doesn't need to know this. All she needs to know, or rather believe, is that my reason for wanting to collect her clothes isn't necessarily related to any suspicions I have toward her. I do have suspicions, of course. As the spouse of the victim, odds are high that she is the culprit based on statistics alone.

"So you need me to go and change into something else?" Summer asks. There is an eagerness to both her voice and her expression that puzzles me for a second. Then I realize she likely sees it as an opportunity to sneak in a smoke.

"I will need you to change, but not into any of your own clothes. Officer Joiner is getting some paper scrubs you can put on."

This earns me a pout. "Can't I just put on my own clothes?" she whines.

"I'm afraid not." I give her an apologetic look, even though I don't feel particularly empathetic toward her at this point. There is something off about this woman. "We need to search the house for evidence and that includes the rest of your clothing. Until that's done, I'm afraid it's all off-limits."

Summer's pout deepens, and when she opens her mouth, I sense another objection coming. I quickly head it off by giving her a new annoyance to focus on. "Do you have somewhere you can stay for the next few days?"

It doesn't take her long. Her jaw drops, and her tone shifts from whiny to plain old irritation mixed with disbelief. "Are you telling me I can't stay in my own house?"

"I am. For a few days anyway. For now, your house is a crime scene we need to process, and that means limiting access to it. Hopefully, it won't be for very long."

Summer rolls her eyes again and huffs irritably. "Unbelievable," she mutters under her breath. She is squeezing the life out of that pack of smokes, enough that I'd be surprised if any of them are still intact.

I hear the front door open and close and Brenda appears at the end of the hallway. "I saw a guest bathroom out in the main living area," I say to Summer. "We can do this in there."

"Whatever," she says irritably, pushing away from the wall. "Let's get it over with."

She walks with quick purpose down the hall, across the main living area, and into the bathroom. Brenda and I follow her. As guest bathrooms go, this one is generous in size, but it's still cozy with three of us in this one small room, once I shut the door. I slip my still camera into my pocket and set the video camera on the counter area around the sink. I don a fresh pair of gloves, hand a pair to Brenda, and then open the evidence kit Brenda brought in with her. Brenda opens the plastic-wrapped paper scrubs while I remove a folded square of paper resting atop the other items in the evidence kit and unfold it. When I'm done, I place the three-foot-square sheet on the floor and tell Summer to stand at the center of it. She does so, and I then remove a folded paper bag from the evidence kit and open it.

"Drop your cigarettes and lighter in here, please," I tell her. She gives me a look of smug disappointment, one that makes me think she has another pack stashed somewhere. She drops the items into the bag, and I grab another one.

"Please remove your shoes and place them in here," I say.

She quickly steps out of the shoes—cute black ankle boots with three-inch spike heels and bright red soles—with a huff of annoyance. She bends over to pick them up and drops them in the bag. "I better get those back," she says with a hint of threat and indignation. "They're Louboutins and they set me back more than eight hundred bucks at Nordstrom."

Her comment triggers a flash of jealousy and irritation in me. I can't imagine spending that much money on a pair of shoes, and even if I could, I'd never be able to wear them. My feet are a size twelve, double-E width, and expensive, fashionable designer shoes don't come in Sasquatch sizes. Plus, I'm six feet tall in my stocking feet. Put me in a pair of spike heels and I'd be subject to jokes about Amazonian women and thin air all night long.

I focus on her perfectly manicured toes, polished in a shade of red that looks like the one my stylist, Barbara, once showed me that's called Charged Up Cherry. We laughed over several of the polish color names during one of my earlier appointments with her, back when her "salon" still made me nervous. It helped to break the tension for me. I should probably tell you at this point that most of Barbara's customers are dead and her salon is in the basement of a local funeral home. She started out as a mortuary cosmetologist—someone who does makeup for the dead—but then received specialized training in facial reconstructions. Since Barbara can put Humpty Dumpty back together again, I suppose it's no surprise that she manages to make me look as good as she does. I've been going to her for nearly four years now. She serves her living clientele in the same place where she takes care of the dead ones, and does her best work on you when you're lying down. The creep factor of this got to me a little in the beginning, and that's how we ended up laughing at nail polish names, including the Silent Mauvie shade she was applying to a deceased woman that day, something that in my nervous state struck me as hilariously appropriate. These days, I consider it no big deal to lie down among the dead to get beautiful, but I can't deny that Barbara has been an acquired taste for me.

My Barbara flashbacks allow me to swallow down my irritation, so I open another bag and have Summer remove her slacks and place them in it. She does so without complaint and next she removes the nylon knee-highs she is wearing. When I ask her to take off her underwear for the next bag, she balks.

"Why on earth do you need my underwear?"

"Please, Mrs. Dixon," I say in my best calm voice. "This is awkward for all of us, but it has to be done."

Her lips thin to a barely visible line and she removes her panties with such vigor I half expect to find them ripped later. As soon as she drops them in the bag, I grab another one and we repeat the process with her blouse and then her bra. Once she is naked, Brenda hands her the paper scrubs, which she pulls on with prideful nonchalance, as if trying now to convince us that her nakedness is no big deal. Her body is trim and taut, and if I had a build like hers, I might take my time and show off my body, too. But I have a build that an ER patient I once cared for referred to as that of a "sturdy girl."

As Summer fidgets with the paper scrubs, I notice something. There is a sheen on her hands, and she is leaving faint, oily stains on the paper scrubs wherever she touches them. I take out an evidence swab and run it over both of her palms and in between her fingers.

"What's that for?" she asks.

"There's some sort of oily substance here," I point out.

Summer stares down at her hands, turning them over a couple of times. "Right," she says, nodding slowly. "Olive oil, I imagine. I attended a cooking class this evening. That's where I was when . . ." She doesn't finish the sentence, but she doesn't need to.

"There also appears to be a small puncture wound on your right palm," I say, swabbing that as well. "I need to take a picture of it."

Once again, Summer stares at her hands, focusing on the palm of the right one as I take my camera from my pocket and prepare for the shot. Once I've taken several pictures of the wound from different angles, I slip the camera back into my pocket and then take the small brush that's in the evidence kit and hand it to Summer. "Run this through your hair, please," I tell her. She does so impatiently, and when she's done, I have her drop it into a bag. Then I pick up the video camera and hand it to Officer Joiner.

"You can step out now," I tell Summer.

"You didn't make some kind of movie of me naked, did you?" Summer asks, eyeing the video camera.

I can't tell if she's concerned or titillated at the prospect.

"No," I assure her. "I just brought it in with me because I want Officer Joiner to have it when you leave this room. She's going to record your interview with the detective on the case."

Brenda opens the bathroom door and Summer walks out. Brenda follows and I fold up the sheet of paper Summer was standing on, making sure the upper surface is all to the inside, and bag it. I quickly seal and label all the bags I've collected, and when I'm done, I carry them out to the living room and set them on the floor along one wall. Summer and Brenda have settled onto stools at the large granite-topped island that separates the kitchen from the living area, and I join them.

Summer is leaning forward, elbows on the countertop, face buried in her hands. I'm about to say something when I hear the front door to the house open and the man who walks in makes my heart skip a beat.

CHAPTER 2

My husband, Steve Hurley, emerges from the foyer and steps into the great room. In addition to being my husband, Hurley is also a homicide detective here in town. I knew he was coming here because we were at home together when the call came in, though Hurley had just arrived mere minutes before after spending the evening at the police station. The other homicide detective in town, Bob Richmond, had been called out to assist on one of the county deaths, along with Christopher, because the sheriff's department had more than it could handle alone. This sort of cross-jurisdictional aid is common in rural areas, and our office has been responding to calls in the county for over a year now, part of a plan to channel all the autopsies and suspicious deaths through us at the medical examiner's office. It's a move in the right direction, but staffing is always a challenge. So, while my husband understood the need to step up on his night off, he, like me, was none too happy about it, even though we both understand it's the nature of our work.

We have two kids and, normally, when we're both on call and need to go out, my seventeen-year-old stepdaughter, Emily—Hurley's daughter from a previous relationship—

babysits for our toddler son, Matthew, who is almost three. But as luck would have it, it's a Saturday night and Emily is out on a date with her longtime boyfriend, Johnny Chester. That meant we would have to wait for my sister, Desi, to come over, since it was after ten and Matthew was already in bed for the night.

Hurley and I considered doing rock-paper-scissors to see who would go right away and who would wait—since the site was secured by our own police officers, it didn't matter as long as one of us got there reasonably soon—but in the end, Hurley said he wanted to be the one to go second. He hadn't had any dinner and he wanted to grab something quick and easy, like a sandwich, while waiting for Desi to arrive. Most of the time, we take Matthew to Desi's house for babysitting needs outside of regular work hours, but Desi has always insisted that she come to us if Matthew is already down for the night rather than wake him up and drag him out. She says it's healthier for the kid this way, though I suspect she has an ulterior motive. Matthew doesn't wake up happy, and once he's up, it's hard to get him back to sleep. I'm sure the short drive to our house at any hour is less of a hassle than dealing with a cranky, fussy kid.

I'm glad Hurley is finally here. He walks up to Brenda, Summer, and me in his slow, gangly way, quickly sizing up the scene before him. He moves in on Summer's right side, and she raises her head to check him out.

"This is Mrs. Summer Dixon," I tell Hurley. "She's the wife of our victim."

"Hello, Mrs. Dixon," Hurley says in his deep, soothing voice. "I'm Detective Steve Hurley and I'm here to try to determine what happened to your husband. I'm sure this must be a huge shock for you."

I watch Summer's head go up and then down as she eyes Hurley from the top of his head to the bottom of his shoes. I can't see the expression on her face, because her back is to me, but I can imagine what it looks like. I've seen it dozens of times on the faces of other women who meet Hurley for the first time. Or the second time. Or the bazillionth. Hurley makes quite an impression with his tall, lean build, thick black hair, and cornflower-blue eyes. He gives Summer a hesitant smile and I know I'm right about her reaction to him. Hurley has that pleased, but slightly uncomfortable, look he always gets when he's ogled by a woman. Unless I'm the one doing the ogling—then his expression is altogether different.

Hurley and I don't try to hide the fact that we're a married couple, but we don't advertise it, either. And the fact that we have different last names—a bit of a thorn in Hurley's side, if truth be told, since Winston is the last name of my ex—helps obscure the situation. I'm often amused by other women's reactions to Hurley when they don't know I'm his wife. Though I have a feeling that Summer's reaction would be the same regardless.

"Please call me Summer," she says in a breathy voice. Then she turns in her seat, facing forward, and assumes a beleaguered posture and tone. "Can we just get on with it?" she whines, massaging her temples. "Do what you have to do and let's get this circus over with. Please."

Hurley and I exchange looks over Summer's head, both of us taken aback by Summer's response, as if this is some annoying task that she wants out of the way.

"I will do my best," Hurley says. "First I need to go and examine your husband." He gives me a questioning look and I point down the hallway toward the game room. "I'll be right back, Summer," he says in his most soothing voice.

As he takes off toward the game room, Summer turns and sneaks a peek at his retreating form. I gather she approves, if the beatific expression on her face is any indication. I should probably be annoyed, but I agree with her. Hurley's backside is mighty fine-looking.

Once Hurley is out of sight, Summer goes back to staring

at the countertop in front of her and massaging her temples. I spare a second to more closely admire the Dixons' kitchen, which is huge and Spic and Span clean, gleaming with stainless-steel appliances, lustrous granite on all the counters, glossy white cupboards, and strategically placed lighting. It's a chef's kitchen based on the large stove, double ovens, and prep sink area built into the island, and I wonder who the cook in the family is. I suppose it's Summer, since she told me she went to a cooking class earlier this evening. Or maybe she and Monty both like to cook.

Making a sweeping gesture of the room with one arm, I give Brenda Joiner a look and she nods, turns on the camera, and does a quick panoramic shot of the area before aiming the camera at Summer. I slide onto the stool beside Summer, sitting sideways so I can face her. I don't want to ask her any questions until Hurley comes back, but the silence surrounding us is deafening.

"Is there anything I can get for you, Summer?" I say, placing a hand on her arm. "A glass of water, perhaps?"

She shakes her head, keeping it sandwiched between her hands, fingers massaging those temples. "Just a bit of a headache," she says.

"Your kitchen is lovely," I say. "It looks like it belongs in a magazine photo."

"It was featured in some Wisconsin magazine a couple of years ago," she says, finally lifting her head and looking around the room. "Not sure why we have such an elaborate cook's kitchen, since the only person who ever uses it is Damien."

"Who is Damien?"

"He's our chef. He comes every day, except Sundays, and prepares a day's worth of meals for us."

I'm admittedly jealous. The only thing I can cook with the promise of any reliable outcome is hot dogs and boxed macaroni and cheese, Matthew's favorite meal. "I thought you said you were at a cooking class tonight," I say.

"What?" she says, squinting like she has a headache. "Oh, right. I'm trying to learn." She grimaces and shifts her position.

Hurley returns from the game room, walks around to the other side of the island, and stands there, facing Summer and me. He removes a small notebook from his jacket pocket and flips it open. Then he digs in the pocket again and comes up with a pen.

We hear the front door open and everyone, except Summer, turns to look. This time, it's Jonas Kriedeman, the police department's evidence tech, and he's carrying two very large suitcases that contain the tricks of his trade. We point down the hall toward the game room and he nods his understanding before heading in that direction.

I start things off, figuring I can give Hurley something of a lowdown with a few key questions. "You said you were the one who found your husband?" I say, turning my attention back to Summer, making it sound like a question in the hope that she'll elaborate. But all she does is nod.

"Can you tell us about it?" I prompt, thinking this is going to be a long one. But Summer proves me wrong. She raises her head, looks at me, and spills her guts.

"I came home from . . . that cooking class, and when I didn't find Monty in the TV room, I called out to him. He didn't answer and I thought at first that he might have gone to bed early. But he wasn't in the bedroom, either, so I kept looking until I found him in the poolroom there."

"This was what time?" I ask.

"I called the police right away, so it would have been right before that. I used the landline there." She nods in Hurley's direction. "Check the history on it. It should show the call." Hurley looks around, sees the landline phone on the counter behind him lying in front of its charging station. He picks it up, pushes a few buttons, and then says, "Looks like you called 911 at ten-eighteen." Hurley sets the phone down on the island and jots this information into his notepad.

"That jibes with what Devo told me," I say. "EMS arrived and immediately pronounced at ten twenty-eight."

Hurley nods and writes some more.

"Why did you come all the way out here to call?" I ask Summer.

"Because that's where the phone is," Summer says with a tone one might use on a two-year-old. "There isn't one in the game room."

"You don't have a cell phone?"

"I do, but it was in my purse, and my purse was in the living room. I dropped it on the couch when I came in."

Reasonable answers and I nod accordingly.

"Did your husband have plans to entertain someone this evening?" Hurley asks.

"I have no idea," Summer says. "He doesn't typically share his schedule with me."

I sense something, an undercurrent beneath her words. "Why is that?" I ask.

She casts an impatient look toward me and then rolls her eyes. No wonder the woman has a headache. Her eyes roll more than the dice at a casino. "Our relationship has been a bit tense of late," she says. "Things haven't been ideal between us for a while now."

I pause for a beat, and then in a friendly tone, I say, "Marriage can be quite the challenge at times, can't it?" She casts another glance my way, this one more curious. "I'm going through some things in my own marriage," I tell her. "We're in counseling."

Hurley raises his eyebrows at me. We prefer to keep our relationship out of the equation as much as possible, and now I've just tossed it right into the middle of things like a lit stick of dynamite.

"Is it helping?" Summer asks. Before I can answer, she holds up both her hands as if she's warding off an attack and shudders. "Never mind. It's none of my business, and it's not like it matters for me anymore anyway. My marriage is well beyond anything a counselor can help with now, isn't it?" She gives me an ironic but painful smile before returning to her head-massaging position.

There is a hitch in her breathing that sounds like a stifled sob and I'm tempted to reach over and put a hand on her shoulder. But I don't. Something tells me she wouldn't like it and I trust my instincts. One thing my career in nursing taught me was to trust my gut. It rarely lets me down.

Hurley says, "What does your husband do for a living?"

"He sells real estate."

I gather Hurley asked this question as a matter of routine, since it's hard to go anywhere in Sorenson without seeing Monty Dixon's name plastered all over billboards around town.

"Does he have a home office?" Hurley asks.

Summer nods. "Down there," she says, pointing off to her right, where another hallway branches off the great room. "In the back wing."

"Does your husband often entertain guests or clients here at the house?" Hurley asks.

Summer shrugs. "Yeah, I guess. Like I said, he doesn't keep me apprised of his plans."

"So you have no idea who might have been here tonight?"

Summer gives him a tired shake of her head.

Hurley shifts gears a little. "Did you touch your husband at all when you found him?"

Summer doesn't answer right away, but I see her take hold of the fingers on her right hand with her left. A tiny shudder runs through her. "I checked on his neck for a pulse," she says finally. "I didn't find one and he felt and looked . . . well, dead, so I called for help."

"Summer has a wound that looks like a puncture on her right palm," I say to Hurley. "And some kind of oily substance on her hands that she thinks might be olive oil."

Summer separates her hands and holds them out, palms up, for display.

"That wound looks fresh," Hurley observes. "How did it happen?"

A hint of a smile turns up the corners of Summer's mouth. "It was during the cooking class I attended tonight. We were doing a London broil and I accidentally stabbed myself with a meat fork."

Hardly an amusing event, unless Summer is one of those people who gets off on pain.

"Where was this cooking class?" Hurley asks.

Summer names Cut the Cheese, a kitchen supply store in town that regularly offers such classes. I've been tempted to attend a few of them myself, though I haven't yet managed to find the time to follow through on the idea. Hurley jots down the name of the store in his notebook so he can check out the information later.

"Do you know of anyone who would want your husband dead?" Hurley asks. "Or anyone who has recently had any run-ins with him?"

Summer scoffs. "Well, you can start with that ne'er-do-well son of his, Sawyer. Ever since he moved in here, things have been rather tense. I think his mother was glad to see him go, especially since she's no longer getting the child support money Monty's paid out over the years." There is a hint of bitterness in Summer's voice. "Sawyer lives here rent-free, and despite that, he seems to think his father owes him a leisurely and wealthy lifestyle."

"Sawyer isn't your son?" Hurley asks.

Summer shakes her head. "God, no. That brat is the offspring from Monty's first marriage to a woman named Linda Shoop."

"Does Ms. Shoop live near here?" Hurley asks.

Summer shakes her head again. "No, she lives up north, just outside of Bayfield. Between all the child support money she collected over the years, she's managed to buy herself a house on the shore of Lake Superior. Quite the nice little racket, wouldn't you say?" There's more than a hint of bitterness in her voice now.

"This house is quite lovely, too," I say. "Monty must be doing very well in his business."

Summer shrugs. "I don't know, to be honest. He handles all the money and the bills. I guess he does well enough, because I've never been told we need to cut back or felt like we didn't have enough. At least not until the devil spawn moved in."

"Where is Sawyer now?" I ask.

Summer shrugs again. "Don't know, don't care. He does whatever he wants, comes and goes whenever he wants." She bows her head, but looks up at Hurley through her lashes. I imagine she's trying to look coy or coquettish, but the result is more along the demented spectrum. "I'll tell you something about Sawyer," she says, her tone hinting at great secrets about to be divulged. "I overheard him on the phone once, telling someone that he couldn't wait for his old man to kick the bucket so he could inherit some money."

Hurley scribbles in his notebook, while I remain silent. Summer, still employing her demented look, waits for a reaction. When she doesn't get one, she pouts and lets out a huff of irritation, folding her arms over her chest and abandoning her attempts to look coy.

"Was Sawyer here when you left for your cooking class?" Hurley asks.

"He sure was," Summer says bitterly. "He and Monty were going at it, arguing about money for the hundredth time."

"What time was that?"

"Around six-thirty, maybe six-forty."

"How long have you and Monty been married?" I ask, curious as to how long it took to grow this level of animosity and bitterness.

"Ten years."

"Your first marriage?" I probe, half expecting her to get angry with me for asking such personal questions.

She nods.

"No children of your own?"

She shakes her head and I see something flit across her face . . . regret? Remorse?

"You didn't want any children?" I ask, pushing a little deeper. I see Hurley give me a warning look.

"We tried," Summer says, no emotion in her voice. "It wasn't meant to be."

"Do you have contact information for Sawyer?" Hurley asks. "Like a cell phone number?"

Summer slides her cell phone across the island toward him. "It's in there, in my contacts."

"Does Sawyer have his own car?" I ask as Hurley snatches the cell phone. He gives Brenda a sideways nod of his head and she moves closer to him, video camera still rolling.

Summer scoffs at my question, but this time there's less energy behind it. "He sure does," she says wearily. "Daddy dearest bought him a brand-new car last year, thinking that might satisfy the greed in him, but all it did was make him want more." She manages a woeful shake of her head before once again burying her face in her hands.

Hurley is thumbing through the contacts and recent phone calls in Summer's phone as Brenda films the screen display. This is a major coup to have information on a potential suspect offered up like this without objection or subpoena, and I'm surprised Summer has allowed it.

Lady Luck doesn't hang with us for long, though. The front door opens with a loud bang and we all turn to see who the new arrival is. The officer stationed outside looks surprised and it's not hard to see why. A man dressed in khaki slacks, a long-sleeved sweatshirt, and athletic shoes steps over the threshold. There is a collective gasp from everyone, except Summer, as our dead man, Monty Dixon, walks in.

CHAPTER 3

I'm so stunned that I hop off my stool and take a few steps toward the game room, as if my brain is urging me to go there and verify what I think I saw a short time ago.

The new arrival stops me as he bellows, "What the hell is going on here?" His gaze falls on Summer and he looks peeved, his shoulders sagging. "Aw, hell, Summer, you haven't been talking to the cops, have you?"

"Who are you?" Hurley asks before Summer can answer.

I hold my breath, as I'm afraid to hear this man's answer.

"I'm Summer's lawyer," he snaps back, and I can't tell if he's being purposely vague just to annoy us or if that's how he always identifies himself.

Before he can elaborate further, Summer says, "Folks, meet Harrison Dixon, Monty's twin brother."

I feel a modicum of relief, but it doesn't last long. It's not Monty; it's his twin, his identical twin, no less. But his existence complicates our tentative ID of the victim. Hopefully, there will be fingerprints on file somewhere for one or both brothers, as this is the one thing that is different in identical twins, though sometimes the differences can be so slight as to be useless. Another option is to review the medical records to look for specific scars that one twin has, and the other doesn't. The primary things we use for identification—DNA, photos, and third-party identification—aren't going to help here. Dental records might help, and the thought makes me focus on Harrison's teeth, where I see an immediate and obvious difference between him and his brother. Harrison has a space between his two front teeth. Monty doesn't.

My thoughts are interrupted by Harrison's demands. "I insist you stop talking to these people right now, Summer," he says. Then he pins Hurley with his gaze. "Where is my brother?" He looks around frantically, like he thinks we might have Monty's body stashed in a corner of the room somewhere. "Where's Monty?"

From where I am, I see Devo plant himself in the middle of the doorway to the game room at the end of the hall, no doubt because he heard the ruckus. He shuts the door behind him and stands in front of it. Fortunately, he has abandoned his phone, at least for now.

"Mr. Dixon," Hurley begins, but Harrison has seen Devo, too, and he bolts toward the game room. Brenda sets the video camera down and goes after him. Hurley slides Summer's cell phone across the counter toward her and does the same.

I brace myself in anticipation of Devo getting run over by Harrison, who has several inches and about forty pounds to his advantage. But if Devo is worried, it doesn't show on his face. He spreads his legs a bit, plants his feet firmly, and stretches one arm out in front of him, palm facing Harrison. Then, in a deep voice I've never heard from Devo before, he says, "Stop! Sir! Now!"

Amazingly, Harrison screeches to a halt right in front of Devo, inches away from that outstretched palm. Looking like he wants to cry, Harrison turns around and looks at Hurley, who has also skidded to a halt with Brenda beside him.

"I need to see my brother," Harrison says.

Hurley, looking genuinely sympathetic, says, "I'm sorry, sir, but I can't allow that."

I expect Harrison to object, but his shoulders slump, his face sags, and he steps to one side and leans against the wall. "I can't believe he's gone," he says woefully.

I walk down the hall toward the others. "Mr. Dixon," I say, "I'm very sorry for your loss."

He nods, his face buried in his hands. There is dampness seeping between his fingers and that makes me think he's crying. If so, he's the first person to shed a tear for the dead man.

I walk over and put a hand on his shoulder. "May I ask how you found out about your brother?"

Before Harrison can answer, Hurley does. "Summer called him. I saw the name and number in her cell under recent calls. It was at . . ." He pauses and consults his notebook. "Ten thirty-five."

With this tidbit of information, Harrison drops his hands, revealing that I was right about his tears. He gapes down the hall at Summer and makes a little sucking noise with his tongue on the space between his teeth. "You gave them your cell phone?" he says to Summer. "Are you nuts, woman?"

Summer, who is still sitting on her stool, finally smoking that cigarette she's been craving, shrugs. "I've got nothing to hide," she says.

I have no idea where she got the cigarette from, or even when, but it had to have been in the last minute or so when I moved down to this end of the hallway. Did she have stashes around the house?

"Why bother to call me and ask for my advice if you're not going to follow it?" Harrison asks her, clearly annoyed. "I can't be held responsible for whatever happens to you now." He swipes his palms together a couple of times in a clear *I wash my hands of you* gesture.

In an apparent attempt to take charge of this somewhat unruly group, Hurley says, "Mr. Dixon, why don't we go back out to the kitchen. I need to ask you some questions."

Harrison sighs, wipes the tears from his cheeks, and pushes himself away from the wall. Like a kid who's just been chastised and told to go stand in the corner, he shuffles toward the kitchen, head hanging low, shoulders slumped. He walks up to the stool on Summer's left and slides onto it.

Hurley's frowning and looking around the great-room area. I know what he's thinking. He wants to talk to these people, but he needs to do it privately, not all together. He also needs to have a look around the house. It's a crime scene. I rack my brain trying to think of a solution and then the situation worsens. The front door opens and someone new walks into the house. This time, it's a young man about five-eight with slicked-back brown hair, large hazel-colored eyes, and a persistent case of teenage acne that has stalked him into what I figure is his early twenties. He walks up to all of us in the kitchen and blinks hard several times.

"What the hell is going on?" he asks. "Who are you people?"

"This would be Sawyer," Summer says in a world-weary voice.

Sawyer zeroes in on Brenda Joiner, who has zeroed in on him with the video camera. "Get that thing off me," he snaps. "I didn't give you permission to film me."

Brenda keeps the camera aimed at him.

Hurley says, "You are Sawyer Dixon?"

"Who wants to know?" Sawyer asks belligerently.

"I'm Detective Steve Hurley with the Sorenson Police Department."

"*Detective?*" Sawyer says with a sarcastic snort. He shifts his gaze toward his stepmother. "What did you do now, Summer?"

Summer raises her head long enough to give me a pained look. "See what I mean? Quite the charmer, isn't he?"

Clearly, no one has bothered to share the news of his father's death with Sawyer. Things are about to get sticky.

"Mr. Dixon, I'm afraid we have some bad news," Hurley says.

The first crack appears in Sawyer's veneer as he looks at all of us and registers the person who isn't there. "Where's my father?" He walks behind the island, as if he expects to find the man hiding there.

The door to the game room has been reopened so Devo could go back in, and he and Jonas are talking. Sawyer hears the low murmur of voices emanating from that direction and starts to head that way. He doesn't get far before Hurley steps in front of him, blocking his way.

"Why don't you have a seat on the couch," Hurley says, nodding toward the living-room area.

Sawyer looks like he's about to say no, but then he seems to think better of it. Still, he can't resist one tiny show of independence and, with a smug look, he turns around and heads for the stools where Summer and Harrison are sitting, sliding onto the one to the right of Summer.

Hurley walks up on the other side of him and, with uncharacteristic bluntness, says, "I'm sorry to have to tell you this, but your father is dead."

The delivery is harsh—I suspect this is because of Sawyer's refusal to do what Hurley asked of him. Judging from the smug smile Sawyer had aimed in Summer's direction a moment ago, I gather he thought she was the reason the police were here and that her imminent arrest or some other embarrassing event was about to happen. As he digests what Hurley just told him, his skin pales, making those pimples stand out even more, and his expression goes blank. He stares at Hurley unblinking, not reacting, for an amazing amount of time. I start to wonder if he's become catatonic. Granted, Hurley delivered the news with less than his usual amount of prep and tact—he's typically gentler with this kind of thing— but I suspect he's trying to get a reaction from the guy. If so, I imagine he's disappointed.

"Dead how?" Sawyer finally manages to ask.

"Someone killed him." Hurley tosses it out there with no empathy in his voice.

"What? Wait. You mean he was murdered?" Sawyer says as things start to sink in. "Where? How? When?"

I notice he didn't ask "who."

"Where have you been this evening?" Hurley asks.

Sawyer looks scared. His eyes dart back and forth, and I can tell he's replaying some scenario in his head. "Why?" he asks, jutting a provocative chin toward Hurley. "You think I had something to do with it?"

"Did you?" Hurley asks calmly.

Sawyer gapes at him with disbelief. "Man, are you seriously asking me if I killed my own father?"

"I would advise you to keep your mouth shut," Harrison says.

"Please tell me where you've been this evening," Hurley says again.

Sawyer scowls at him. "I've been out driving around, doing some thinking." At this, Harrison closes his eyes and shakes his head dolefully.

"Driving where?" Hurley pushes.

"Wherever," Sawyer says with a shrug. "Just driving. I like doing that. It helps me think."

"Is there anyone who can verify where you were and what you were doing?" Hurley asks.

"Nope," Sawyer says. "I was alone."

"When did you leave the house?"

"A little after seven. My father and I had a . . . discussion about things and I needed to get away, have some time to sort things through in my mind."

Summer provides a snorting laugh as commentary and Sawyer gives her a dirty look.

"Was there anyone here when you left the house, besides your father?"

"Nope," Sawyer says with casual indifference. "Summer was here, but she left during the . . . um . . . discussion Dad and I were having."

"It was an argument," Summer says. "Quit trying to hide the truth and admit it. The two of you were going at it, hot and heavy, when I left here."

"I would advise you both to shut up and ask for a lawyer," Harrison says again.

"You're a lawyer," Summer says to Harrison.

"If you're looking for someone who wanted my father dead, you should take a closer look at her," Sawyer grumbles, gesturing toward Summer.

"For God's sake," Harrison says, planting his elbows on the island top and planting his face in his palms. "Why do I even bother?"

Hurley looks exasperated and he runs his hands through his hair, something he often does when he's thinking. He looks at me and nods toward the living room, then heads that way. I follow him. Brenda sets the video camera on the island countertop, but I note she doesn't turn it off. Smart girl. That way, she will capture anything that gets said while Hurley and I are out of earshot.

"I need to question all three of these yahoos," Hurley says to me in a low voice when we are at the far end of the living room near the front foyer. "I have three persons of interest at this point and I don't want to give them time to collaborate on their stories, not that any of them get along well enough to do that, but I also don't want to have to haul them down to the station right now. I need to look over this house while everything is fresh." He pauses and sucks in a deep breath. "God, the smell of those lilacs is so strong here," he says with a grimace.

"Why don't we question all three of them, here and now, on the basics, like when they last saw the victim, where they were this evening, and what they were doing? We can record it on video. Then have each of them come into the station tomorrow for a more thorough talk. Except for Harrison, they all seem eager enough to talk now without a lawyer present, so why not take advantage of that? Besides, it might be interesting to see the interplay among them. And we should probably process Sawyer for evidence here, like we did with Summer, since he admits to being here this evening and he lives in the house. I don't know if you noticed it or not, but he's got something in his hair that looks like a wood sliver."

"No, I didn't notice. Good eye, Squatch. I knew there was a reason why I married you."

"Clearly, you married me because you have a big-foot fetish," I tease. "And I'm using 'big' in reference to the size of the foot, rather than the enormity of the fetish. Otherwise, why keep calling me *Squatch*?"

He smiles a lazy, sexy smile I typically only see in bed. "It fits you. And you fit me."

No arguments there.

"This is looking like an all-nighter," he says with a perturbed sigh, his facial expression changing in a flash. And just like that, we are back to reality. "Hell of a thing when it's our night off. And those damned lilacs." He shakes his head like a dog trying to shake off water.

"I'm sure Desi is fine with staying at the house until Emily comes home. In fact, she'll probably just sleep over."

Hurley gets a wary look on his face. "I don't want to do anything that will tick Lucien off," he says, wide-eyed.

Lucien is my sister's husband. He's also a criminal defense lawyer and a politically incorrect, obnoxious sleazebag. He can be hard to take, particularly if he's not on your side, but I've learned over the years that most of his insufferable persona is an act, one he uses to great advantage to unsettle his opponents. At the mention of lawyers, a question pops to mind.

"Do you suppose Monty had a will?"

"I would imagine so. A successful businessman like him?"

"Based on what I see here, the man is quite wealthy. I wonder who stands to inherit, and if they know it."

"Let's go find out, shall we?" Hurley says with an eager light in his eyes.

CHAPTER 4

We return to the kitchen and the "three persons of interest," as Hurley referred to them. Given the way they are bickering and sniping at one another when we return, I think they're more in line with the Three Stooges.

"I take it Monty had a will?" I say to no one in particular, and that shuts everyone up right quick.

"Yes," Summer says.

"He does," Sawyer says at the same time. The two of them glare at one another. Harrison doesn't answer.

"Do you know who the lawyer is that drew it up?" I ask.

"Lucien Colter," Summer says, and I hear Hurley groan.

"Are you sure?" I ask. "He's primarily a criminal defense lawyer."

"Yes, I'm sure," Summer says. "Mr. Colter is not the sort of person one forgets or mistakes for anyone else." She has that right. "Apparently, Mr. Colter branched out into some other areas a couple of years ago when he was having some financial difficulties."

Ah, yes. I recall that period in Lucien's life. He'd tried to take on some investment opportunities and convinced some clients to join him. When things didn't pan out the way he had hoped, he was determined to pay back what his clients lost. Despite his often disgusting and shocking outward persona, Lucien really does have a big heart and a strong sense of right and wrong. I loaned Lucien and my sister some money during that period, money that Lucien dutifully paid back with interest, aided in part by his willingness to work hard and expand his office functions. It seems Monty Dixon took advantage of that and used Lucien to draft a will.

"Did your husband keep a copy of his will here in the house?" Hurley asks. No doubt he's hoping the answer will be "yes" and this will enable him to avoid an encounter with Lucien.

Summer shrugs; Sawyer simply looks oblivious. Harrison looks like he has a headache. "If he did," Summer says, "it would be somewhere in his home office."

"I'll look for it later," Hurley says.

Sawyer frowns. "What do you mean, you'll look for it later?"

"I'll be going through the entire house."

"I don't give anyone permission to invade my space," Sawyer says, thrusting a belligerent chin at Hurley.

"Too bad this isn't your house and you don't get a say," Summer counters in a smug tone.

"It's as much my house as it is yours," Sawyer snaps back. "We both live here."

"For Pete's sake, you two," Harrison moans. "This house is a crime scene and the police are going to kick you both out of here until they have a chance to look the place over to their satisfaction."

Sawyer ignores him. "Dad told me last year that I inherit everything based on his will, and that means this is my house and no one is kicking me out of it."

"Is it?" Summer says with a knowing smile. "I believe if you search the public tax records, you'll see that my name is on the deed, along with your father's, as a joint tenancy with the right of survivorship, which means that if either of us dies, the other is left as the sole owner. Plus, Wisconsin is a marital property state." She shoots one last triumphant look at Sawyer, who mouths an expletive.

"You two stop it, now," Harrison carps. "Show the detective some respect, for heaven's sake, and quit the bickering. You're embarrassing yourselves."

"You mean we're embarrassing *you*," Sawyer snipes. "Don't presume to—"

Hurley cuts him off. "Mr. Dixon, I'm going to need you to give us the clothes you're wearing."

"Say what?" Sawyer says with incredulity.

"Welcome to reality," Summer says, her voice just shy of a sneer. She plucks at the collar of her paper scrub top. "I've already been there and done that."

Hurley tells Sawyer to stay put; then he disappears down the hall to the area of the game room. When he returns a moment later, he has Jonas in tow, and Jonas has a package of paper scrubs and a scene-processing kit in his hands. Hurley directs Sawyer toward the same guest bathroom off the living area that we used with Summer, Jonas following. A moment later, the three of them are enclosed behind the bathroom door and we hear Sawyer letting forth with a string of invectives that tells us he's none too happy about the situation.

Summer chuckles. I look at Brenda and then at the video camera. She nods and picks it up.

"You and Sawyer really don't like one another, do you?" I say to Summer.

She tilts her head to one side and eyes me with a derisive grin. "Ooh, did you figure that out all by yourself? You could be a detective."

"Try to be nice for once, Summer," Harrison chastises. "Or is that impossible for you?"

The only answer is the sound of the grandfather clock in the living room striking midnight.

"How long has Sawyer been living here?" I ask, once the clock is done. I know the answer from what Summer told me before, but I want to keep her talking to see if she'll say anything new or useful. Or incriminating.

"A little over two years," she says with a world-weary sigh. "He showed up right after his nineteenth birthday when he graduated from high school, which also happens to be when the child support payments ended. I think Sawyer envisioned a decline in his future level of living when that money train ceased for his mother, and he decided to move to where he could change it up for the better. Monty offered him room and board, and said he'd pay for him to go to college, but Sawyer insists he doesn't need a college degree to learn how to sell real estate. He's seen what a success his father has made of the business and he thought all he had to do was get a license and he'd be just as successful. But Monty is making him put in the hard work, not just handing anything to him, and it hasn't set well with Sawyer."

"Did you spend much time around Sawyer before he moved in?"

"When he was nine, and Monty and I had just started dating, we used to spend time together, the three of us. But when we got married, Sawyer's attitude toward me changed. I think his mother might have poisoned his opinion of me by making me out to be a gold digger, who was after Sawyer's inheritance."

"And are you?" I ask.

"You don't have to answer that, Summer," Harrison says. "Though you seem determined to keep on blabbing, no matter what I say, so go ahead and hang yourself."

Summer shoots him a weary look before answering me. "I married Monty because I love him, not for his money," she says, and I notice she is still referring to him in the present tense, as if he were still alive. "But there will always be people who believe I'm in it only for the money. Mind you, I've been smart and savvy when it comes to money. I've been careful to make sure I'll never be left out in the cold if our marriage falls apart . . ." She pauses, a stricken look flitting across her face. "Or if something like this happened," she adds, looking sad. "That's why the mortgage on this house is in both our names, as are our cars."

Summer is far more money savvy than I was with my first marriage. My husband, David Winston, was—still is—a surgeon here in town, who practices at the hospital where we both worked at the time. In my starry-eyed, romantic naivete, I allowed him to handle all our finances and purchases. Consequently, this left me virtually destitute when I discovered he was cheating on me and decided to leave him. I eventually received a nice settlement in the divorce, but things were dicey for a while, and if David had wanted to screw me over financially, he likely could have done so. Fortunately, he was kind enough to be somewhat fair. And I am older and wiser now.

The door to the guest bathroom flies open, slamming against a doorstop screwed into the floorboard. Sawyer strides out, dressed in paper scrub pants and top, his face beet red, his pimples dark, his hair standing up on end. His face looks like a pepperoni pizza. As he storms toward the front door, Hurley hollers after him.

"I need you to stick around."

Sawyer's expletive is loud enough for all to hear. He exits through the front door, slamming it behind him.

I half expect Hurley to go after him, but then Summer says, "Don't worry, he can't go far. He left his car keys here on the island." She slides off her stool, walks toward the fridge, and takes a bottle of vodka out of the freezer. Then she gets a highball glass from one of the cabinets and pours herself a good two fingers or more of the vodka, which flows from the bottle like syrup. Grabbing the landline phone from its charging cradle at one end of a kitchen counter, she makes her way toward the sectional couch. She flops down on the end piece that forms a chaise lounge and takes a long swig of the vodka. Then she finds a number in the phone and calls it.

When whoever she has called answers, Summer starts in without any nicety like a greeting. "You are not going to believe what is happening to me. I don't think anyone could have had a worse day."

"Classic narcissist," Harrison mutters, shaking his head. "Seems to me, my brother has had a much worse day." He pauses, his brow furrowed in thought. "You know, there is someone else you should be looking at for this. There's a woman named Taylor Copeland, who worked in my brother's real estate office until recently. Something happened, and he ended up firing her, though it wasn't your classic firing in this situation. Real estate agents work for themselves to some extent, but for a share of their commission, they get a lot of services provided by the brokerage they're associated with, as well as use of the brokerage name if desired. My brother opened his own brokerage a decade ago and he's been very discriminating in whom he hires to work in his office. That pickiness has served him well, because he makes a very nice profit every year. And, apparently, those who work with him do well, too. Being associated with Monty's name is a coup in this area. His reputation is stellar."

Hurley, who has been writing down some notes as Harrison talks, says, "People get let go from jobs all the time. What is it about this situation that makes you think it rises to the level of murder?"

"Because Monty also reported her to the licensing board for unethical behavior and they may yank her license as a result. Ms. Copeland didn't deal with the situation well and, apparently, there was quite the showdown at the brokerage office last week." He gives Hurley a quizzical look. "Surely, you know about that already," he says. "Monty told me the police were called."

"That isn't my area," Hurley says. "I'm a homicide detective. Something like that would have been handled by the regular duty cops."

"Seems to me it should be in your area," Harrison says in a mildly chastising tone, like a teacher admonishing a pupil who hasn't done his homework. "Monty said Taylor told him to keep looking over his shoulder because she was going to be coming to get him." He pauses, looking sad. "And it looks like she may have kept her promise. A few days after the firing incident, Monty said he got a threatening letter, anonymous, of course, but he had no doubt who it was from."

"Do you have any contact information for this Taylor Copeland?"

"I don't, but I'm guessing there will be some sort of info on her in the police report, right?"

Hurley nods, scratching out more notes.

Harrison slides off his stool and says, "I'd like to go home."

Before Hurley can respond, Jonas emerges from the bathroom with a collection of evidence bags. He sets them on the floor in the foyer next to the ones I collected from Summer; then he goes back into the bathroom and emerges carrying a small computer tablet.

"Just a couple of quick things," Hurley says to Harrison. "I need to get fingerprint samples from all of you. We collected Sawyer's while we were in the bathroom, but I need yours and Summer's."

"What good will that do you?" Harrison says. "Our prints are going to be all over this house."

"We need them for elimination purposes."

Jonas walks over and sets the tablet on the counter in front of Harrison and proceeds to scan his fingers in, one at a time.

"When is the last time you saw or heard from your brother?" Hurley asks while Jonas works.

"A couple of days ago. I stopped by his real estate office so he could sign some forms."

"What kind of forms?"

"Just some routine business stuff."

"Do you perform legal functions for your brother, or for his business?"

Harrison shakes his head. "There have been times when I've worked with him on a closing, because I was the attorney of record for the buyer or seller on a deal he made, but otherwise Monty preferred to keep business and family separate as much as possible. I think that's why he wasn't happy about Sawyer's decision to go into real estate, not to mention Sawyer's insistence that his father help him achieve instant success."

Jonas finishes printing Harrison and, after thanking him, he moves over to Summer, who is no longer yakking on the phone. She is lying on her side on the couch, a throw pillow beneath her head. Not surprisingly, she acts quite put out when Jonas tells her what he needs to do, but despite the display of displeasure, she cooperates with him.

As Hurley jots down more notes, Harrison closes his eyes and massages the area of his forehead above them.

"Does this house have some kind of security setup?" Hurley asks.

"It does, or rather it did," Harrison says. "There is an alarm system on the doors and cameras in the front and back of the house, but Monty had the whole thing disabled shortly after Sawyer moved in."

"Why?" I ask.

"Monty said Sawyer complained about the cameras being an invasion of his privacy, saying they made him feel like he was being watched all the time. And, apparently, the kid was too stupid to remember to disarm or rearm the alarm system when he came and went. After he set the thing off more than a dozen times, Monty finally canceled the service and disabled the whole system."

"That's unfortunate," Hurley says.

"I suppose it is, in retrospect, though I'm sure Monty thought it was the right thing to do at the time." Harrison's brow furrows and he massages his forehead again. "I have a splitting headache, Detective. Can the rest of this wait?"

After a few seconds' hesitation, Hurley says, "Sure." He takes out a business card and hands it to Harrison. "I think that's all I need for now anyway. Give me your contact information and I'll call you and arrange a time for you to come down to the station if I need to chat with you about anything else."

Harrison offers the requested info and Hurley scribbles it into his notebook. When that's done, Harrison takes his leave without another word or look to Summer.

Summer is on her phone again and I've been eavesdropping on her end of the conversation to make sure she isn't cooking up more than whatever was on the menu at her class this evening.

Hurley stares at her for a moment and sighs. "I don't think I have the strength," he says quietly. "I'm going to tell her and Sawyer to come into the station tomorrow and give their official statements then, so I can get started on this house."

"And I need to get Monty's body to the morgue," I say. I look over at Brenda. "Do me a favor. My gut tells me Summer Dixon is hiding something. Keep an eye on her and eavesdrop on her conversation. It sounds like she has an alibi for the time of Monty's death, but until we know for sure, I don't want her chatting with anyone and making one up." I pause, frowning. "Try to get her and Sawyer to leave as soon as possible and go somewhere else for the night. I don't know where Sawyer is, but he must be on the grounds somewhere. Unless he called a friend or an Uber."

"I'm on it," Brenda says. I take the video camera from her and hand it to Hurley, who has pocketed Sawyer's keys, so he can start his search of the house. He heads for the hallway that leads to the bedrooms. I go back to the game room. I have a dead body I need to tend to.

CHAPTER 5

Devo is playing on his cell phone again, while Jonas Kriedeman, decked out in a white Tyvek suit, which has him sweating bullets, is busy dusting the pool table edges for fingerprints.

"How's it going, Jonas?" I ask.

"Interesting." He pauses with his fingerprint brush and looks over at Monty Dixon. "Someone sure got ticked off, didn't they?"

"Certainly looks that way. How did it go when you collected Sawyer Dixon's clothes?"

"About how you'd expect," Jonas says. "He wasn't very happy."

"Yeah, Brenda and I did the wife, and she was none too pleased, either."

"She the one who called it in?"

I nod. "Hurley and I talked to her already and it sounds like she has an alibi. Says she was at a cooking class all evening, came home, and found our victim just like he is."

"Any idea on the time of death?" Jonas asks.

"I don't have a cue," I say with a sly smile.

Jonas groans but grins, shaking his head. It's a bit inappropriate to crack jokes at the scene of someone's murder, but it helps to relieve the tension, assuming there isn't a family member or someone with a significant connection to the victim within earshot. It happens with some regularity. Those of us who deal with this sort of stuff on a regular basis tend to have dark senses of humor.

"Best guess, based on the onset of rigor and body temp, is between eight and nine this . . ." I pause and make a correction. "Between eight and nine *last* evening."

Jonas stands, arches his back, and stretches, letting out a little moan. When he's done, he studies Monty's body for a few seconds. "I have to admit, this is my first death by pool cue," he says. "There's a small gouge in the pool table over there at the end that looks fresh. I'm thinking someone got angry and broke that cue stick there on the table before wielding it as a weapon."

I walk over and look at the mark he has pointed out. "Any way to tell for sure if that's where the stick was broken?"

Jonas shrugs. "I swabbed that area, thinking maybe some minute bits from the cue stick might show up, but even if they did, who's to say it came from that particular cue stick on the night of the murder, as opposed to any other cue stick that some frustrated person might have banged against the table?"

"Good point," I say, frowning. "Clearly, someone broke that cue stick and stabbed our guy with it. The question is, who broke it? And did the same person who broke it, then stab the victim? Maybe Monty broke the cue stick and someone else picked it up and stabbed him with it."

"My money is on the same person for both," Jonas surmises. "The kind of anger required to break the stick in the first place could easily segue into a murderous rage. The question then becomes how we can prove it."

"By slowly building a case and studying all the evidence," I say. I nod toward the two beer bottles on the side table. "Be sure to grab those and anything that might be left in them.

The bottles should be good for prints, and the rim and contents for DNA."

"Yep, it's on my list," Jonas says.

"You have a list?" I say, looking around.

Jonas taps the side of his head. "It's up here. I'm thinking we should also collect the unbroken cue stick on the table and all the balls, both on top of the table and in the pockets. Who knows what prints we might find? Do you agree?"

"Absolutely."

"I'll dust all of them here and lift what I can, then bag them and take them back to my work area."

Jonas has a work and laboratory area in the basement of the police station, but in our office, there is also an evidence lab on the second floor. Our evidence technician is Arnie Toffer, and evidence processing is often shared between the two sites. Arnie's lab has the fancy machinery necessary to do chemical analyses and detailed microscopic examinations, whereas Jonas deals with more superficial stuff. Both can collect and process fingerprints, and while we do collect DNA evidence, the actual analysis of that is done at the labs in Madison or Milwaukee. It's a piecemeal system, but it works well enough.

"Sounds like you have it all well under control, as usual, Jonas," I say with a smile. Jonas may be a one-man department, but his work is always thorough and timely. He's good at what he does. Technically, these days he's more of a one-and-a-half-man department because there is another employee, Laura Kingston, who is shared between the police department and our office. "Feel free to get Arnie to help as needed."

"Will do."

I squat down next to the body and examine it again. There is a design on the thicker end of the broken cue stick that was used to kill him, and I take out my regular camera from my pocket and shoot a couple of close-up pictures of it. There is a slight sheen on the side of Monty's neck that I suspect might have been left by Summer when she checked him for a pulse, but I don't see anything on the handle of the cue stick. Still, I suppose it might be there and just hard to see. I'd like to get a sample swab on the cue stick handle, but there are likely to be fingerprints on it, too, and I don't want to mess those up.

"Jonas, let me run something by you," I say. I explain my dilemma and the two of us stand there, eyeing the cue stick handle for a moment, debating the best way to get any evidence we might need from it.

Jonas says, "If the wife touched the handle of that cue stick with enough oil on her hands to leave behind a sheen like the one on his neck, I doubt you'll have any usable prints, because her hands would have slid all over that shiny wood surface. Frankly, I doubt she could have thrust that thing into his chest with even a tiny amount of oil on her hands. That takes some strength. So I'd say to secure the thing the best you can for transport, and when Izzy or Doc Morton pulls it out, have them try to do it down low, close to where it enters the body. Then get Arnie to look at the thing and see what he can do. His machines can work miracles."

After considering my options, I use some gauze to secure the extruding end of the cue stick where it is and minimize any movement, so it won't mess up the wound track, and then I place a plastic bag over the stick. When that's done, I fetch a body bag from my scene kit, take it out of its package, and unfold it on the floor beside the body. I'm going to need help with this part.

"Hey, Devo, can you give me a hand, please?"

Devo looks at me, tucks his cell phone in his pocket, and claps his hands.

"Very funny," I say with a smirk.

"Hey, you started it with that cue pun," he says with a laugh as he walks over to me. "What do you need me to do?"

"Help me get this guy bagged up, if you would."

With both Jonas's and Devo's help, we manage to get Monty's body in the bag and ready for transport. I end up having to cut a hole in the bag to allow for the cue stick to protrude, but by the time we're done, things are relatively secure and protected. Devo, whose stomach is about as iron-clad as a roll of plastic wrap, looks pale and sweaty, and I send him back to his corner as soon as I can.

Before calling the funeral home service that provides our transport, I go back to the main part of the house in search of Hurley. The great-room area of the house is deserted and there is an empty silence to the place that tells me Sawyer and Summer have left. I find Hurley in what appears to be the master bedroom.

"Need any help? I've got the body ready for transport, but wanted to check with you before I call for the Johnson twins." The Johnson twins, who go by the nicknames Cass and Kit, monikers that cause them to be referred to as the CassKit twins, work for a funeral home that provides the local transfer of bodies to our morgue. In order to ensure the chain of evidence, I'm required to follow them to our office and take delivery of the body once there. It's a bit comical, given that I drive a hearse as my primary vehicle, though I never transport bodies in it. At least not dead ones. My reasons for driving a hearse have nothing to do with my job and everything to do with basic practicality and my stupidity when it came to financial matters in my first marriage. A bad wreck left the car I took with me from the marriage totaled, and since it, like everything else, was in David's name rather than mine, I was left with no car and no way to buy much of one, since my cash assets were rather slim. The used hearse was the only thing on the lot I could afford. I was skeptical of the car initially, but I've come to love it. It's a smooth ride with plenty of room in the back for all the tools of my trade—except the dead bodies . . . there's room for them, but I don't carry them—and my dog, Hoover, loves all the funky smells it has in the back area. A couple of years ago, when I was being stalked by a crazy man, Hurley had the thing reinforced with steel side panels, bulletproof glass, and run-flat tires. The extra weight this added to the car diminished my gas mileage, but I feel safer than our president when I drive the thing.

"I can handle things here for now," Hurley says.

"Did you kick the Dixons out?"

"I did. They are both going to stay at the Sorenson Motel for now."

"Not together, I hope. Otherwise, we'll have another murder to investigate and Joseph Wagner will be mad as hell. He already thinks we're purposefully trying to put him out of business by planting killers and dead bodies out there."

Joseph is the owner of the Sorenson Motel and a cantankerous old coot on his best days. I understand his animosity. There have been several cases that involved his motel in some way, either because a killer was staying there, or one of his guests was killed while staying there. Since I've been involved in every one of these situations—darned near becoming a victim myself on the most recent one—he holds me personally responsible. All my attempts to assure him that my proximity to these cases is by chance and not by intent have fallen on deaf ears. Though if Joseph would take the time to get rid of all the hair growing out of his ears, I suspect his hearing would improve substantially.

"I doubt those two will room together," Hurley says. "In fact, I'm surprised they're willing to be in the same town, much less at the same motel." He sighs and shakes his head. "I'm going to have them come down to the station for more questioning beginning at noon. You're welcome to join me for that, if you like."

"I would." I look around the room, which is messy—bed unmade, clothes tossed over furniture and on the floor. "Find anything of interest?"

"Well, it appears our couple has been sleeping in separate rooms."

I look again and see that only one side of the bed has been slept in, all the clothes lying around are men's, and in the attached bathroom, all I see are men's toiletries. There is a large walk-in closet off to one side, its door gaping open, and everything I can see on the shelves and hanging from the rods looks like men's dress shirts, sports coats, suits, and slacks. There are ties everywhere: draped over furniture, hanging on doorknobs, piled on the dressers, hanging in the closet, and even lying on the floor. It seems as if every color, material, finish, and design one can imagine is represented somewhere and I start to think Monty had something of a tie fetish.

"Looks like the missus has been sleeping in the guest room," Hurley explains.

"Have you looked in Monty's home office yet?"

"I have. He doesn't have a desk calendar, but there's a laptop in there. I'll have Jonas take it in, and maybe between the computer and his cell phone, which is on a credenza in the office plugged in and charging, we can establish a schedule. Hopefully, they aren't password protected. I'll need to visit his real estate office, too. Sawyer told me there is an office manager and a handful of other Realtors who work there." He pauses as a yawn overtakes him. "I should probably try to visit the office before it opens up in the morning. I don't know if Sawyer has a key to the place, but if he does, I want to get there before he does."

"Do you have keys to the place? We could go there tonight."

Hurley reaches into his pocket and pulls out a key ring. "Keys to Monty's office, his car, and this house."

"Sweet."

"I had Brenda look up the police report on the incident involving this Taylor Copeland woman and she was overheard by several people threatening our victim. Her address was in the report and I'm thinking we might surprise her with a middle-of-the-night visit, see what she has to say for herself."

"You're thinking that's where you'll go next?"

Hurley nods.

"Can I come along?"

"Of course."

"I need to get my body transported and checked in."

"Do it. You should be fine. I'll be another hour here at least. I'll call you when I'm done."

"Got it."

CHAPTER 6

I leave the room and use my cell phone to place a call to the Johnson twins. As I'm relaying the specifics over the phone to them, I wander down the hallway and peek into the other rooms. The front hallway has another that ells off it toward the back of the house. Going down it, I find what I guess is Sawyer's bedroom, based on the toiletries and clothing I can see; though upon entering the room, I discover that it's more of a suite. There is a small sitting area off the bedroom, outfitted with a large-screen TV mounted on the wall, a gas fireplace, a wet bar, and two leather reclining chairs. And from this room, one has access to a kitchen area that is simple and small, but equipped with all the basics: stove, refrigerator, microwave, and even a dishwasher. Unlike the kitchen in the main part of the house, this one is a bit messy with dirty dishes in the sink, used coffee mugs on the counter, and crumbs scattered on the floor.

The reason for this second kitchen becomes clear when I look out a window and see that the yard here contains a large stone patio area, with seating for dozens of people once you count the built-in stone benches, several cocktail-sized tables, a large picnic table, and a half-dozen outdoor recliners that

are situated around an inground pool. A handful of strategically placed solar-generated ground lights, along with the
underwater pool lights, lends the area a warm, ambient glow
that is almost otherworldly when the night breeze ripples the
surface of the pool water and creates undulating waves of
light.

I would think Monty used this part of the house for enter-
taining in his real estate business and wonder if Sawyer's arrival affected that. It's certainly a nice setup for Sawyer. This
section of the house is like a separate apartment, with its own
entrance into the sitting room, and the backyard patio area is
accessible through a side gate, so Sawyer can come and go as
he pleases.

Monty's home office is also in this part of the house,
though separate from Sawyer's area, and it's as messy as the
master bedroom was. The desk is covered with folders and
papers, and there are stacks of files on a side credenza next to
the charging cell phone Hurley mentioned. On a small table
in front of a window, there is a philodendron, its leaves yellow, brown, and wilted, and there is a collection of dead
leaves on the floor beneath it. There is a bookcase, most of its
contents related to real estate, business management, and
motivational philosophies, but there are collections of folders
and papers stuffed between and on top of the books. Two
large bookends carved out of marble in the shape of houses
hold one shelf's worth of stuff in place. The other shelves are
crammed in tight from one edge to the other. Curious, I lift
the cover of one folder with the tip of my fingernail and see
what appears to be some sort of financial report.

I head back out to the front hallway and come across a
bedroom that is filled with women's clothing. It's a small
room, compared to the others in this house, with an ordinary-
sized closet. Summer Dixon, however, is clearly not an ordi-
nary dresser. There are clothes all over the place, crammed in
the closet, laid out on the bed, draped over a chair, and in the

case of shoes, scattered around the room. This bed, like the one in the master, is unmade. Seems neither of the Dixons was a neat freak, though I'm not one to cast aspersions in that regard. There are plenty of days when the beds in our house are unmade, and messiness is a common state of being. Our two cats have been known to scare up dust bunnies nearly as big as they are from under the beds, and between a toddler, a teenager, and a dog, there is enough clutter and mess in our house at any given moment that on some days I feel like we're one shopping bag away from being featured on an episode of *Hoarders*.

I've struggled to keep up with the housekeeping duties, along with my job and the childcare, but I never seem to be able to get caught up. This has caused some strife between Hurley and me, and after a couple of sessions with our counselor, Dr. Maggie Baldwin, we agreed to hire someone to help with some of the household tasks. In fact, we have two interviews set up for this weekend, something that would have been a lot easier if we hadn't had to go out tonight on this case, one that will likely keep us up and busy most of the weekend.

As I survey the room Summer has been using, I think she could use someone to clean for her, too, but at least she and Monty had someone to cook for them. I can't help but wonder if Summer resents Sawyer's presence and his occupation of the much nicer and roomier suite in the back of the house. Clearly, there is plenty of animosity between those two, and I doubt the current living arrangements have done much to help with that.

I hear the front door open and a familiar squeak that tells me the Johnson twins have arrived with their stretcher, the wheels of which have needed a good oiling for as long as I've known them. I meet them in the great-room area and direct them down the hall toward the poolroom. Looking at the kitchen, I'm once again struck by how shiny and clean it is, particularly now that I've seen the cluttered mess that is most of the rest of the house. I imagine the kitchen would look like a food bomb went off if either Summer or Monty ever used it.

The twins prepare to load Monty's body onto the cot with some eager help from Devo. Given that Devo normally shies away from this kind of stuff, it's amusing to watch him trip all over himself to assist the twins. The fact that the body is now neatly tucked inside a body bag no doubt makes Devo's tolerance of the task easier. The twins, with their big brown eyes, long black hair, knockout figures, and tight clothing, tend to turn male heads wherever they go. The fact that Devo is currently dating Laura Kingston, the evidence tech we share with the police department, is something he seems to have temporarily forgotten—though if she was here processing the room instead of Jonas, things might be different.

"Hello, ladies," I say. "How are things in your world?"

"Can't complain," Cass or Kit says. I've never been able to tell them apart.

"And if we did, who would listen?" the other one says archly.

"I'd listen," Devo says, punctuating the comment with a grunt as he helps the girls hoist the body up onto the stretcher.

"With Laura at your side, right?" I say, and Devo has the decency to look abashed. I see Jonas shoot Devo a look of disgust and I shake my head at the dynamics in this room. Jonas was vying for Laura's attentions at one time, as was Arnie Toffer, our evidence tech. The two of them thought they were in competition for the girl's affections, and even had a fight over it, only to learn that she'd been seeing Devo for some time behind their backs.

"How are your parents?" I ask the twins. Kit recently had an abusive boyfriend, who turned violent, pistol-whipping the twins' parents when he was trying to find Kit. Cass had been hurt, too, but she healed quickly. Their elderly parents hadn't fared quite as well.

"They're doing great," one of the girls says. "Mom is nagging Dad, and he's complaining about it, so things are more or less back to normal."

"I'm glad to hear it."

Eyeing the obvious protrusion in the body bag, the other of the girls says, "I take it someone was a poor sport?"

"You could say that," I tell her.

"Are you ready to roll?" she then asks.

"I am." I follow the girls out and watch them load the body into their hearse, while I load my scene kit and some of the evidence into mine.

Once all the items are loaded, I follow the Johnson twins back to my office. We pull into the underground garage and I grab the evidence bags from my car and walk over to summon the elevator with my key card as they unload the body and wheel it over. It only takes us ten minutes to check the body in, a process we have done together many times. Once the Johnson twins are done, they leave, and I set about the process of admitting Monty's body to our morgue. This requires opening a chart for him, recording the basics of his physical characteristics, such as height, weight, hair and eye color, and a summary of where, when, and, if known, how the death occurred. I haul his body into the X-ray room and get a set of head-to-toe films, and then I do my least favorite part of the job: gathering samples of his vitreous fluid. Vitreous fluid is the liquid inside the eyeball, and it can provide a wealth of information useful for determining the time of death and, in some instances, the means. Unfortunately, it is obtained by inserting a needle into each eye and aspirating the fluid into a syringe. It's a task that never fails to give me a case of the heebie-jeebies.

When all of that is done, I wheel Monty into the morgue refrigerator and park him beside two other bodies currently residing there. One is new and I know nothing about it, no doubt one of Christopher's victims. The other is a fifty-two-

year-old husband and father of three who had the unfortunate luck of running into a large deer while riding his motorcycle. Neither he nor the deer survived, though the man
might have if he'd been wearing a helmet. Izzy and I did his
autopsy earlier today, and while we found plenty of injuries
from the collision, the only ones that were fatal were the ones
to his head. Wisconsin bikers aren't required to wear helmets
and plenty of them enjoy the feeling of freedom they get by
not doing so. But at times, that freedom comes at an awful
price.

I spend another ten minutes logging in the evidence I
brought back with me and leaving the packages in Arnie's
lab: the end of the cue stick that wasn't part of Monty, and
all the items I got from Summer.

With perfect timing, Hurley calls me just as I'm turning
out the lights in preparation for heading back down to the
garage. Fortunately, his call comes before I descend in the elevator, because the garage is a dead zone for cell signals, as
well as humans.

"Are you close to finishing?" he asks me with no preamble
as soon as I answer the call.

"Just did. Should we ride together, or do you want me to
meet you there?"

"I'm two minutes away from your office. Meet me at the
gate to the garage?"

"Will do."

"Bring your scene kit and some evidence bags. You never
know what we might find."

CHAPTER 7

No sooner do I grab my scene kit and some extra evidence bags from the back of the hearse and step outside the underground garage than Hurley rolls up in his blue pickup. I set my scene kit and the evidence bags on the back floor of his king cab and then slide into the front passenger seat. Hurley takes off the second I've shut the door.

"Tell me what you know so far about this Copeland woman," I say.

"She's forty-two, has blond hair, brown eyes, and weighs one-sixty. At least that's what her driver's license info says."

"Which means she weighs at least one-seventy, probably more. Women always lie about that."

"Do they?" He looks over and winks at me.

I know from eavesdropping when I've been hanging out at the police station that this is common knowledge among the cops, so I let the matter drop. "Anything else about Ms. Copeland?"

"Just what was in the police report. It seems that Monty confronted her about this incident—though just what the incident was isn't clear—and he wanted her to pack up her things and leave the office because she was no longer going to be allowed to work there. He also informed her that he had filed a complaint with the state licensing board, and they were likely going to yank her license to practice.

"Ms. Copeland denied the incident happened and got angry when Monty wouldn't believe her. She accused him of making things up to get rid of her so he could make space for his new girlfriend, a brand-new real estate agent that he brought into the firm."

I raise my eyebrows at this. "That helps explain the separate bedrooms," I say.

Hurley nods. "Monty denied it, Copeland continued to yell at him, and he then threatened to have her physically removed from the property. At that point, Monty put together a box of Copeland's personal items from her office and carried it outside, leaving it beside her car. Copeland followed him to the parking lot, yelling the whole way, and then they engaged in a shouting match, where some unkind words were shared. Others from the office were there at the time and were witness to the whole thing. They claim that Copeland swore she'd make Monty pay for what he was doing to her and then warned him that he had better watch his back."

"Not very friendly, but not exactly a death threat, either," I say.

"But I'm not done," Hurley says with a teasing look. "It gets better."

I rub my hands together with glee. "Do tell."

"There was an addendum to the report. Two days ago, Monty received a letter in his office inbox."

"Yeah, Harrison said something about that."

"It wasn't mailed. It was in a plain white envelope with just his name on it, obviously hand delivered. Inside the envelope was a simple one-sheet letter computer-printed on regular copy paper. It said, 'I'll make you pay for this. You're a dead man.' "

"Now we're getting serious," I say.

"Monty was genuinely afraid because he knew that Copeland had a gun. She bought it last year after that real estate agent in Madison was killed while showing a house to some guys who posed as potential buyers. She carried it with her whenever she met new clients. Monty called the police again, gave them the letter, and told them about the gun. The officers followed up with Copeland, who, not surprisingly, denied writing and sending the letter. She did admit that she still had a key to the office, and since Monty didn't bother to change the locks after firing her, she could have put the letter there. The cops asked her if they could look around her house, but she refused and told the officers that if they wanted to talk to her anymore, they could contact her attorney."

"And that's where it was left?"

"Pretty much. The letter and the envelope were processed for prints, but there weren't any. Both are generic stock that a person can buy at any big-box or grocery store. Even if we had Copeland's printer, it likely would be of little use because the letter was printed on an inkjet printer. Lasers sometimes leave tiny marks on the page that can identify a printer, but inkjets don't, so it can be difficult to pinpoint a specific printer as the source."

"It doesn't sound like Ms. Copeland is going to cooperate with us," I say.

"Maybe not. We'll see. Maybe the fact that she's now facing an actual murder charge with a potential life sentence, rather than a death threat charge with a maximum of five years, will make her more amenable."

I scoff at this. "And just when I'm starting to think you know women," I tease.

Hurley doesn't have time for a comeback because we have arrived at the Copeland woman's home.

It's a little after two in the morning, so I'm surprised to see light shining through a narrow gap in the drapes hanging in a first-floor front window of the cute little Cape Cod. We climb the steps to the front porch and Hurley rings the doorbell. I hear it chime inside, and we wait. Hurley takes out his badge; he'll be ready to show it to Copeland when she answers the door. When nothing happens, Hurley rings the bell again and knocks hard on the door, for good measure. Again we wait, but nothing happens.

I look over at the front window with its meager sliver of light and climb down from the porch to walk over there and see if I can peek inside. There is a privet hedge to navigate—it's about two feet high and nearly as wide—and as I try to step over it, one of my gigantic feet gets tangled in the branches and I lose my balance. I fall, landing on top of the bushes at first and then rolling down behind them. The stems and leaves scratch my arms and part of my side as my shirt rides up, and I end up wedged between the house and the hedge, my legs trapped in between the branches.

"Damn it," I mutter, twisting my body around in the narrow space until I'm on my side. Sort of. I try to free my legs, but I'm too confined and can't get the right movement going. I finally give up and curse again.

Hurley watches my futile efforts and I see the corners of his mouth twitch.

"Are you going to stand there and laugh at me or help me up?" I say, feeling perturbed.

With one last glance at the still-unanswered door, Hurley climbs down from the porch and comes over to me. He frees my legs, untangling them one at a time and tossing each one behind the hedge like they're sacks of sand. Then he proffers a hand. After a scramble to get my legs in a better position, he gives one mighty heave and I'm able to get to my feet.

"I can't take you anywhere, Squatch," he teases as I try to tug my shirt back into place. He reaches up and pulls a twig out of my hair.

"At least you're never bored," I say with a wry smile.

Then I turn and try to peer in through the small opening in the drapes. The room is well lit and I can see the back of a chair and, beyond it, part of a couch that faces the window. On the floor, in front of the portion of the couch that I can see, is a foot wearing a feminine shoe, and part of one leg.

"Hurley, something isn't right. There is a person lying on the floor in there."

"You're sure?"

"Positive."

He retreats and climbs back onto the porch. Then he tries the doorknob; more, I suspect, just to rule out an unlocked door before he breaks it in. Surprisingly, the door opens, and Hurley disappears inside.

I scramble back over the privet hedge and follow him. Inside is an unwelcome surprise. There is a woman on the floor, on her back, staring up at the ceiling with lifeless eyes. Beside her is a pile of what looks like vomit.

"Oh, crap," I say as Hurley takes out his phone and calls it in. I squat down next to the woman, taking care not to disturb anything that might be evidence, and check her neck for a pulse. It's a reflexive act, even though I'm certain she is dead. Very dead. Her color tells me that much. A second later, I withdraw my hand. No need to look for a pulse. She's cold.

I get back to my feet and wait for Hurley to get off his phone. "She's long dead," I say, and he nods. "Is it the Copeland woman?"

"She looks like Copeland's DMV picture." He tears his eyes away from the dead woman and looks around the room. Over next to the couch is an end table and on it is an envelope propped up next to a lamp. Beside it is a highball glass with a tiny amount of brown liquid in the bottom, and next to that is a prescription bottle.

"Do you have any gloves on you?" Hurley asks.

"No, but I'll run out to the car and grab some." I do so and return a moment later carrying my scene kit. I hand a pair of gloves to Hurley, and then I don a pair myself and take out my camera.

"Shoot that first," Hurley says, nodding toward the end table. I do so, and when I'm done, Hurley picks up the envelope and examines it. There is nothing written on the outside, and the flap hasn't been sealed. Carefully, Hurley opens it and removes the single sheet inside. It's folded into thirds, and after carefully unfolding it, he reads it. It doesn't take him long, and when he's done, he shows it to me.

It's a computer-printed suicide note, short and sweet: *I'm sorry for what I did to Monty and can't live with the guilt. Please forgive me.*

There is no signature at the bottom, but *Taylor* is printed there in the same computer font. I get out a clear evidence bag for the note and hold it open for Hurley. He drops it in, and I seal and then label it. We do the same with the envelope.

Then we focus on the prescription bottle. It's labeled with Taylor Copeland's name and a date from a few days ago. According to the prescription, it contained sixty tablets of trazodone, a sleeping pill. It's empty and I calculate quickly in my head.

"Assuming she took one pill a night as prescribed, she could have taken more than fifty of these," I say. "Definitely enough to do the job."

I look from the note back to the dead woman. "So, are we supposed to assume from this that she killed Monty Dixon?"

"It looks that way. Makes sense, I suppose, but let's not make any assumptions until we've had time to thoroughly examine the scene and the evidence."

"Given that everyone is already busy processing the Dixon house, that task is likely going to fall on us."

"I called Jonas when you went outside to get the gloves and he's going to call both Laura and Arnie in to help. I'll secure the Dixon house for now with an officer, and, if need be, Jonas can help here even if he isn't finished there. We have plenty of folks looking for overtime, so it shouldn't be a problem. I can get some officers to chip in and help with evidence collection."

"Still, it's going to be an all-nighter for us."

"Yeah, looks that way," Hurley says with a sigh. Then one eyebrow cocks upward. "People are just dying to meet the Grim Reaper tonight."

This time it's my turn to groan.

Two hours later, there are two off-duty police officers onsite helping us, along with Arnie Toffer and Laura Kingston. I have photographed, examined, and secured Taylor Copeland's body inside a body bag and I'm waiting for the Johnson twins to arrive.

Hurley has made a bunch of calls to try and track down a next of kin, and so far, all he's been able to find is an ex-husband from ten years ago, who lives on the West Coast and hasn't seen or heard from Taylor in four years. He informs Hurley that both of Taylor's parents are dead, she's an only child, and, as far as he knows, she has no children. As to whether she is seeing anyone romantically, no one seems to know, though we don't find any evidence of any close relationships after looking through her cell phone, which fortunately isn't password protected. At least the gods are smiling on us in that regard.

We do find an e-mail on a laptop set up on Copeland's dining-room table that is from the state board of licensure informing Copeland that her license is temporarily suspended pending an investigation of the allegations made by Mr. Dixon. But it doesn't state what those allegations are.

"Bag and tag that computer, the printer, all the paper, and envelopes you find," Hurley says to one of the police officers. "She sent a threatening note to our earlier victim and we'll need to see if all of the printed notes match."

"Got it," the officer says.

"Has anyone found a gun?" Hurley asks.

The officer shakes his head.

"There should be one here somewhere. Check her car, too."

The Johnson twins arrive, and after looking at the body on the living-room floor, one of them—I really cannot tell them apart—says, "Are we offering a special on dead bodies this weekend?"

"Seems that way, doesn't it?" I say.

As the twins prep their stretcher for loading up the body, Hurley says to me, "I want to go and visit Monty's real estate office before anyone else gets there. Brenda Joiner said she can meet me there. How long will it take you to check in Copeland's body?"

"I'll need to ride with the twins, since I don't have my own car here. Once I'm at the office, I'll need about an hour, give or take."

"Tell you what." Hurley reaches into his pocket, takes out his truck key, and hands it to me. "Why don't you take my pickup and then come back here and get me when you're done. We can ride over to Monty's office together, and when we're done there, I'll take you back to your office to pick up your car."

"Okay." I try, unsuccessfully, to stifle a yawn. "Can we schedule a nap in there somewhere?"

Hurley smiles and kisses me on my forehead. "Maybe we can sneak in a couple of hours once we finish at the real estate office."

"That sounds wonderful, though we'll have to touch base with my sister and Emily to make sure Matthew is taken care of. I spoke to Christopher a bit ago and he said Doc Morton was planning on coming in at noon to start the autopsies."

Hurley sighs. "We'll play it by ear and do what we can," he says. "See you in a bit."

With that, I head outside with the Johnson twins and my second body of the night, hoping that adage about things coming in threes doesn't hold true.

CHAPTER 8

It's a little before five in the morning when I pick my husband up from the Copeland house and drive us to Monty Dixon's real estate office. The sun hasn't appeared yet, but it's bathing the eastern sky in a gorgeous pink-and-yellow glow. As I park and turn off the truck, I try to stifle a yawn, but it overpowers me.

Hurley looks over at me. "Tired?"

"You think?" I say with a smile. "To be honest, I'm exhausted. If it hadn't been for getting called out for that motorcycle accident Friday night, I'd be fine. I used to do this when I worked in the OR and had to take a call. There was one weekend where I was up for fifty-some hours with no sleep, except for a two-hour nap." I pause and yawn. "I guess I'm out of practice," I add with a tired smile. "And I'm older. And I have two kids."

Now it's Hurley's turn to yawn.

"I should have tried to take a nap yesterday," I go on, "but there was too much to do. Emily had a date with Johnny, so I had Matthew to deal with, and even if I'd pawned him off on Dom or my sister, there was tons of laundry that needed to be done, vacuuming, the animals to tend to, and a dishwasher to empty." I pause, yawning again. "I figured I'd catch up on my sleep tonight. I wasn't anticipating having to go out, since we weren't on call."

Hurley looks at me warmly and pushes a strand of hair back from my face. "Are you sure you want to do this with me? I can drive you home and you can go to bed now."

"Thanks, but no. This investigative stuff is part of my job and it revs me up. Plus, it helps knowing that the end is in sight regarding the housework."

Hurley's loving expression falters. "Right," he says. "When is our first interview again?" he asks, turning to face forward.

"Tomorrow . . . oops, make that today. We have two of them, one at four and one at five." I see Hurley's brow furrow. "What's wrong? Do you want me to reschedule them?"

He gives me a brief sidelong glance. "I don't know. I'm not crazy about the idea of some stranger poking around our house. I've got a lot of confidential stuff in my office."

I'm tempted to snap back with a comment about how housecleaners clean, they don't poke around, but I bite it back for two reasons. One, I can't be sure some of them don't snoop, and, let's face it, you can't clean someone's house without learning a few things about them, potentially intimate things. I know I've learned things about the dead people I've tended to by looking around their houses. What's in the medicine cabinet? Antidepressants? Viagra? Birth control pills? Hemorrhoid cream? What sort of reading material is in the house? *People*? *National Geographic*? *Guns & Ammo*? *Playboy*? Heck, even the contents of a refrigerator or kitchen cabinet can tell you things. So can the dirty dishes in the sink. So, yeah, our privacy will be invaded to some extent.

The second reason I bite back my comment is because of something our marriage counselor said. Maggie told me that I tend to bite Hurley's head off when he says something I don't like, rather than take the time to calm down and consider what he's saying. "He can't be wrong all the time," she had said with a smile. Her point was a valid one, but the comment about biting Hurley's head off made me see myself as a blond-haired, blue-eyed praying mantis with feet the size of a Sasquatch. It was a horrifying image, the stuff of nightmares, and it stuck with me. It's this image more than Maggie's words that makes me pause and think now.

I decide to validate Hurley's concern. "I get it," I tell him. "But we can mitigate it some by making parts of the house, like your office, off-limits. Just lock the door."

Hurley rakes his teeth over his lower lip. "There will still be a stranger handling my underwear." He shivers. "It feels weird."

I feel my anger start to flare again and see that hideous praying mantis. I force the image out of my mind and do what Maggie taught me. I count to ten in my head before I respond. Then I remind myself that I'm tired, and my patience on this matter would be dicey on a good day.

"If it will make you feel better, I'll handle all of your underwear personally," I tell him in my best flirtatious voice.

He looks over at me with a rakish look that makes me feel all squishy inside. At least that part of our relationship has always worked well.

This housekeeping stuff is only part of the stress that led us to counseling. Another part stemmed from my ambiguity over the idea of having another child, something I knew Hurley wanted and I agreed to. Then I discovered my commitment had all the stability of a sand castle at high tide when a pregnancy test came back positive. The wave of reality it brought with it demolished my house of sand, eroding my convictions. Already too busy to be able to keep up, the idea of adding another kid to the mix suddenly seemed unwise.

I tried to work out my feelings without Hurley knowing about it, not wanting to crush his hopes unnecessarily and uncertain if my reaction was real or just the hormones talking. I did some things that made it seem like I was being sneaky and lying to him, which, in all fairness, is what I was doing, though not in a way I thought would be harmful to him or our relationship. I just wanted to see Dr. Maggie alone and have her help me sort out my doubts and fears before I shared any of it with Hurley. In hindsight, I should have just told him what I was thinking from the get-go, but in a misguided attempt to spare his feelings, I ended up hurting him. That was never my intent, but how does that adage go? "The best of intentions . . ."

Then I had a miscarriage and realized just how much I *did* want another child. The loss hit me hard, much harder than I expected, and it brought with it a lot of clarity.

Any more discussion on the matter is tabled for now, for we have arrived at Monty Dixon's office. It's located in what was once a private family home, a large, old Victorian that might have been a showcase house for someone prominent in town a century ago when it was first built. Now its location on the main thoroughfare through town makes it less than ideal for a family but perfect for a business willing to work within, and adapt to, its limitations. There is a sign hanging from the front porch ceiling that has a house-shaped icon on it in bright red, alongside the words DIXON HOMETOWN RE-ALTY.

The house appears to have been converted into a two-flat, as there are now two front doors, side by side, each with its own mailbox. A peek through the window in the door on the right reveals a staircase that, most likely, was once the primary access to the second floor. Now a wall separates it from the rest of the first floor.

Brenda Joiner pulls up, gets out of her car, and walks up onto the porch as Hurley wades through the keys he has on the ring that he got from Monty's house.

"I've been here before on a call," Brenda says. "More than once, in fact. The first time, it was for the upstairs apartment, which is rented out. The second time was the one you spoke to me about, involving our latest victim."

"You were here for the call when Taylor Copeland was fired?" I say.

"I was. It got rather nasty. That Copeland woman was furious."

"Furious enough to kill Dixon?" I say.

Brenda shrugs. "It's starting to look that way, isn't it?"

"Don't jump to conclusions," Hurley says as he finally finds the right key and unlocks the door to the real estate office.

"Did anyone find a gun at Copeland's house?" I ask as he opens the door.

With a worried look, he shakes his head.

I hand Brenda a video camera and we enter a part of the house that used to be a large foyer, but has now been set up as a reception area with a desk, two comfy-looking stuffed chairs, and a small bookcase, on top of which there are several business card holders filled with cards for the agents who work here. Monty's cards are front and center, and there are four other business cards on either side of them, each one with the agent's picture on it. Recalling Taylor's accusation that Monty was trying to get rid of her to make room for his new girlfriend, I look over the pictures. There are two male agents, one of whom is Sawyer, and two female agents, one of which is a gray-haired woman, who looks to be in her late fifties or maybe even sixties. I recognize her name as one I've seen around town for years. I figure that's not likely to be Monty's girlfriend, so that leaves the other female agent: Jessica Leavenworth, a very pretty woman, who looks about twenty-five to thirty, with huge, round blue eyes and long black hair. She bears a strong resemblance to Summer. If this is Monty's new girlfriend, he has a type.

We cross the foyer/reception area and enter a hallway straight ahead that runs to the back of the house. Before the wall was put up, this hall would have followed the staircase to the second floor. Hardwood floors creak beneath our feet as we pass large, high-ceilinged rooms that I imagine once served as a parlor, living room, and dining room. Now they are being used as office space, with one large desk occupying the first room, and two desks in each of the other two rooms, along with several filing cabinets, chairs for clients, and bookcases. Each room has a different color of paint on the walls: forest green for the first room, Colonial blue for the middle one, and the final one in a rich plum. The crowded furniture and dark colors on the walls might have made the rooms feel cavelike, but thanks to the ten-foot-high white ceilings, windows that reach from a foot below the ceilings to a foot above the floors, and the bright white of the base-boards, door and window trim, and crown molding, all the rooms feel bright and airy, even at this time of the day.

The kitchen is at the back of the house and it has been left relatively untouched. It boasts the same polished hardwood floor and high white ceiling as the other rooms. The kitchen cupboards are painted white and they are tall—so much so that I wouldn't be able to reach the upper shelves without a stool—and I measure in at six feet. Hurley has a few inches on me in height and I don't think he could reach them, either. Along the back wall is a huge old porcelain sink beneath a window that looks out onto the backyard. I walk over and look outside. There is a large expanse of green grass with a majestic old oak tree off to one side that boasts a large lower branch that would be ideal for a child's swing, and a big knothole that would make an ideal hiding place for a kid's treasure or a secret note. On the other side of the yard is a maple tree that would be perfect for climbing. It seems a waste not to have one or two kids running around in this backyard, and I wonder if the tenant upstairs has any.

There is a small bathroom off the kitchen, and another

room that I suspect was once a butler's pantry that has been converted into a copy-and-mail room. It's a lovely old home, and while it saddens me that it no longer serves in that capacity, the place still retains a lot of its original charm and character.

"I'll bet this place was magnificent in its heyday," Brenda says, lowering the video camera and turning it off for the moment. "If you stand still and listen, you can almost hear the running feet of little children, laughing as they raced through these rooms a century ago."

We all do as she says, and I swear I *can* hear the laughter and the footsteps. Hurley looks uncomfortable at the idea of little kid ghosts scampering through the house, so I don't say anything, but I'm quite comfortable with the idea of ghosts. I'm a fairly rational person who chose a profession strongly based in math and science, so I'm not inclined to believe in ghosts. But I've also seen some things in my nursing career that have left me to wonder, and I try to keep an open mind. Now that I've been working with the dead for a few years, I've become convinced that if there is some form of afterlife that lingers on this plane of existence, it or they mean us no harm. While I don't generally believe in ghosts, I do have a habit of talking to the dead I care for. I find it comforting.

"Any idea which of these rooms is Monty's office?" I say to Hurley.

"I'd guess it's the one closest to the front because it's the most strategically located and the only one that doesn't appear to be a shared space."

Brenda starts the video camera up again and we make our way back to that office—the one painted forest green—and scope out the stuff on the desk. There is another business card holder filled with Monty's cards, promising "personalized, professional, and principled" service. His cards are quite elegant, printed on thick cream-colored cardstock, with Monty's smiling face in the top left corner, and the pertinent information printed in rich gold-and-black lettering, with the bright red house icon watermarked in the background.

There is a laptop on the desk, and when we open it, I'm surprised to discover that not only isn't the machine password protected, but Monty has let the computer memorize and save all his passwords for the various programs loaded on it. This gives us quick and easy access to his e-mail.

Hurley settles into the chair behind the desk and starts wading through it all with Brenda filming video over one of his shoulders, while I watch over the other. Our use of the video cameras has made our investigations much easier, as it creates a visual and audio report of everything that is seen, said, and done. We started using them a little over three years ago when Chief Hanson got a grant to purchase several cameras and hire a temporary videographer to use them, manage the resultant footage, and teach the rest of the staff how to use them. The videographer we had initially was a young, gorgeous redhead named Charlotte, who insisted that everyone call her Charlie. She was smart, attractive, easy to get along with, and had a knockout figure. Basically, she was everything I felt I wasn't at the time as I was still struggling with David's betrayal and the disintegration of our marriage. My self-image and self-confidence were both at an all-time low. I wanted to hate Charlie on sight, particularly when she started cozying up to Hurley—my relationship with him at that time was about as straightforward as string theory—but Charlie was too likable and too nice a person. To her credit, once she learned I was interested in Hurley, she backed off and, eventually, became a good friend. She's gone now, having moved on to bigger and better things, but the legacy of the video cameras that she brought with her has remained. At this point, every police car, every detective, and every scene processing kit carried by anyone in my office or the police department contains a small video camera, and everyone knows how to use them.

There are fifty-two unread e-mails in Monty's inbox that have arrived since five o'clock yesterday—and they all appear to be business related. Monty has organized his e-mail account with dozens of folders, most of them bearing what I suspect are client's last names. They are alphabetically arranged, and I scan the list, recognizing a few names. Then I see one that makes me pause and I point to it.

"Hurley, look at this folder. What do you suppose is in there?"

The folder is titled *Summer* and Hurley clicks on it. There are dozens of e-mail exchanges and a quick scroll through the list makes me think it's something better perused later. But then I see a header on one that makes my heart quicken.

"Is that who I think it is?" I say to Hurley, pointing at a sender name that is not Summer's.

"Ooh, doggies," Hurley says excitedly, and he clicks on the e-mail.

"Who is Peter Carlisle?" Brenda asks. "Should I know that name?"

"He's a private investigator," Hurley says.

"Hurley hired him to follow me recently," I add, and I see Brenda give me a curious side glance. "Long story," I say with a dismissive wave, remembering that this is all being recorded.

Hurley, meanwhile, is reading the e-mails. "It looks like Monty Dixon hired Peter to investigate both his wife and his son," he says. "There is a report attached." He clicks on the attachment and sends it to the office printer. Several pages spit out almost immediately, making me envious of Monty's printer and his Wi-Fi setup. Our home Wi-Fi is sketchy at best and slow as molasses on a good day, a price we pay for living out in the country where internet service options are few and far between. Whenever our printer has to do its thing, it makes a sound like a patient with a bad case of asthma, kind of the way I sounded when I thought I'd try jogging as a form of torture . . . I mean, exercise. It huffs and wheezes for several seconds before starting to print, and then it pauses every few lines, as if to catch its breath.

I walk over to a small file cabinet and remove pages from the printer sitting on top of it. A quick scan is revealing. "It seems young Sawyer has a teensy gambling problem," I say, feeling a twinge of discomfort. I'm minimizing the situation with the word "teensy" out of defensiveness, because I love to gamble. I've proven that I can blow through a lot of money if left to my own devices inside a casino. I don't know when to quit, and there are times when I feel an itch of a lure to hit up one of the casinos in the state for a random visit with Lady Luck. It seems Sawyer has a similar problem, to the tune of tens of thousands of dollars he apparently couldn't afford to lose.

More pages spit out of the printer as Hurley continues combing through Monty's e-mails. The report on Summer comes up next, and I don't think any of us are surprised to learn that she is having an affair. "Summer's not-so-secret affair is with a man named Damien Cook," I announce to the others in the room after summarizing the report. Then I snort a laugh.

"What's so funny?" Hurley asks.

"Summer told me they have a cook who comes every day and prepares meals for her and Monty. She said his name was Damien. She didn't give me a last name, but how ironic is it that this guy's last name is *Cook*? Is she having an affair with *a cook* named *Cook*? It must be the same guy. I mean, how many Damiens can there be in town?"

Hurley shrugs.

"Don't know a one," Brenda says.

Then another thought comes to me. "I'm willing to bet

that when you call Cut the Cheese, they're going to tell you
that they didn't see Summer Dixon last evening."

"If that's true, it was a ridiculous alibi to offer," Hurley
says. "It's easy enough to check."

"It is, but I'm betting Summer figures you won't check on
it, or if you do, you'll simply check to see if there was a class
and not inquire as to whether she was there."

"We're not that stupid," Hurley says.

"Of course not, but I'm betting Summer Dixon thinks you
are. Or perhaps hopes you are. And anyway, if she's caught
out, I'm also betting she has a ready excuse, one where she
can honestly say she wasn't lying." I pause, suddenly hearing
myself and the number of times I've used the term "betting."
I swallow, and then say, "I'm going to go out on a limb and
say that Summer spent the evening with Damien and that
was her"—I make air quotes with my fingers—" 'cooking
class.' "

Brenda giggles and says, "Ooh, I can just imagine what
kind of hot stuff was served up for the main course. Do you
think she got saucy?"

"You butter believe it," I counter. Hurley groans. "And I'll
bet there were wieners on the menu," I continue.

Brenda snorts a laugh and then, with a sly look, adds, "Or
maybe some salami."

"Need I remind you two that this is being recorded?" Hurley says.

Brenda looks properly chastised, but gives me a wink
when Hurley isn't looking. I grin back at her and then shift
my attention to the rest of the office. I peruse the book-
shelves, which contain everything from a handful of paper-
back novels to hardcover books on business, real estate, and
the many areas associated with it, and some ledger-sized
books. It's a mishmash of information and topics, and again
I'm struck by Monty's apparent lack of organizational skills.
Though maybe he was one of those people who functioned

well in controlled chaos and knew where everything in his messy life was located.

Aside from the private-detective files, Hurley doesn't find anything else of interest in his brief perusal of the e-mails, though there are too many to wade through to be sure. That task will likely fall on Jonas or Laura. We bag up and label everything we can, including Monty's laptop, and haul it out to Hurley's truck, piling it in the backseat. By the time we unload our evidence at the station and log it all in, it's nearly seven in the morning.

When we get home, I check on Matthew and Emily, both of whom are safely tucked into their beds sound asleep. My sister is gone, but she has left a note on the island in the kitchen:

> *Mattie,*
> *Matthew slept the entire time. Em came home at*
> *one, as promised, and after chatting with her for a*
> *while (I think she behaved on her date, as did Johnny),*
> *I decided to go home. But you can bring Matthew over*
> *to my house today, if need be. I'm guessing you and*
> *Steve will have more work to do, and Em said she had*
> *plans to meet up with some friends and study for*
> *finals. Let me know either way.*
> *Love you,*
> *Desi*

I say a little prayer of thanks—not for the first time—for my sister. She is an angel, at least these days. When we were younger, though, there were times I swore she was the devil's spawn. I show the note to Hurley, and when he's done reading it, I tear it up into tiny pieces and flush it. I don't want Emily to think Desi is spying on her in any way, even though Desi does report to me on occasion about what Emily is up to. While Emily is open and willing to discuss things with me that she would never talk to her father about, I'm not sure she's convinced that I won't share everything she tells me with Hurley. There are a few topics I've promised her will stay between us—a promise I've kept because I only make it once I know what the topic at hand is—but I've also told her that if she shares something with me that I feel her father really needs to know, I won't keep it from him. Because of this, she has confided in Desi a time or two about things she must have felt uncomfortable running by me. Desi and I discussed this and agreed to share information, but not let Emily know so she would feel she had someone outside of Hurley and me to go to if she needed to. So far, I haven't felt compelled to share any of it with Hurley. It's just as well, since most of the topics have been girl stuff or questions about dating and sex, and these topics are hot-button items for Hurley when it comes to his daughter.

I touch base with a call to Christopher to see what's planned for the day and to tell him about the Copeland woman. Technically, since it's his weekend on call, her death should be his to deal with. Since it appears the case might be connected to Monty's, I make the decision to handle it. Besides, Christopher is still tied up out in the field with one of the other deaths that occurred. It's up in the air as to who will handle the three autopsies now pending—Monty's, Taylor Copeland's, and Christopher's body in the morgue fridge—and when they'll get done. Chris tells me he'll talk with Doc Morton and call me back. While waiting for his call, I write a note to Emily, telling her that we are napping and plan to get up at eleven after being out all night and would she please watch Matthew for us until then, and if she can't for some reason, to wake me.

Chris calls back and informs me that Otto Morton will do both of my autopsies today, as the one they have from their calls can wait. "He'll start at noon with Monty and then do Taylor Copeland. Barring any unforeseen problems, he should be done by five. You are welcome to assist if you want, but I told him you have interviews at noon and one and need to be home by four, so he said he's fine working alone if he has to. I'll help him as much as I can, assuming I don't get called out."

"Thank you, Christopher," I say, hearing the Siren song of my bed.

"No, thank *you*. What a crazy weekend."

It certainly has been, and I have a strong feeling it's going to get worse. But crazy will just have to wait because I have a hot date with my bed.

CHAPTER 9

When Hurley's alarm goes off, he slaps it quiet and bounds out of bed, heading for the bathroom. He always wakes up full of energy and raring to go, a characteristic that can be surprisingly annoying. I, on the other hand, tend to lie in the bed trying to convince myself that I need to leave its warmth and comfort while the soft and soothing voice of Hypnos tries to lull me away to his underworld.

Today Hypnos is easily cast aside, perhaps because the hours of sleep I've had are so short that I never fully rested. Years ago, when I was working as an OR nurse, I learned how to wake up fast and get my brain functioning well, despite the lack of sleep. Things aren't much different these days, since I still pull call duty and get awakened at all hours of the night. Functioning on little sleep is something I'm well-heeled in. But that doesn't mean I like it.

I get out of bed as Hurley emerges from the bathroom barefoot but dressed in jeans and a T-shirt, his hair wet and combed into place, a five o'clock shadow and then some on his face. He's able to shower and dress in ten minutes flat most days if he doesn't shave, something that makes me jealous. I can tell he has brushed his teeth when he walks over and kisses me on the forehead.

"Rise and shine, Squatch," he says in an annoyingly chipper voice. With that, he heads off down the hallway.

I shuffle into the bathroom and catch sight of myself in the mirror, surprised that Hurley was able to look at me, much less kiss me. Since I didn't bother to remove my makeup before dropping into bed, I have raccoon eyes. My hair is sticking up and out like Medusa snakes, and my face is puffy and pale. I sit on the toilet to empty my bladder, and our two cats, Tux and Rubbish, stroll into the bathroom and sit at my feet, watching me. I don't understand why cats feel compelled to provide an audience to my toilet time, but they do so regularly. Sometimes Hoover even gets in on the gig. I shoo the cats away when I'm done, take a quick shower, blow-dry my hair, and decide to go without makeup for the day. My speed routine takes me twenty minutes.

By the time I dress and make it downstairs, Hurley, Emily, and Matthew are sitting at the kitchen table eating. Even though it's lunchtime, everyone is eating breakfast: Cheerios with apple juice for Matthew because he doesn't like them with milk, Cheerios with milk for Hurley, and a toasted English muffin with a fried egg on it for Emily. Our dog, Hoover, is in his usual spot next to Matthew's seat. He lies here because he knows Matthew drops food often, though sometimes the kid simply tosses the dog tidbits. I see that Matthew is dressed in denim pants, a button-up shirt that he has on backward, and mismatched shoes and socks.

I give Hurley a questioning look and he shakes his head, his lips pursed, letting me know to let it go. Matthew has been experimenting with his dress of late and he gets quite upset if we don't let him wear what he wants. Most of the time, it's not worth the turmoil it causes to argue the matter with him, even though he often ends up looking like a Picasso painting.

Grabbing a cereal bowl from the cupboard, I pour myself some Cheerios. The box feels suspiciously light and, sure enough, I get five whole Cheerios out of it.

"Sorry," Hurley says with an apologetic wink. "I just used the last of the apple juice, too."

I add "apple juice" and "Cheerios" to the mental shopping list in my head even as I push down a surge of resentment that Hurley has relayed the information to me as if it's assumed to be my job to take care of these shortages. *Help is on the way,* I remind myself, assuming we ever hire someone to help with the housework. I opt for a cup of coffee and a piece of buttered toast for breakfast and settle in at the table with the others.

"Thanks for watching your brother, Em," I say.

"No problem, especially since we agreed these short-notice sessions deserve double pay." Emily is saving up for college and has a fund she uses for gas money and entertainment expenses. Thanks to our frequent need for a last-minute babysitter and Emily's clever bartering skills, she's saved up an impressive amount.

"I can't watch him for the rest of the day, though," she says. "I'm meeting a group of friends so we can study for finals."

"That's okay. Desi can do it. I'll give her a call and let her know I'll be dropping Matthew off."

"Already did," Hurley says. "She's expecting you."

Desi is a peppy early riser like Hurley, and I'm sure the fact that she didn't get home until bar closing hours last night hasn't slowed her down one whit. We rely on Izzy's partner, Dom, for most of our day-to-day childcare needs because he, like Desi, is a natural parent at heart. Plus, he and Izzy have an adorable daughter, Juliana, who is a year-and-a-half old and Matthew's favorite playmate. I'm very conscious of not using Dom to the point where he feels like we're taking advantage of him—though I doubt he would ever think that.

My sister happily helps to keep things in balance because, in addition to Juliana, Dom and Izzy also have Izzy's elderly mother, Sylvie, to care for. And these days, Sylvie is as much of a challenge as any toddler, probably more so. She's tiny, frail, and in the throes of dementia, though she hasn't forgotten how to fling verbal assaults at people. Last week when I was driving her to a hair salon for her bimonthly perm of the few hairs left on her head, she informed me that I needed to drop a few pounds. "Men, they don't like the chunky girls," she said.

I glared at her and suggested that I could instantly rid myself of a few pounds by pulling over and letting her out. She said I was a nasty girl and slapped me on the arm.

"There's something your sister wanted me to tell you," Hurley says in an ominous tone.

"Okay." I brace myself, wondering what it might be. Has she tired of the babysitting routine? Are she and Lucien getting a divorce? They've had some hard times over the past couple of years and things were strained there for a while. Could it be a problem with one of their kids, Ethan or Erika? Ethan, who is twelve, is a quiet, withdrawn kid whose primary interests lie along the lines of entomology. He has a hair-raising collection of dead bugs on display in his bedroom, and if that isn't enough to make your goose bumps rise, he also has a couple of live ones: a tarantula named Fluffy and a three-inch-long Madagascar hissing cockroach named Hissy. The only thing I can imagine Desi wanting to tell me about Ethan is that one of these "pets" is again on the loose—something that happens more than I like.

Erika is the more likely candidate. At the age of fifteen, almost sixteen, she is like many teenage girls who are often at odds with their mothers. She and Desi have had some heated arguments recently over Erika wanting to extend her curfew, her choice in friends, and her choice in clothing (too revealing for Desi's taste and, frankly, mine as well, unless she wants to start working in a brothel). The only thing Erika hasn't made an issue of yet is dating, and I've started to wonder if she might be gay. She has several girlfriends that she hangs with all the time and, at her age, I would expect her to be much more interested in boys than she is. When I was her age, I was all about dating and flirting, both of which were made difficult by the fact that I was taller than nearly every boy I knew. While I reconciled myself to the disproportions, most of the boys didn't. They felt intimidated, and at times even emasculated by the disparities in height, and often dismissed me as potential girlfriend material as a result. The fact that I was something of a klutz (and still am, if truth be told) didn't help. I earned the moniker of Blunder Woman one year, and the nickname Sequoia in another. Whispered calls of "Timber!" followed me all year long.

By the time high school ended, a lot of the boys had finally caught up to me in height and things got a little easier, but in middle school and my early high-school years, the only thing boys seemed interested in doing with me was slow dancing. I think the fact that their faces often hit around the level of my boobs had something to do with that. There's a reason my sister nicknamed me Boobzilla in high school.

I put my mental money (there I go betting again) on Erika's sexual orientation being the topic at hand my sister wants to address, but I'm far off the mark.

"She has invited your father to live with them and he has accepted," Hurley informs me.

"Oh." I digest this tidbit of information, unsure how I feel about it. My relationship with my father is complicated, and that's putting it mildly. His name, at least the one he uses now, is Cedric Novak and he left my mother and me when I was four years old, or at least that's the history I grew up believing. This made me resentful and angry toward him most of my life, though there was also a small part of me that felt hurt, abandoned, and flawed, wondering what it was about me that made my father want to leave me.

In recent years, I have come to learn that the situation wasn't what I'd always believed. While it was true that my father left us back then, he did so because he was a key witness in busting up a huge crime ring in Chicago, and he entered the Witness Protection Program. My mother, who was pregnant with Desi at the time, though she didn't inform my father of this, declined to accept that lifestyle. My father was also a member of a traveling group of "family" that roamed around the countryside running stings and scams on people. He had several other aliases he used while committing his crimes, a common ruse among his people. His marriage to my mother was something this "family" didn't approve of, so he kept it a secret and lived a double life for most of the time that they were married.

Desi and I grew up thinking that our mother's second husband was Desi's father, a subterfuge that this man agreed to play out for my mother. We didn't learn the truth—that Desi and I are full sisters, not half sisters—until two years ago. It was easy to believe that we were only half related, as we look very different. I inherited my mother's pale coloring, blond hair, and blue eyes, but my father's large build. Desi got our father's dark complexion and hair, but our mother's petite build. Strange how genetics work out sometimes.

Desi has taken to my father much faster and easier than I have. She has forgiven him for his past, for the lies—though those were perpetrated and perpetuated as much by our mother as our father—and Desi has embraced her relationship with him. I, on the other hand, have had a difficult time letting go of all the resentment I've carried around for decades. When my father had a heart attack recently, it softened my own heart a lot, and Desi's gentle but persistent coaxing has gone a long way toward convincing me to give him a second chance. Yet some small part of me still resists, and I don't fully understand why.

Since his return, our father has been living in a rented trailer on some farmer's property, but he has made a concerted effort to be involved in our lives, to get to know us and his grandchildren. The fact that Desi has taken this last step of inviting him to live with her, Lucien, and the kids bothers me a smidge, but not as much as it might have a year ago.

"Are you okay with that?" Hurley asks me, aware of my history with, and convoluted feelings for, my father.

"I suppose I have to be. It's her choice."

"He and Matthew seem to get along well," Hurley says, testing the waters a little more.

"Yes, they do," I say with a smile at my son.

I don't know how much of what we're discussing, and all the undercurrents that go with it, Matthew understands. But he proves to me that those little ears aren't missing much when he says, "I get to see Pop-pop today?" His eyes are wide with excited anticipation.

"Sounds like you might," I tell him.

"Goody, goody, goody," he says. Then he embellishes a little by using a singsongy voice: "Goody, goody, good, good, goody." His legs kick in rhythm with the words and his head bobs back and forth.

I look at Hurley and he gives me a conciliatory nod. I nod back and then he says, "Should we ride together or take separate cars?"

"Best take separate vehicles," I tell him. "Who knows where this case is going to go, and I might have to help with the autopsies.

"When will they be done, do you think?" I summarize my phone conversations with Christopher. When I'm done, Hurley glances at his watch and gives me a sympathetic look. "You okay to take Matthew to your sister's?"

"I am. I know I've been slow to come to terms with all of this, but I've made a lot of progress. I'm not all the way there yet, but I'm getting close."

"Okay. I'll meet you at the station then?" he asks as he gathers up his empty bowl and puts it in the sink.

"That will work."

Hurley heads upstairs to finish getting dressed. It will take him all of five minutes. He looks good in everything he wears. I, meanwhile, often agonize over what to wear, depending on what state my body image is in for the day. There are days when I feel fat. There are days when I am fat. There are days when I feel like my thighs are a percussion instrument, and days when I feel like my butt needs its own zip code. I can't wear corduroy pants because I'm afraid the friction created by those wales rubbing together on my inner thighs might start a fire. And then there are the days when my boobs behave like football players running onto a field and bursting through a paper banner. It came as a shock to me to learn that my boobs aren't both the same size and can change from one day to the next, more so now that I've had a child. A blouse that fits fine on Tuesday might be straining at the buttons on Saturday.

My son has a thing with his clothes, too, though not for the same reasons. His issues seem to stem from some arbitrary preferences he has regarding the colors in the fabrics, the way they feel on his body, and a complete and utter lack of fashion sense. Some of his recent combinations have been downright bizarre. He confiscated one of Emily's bras, strung it around his waist, tucked some toys into the cups, and declared himself a superhero with the bra serving as his utility belt. Except Matthew called it a "futility" belt, an accidental but apropos bit of insight on his part.

I just hope he outgrows this phase before he starts school, because I feel certain that a kid who wears things like mismatched shoes, a bra futility belt, and shorts over pants is just begging to get his ass kicked by the other kids. Then again, what would one expect from the offspring of Blunder Woman but a superhero who will probably be called something like Braman, or perhaps his sidekick, Boobin.

CHAPTER 10

When I get to Desi's, any anxiety I was harboring over another encounter with my father proves to be for naught. He is asleep on the foldout bed kept in Lucien's home office, a space Desi informs me is going to become a permanent room for him, and a space I'm sure Lucien isn't happy about giving up. The additional upside for me, however, is that Lucien is seated at the dining-room table doing something on his laptop instead of being hidden away in his office, which is usually the case whenever I come over. Normally, it's a relief when I don't have to deal with Lucien, but today I have a reason to talk to him.

Desi takes Matthew from me, biting back a smile at his outfit of choice. "Hey, if you think this one is goofy, you should have seen the one he had on the other day," I tell her.

"Well, at least he's willing to wear clothes," Desi says. "Ethan went through a phase when he was four where he wanted to be naked all the time. He ran around the house naked, ate all his meals naked, wanted to play outside naked—I put my foot down on that one—and one morning he wanted to go to daycare naked. He was fascinated with insects even then and he said, 'Bugs don't wear clothes, so why should I?'" She smiles and shakes her head, looking wistful with the memory. "We had a long talk, several in fact, about the appropriateness of nudity in certain segments of society and eventually he outgrew it. I worried that he would grow up to be a pervert, but I've since come to realize it was just one of the many stages kids go through."

"Thanks for reminding me that it can always be worse," I say with a wan smile. "Think Lucien will mind if I interrupt him?"

Desi makes a fleeting V with her eyebrows, letting me know she is curious about my sudden change of topic, not to mention my asking for Lucien. My relationship with my brother-in-law has been, well, challenging, to say the least. In the work arena, the man is known for his crass behavior, but I have seen a different side of him here in his home. He is a wonderful father to his kids and, while far from perfect, he has been a good husband to my sister. He's been kind and polite with me on occasion, but for some reason, he tends to default to his crass work persona when he's around me, peppering our conversations with crude sexual innuendo and inflammatory comments. Desi once told me that this behavior is his way of hiding the fact that he's feeling threatened, or worried, or intimidated. If he makes people uncomfortable and unsure of how to behave around him, it gives him an edge.

"Lucien is a little frightened of you," Desi once told me.

When I asked her why on earth he had any reason to feel that way, I half expected her to say it was because of my size. I have Lucien by a couple of inches in height, and while I don't know how much he weighs, I'm certain I have him in that category, too, by a good margin.

"It's because he knows how close you and I are," Desi said. "He knows I listen to you, and that you have influence over me. He thinks that if you told me to leave him, I'd do it, no questions asked."

"Is that true?" I'd asked.

She shook her head and gave me a sly smile. "I'll always listen to what you have to say, but I make my own decisions. Still, it doesn't hurt to let Lucien believe it's true, now does it?"

My sister has the face of an angel and a gentle, singsongy voice that evokes images of Disney heroines, making her seem like an easy pushover at times. But I know from growing up with her that her personality is anything but sweet and subservient. She is the sister who once made me a canned dog food and tomato sandwich, telling me it was a sloppy joe. Since we had no pets—my mother is and always has been a hypochondriac of the first order and, to her, any animal is nothing more than a vector for germs—I had no reason to suspect the substitution. She also dumped ice water over my head once when I was taking a bath, and on another occasion, she broke all the posts off my earrings because my ears were pierced and hers weren't. That was the mild price I paid for an impulsive decision, one I did without my mother's knowledge or permission. I lied to the girl at the ear-piercing kiosk at the mall and told her I was eighteen. For situations like that and, in later years, for getting into bars before I was of age, my height was an advantage because I could pass for older than I was. When Mom found out what I'd done, she spent weeks telling me about all the horrible infectious processes, like flesh-eating bacteria, that could now take hold, starting with my ears, and rapidly spreading throughout my body. This became even more likely when I was required to wear the same earrings for weeks on end because Desi had destroyed all but the ones I was wearing, and I didn't have the money to buy more. I had nightmares for weeks about my ears rotting off, followed by the flesh on my face.

Desi is a much different person these days, thank goodness. So she doesn't come right out and ask me why I want Lucien, even though I know she's curious. "He's in the dining room," she tells me.

I decide to reward her politeness with some answers. "He might have some knowledge about that case we got last night that I want to discuss with him."

She waves a hand toward the dining room. "Have at him," she says. "And while you do that, I'm going to take this guy out to the kitchen so he can help me make strawberry pancakes."

"Pancakes!" Matthew yells, and with the eagerness he's displaying, you'd never guess he ate breakfast fifteen minutes ago. He may have his father's looks, but he has my appetite.

As they disappear into the kitchen, I make my way into the dining room and find Lucien sitting in one of the chairs, frowning at his laptop.

"Mattiekins!" he says when he sees me. "What brings you my way?"

"A case. I understand you handled the will for Monty Dixon."

"I did," he says, his brow furrowing. "And I'm guessing you don't come with good news if you're asking about a will."

"You guess right. Monty is dead."

Lucien shakes his head, looking mournful. "What happened?"

"Someone stabbed him with a broken pool cue."

"Really?" Lucien now looks intrigued rather than sad. "Any idea who did the deed?"

"Not yet. But there are a couple of likely candidates in the mix already, his wife and his son. I'm heading into the station to meet with Hurley now to talk to them."

"Interesting," he says.

"Any surprises in the will?"

Lucien scratches the side of his head, leaving his strawberry-blond hair sticking straight out above his ear. "I did that will a few years ago, back when I was branching out into other areas of work, and I don't recall the specifics off the top of my head. I don't think there was anything that would make for high drama, but it doesn't matter. About six months ago, I got a notice from a lawyer in Mauston that he had redone the will, making mine null and void."

"Do you happen to recall that lawyer's name?"

Lucien shakes his head. "I know I have it in a file at the office. If it's urgent, I can go in there today and try to dig it up. Or if it can wait until morning, I'll do it first thing when I go in."

"Tomorrow morning should be fine. Give Hurley a call when you find it."

"Will do, Mattiekins."

"Thanks."

With that, I start to leave, but stop and turn back. "I hear you've invited my father to live with you."

Lucien rolls his eyes. " 'Invite' might be too strong a word," he says. Then he shrugs. "But to be honest, I like the guy. He's really trying to make a go of things, and it can't be easy for him with all that's happened. He and Desi seem to be bonding. And 'happy wife, happy life,' " he concludes.

I'm not sure what to make of the fact that Lucien thinks my father is an okay guy. It's not the greatest recommendation I could ask for, but Lucien does have a keen sense for people. Then I hear a door open in the direction of Lucien's home office and heavy footsteps clomping down the hall toward the bathroom. I realize it's probably my father getting up for the day—he's a self-proclaimed night owl—and I panic at the thought of having to talk to him.

I glance at my watch and tell Lucien, "Talk to you later." Then I hightail it out of the house at a near run.

My history with my father is so complicated that I'm not sure I'll ever be comfortable around him. After so many years of hating him, I'm finding it hard to trust my heart to him now. I spent nearly my entire life yearning for a father, and now that I have one, I don't know what to do with him. It doesn't help that the desertion that led to my feelings of resentment and animosity wasn't for the purely selfish reasons I'd come to believe. Yet there is a part of me that feels he deserved what he got because he chose a life of criminality and cons. Some of that was because it's how he was raised, but at some point he made choices that ultimately put him—and potentially my mother and me—in harm's way.

I'm making progress in my relationship with him, but it's all baby steps. Maggie Baldwin has told me it's a wonder I'm sane at all, given my upbringing. My mother was hardly a stabilizing influence with her severe hypochondria and obsessive-compulsive disorder, both of which worsened over the years. I was often left in charge of the household when my mother would take to her sickbed, and I figured it was good practice for the future, since I spent a good portion of my childhood thinking my mother was going to die any day and leave me to raise myself and Desi.

There were some periods of respite over the years. After divorcing my father, my mother remarried three more times and her choice of husbands was surprisingly good. My stepfathers provided the only stability I had in my life growing up. Unfortunately, Mom's instabilities led to short relationships, and her longest marriage only lasted three years. She's in the running for tying that one now, though the man she is living with currently is not married to her. William (not Bill) Hanover was a blind date I saw once, even though he was fifteen years older than me, but his allergy to cats and his obsessive need for neatness and order doomed us right from the start. It made him a perfect match for my mother, however, and they have been together now for nearly three years and I've heard Mom boast a time or two about how she snagged herself a younger man.

Given my history, it's no wonder I have trouble handing my heart over to my father. I don't trust myself to rely on people. My mother was unreliable throughout my childhood;

my history was rewritten so that much of what I once believed to be true has now been proven wrong; and every serious romantic interest I had before Hurley has let me down and hurt me in some manner, my ex-husband being the most recent example. I learned to trust Hurley, but it didn't come easily, and I feel that shucking the past and embracing this new truth with my father is a bit more than I can handle right now.

I just hope he's patient and will wait for me.

CHAPTER 11

I believe in tough self-love and I chastise myself all the way to the police station, talking aloud and labeling myself a judgmental, lily-livered chicken, and an insecure nitwit among other things. I'm really getting into it at a stoplight when I look over at a pedestrian waiting to cross in front of me. I recognize the fellow as Tim Bartlett, an old high-school acquaintance and someone I once had a crush on. But Tim was one of those guys who never achieved enough height to equal or outdo me and therefore wouldn't give me the time of day. Though now, as I see the way he's looking at me as I'm lecturing sternly to myself in my hearse, I start to think that it might have been more than my height that scared some of the boys away. Whatever thoughts are driving his reservations at the moment must be powerful, because he won't cross in front of me even when the light gives him the right of way.

When the light finally changes, I spare a few words of tough love for Tim Bartlett before leaving him behind. By the time I park my hearse in the public lot out front and head inside, I've thoroughly flogged myself verbally and have promised to try and do better in the future.

The dispatcher on duty, a woman named Heidi, is on the radio handling a call and she greets me with a nod and buzzes me into the back area of the station without a word. I walk down a long hallway with offices on either side, all of them empty on a Sunday morning, except for Hurley's, which is the last one on the left. He is seated at his desk, jotting some things down in his notebook, and I walk over and kiss him on the back of his neck.

"Hmm," he mutters, sitting back in his seat and closing his eyes. "A little more of that and we'll never get anything done." He reaches one arm around behind him and pats me on my thigh.

"Okay, back to business," I say, stepping around to his side. "Who's first on our agenda?"

He looks up at me, all dreamy-eyed for a moment, before sighing and leaning forward, arms on his desk, back to work. "Summer is first. She's due here in five minutes. I've got The Hole set up already. I was just jotting down some questions before she gets here." He nods toward the coffee mug on his desk, currently half empty. "And I put a fresh pot of coffee on in the breakroom, if you like."

"Ooh, you do know the way to this girl's heart," I say. I give him a kiss on top of his head and I'm about to head for said breakroom when I see that Hurley has written *cooking class* in his notebook with a big question mark behind it. Following that is <u>NO!</u> in caps and underlined. "Did you check on her alibi?" I ask him, pointing to the note.

"I did," he says. "I was able to reach the store owner right before you came in and she said Summer wasn't signed up for the class last night and wasn't in attendance. So we have lie number one."

"Interesting, though not particularly surprising. I've already told you where I think she was."

"Did you see your father at Desi's?"

The sudden change of subject throws me for a second and another wash of shame comes over me at my yellow-bellied departure. "No, he wasn't up yet," I say, only a partial lie. I justify this response in my mind by telling myself that, technically, I can't be sure it was him I heard, so as far as I can prove, it's the truth. Never mind the fact that there is no one else in that house that is big enough to walk with the type of thunderous footsteps I heard coming down that hall. Since my father stands about six-four and weighs around three hundred pounds, it's a safe bet that it was him. But Hurley doesn't need to know that.

"I did have a brief chat with Lucien about Monty's will, though," I say, eager to change the subject. "Apparently, Monty had a new one drafted about six months ago through a different lawyer up in Poynette. Lucien is going to look up the guy's name in the morning when he goes into the office and pass it on to you. He offered to go in and dig it up today, but I figured it could wait until morning. If that's not okay, give him a call."

"No, that should be fine. I've got plenty of stuff to do today and I figure I'll start to flag early, thanks to the lack of sleep. Did Lucien recall if there were any surprises in the will?"

"He doesn't remember it that well, which suggests to me that there weren't any. I think Lucien would have remembered if there had been any nasty surprises written into it."

Hurley's desk phone buzzes then, and Heidi announces that Summer Dixon has arrived, along with her lawyer. Mention of a lawyer is news to me and to Hurley, if the scowl on his face is any indication. He tells Heidi, "I'll be up in a minute," and then looks at me. "Interesting that she brought a lawyer today after spilling her guts last night, despite Harrison Dixon's cautions."

"It's probably a smart move on her part, given that she lied to us about her whereabouts last night and has to know we're going to figure that out."

"Well, this might make things more interesting," Hurley says. "Or a lot quicker. Are you ready?"

I nod. "I'll grab a quick coffee and meet you in The Hole."

Hurley accompanies me to the breakroom so I can get my coffee and then we walk back down the hallway together to what has come to be fondly referred to as "The Hole" in recent times. It's a multipurpose space that serves as meeting room, conference room, interrogation room, and proof of one woman's horrible taste in home décor. It's equipped with comfy chairs, a hideous color scheme, ugly pictures on the walls, and is as far from anyone's idea of an interrogation room as you can get. It does have audio-visual–recording capabilities, and there is even a ring in the floor beneath the table and one on top of the table for securing handcuffs, if necessary, but aside from these accoutrements, it looks like any other conference meeting room designed by someone doing too much LSD back in the sixties. A recent police officer hire, upon seeing the room for the first time, gaped at it for several seconds and then asked if he'd just fallen down Alice's rabbit hole. Somehow that analogy struck a spark with the others and the room has been called "The Hole" ever since.

Hurley parts company with me to go and fetch Summer and her lawyer. His furrowed brow and pondering silence, while I was getting my coffee, tell me he's rethinking this meeting now that there is a lawyer involved. I'm certain Hurley was going to make this conversation with Summer official and read her the Miranda prior to starting, but given the way she behaved last night, it's a bit of a surprise that she suddenly feels the need for a lawyer.

I enter The Hole and stand behind a chair just inside the door and to the left of the seat the person in charge of questioning always takes. The controls for the A-V equipment are located beneath the table's edge at that prime seat, and the people being questioned will typically be seated across the table from the interrogator, though sometimes they will sit at the head of the table. I don't want to sit yet because I don't want Summer Dixon looking down on me when she enters the room. Standing, I will tower over the woman, a small but useful psychological edge that I've grown used to over my lifetime. With any luck, I'll also tower over the lawyer. I figure if I'm stuck with this body, I might as well work it to my advantage whenever I can.

I'm in The Hole for maybe a minute when the door opens and Summer walks in. She spares me a glance before taking in the rest of the room and wrinkling her nose as if the room has a foul odor. Her eyes widen as she takes in the décor, and she gives the subtlest shake of her head, as if in disbelief. Right behind her is her lawyer, and any advantage I thought I might have has vanished faster than the mac and cheese Matthew threw down to Hoover the other day.

"Hello, Mattiekins," Lucien says with a smile and a wink.

"What the hell, Lucien?" I say.

He shrugs, his smile widening. "Literally seconds after you left, I got a call from Summer here asking if I'd be willing to represent her during this little chat."

I look at Summer suspiciously. "You called him? He didn't call you?" If Lucien is going to use information that I provide to him about cases to build up his client base, there's going to be a lot more to chat about here.

"I did," Summer says. "Harrison talked me into it. He wanted to represent me himself, but I didn't like that idea. He doesn't do this kind of law, and I figured if I'm going to get someone, it should be someone who knows what they're doing."

Hurley is standing behind Lucien and he says, "Would you two please take a seat on that side of the table?"

Summer walks around the end of the table to the other side, eyeing the pictures on the wall and the coverings on the chairs with a look of horror mixed with disgust. Lucien, who has been here before, ignores the décor and quickly positions himself at the head of the table, telling Summer to take the seat to his right. She does so and, with a weighty sigh, settles herself in. Lucien does the same, and I note that he managed to find time enough to change his clothes from when I saw him at the house. Then he was wearing sweatpants and a sweatshirt, now he's dressed in a tan suit, albeit a wrinkled one, and the pale blue dress shirt he has on beneath the jacket has a large pink smear on one side of it that I'd be willing to bet is from the strawberries Desi prepped to go on her pancakes. Whenever I see Lucien in his professional mode, he's always wearing clothes sporting food stains. It makes me wonder if it's become such a standard element of his professional character that he purposely smears something on himself as part of his daily dress routine. I know he thinks, or at least hopes, his lazy, sloppy appearance will make his opponents think he's a lazy, sloppy lawyer, but it's a wasted effort on Hurley and me. We know all too well that Lucien is sharper than most, and darned good at what he does.

Lucien is carrying a battered briefcase, which he sets on the table and snaps open. He lifts the lid carefully, since only one of the hinges is fully attached. He removes a pen and a writing tablet, and then lets the lid drop. It lands cockeyed atop the bottom half of the briefcase, but Lucien ignores it and, instead, looks expectantly at Hurley.

Hurley and I take our seats, and Hurley flips a switch under the table to start the recording equipment. He states the date, time, and case that's being investigated, and then names everyone in the room. Then, as I expected, he recites the Miranda warning to Summer. Sometimes the mere sound of those words, which are known to anyone who watches TV, strikes fear into the listener when they realize they're a potential suspect. I have no doubt that Summer already knows she's a suspect. Yet I don't get the sense that she's overly concerned about it.

"Mrs. Dixon, I'd like to begin by asking you again as to your whereabouts last evening."

Summer Dixon leans back in her chair and glances at Lucien, who gives her a subtle nod. Summer then looks at Hurley, a hint of a smile on her face. She studies him without answering for long enough that Hurley gives her another prompt.

"Mrs. Dixon?"

Her smile broadens and she leans forward, clasping her hands and resting them on the tabletop. "Yes, yes, I told you a teensy bit of fabrication last night." She emphasizes the *teensy* aspect by holding up one hand and making a pinching gesture with her thumb and forefinger. "I *was* at a cooking class of sorts, but not the one that I mentioned to you. I panicked there for a second because I didn't want the truth to come out. That comes from months of needing to lie about such things, and even though I didn't need to lie anymore last night, old habits are hard to break, you know?" She shrugs her shoulders dismissively and smiles coquettishly at Hurley, who stares stonily back at her. Not seeing a softening on Hurley's face, she shifts her gaze to me.

"You know how it is, right? You have a secret that you've been keeping for so long, and when suddenly you don't need to keep it anymore, it's hard to let it out."

I feel my cheeks redden at her words; they strike a little too close to home for me. Hurley shifts in his seat and I suspect he feels the same slightly uncomfortable level of aptness in her words.

"Where were you, Mrs. Dixon?" Hurley repeats, his impatience clearly communicated in his tone and his expression.

Summer's smile vanishes. "I was with Damien, our chef, at his apartment," she says. She tries the smile again, but it looks forced and fake and she seems to sense this because she gives up on it after a second or two. "He really was teaching me how to cook something, but that isn't the main reason I was there. We have a relationship."

"A *relationship*?" Hurley says.

"Yes." Summer's eyes dart toward me with an imploring look. If she's hoping I'm going to help her through this awkwardness, she's about to be disappointed. "A romantic relationship," she concludes.

"You're having an affair with your chef?" I say, and Summer shoots me a look of utter disappointment, as if I'm a traitor to some secret club we both belong to. I'm not bothered by it, since I have no desire to join that particular club. I might not tell Hurley every little thing that's on my mind or bothering me, and I might have participated in one or two minor deceptive acts recently, but they were white lies compared to Summer's black level of deception with infidelity.

Some mean little voice inside my head asks me, *Does it really matter what type of deception one practices, because it's all betrayal, isn't it?* I tell that voice, *Shut the hell up,* and then remind her, *I know lots of clever ways to kill people, and likely get away with it, so if you know what's good for you, you'll crawl back into whatever mind cave you emerged from and stay there. Silently.*

Summer continues with her explanation. "My husband and I haven't been very close over the past two years, in part because of that idiot son of his and Monty's stupid decision to let him move into our house."

"What was Monty's reaction to your affair? Were the two of you planning on a divorce?" Hurley asks.

"Oh, Monty didn't know," she says with a dismissive smile, looking at Hurley like he's an idiot child for even asking the question. "He thought I was trying to learn how to cook. And I was, truth be told. That's how the whole thing started. I asked Damien for some cooking lessons and things ended up getting a little more heated than we originally planned." She shrugs and the smile widens.

"Monty did know," I inform her, and I have the satisfaction of seeing her smile fall apart. "He hired a private investigator to check up on you and we found reports from that investigator informing Monty of your indiscretion."

Summer looks genuinely stricken. "He knew?" she says, her voice bearing a hint of tremble. "Are you sure?"

"Quite." This from Hurley. "We found e-mail exchanges between the PI and Monty that were quite . . . um . . . explicit."

If he's hoping to embarrass the woman, he'll have to try again. Summer doesn't look at all ashamed by her behavior. Rather she looks worried, and I think I might know why. "Mrs. Dixon, how long have you and Damien been an item?"

"We are not an item," she says with distaste. "We were very discreet and never acted like a couple in public. I would never dis Monty like that."

Interesting set to her moral compass, I think. "How long?" I repeat.

"A little over a year."

"Did it start after he invited Sawyer to come and live with the two of you?"

There is the faintest hint of a frown on her pretty face, a twitch of the eyebrows that draws them together, a brief downturn at the corners of her mouth. It's there and gone in a flash. "It did," she says. Then, with an air of suspicion, she asks, "Why do you ask?"

I think she knows why I'm asking. I think she knows I'm going down the path she is steadfastly avoiding. She just can't verbalize it.

"Just wondering if perhaps Monty was rethinking his will," I say, watching her face closely. I shoot a glance at Lucien. "I understand he recently revised it." Judging from the look on Summer's face, I have struck at the heart of what matters to her. Her desire to hide her affair from her husband had nothing to do with his peace of mind or standing in the community. It was all about maintaining her financial position with him.

"Is that true, Lucien?" Summer says, eyeing him with a look of betrayal.

"Probably," Lucien says, squirming in his seat. This makes me like Summer a tiny bit more because not many people can make Lucien squirm.

"Probably?" Summer screeches. "You can't do any better than *probably?*"

"I do know that I was called by a lawyer who said Monty had redone his will, making the one I did null and void. But I have no proof it happened."

"And you were going to tell me this when?" Summer asks accusingly.

"Sorry, Mrs. Dixon, but I wasn't obligated to share that information with you. Presumably, the police or someone else will dig up a more recent document, but if nothing turns up, it's possible that the one I drew up will still hold."

"I need contact information for Damien," Hurley says, the unexpected segue making both Summer and Lucien whip their attention toward him. There is a moment of silent staring until Summer snaps out of it and removes her cell phone from her purse. She jabs angrily at the screen while muttering about "wills . . . the gall . . . stupid lawyers," and a few other things that might or might not get picked up by the room's mike. Once she has Damien's info up on the screen, she slides the phone across the table to Hurley.

"Whoa!" Lucien says, grabbing the cell phone. "Let's not provide information we don't need to."

"Oh, it doesn't matter," Summer says churlishly. "I let him scroll through the whole thing last night."

"You did what?" Lucien says with deadly calm, his eyes nearly bulging out of his head.

"I gave him my phone and let him look through it."

"Oh, for cripes' sake," Lucien mutters, running a hand over his head. It leaves his strawberry-blond hair standing up in little tufts everywhere. He then slaps the hand to his chest, as if he's about to have a heart attack. From the apoplectic look on his face, he just might.

"Cool your jets, Lucien," Summer says. "I didn't kill Monty, and now that I've confessed about Damien, I have nothing to hide."

"Can I get Damien's info?" Hurley says to Lucien. "I didn't write anything down last night. I just looked at her call and message history." I'm pretty sure my husband is lying because I'm almost certain Brenda got it all on video last night when Hurley was looking at Summer's phone.

"*Just?*" Lucien echoes. "You *just* looked at her call and message history?" He shakes his head miserably and pins Hurley with a classic Lucien glare. "Did you Mirandize her first?"

"Nope, I was simply gathering information at that point. I do have audio and visual of Summer giving me the phone and agreeing to let me look at it."

Lucien is about to say something else, but I decide to side-track him.

"Did Monty say anything to you about changing his will

recently?" I ask Summer. This has the desired effect of riveting her attention on me.

"Obviously not," she says, that fleeting-frown face of hers putting in another appearance.

"Did he discuss his plans for Sawyer's inheritance with you?"

Summer rears back in her seat. "He had plans for Sawyer to inherit?"

"Why wouldn't he?" I ask, deftly avoiding any answer to her question and upping the ante with one of my own. "Sawyer is his son, his only child, right?"

"Yes, but . . ." She hesitates, and I can tell her brain is scrambling for a way to say what she wants without it making her look like a greedy, bitter, selfish witch.

"But what?" I encourage. Lucien is busy writing down Damien's contact info for Hurley and I figure I might as well continue while the two men are distracted.

"As the spouse, I automatically inherit half," Summer says.

"Wisconsin is a community property state and you are entitled to half of the estate he established while you were married to him, but not necessarily any monies made before that. Did you sign a prenup?"

"Of course not. Monty knew I wasn't after his money."

I let that one go. "I imagine Sawyer could reasonably contest any will Monty made if he feels he might be able to get a larger share of the estate. He might not win, but he could tie things up for a long time by doing that."

My goal is to rattle Summer, because people who are unsettled tend to blurt out things they might not otherwise. Summer tries to look nonchalant, as if what I'm saying doesn't bother her in the least, but I can tell she's on edge. I decide to switch gears on her again.

"Was Monty also having an affair?" I ask.

Summer looks stunned, as if the idea never occurred to her.

"Not that I'm aware of," she says. Her brow furrows in thought for a moment. "Why did you ask that?" she says, her voice rife with suspicion.

I shrug it off. "No reason really."

Summer glares at me and I know I've piqued her interest. Odds are, she'll be investigating that rumor on her own as soon as she leaves here.

Lucien tries to regain control. "Mrs. Dixon, given certain revelations here, I am advising you to not say anything more." He switches his gaze to Hurley. "We are done here." He rises from his chair, tosses the notepad he had in front of him into his cockeyed briefcase, and then looks at Summer expectantly.

Summer blinks at him, and then looks at me with a bemused expression. "I guess that's it," she says with a shrug. She stands, and then addresses Hurley. "Do be kind to Damien when you talk to him, will you? He's a gentle soul and bruises easily."

With that, Lucien walks out of The Hole, with Summer on his heels.

Hurley stops the recording and looks over at me.

"I think that went well, considering," I say.

"You mean considering that your brother-in-law was involved? Rather convenient that Summer called him this morning, don't you think?"

I shrug. "I don't think it matters, because I don't think she killed Monty."

Hurley makes a face. "Yeah, neither do I. But I still have to do my due diligence and check on her alibi."

"I don't suppose her alibi with Damien will be worth much," I say. "He's bound to say she was with him, even if she wasn't, don't you think?"

"Maybe, but it doesn't matter, because based on this address, Damien's apartment is located downtown, and that area has lots of security cameras. We should be able to find out if she's telling us the truth." He glances at his watch. "We have a little over ten minutes before Sawyer arrives. I'm going to make some phone calls."

"Who to?"

"I want to talk to Jessica Leavenworth to see if the rumors of Monty's affair are true. And I also want to talk to the PI Monty hired."

"The PI you also hired?" I remind him.

He looks at me with shame. "I'm sorry about all that, Mattie. I don't know how we got so far off track."

"Well, part of it was my unwillingness to tell you some things. I guess I'm not wholly comfortable with sharing every little thought and doubt I have yet. I have trust issues, I think. Too many people in my life have let me down or abandoned me, and that makes me want to keep all my feelings locked up inside."

Hurley takes my hand and kisses the back of it. "I will never abandon you, Squatch. I hope you believe that."

"I do. Well, most of the time," I add with a pained grin. "I promise to do better. I think the counseling sessions have helped."

"I suppose," he says with little conviction. Hurley hates what he calls "psych speech" and I've known all along that he wasn't keen on the idea of marriage counseling. It wasn't a surprise, because he wasn't keen on it two years ago when we were doing family counseling with Emily when she was acting out. But the changes Maggie was able to bring about in Emily helped convince Hurley it wasn't a total waste of time and money. I'm not sure he's convinced about marital counseling yet, but it's helping me and us as a couple, even if he isn't as fully vested as I'd like at times.

"That reminds me," Hurley says. "Tell me again what time we're doing these housekeeper interviews?"

"At four and five today."

Hurley's phone rings then and he glances at the caller ID. "It's Monty's accountant. I found his card in Monty's home office and left him a message earlier this morning asking him to call me. Didn't think I'd hear back from him so soon." With that, he answers the call and puts it on speaker. "This is Detective Hurley."

"Detective, this is Aaron Baker, returning your call."

"Thanks for getting back to me so quickly. I didn't think I'd hear from you until Monday."

"I'm playing catch-up on the heels of the tax season," Baker says. "I do a lot of work from home on the weekends. What can I do for you?"

"Can you hold on for a second while I get to my office?"

"Sure," Baker says.

Hurley heads that way and I follow. It only takes a few seconds, and as soon as we are there, Hurley settles in his desk chair and sets the phone down so he can write in his notebook. I stand against the wall and listen.

"I'm calling about Monty Dixon," Hurley says. "I don't know if you've heard yet, but he was killed last night, murdered."

There are several seconds of silence followed by, "*Murdered? Really?*" Apparently, Baker isn't well connected to the local gossip mill. News like Dixon's murder typically travels through town at the speed of light. Or maybe Baker's so buried in his work that he hasn't surfaced long enough to catch up on that part of his life.

"Yes, I'm afraid so," Hurley says.

"Who did it?" Baker asks.

"Don't know yet," Hurley says. "But I'm working on it. Did you provide accounting services for Monty's personal finances or his business?"

"Both, and neither," Baker says. "I handled everything for

him, except some investment funds, up until two years ago, and then he switched everything over to his brother, Harrison. Apparently, Harrison has a friend with an accounting and an investment background who works as a financial consultant." His pronunciation of the word "friend" is rife with skepticism. "There's no loyalty in business anymore," he concludes with mild disgust.

"Did you notice anything unusual with Monty's finances when you were doing his books?" Hurley asks.

"No, just a profound lack of knowledge when it came to money matters. I hope Harrison has had better luck than I did. Monty Dixon has . . . had no financial sense at all."

"Any idea what his estate might be worth?"

Baker scoffs. "Keep in mind that my information is at least two years old, so I can't say what kind of financial state Monty was in when he was killed, but when I was working with him, he was raking in the dough with his real estate business. He always maintained a balance of fifty grand or more in his checking account, and he had several investment funds that totaled around two million, if I remember right. Plus, he owned his house and all his vehicles outright. Oh, yeah, and there's a vacation home on an island in the Caribbean somewhere. I don't remember the exact location, but it's a hacienda right on the ocean. Worth at least two mil would be my guess. The guy was talking about retiring there in another five years, if you can imagine that. Retirement at the age of fifty." He lets out a humorless laugh. "Clearly, I chose the wrong profession."

"That makes two of us," Hurley says with a wink at me. "Thanks for getting back to me so quickly, and if you think of anything else that might be useful, give me a callback."

"Will do. You have a nice day."

Hurley disconnects the call and starts to say something to me, but before he can, the intercom on his desk phone buzzes again.

"Yes, Heidi?"

"Sawyer Dixon is here . . . um, also with his lawyer."

Hurley's brows form a V at that, and he looks at me. Then he asks Heidi, "Who is his lawyer?"

"That would be Mr. Colter again," Heidi says.

"I'll be out in a minute," Hurley says. Then he leans back in his seat, stares at the ceiling, and says, "God, give me strength."

CHAPTER 12

"I don't know if I can take another round with Lucien," Hurley says. "What the hell did he do, give them a family discount?"

"Speaking of family," I say, "why didn't Harrison let on that he's handling his brother's finances?"

"Who knows? Getting information out of that bunch has been like watching a movie trailer. Little tidbits that only hint at the full story."

"Maybe Sawyer will be calmer and more forthcoming today," I suggest.

Hurley scoffs at this. "He acts like he's owed something, and who are we to question his needs, his ideas, his life?"

"He definitely has an air of entitlement about him."

"That, he does," Hurley says with a thoughtful frown.

I can tell from his expression that something is troubling him. "What are you thinking?"

He looks at me with genuine concern. "Do you think we're spoiling Matthew? Do you think he'll grow up to have that attitude of entitlement?"

"I hope not," I say with less certainty than I like. It's a disturbing thought. Matthew isn't exactly living a life of dearth and need. We live in a big house, where he has his own room, and plenty of clothes and toys. He doesn't lack for anything . . . except maybe parental time. But when we aren't with him, he has Desi and Dom, both of whom are good influences, even if they do indulge him on occasion.

"I think that's one of the things that having another child might mitigate," Hurley says. "Right now, he doesn't have to share anything with anyone. Everything revolves around him. Having a sibling might teach him to share, don't you think?"

"I think he can learn about sharing without having a sibling," I say, placing my hand on Hurley's arm. "Besides, he has one with Emily, though I grant you it's not the same as it would be if he had a sibling closer to his own age, one he had to share toys and parental attention with. One who would play dirty tricks on him and try to get him into trouble."

"I take it you're speaking from personal experience?"

"Desi and I had our moments, for sure. But we turned out okay, didn't we?"

"You did," he says, his gaze growing oddly heated. "But your sister married Lucien. That's a clear sign of brain damage, if ever I saw one."

I laugh. "He's not all that bad really." Hurley gives me a look that suggests I have brain damage as well. "He's different at home," I insist. "That annoying side of him is just a work face. Desi says it's his way of dealing with feeling intimidated." Hurley still looks skeptical. "Come on, how bad can he be if Desi married him? And look at Ethan and Erika. They turned out okay."

Hurley arches one eyebrow at this. "One might argue that being antisocial and reclusive, and having a tarantula and a giant cockroach for pets, are something other than okay," he says.

"Yeah, okay. Ethan is a little different," I concede. "But if we do have another child, who's to say we won't end up with two spoiled, entitled kids? Or a kid who wants a cockroach for a pet? Matthew wears his teenage sister's underwear as a superhero outfit, for heaven's sake. Wouldn't you call that a little strange?"

Hurley doesn't answer me, because his desk phone buzzes again. He hits the intercom button. "Be right there," he says, and then he gets up and heads for the hallway without waiting for a reply. "Meet you in The Hole?" he says as he passes me.

I nod and go that way as he heads for the front reception area. I'm not in the room long when the door opens and a surly-looking Sawyer walks in, with Lucien right behind him.

"Have a seat on the other side of the table," Hurley says from behind Lucien.

Once again, Lucien opts for the head-of-the-table location, while Sawyer settles into the same seat his stepmother had earlier. Lucien gives me a smile that is part smirk, part apology, as he once again opens his damaged briefcase.

Judging from the way Sawyer looks, I suspect he spent the better part of last night indulging in some spirits. His eyes are red and bloodshot, his skin has that pasty, puffy look that a hangover gives you, and even at this hour of the day, he reeks of alcohol.

"Are you offering a family discount?" I ask Lucien.

"As Mrs. Dixon and I were leaving, we ran into Sawyer in the parking lot," he says. "After a brief conversation, he decided it would be in his best interests if he engaged my services for this session."

I glance at Sawyer, who looks like he's in so much pain that any thought would make him pass out, much less a hiring decision. "Can I get you something, Sawyer?" I offer. "A glass of water or a cup of coffee?"

He swallows hard and shakes his head. It's probably just as well, because I have a feeling anything Sawyer took in right now would soon demand its release, and while I don't think a bit of barf would do the décor in this room one bit of harm, I'm not eager to have to deal with the smell or the cleanup.

Lucien scoots his seat up to the table and says, "I'd love a cup of coffee, Mattiekins. Cream and sugar, please." He doesn't wait for an answer. Instead, he pulls his shirt out from his chest where the red stain is and then licks his fingers and rubs them on the area.

I decide Hurley is right. My sister is clearly a madwoman. She must be, to have married this manipulative cretin. I consider ignoring his request, but decide to take the high road. I make a mad dash to the breakroom and pour a cup of coffee from the pot. It's starting to smell a little old, but I'll be damned if I'm going to make a fresh pot for Lucien. I grab a stir stick, two packs of sugar, and two containers of artificial creamer and carry them back to The Hole. By the time I get there, Hurley has turned on the AV equipment and he is finishing up stating the usual preliminary introductory information, including a recitation of the Miranda warning.

As I slide Lucien's coffee and its accompanying accoutrements in front of him, Sawyer leans forward, elbows on the table, and buries his head in his hands.

Hurley begins his questions. "Mr. Dixon, can you please tell me where you were yesterday evening between the hours of four and eleven-thirty when you came back to the house?"

He doesn't answer.

"Sawyer?"

Still, no answer.

After waiting about ten seconds, Hurley bangs both of his hands hard on the table.

Sawyer's head rockets up from his hands, his eyes wide. "What the hell, man?" he whines. Then he closes his eyes and winces. "Go easy, would you? My head is killing me."

Lucien scowls at Hurley. "Please don't browbeat my client."

"I'm not browbeating him. I'm asking simple questions and it would help if he would at least attempt to answer them."

"One more outburst like that and I will recommend to my client that we leave immediately and answer nothing more," Lucien says.

The two men stare at one another for several seconds and it's Hurley who looks away first, shifting his attention back to Sawyer.

"Sawyer, can you please give me a rundown of your activities and whereabouts last evening?"

"All right, all right, already," Sawyer snaps irritably, despite Hurley's question being framed in a calm, moderate tone. "I was out showing a house to a client early in the evening."

"At what time?"

"The showing was scheduled for four, but they were late and didn't get there until just before four-thirty. We left the place at five-thirty, maybe a little before." Now it's Sawyer's turn to roll his eyes. "I could tell they knew from the moment they entered the front door that the house wasn't for them, but did they say so? Of course not. They wanted to waste my time and go snooping through the place to check out all the rooms so they could see how the owners lived." He starts to shake his head in disgust and then seems to think better of it, wincing and closing his eyes. "So many people are like that," he says. "They pretend to be potential buyers, but they're really just Nosy Nellies who want to see how the other half lives. It's a huge waste of my time."

"What did you do after the showing?" Hurley asks.

"I went back to the office, returned some phone calls, and then left a little before six. There's a sandwich shop across the street and I went there and got a sub, which I ate at one of their tables. After that, I went home, changed my clothes, and went back out."

"What time was it when you arrived at the house? And when did you leave?" Hurley asks.

"I don't know. I got there around six-fifteen or six-thirty maybe? Somewhere in there. I changed my clothes and then left sometime after seven."

"You told us last night that you had a discussion with your father. Summer called it an argument?"

Sawyer sighs, puffing out his cheeks as he exhales. "Right," he says. "I forgot, because it was the same discussion we've had a million times before. It was about the business."

"Real estate?"

"Yeah." He offers no elaboration.

"Did the argument start as soon as you got home?"

"No, I can access my area of the house without going through the main part. After I changed my clothes, I went into the main house looking for my father because I wanted to talk to him. I was frustrated with those Nosy Nellies I'd had to wait on and I'm tired of dealing with people who aren't serious about buying or selling. Dad keeps making me take these leads generated by random phone calls, and most of them don't play out. Either that, or they're first-time home buyers with unrealistic expectations and little money."

"In what part of the house did you and your father have this discussion?" Hurley asks.

"In the kitchen."

"You saw Summer while you were there?"

"Yeah," he says a bit hesitantly, wrinkling his forehead, though it's hard to tell if he's doing so because of thought or pain. "Yeah, I remember now. She breezed through and said she was headed out to some cooking class. Then she left."

"How long did you and your father, um, talk?"

"I don't know, maybe fifteen minutes or so. It started off with me asking him if I could drive his Mercedes for the evening. It's a convertible and it was nice outside. Plus, there's a girl at a bar I'm seeing and I thought that the Mercedes might impress her. It's a sweet little ride."

I roll my eyes at this. Clearly, the guy has no clue how to woo a woman, or how to take no for an answer.

"I take it your father said no?" Hurley says.

"He did. He made some comment about how I needed to work harder and make enough money to buy one of my own." He pauses and rubs his nose. "The guy can be such an asshole at times, you know? I keep asking him for help at work, to give me some decent leads. He has plenty and it would be easy enough for him to share, to give me a leg up, you know? But *nooooo*." He rolls his eyes. "The high-and-mighty Montgomery Dixon thinks he knows best. He insists that I should make my way in the business the same way he did, starting at the bottom with nothing and working my way up." He lets out a little *pfft* of exasperation. "I mean, it's not as if I'm asking him to hand me success on a platter, you know? All I want is a little help. Is that too much to ask?"

Neither of us answers what we assume is a rhetorical question, though I do note that Sawyer is talking about his father in the present tense.

Hurley asks him, "Where did you go last night when you left the house?"

"I already told you, I drove around. I don't remember where. I was ticked off with Dad, and then Maribel wasn't at the bar, and I was just so angry at everyone and everything."

"You stopped at the bar?" Hurley asks.

Sawyer shakes his head, but quickly halts the movement with a wince. He reaches up and pinches the bridge of his nose for a second before answering. "I didn't go in or anything. I just drove around in the parking lot looking for Maribel's car. But it wasn't there."

"Maribel is this girl you like?"

Sawyer nods.

"What bar was it?"

"The Nowhere."

"Did you stop anywhere else during your drive?"

Sawyer frowns. "I stopped at the Quik-E-Mart on the east end of town for gas. Bought a soda there. But other than that, no."

"So you just drove around for four or more hours?" Hurley asks, a hint of skepticism in his voice.

Sawyer stares at him, sensing the challenge behind that question. He licks his lips and then juts his chin out. "That's what I said, isn't it?" he says, his voice laced with arrogance.

Hurley smiles, but it's brittle and humorless. "Yes, that is what you said. Is it what you did? Just drove? No other stops?"

"How many times are you going to ask me?" Sawyer asks irritably. He wrings his hands a few times and then seems to realize what he's doing and shoves them down in his lap.

I get a strong sense that he's hiding something, that he's lying to us.

"Please stop badgering my client," Lucien says.

Hurley's jaw muscles start popping and I can tell he's getting frustrated, so I decide to jump in.

"Last night, when they took your clothes, they found a tiny wood splinter in your hair," I say. "Any idea where that came from, if all you were doing was riding around in your car?"

Sawyer doesn't answer right away. His gaze shifts off to the side for a few seconds and I suspect he's recalling something from last night. But whatever it is, he isn't telling.

"How the hell would I know?" he asks. "And why does it matter? It could have been there all day, for all I know. Maybe I picked it up at one of the houses I showed yesterday." His eyes widen suddenly, and his face brightens. "Yes, of course," he says, snapping his fingers. "One of the houses I showed yesterday around lunchtime had some construction going on at the time. There were guys in the driveway cutting plywood with a table saw. I probably picked up a flying splinter from that."

I'm not buying his explanation. Sawyer strikes me as too vain to have gone all day without running a comb or brush through his hair, particularly if he had plans to try and find this girl Maribel last evening. But until the wood splinter is analyzed, there isn't much more we can do with that bit of evidence.

"Is there some relevance to this wood splinter?" Lucien asks.

"Not sure," I say. "We haven't had it analyzed yet, but given that Monty was stabbed to death with a broken and splintered cue stick, I'd say it's definitely a point of interest."

"What?" Sawyer says, pinning me with wide eyes. He pales noticeably, making those pimples stand out even more. "What did you just say?" he says, his voice shaky.

I think back to the night of the murder and realize that Sawyer was told his father had been stabbed, but I can't remember if anyone mentioned what was used.

"Your father was stabbed with one end of a broken cue stick," Hurley says.

Sawyer turns his gaze toward Hurley. He looks . . . scared? Shocked? Disbelieving? I can't quite put a finger on it. But something has clearly rocked his world in the past minute, rocked it like a 9.0 earthquake on the Richter scale.

"You didn't tell me that," he says.

Hurley shrugs. "I would have thought your stepmother told you."

Sawyer doesn't respond. He slumps back in his chair, his eyes staring at the tabletop. It looks as if he's thinking hard about something. Hurley lets him stew until Sawyer raises his gaze and leans forward again, apparently having resolved something in his mind.

"Can I ask you a question?" Sawyer asks.

"Sure," Hurley says.

"How long is this investigation thing going to take? Because I've been told that the settling of Dad's estate might be delayed until it's done."

Clearly, there is little love lost between father and son, since it seems Sawyer's primary interest now isn't in solving his father's murder—assuming he isn't the culprit—but rather in settling his estate.

Hurley leans back in his chair and narrows his eyes at Sawyer. The two men stare at one another for an impressive length of time, and I watch to see which of them will cave first. My money is on Sawyer, but he's looking mighty sure of himself. Surprisingly, it is Hurley who looks away first and Sawyer's expression gets even cockier.

"I can't tell you how long our investigation is going to take," Hurley says, picking up his notebook and flipping through it.

I realize it's a beat, a stunt to keep Sawyer a little off his mark, because I can see that the pages Hurley is flipping are empty, even though he stops on one of the blank pages and peers at it as if he's reading something noteworthy. He finally closes the notebook and sets it on the table. Then he pins Sawyer with a steely-eyed gaze.

"What kind of car do you drive?" Hurley asks.

"It's a Subaru Outback."

"What year?"

"It's a 2020. Why?"

"Did you buy it?" I ask, recalling Summer's claim that Monty bought Sawyer a new car.

Sawyer gives me an annoyed look. "My father bought it for me."

"So he buys you a brand-new car to drive and you got mad at him the other night because he wouldn't loan you his car?"

Sawyer doesn't answer, but the question does cause some color to return to his cheeks.

"I need you to write down the route you drove last night," Hurley says.

"I didn't have any route," Sawyer says, punctuating the comment with an exasperated sigh. He rubs the side of his head with his fingertips. "I told you, it was aimless driving."

"Then write down as many of the streets, roads, and turns you took, as you can remember," Hurley says.

"Can I ask why?"

"Because he isn't sure he can get a warrant to search your car's GPS," Lucien says.

"I want it by tomorrow morning," Hurley says, ignoring Lucien's comment. "And don't leave town unless you check with me first. That's all . . . for now."

"We're done?" Lucien says, looking surprised.

"For now," Hurley repeats.

This makes Lucien frown. He narrows his eyes at Hurley, clearly suspecting that he's up to something. I don't think Hurley's up to anything other than trying to unsettle Lucien. Turnabout is fair play and it appears it's working. Lucien closes his briefcase—though not without some difficulty because of the broken hinge, resulting in a fumbling feat of frustration that temporarily rivets the attention of all of us in the room—and then says, "Let's go."

He and Sawyer both get up and leave, but Lucien's brow is furrowed in worry, something I know from experience is unusual. Lucien doesn't let his emotions show if he can help it and the fact that he's showing them now tells me his confidence has been knocked down a peg.

Once they're gone, and Hurley has turned off the AV equipment, he glances at his watch, leans back in his chair, and stares at the ceiling. He yawns widely and it triggers one in me.

"I got a text from Christopher while we were talking with

Sawyer," I tell Hurley when I'm done yawning. "He and Doc Morton are almost done with the autopsy on Monty. He said they didn't find any big surprises, other than what we already know."

"Sounds good. I'm going to call Harrison Dixon to schedule an interview with him, and then I'll give Jonas a call to see where he is on the evidence processing."

Hurley gets up from his chair and gives me a kiss on top of my head before he exits The Hole and goes back to his office. I follow him and stand by as he calls Harrison Dixon. He puts the call on speaker so I can hear.

"Mr. Dixon," Hurley says when Harrison answers. "Can we set up a time for you to come in for an interview?"

"Will tomorrow morning work? I can be there bright and early."

"How about nine?" Hurley offers.

"That will be fine," Harrison says.

Hurley may be tired, but he isn't about to let Harrison off the hook without a little bit of twisting. "I understand that you handled some of your brother's finances. I'm surprised you didn't tell me that last night."

"I didn't think of it. Why? Is it important?"

"Money is one of the primary motives for murder," Hurley says.

Harrison chuckles at the implication. "To be honest, I didn't handle any of Monty's finances directly. He did that himself. I did recommend someone to manage his investment account, but I don't have any direct dealings with that. I'll see you in the morning." Harrison then promptly disconnects the call, not giving Hurley a chance to ask him any more questions.

"Well, that was abrupt," Hurley says.

"He probably took offense at your suggestion that he had a motive for murder."

"Whatever," he says with a sigh. His exhaustion is beginning to show. "I'm going to call Jonas next, and then Peter Carlisle. After that, I think I'm going to call it a day. There isn't a lot I can get done on a Sunday and I think it will help if I start fresh in the morning."

"Don't forget our interviews this afternoon," I remind him.

He frowns. "Right." No enthusiasm there. "What are you going to do?"

Before I can answer, Bob Richmond walks into the office. As the other homicide detective in town, he and Hurley share call duties, investigative duties, and this office.

"Hey, you two," he says with a tired smile. "Sorry I had to drag you in on your weekend off last night. Got called out for a twofer in the county that they needed help on."

"A double?" Hurley says. "Are your bodies going to bump ours for the autopsy table?"

"No, they got sent to Madison," Richmond says. "It looked like a straightforward murder-suicide and they had been there for a day or two. Older couple. No real family to speak of, so there's no rush on getting results. Sounds like the wife had dementia and the husband decided to put her out of her misery. Then he shot himself."

"Seems straightforward," Hurley says, stifling a yawn. "Why couldn't the county guys handle it on their own?"

"Because they had four other deaths in three other locations," Richmond says, eyebrows raised to indicate his surprise. "Seems it was not a good weekend in the county. One was a doctor who had been diagnosed with cancer and apparently decided to end things his own way with a bullet to the head. That body was also a couple of days old by the time it was discovered. It appeared straightforward and Doc Morton cleared the case on scene. The funeral home came and got the body. Another was an explosion in the basement of a dentist's house night before last, where it appears someone was experimenting with bombmaking. That took out two people, the dentist and his teenage son, who they think was the one who created the bomb. They've got the FBI and Homeland Security helping with that one, and those bodies were sent to Milwaukee. And the third one was some wealthy tech CEO from Chicago who drove his car off the road and into a lake on Friday night. He wasn't able to get out and drowned."

"Wow," I say. "Did Christopher and Doc Morton go to all of those?"

Richmond nods. "They were quickly fired from the bomb scene once the feds took over, and I get a sense they weren't disappointed by that. One of those bodies was in multiple pieces. I think the guy from the car accident is still in your morgue. Doc Morton did his autopsy yesterday, and I don't know if he's released the body to a funeral home yet or not. Your cue stick stabbing case is up first for today, given that it's an obvious homicide, and I believe Otto plans to do the woman who supposedly killed your homicide victim next."

"Sounds like everyone has their work cut out for them," Hurley says. He turns to me as Richmond settles in behind his desk. "You can hang here while I make the phone calls, if you want, but maybe it would be better if you went home and took a nap."

"I think I'll make a quick run to the grocery store instead. We're out of Cheerios and apple juice, and I don't want to deal with one of Matthew's meltdowns tomorrow morning."

"I think we're low on mac and cheese, too," Hurley says. "And chicken nuggets."

"Got it," I say with a weary sigh. "I'll pick up that stuff and then run home and clean the house before these interviews."

Hurley looks at me, his brows raised in question. "We're interviewing people to come and clean our house. Why not let them see what they're getting into?"

"Because the way the house looks when they come should be the way I want the house to look once they've done their job. Otherwise, it reflects poorly on me."

"On *you?*" Richmond says, obviously eavesdropping. "Last I heard, there were four people living in that house."

"That's true," I say, "but like it or not—and I don't—the housecleaning status is always a reflection on the lady of the house. Just one more example of modern society's unfair, archaic, and sometimes misogynistic biases." I see Hurley and Richmond exchange a wary look and figure it will be best if I leave now before I say something I might regret. "See you at home at four?" I say to Hurley.

I don't wait for his answer, striding out of his office and heading down the hall. While trying to dig my car keys out of my pocket, I promptly drop them on the floor. As I bend down to pick them up, I hear Richmond back in the office say, "Must be that time of the month, eh?"

To which, my husband replies, "Sadly, no."

I stand there a moment trying to suss out the meaning of his response and decide I'm too tired and too emotionally volatile. I decide to do an Elsa and "Let It Go."

Easier said . . . or sang . . . than done.

CHAPTER 13

Thoughts of *Frozen* make me think of Matthew—it's one of his favorite movies—and I hesitate as I pull out of the PD parking lot, torn between wanting to spend time with my son and needing to go home and do some housecleaning. A quick glance at my watch tells me I have about an hour and a half, and I figure I can do both. Granted, I won't be able to get the house as clean as I'd like, but it's just interviews and that means I only need to worry about the main floor, right? Unless they want a tour of the house before quoting me a price to see what's involved.

Crap.

I want to see Matthew. It only takes me a little over seven minutes to drive to Desi's house and I consider calling ahead to say I'm coming, but don't. My father is there and I'm curious to see how he and my son interact, if at all. I figure my chances of witnessing that are better if I arrive without advance warning. I pull up and park at the curb in front of Desi's house and head up the sidewalk to her front door. But halfway there, I veer off into the grass and head around the left side of the house, where the dining-room and kitchen windows are located. I want to do a little peeping first. The large front window to the living room shows it as empty, so my money is on one of these other two rooms as the center of any action.

I walk past the dining room and see that it's dark and empty. Then I go by the kitchen window, where I see my sister and Erika seated at the table peeling apples—no doubt to make some kind of yummy apple dessert, the simple thought of which makes my mouth start to water—but no sign of any of the men. I imagine Lucien has left the house and gone into his regular office, now that he has two new clients and his home office space has been taken over by my father, and no doubt Ethan, reclusive little bug lover that he is, is in his room examining his specimens or playing with his tarantula. That leaves my father in charge of Matthew and my heart does a funny little flip-flop at the idea. *Where are they? Would Desi have let our father drive off somewhere with Matthew?*

My father doesn't have a car, but Desi might have let him use hers. Was it in the garage? I don't want to go all the way around to the other side of the house to access the garage and decide, instead, to approach it from the back. But as I near the corner of the house, I hear my son's voice coming from the backyard.

"Make it blow up!" he says. "I want it to blow up."

I hear my father's deep, rumbling chuckle. "Patience, little man," he says. "Patience."

I peer around the corner into the backyard. Desi has a large covered patio that extends off the back of the house and I see my father squatting in the grass near the edge of it, holding a bottle of something in his hand. Matthew is opposite my father, squatting the same way, their two heads nearly touching as they study the thing between them. It's hard to tell what it is from where I'm standing, but it appears to be something vaguely conical in shape, the widest part at the bottom.

"We need to make it bigger, I think," my father says. "Volcanoes are big and ferocious when they blow up." There is an edge of excitement in his voice that infects my son.

"Make it big!" he says, clapping his hands. "Blow up *big*!" He picks up something beside him and I recognize a can of Play-Doh. My father has one, too, and a moment later, they are slapping gobs of the stuff onto the side of the mini mountain between them. Matthew barely gets his gob stuck when he says, "Can we do it now?"

"Not yet, little man," my father says with admirable patience. "Let's add a little green to it. Volcanoes can have grass on them."

Matthew looks around and lunges to his left, coming up with another can of the modeling clay, this time in green. He rips the lid off and sticks his hand into the can, coming out with a big hunk of green clay.

"Put it on carefully," my father says, no doubt aware of Matthew's last application, which is still sitting on the side of this purported volcano like a giant red abscess about to burst. "You don't want to collapse the volcano, because then we'll have to start over. The grass should be spread out and thin, like this." I watch as my father takes a small chunk of clay and proceeds to work it between his fingers, thinning and flattening it out. When he gets it as thin as he can, he carefully applies it to the side of the volcano, pressing it gently into place.

I watch my son, watching my father, his eyes riveted on my father's big hands, Matthew's little hands mimicking the movements with his own piece of green clay. After two pieces each are flattened, thinned, and carefully applied to the sides of the volcano, Matthew stands up, shifting from one foot to the other with eager anticipation.

"Now, Pop-pop? Can we do it now?"

Dad rises slowly to his feet with a grunt of pain and a massage of his lower back muscles. My father, who is wearing shorts, is built like SpongeBob SquarePants and his skinny legs don't look strong enough to hold up his massive torso. He stands there, towering over my son, smiling down at him. "Okay," he says. "I think it's time to blow this bad boy."

"Yeah," Matthew says eagerly. "Gonna blow dis bad boy." He claps his hands again, and then starts doing an excited dance around the volcano. My father bends over and picks up the board I now see is serving as a base to the volcano, and he carries it out a few feet farther into the yard, depositing it on a gravel pathway that meanders through the grass. It's the same path I walked when I married Hurley. Matthew follows him, half skipping, half hopping. I watch my father reach into his pocket and remove a Baggie of some sort of white powder, a small vial, and a second, larger vial that is filled with clear liquid.

"Okay," he says to Matthew. "Stand back a little because this volcano is going to blow."

"Yeah, gonna blow!" Matthew hollers, backing up two whole steps and then taking another one closer again.

My father bends over the volcano and opens the Baggie of white powder, emptying the contents into the middle of the volcano through the hole in the top. Then he opens the small vial and adds a few drops of something from it into the larger one, turning the clear liquid a bright red color. Food coloring, I realize. He looks over at Matthew. "Okay, little man, stand back. She's gonna blow!" My father's deep voice booms through the air.

Matthew looks a little frightened, but his curiosity and eagerness overrule, and he doesn't back up at all. He dances in place, eyes huge, watching my father as he bends over the volcano and pours the red liquid into the hole at the top. For several long seconds, nothing happens, but then a geyser of red foam gushes from the top of the clay mountain and meanders its way down the sides in rivulets of lavalike liquid.

"Look!" Matthew says with unmitigated glee. "It blowed!"

He claps his hands, dancing around the makeshift volcano, laughing. "It blowed! It blowed!" he says several more times, his delighted laughter echoing through the air.

As the reaction dwindles down to a slow ooze, Matthew dashes over to my father, wraps his arms around those skinny legs, and hugs him hard. "Thank you, Pop-pop."

"You are welcome, little man."

The smile on my father's face nearly breaks my heart. I swallow down burgeoning tears and then retreat the way I came, tiptoeing to the front of the house and getting back in my car. As I start the engine and pull away from the curb, tears well in my eyes and I swipe irritably at them, wondering what the heck I'm crying about. Admittedly, my feelings toward my father are muddled and messy because of our history, but tears? Watching him with Matthew just now both gladdened and saddened me. I'm delighted that my son has a grandfather who is involved in his life, one he adores, one willing to spend some quality time with him. It makes me happy to know he has this, so why do I also feel sad?

Then it hits me. I'm jealous, jealous of the relationship Matthew has with my father because it's one I yearned for most of my life and never had. I recognize the emotion as petty, childish, and silly, but I also own it. It's what I feel. I can't deny it, even if it is born of immature feelings and longings. And to make matters worse, I recognize that I've had barriers in place to keep me from developing the very relationship I want with the man. I desperately want to lower those barriers, but it's been such a struggle. Part of that is because I resented and hated him so fiercely for so many years, and feelings that powerful don't disappear overnight, even with the knowledge that they were born of falsehoods.

I need to let go of the past and open my heart to new beginnings. I know this and briefly consider turning around and going back. But while I recognize my need to build a better relationship with my father, I don't want to upset the building rapport Matthew has with him. Better to set aside some time of my own when my father and I can be together, one on one.

In the meantime, I have a house to clean.

I swing by the grocery store and it only takes me a few minutes to get what I need—Cheerios, apple juice, frozen chicken nuggets, and a couple of boxes of mac and cheese—but checkout is another matter. I get into the queue at the ten-items-or-less line, and there are three people in front of me. The first two have a handful of items each, but the woman directly in front of me has a cart with at least thirty things in it.

I tap her on the shoulder, and when she turns around, I say, "I'm sorry, but I'm in a bit of a hurry and I only have five items. Would you mind if I went ahead of you?"

She looks at my meager and odd collection of groceries and bestows a plastic smile on me. In a hypersweet voice, she says, "I'm in a hurry, too. We all have to wait our turns." Then she faces forward again.

She is dressed nicely in a black pencil skirt and white blouse, and as I stare at her back, I envision a bloodstain spreading along that pristine whiteness. I shake it off and raise my gaze to the back of her head—dark hair sprayed into a plastic coiffure to match her plastic smile—and fume. My good angel tells me to channel Elsa; I should let it go. My bad angel kicks my good angel's ass, and before I know it, I'm tapping on the woman's shoulder again.

"Excuse me," I say in a matching, syrupy tone, "but you are in an express lane with way more than the allowed number of items. Since you are clearly violating the rules, the least you could do is let me go ahead of you."

She turns around again, but much slower this time. Her smile is gone. She narrows her eyes at me and gives me a slow up-and-down perusal. There is only one person now between her and the cashier. "Are you the item police?" she says, looking somewhat amused.

"No, but I'm married to a cop," I counter.

She puffs out a laugh. "And what? Is he going to come here and arrest me for getting in the wrong line at the grocery store?"

The cashier and the customer she is currently serving are more focused on our standoff than what they are supposed to be doing and the line has momentarily stopped moving. I am engaged in a stare-off with the woman in front of me, but my peripheral vision tells me folks in the neighboring line are also focused on us. A dozen responses flit through my mind, everything from threats of speeding tickets from my police friends to simply pushing my way past the woman and her stupid cart to get ahead of her. I discard this last idea quickly, fearful I'd get stuck between her cart and the display case beside it and end up thrashing about like a trapped animal, or, worse, knocking the display case over. A few choice remarks come to mind—some of them profane—but I toss those aside, too. In the end, I decide to take what feels to me like a high road.

In a rational, reasoned, but rather loud voice, I say, "You know, I've heard about people like you. People who don't think the rules apply to them, who think they are entitled to special treatment, who think they're better than the rest of us. But I haven't met one until now. Until *you*. I don't know what it is that you think makes you better than all the rest of us here in this store, but it must be quite the little fairy tale. Clearly, you need that for your fragile ego, so you go on ahead and check out your full cart of items here in the express lane."

For the next twenty seconds or so, there is a silence so complete that I can hear the second hand ticking its way around the large clock on the supermarket wall in front of us. The woman before me twitches and her expression has morphed into something explosive. When sound resumes, it is a symphony of *tsks, clucks,* and *harrumphs* from our audience. I glance at those nearby and see they are all glaring at the woman in front of me. She looks and sees it, too.

I half expect her to ram me with her cart and storm from the store—I'm almost hoping she'll do that because it will speed things up—but to her credit and my chagrin, she appears to swallow down her fury. Looking only a little sheepish, she turns from me and starts loading her groceries onto the conveyor belt. Some of the surrounding people continue to stare, but eventually they all go back to their own business.

I'm harboring some begrudging admiration for the calm way my nemesis has handled the embarrassment, but then, just as the cashier is ringing up the last few items, she says, "Oh, darn, I forgot something. Can you wait just one minute?" Without waiting for an answer, she turns around, gives me an evil smile, and then slides past me, disappearing down one of the aisles.

I squeeze my eyes closed, realizing I've just been checkmated. Deciding I've had enough, I toss my items on the conveyor belt, tell the cashier I'm sorry, and leave the store. I mutter to myself all the way home, cursing the woman and my own inability to just shut up and let her break the rules.

CHAPTER 14

Fifteen minutes later, I'm standing in the middle of my kitchen-dining area, looking around and trying to decide where to start. I'm all too aware that the beds upstairs aren't made, but decide that they can stay that way. If a tour of the upstairs becomes necessary, this is the least of my worries. I remember the messy state of the Dixon house and decide I'm at least ahead of them in terms of neatness.

I start at the kitchen sink and load the dishwasher to get rid of the dirty dishes. Next I do a quick wipe-down of the countertops, the island, and the breakfast nook to get rid of crumbs, jelly smears, and coffee rings. I pick up the stray spoon I find on the floor far under the table, no doubt dropped by my son and licked thoroughly by our dog, Hoover.

With that done, I drag out the vacuum and do a frantic run over the first floor. With the warmer weather, both the dog and the cats are shedding like crazy and this results in hair balls the size of tumbleweeds that roll through the house. Just as I'm emptying the vacuum's full canister into the trash—there's enough animal hair to make a whole other pet—Hurley arrives home, coming in through the garage.

"Whoa," he says, eyeing the mass of hair I'm dumping into the garbage can. "What did you do, suck up both of the cats?"

"You'd like that, wouldn't you?" I tease.

Hurley doesn't answer; but he's wearing a conspiratorial smile. He doesn't like cats. Truth be told, he's afraid of them, though he'd never admit to this. He tolerates ours for my sake, because I had them before he and I started living together and he understood it was a package deal. I rescued the one I call Rubbish as a kitten after someone threw him away in a convenience store Dumpster, hence his name. Tux, whose black-and-white markings make the source of his name obvious, was the pet of a murder victim and would have ended up at a shelter if I hadn't taken him in.

Hurley fears the cats are out to get him, and there are times when I understand why he thinks this. They like to hide under the bed and swat at his feet in the mornings when he gets up or leave a trail of cat puke atop any clothes he lays out in our bedroom, and Hurley swears that Rubbish has tried to trip him up on the stairs a time or two. But it's clear to me that the cats bear great affection for him. I know this because they provide him with food all the time: tiny dead creatures that they bring inside and leave on his pillow, or in his shoes.

"What do you want to do for dinner?" I ask Hurley, once I've put the vacuum back together and stashed it in the closet.

"I can grill up those steaks in the fridge, if you like."

"I like." If Hurley is cooking, anything sounds good.

"There is some asparagus and squash in there, too," he adds. "I can toss those on the grill as well."

"You had me at 'I can grill,'" I say with a smile. Then, knowing that our son won't eat any of the items Hurley just mentioned, I add, "Do we have something for Matthew?"

"I think there are some hot dogs in the fridge," he says. "That and some mac and cheese ought to do him."

"We don't have any mac and cheese," I say.

Hurley shrugs. "Let him have Cheerios and apple juice then. It's not a classic dinner, but it won't hurt him."

Won't it? I imagine sitting down with a nutrition expert and explaining my picky son's diet to her and why he had hot dogs and Cheerios floating in apple juice for dinner. The next image that pops into my head is that of Child Protective Services knocking at the door.

"Can't do that because we're also out of both Cheerios and apple juice," I say.

Hurley frowns at me. "I thought you were going to run by the store."

"I was. I did," I say, feeling oddly defensive at the implication—real or imagined?—that I've failed once again in my attempts to maintain my household. "It didn't work out. I'll go back later when I pick up Matthew." I realize my pants have pet hair all over them and I walk over to the broom closet and grab a sticky lint-removing roller I keep in there. As I'm trying to roll myself into some semblance of presentability, I hear the crunch of tires on gravel and realize our interviewee has arrived.

Hurley hears it, too, and he says, "Give me a quick 411 on this person again."

"I've never met her. Her name is Marie Featherstone and she owns a new housecleaning company called Dust Busters, which is based here in town. A couple of the nurses at the hospital have used her service and been happy with it. I'm not wild about the idea of having different people coming each time—I'd rather have one person, particularly since we will likely have to allow them access to the house when we're not here. But the company is bonded, and I suppose we can ask her if it's possible to have only one person assigned to us, since we'll be a regular service."

Hurley nods as the doorbell rings, and since I'm still rolling my pants, he says, "I'll get it. Shall we do this in the breakfast nook?"

"Sure."

I stash the roller back in the closet and close the door just as Hurley escorts our guest into the kitchen.

I hear the woman say, "Wow, you have a lovely home. So big!" and figure she's already adding up the dollar signs in her head. Something about her voice bothers me, and when I turn around, I see why.

"Mattie," Hurley says, stopping a few feet in front of me. That's when he realizes that the woman with him has stopped several feet back. He gestures toward her. "This is Marie Featherstone." He pauses, noting the shocked expression on Featherstone's face. Sensing that something is off, he looks at me. "And· this is my wife, Mattie?" he says in an oddly tentative tone, as if he isn't sure of this fact.

"Turns out we've met before," I tell Hurley as I glare at the woman, "though we never got around to exchanging names." I turn my gaze to Hurley and smile. "Ms. Featherstone is the reason I didn't get any groceries earlier. And because of that, I think this is going to be the shortest interview in history."

Marie Featherstone's mouth opens and closes a few times, but no words come out. Finally she manages to say, "I was trying to get to you and my interview on time. Timeliness and punctuality are important."

"So is common courtesy," I say. "And that includes not getting into the express lane with a cart full of groceries. And if you do that, it would be the kind and considerate thing to let someone behind you, with only a few items, go first."

"I'm sorry," Marie says.

"So am I," I tell her. "Our interview is over." I start to turn away, but Marie stops me.

"Wait! I can make it up to you. I'll give you a discount on

your first six weeks." I look back at her and shake my head, and she ups the offer. "Three months?"

Hurley has watched this exchange without comment until now. "It sounds like you two got off on the wrong foot, but maybe we can talk it out?"

"Yes," Marie says, giving Hurley a grateful smile.

"No," I say at the same time. I look at Hurley. "Trust me on this. We don't want to work with her."

Hurley hesitates and, for one horrible moment, I fear he's going to waffle and try to talk me into interviewing this woman. But the look in my eyes must convince him it would be an unwise move. "Okay, Ms. Featherstone," he says. "I will defer to my wife on this matter and I'm afraid we are done. I'll show you out."

Marie looks so upset by this that for one insane nanosecond I reconsider my hard stance. Then I recall that smug little smile she gave me in the grocery store and that stunt she pulled at the end and I hold solid. "Have a nice day," I say to her, and then I turn and head down to the basement so I can throw in a load of laundry.

I hear the muffled sound of voices upstairs, but can't make out the words. I wonder if Marie is trying to explain what happened to Hurley, or if she's asking him to try to intervene. It doesn't matter to me what the woman says or tries. After that incident in the grocery store, I would never hire her.

When I get to the washer, I'm delighted to see that Emily did a load of towels earlier before she left for the day. I sort through the small mountain of dirty clothes and start a load of colored items. Then I go about folding the towels that Emily laundered.

Hurley comes downstairs and, without a word, grabs a towel and starts folding it. He halves it along the short axis, and then folds it in half the other way. I start to tell him that it's better to fold the towels along the long axis first, because then it's easier to hang two of them side by side over the towel bars in the bathroom, but I manage to stifle myself, realizing how lucky I am to have a husband who folds at all. Hurley is making an effort to help with the household chores as part of our new plan, and I'm grateful for that.

"So, do you want to tell me what happened between you and Ms. Featherstone?" he says as he starts on his second towel.

I fill him in on the grocery store debacle, and by the time I'm done, he's grinning from ear to ear. "Wow, that's some karma for you, isn't it?"

Yes, it was. "I have to admit, it felt very satisfying," I tell him. "Let's hope the next interview will be better."

"Are you sure you want to burn a bridge with Featherstone?" he asks.

I give it an honest few seconds of thought and find I am 100 percent okay with napalming that crossing. "I am," I tell him. "Like I said before, I'm not keen on the idea of using an agency because it likely means several different people would be coming and going. The fewer people we have traipsing through the house, the better. I only considered Featherstone because people I know have used her service and suggested her."

"Okay, then," Hurley says. "Who's up next?"

I take out my cell phone and open up my calendar app. "Cara Solomon, a woman who cleans houses on her own. She lives out in the country. We wouldn't be her only client, but she'll be our only cleaner. I found her through an ad on craigslist and spoke with her briefly to set up the appointment." I look at my watch. "She won't be here for forty-five more minutes. Let me grab a cup of coffee and then you can fill me in on how your phone calls went."

Hurley grabs the stack of folded towels and carries them upstairs. I follow, admiring his backside as he climbs the basement stairs ahead of me. While he heads for the second floor, I detour to the kitchen and start a pot of coffee brewing.

Five minutes later, we are seated in the breakfast nook, sipping our respective cups of coffee as Hurley fills me in.

"First off, Lucien called with the name of the lawyer who redid Monty's will."

"That's great. He said he wasn't going to do that until the morning."

"Yeah, well, I guess things changed once the Dixon clan decided to do a last-minute, family-plan hire of him. Since he had to go into the office anyway, he looked it up and called me. The lawyer's name is Harvey Simpson and he's based out of Mauston. I gave him a call, but the number Lucien gave me was most likely for an office and all I got was voice mail. Hopefully, the guy will call back first thing tomorrow."

"I can't wait to see how that shakes out," I say.

"It could be interesting," Hurley agrees. "I also talked to Jonas, who has been up all night working nonstop, and he also has Laura and Arnie helping. Laura is looking over both of Monty's laptops—the one from the real estate office and the one from his home office—and she found something interesting when she looked at the accounting programs on Monty's home computer. If the information there is to be believed, Monty Dixon's bank accounts were nearly empty when he died."

"Really?" I say, taking a second or two to digest the implications of this.

Hurley nods and says, "His savings account has five bucks and change, and his day-to-day checking account has just three hundred and change in it."

"That's a far cry from the fifty grand the accountant said Monty kept in his checking two years ago. What about the investment account that had the two million in it? And the oceanside vacation hacienda in the Caribbean?"

"No word on those yet. Laura is still looking. She did find some expenses, though, and it appears that Monty was heavily in debt. She found five credit cards with hefty balances on them, two of them in the six-figure range. All five appear to be in arrears. We also found paperwork for a first and a second mortgage on the house, and it looks like Monty owed what it's worth. There's no equity there."

"That's crazy," I say. "The accountant you spoke to earlier said the house was paid off. Where did all the money go?"

"Laura contacted the credit card companies for the two with the biggest balances, and it looks like most of the charges were for women's clothing and jewelry, a lot of air travel, including a couple of excursions to Europe, and countless meals at fancy restaurants. Summer has access to all the cards, though it's possible that Monty might have charged the meals as part of his business. Hard to tell at this point."

"Maybe Monty hid some of his money," I suggest. "He could have set up some offshore accounts or something like that in preparation for divorcing Summer."

"He did make some rather large cash withdrawals over the past year," Hurley says. "But I don't think he hid the money. More on that in a minute."

I can hardly wait.

"Jonas said he processed a number of prints on the cue sticks and pool balls, and he found partials that he can match to Sawyer, Monty, and Harrison. No surprises there, since I assume all three of them played. The broken cue stick hasn't been processed yet because Arnie had to wait to get it from Doc Morton, once he removed it during the autopsy. But Arnie did process the samples you collected from Summer's hands, Monty's neck, and the portion of the cue stick that was used to kill Monty. The oil on Summer's hands is olive oil and it's a match to the residue on the swab you took from Monty's neck."

"That jibes with Summer's story," I say. "She said she checked his neck for a pulse. What about the broken cue stick?"

"He didn't find any trace of the olive oil on the cue stick swab," Hurley says. "That fact puts Summer a lot lower on my list of suspects, though we still need to have a chat with Damien Cook. It's possible that the two of them were in on it together." He pauses and sighs. "I'm going to drop in on Damien this evening as soon as we finish with this next interview. I don't want to delay and give him a chance to clean anything up."

"Makes sense. We can do that before dinner."

Hurley cocks his head to one side and eyes me with a mix of affection and concern. "I can do it alone, if you want. That way, you can try for a nap."

"I'm fine," I tell him with a dismissive wave of my hand. And I mean it. The coffee has perked me up—that, and the stunning revelation about Monty's financial status.

"Okay, if you're sure."

"I am. Continue."

He smiles indulgently. "I also spoke to Peter Carlisle. Apparently, Monty had had him on a retainer of sorts for nearly two years, monitoring Summer's activities, as well as Sawyer's. That explains where one chunk of money went. Carlisle isn't cheap. Then, two weeks ago, Monty canceled Carlisle out of the blue, claiming that he couldn't justify the expense any longer and that he was going to make some changes."

"His bank account balances would seem to justify that," I say, and Hurley nods.

"Carlisle said the thing with Summer and Damien has been going on for nearly two years, and that Monty knew about it and didn't seem all that upset over it. Sawyer, on the other hand, was a thorn in Monty's side. When Carlisle told him about Sawyer's gambling problem, Monty got very angry. It seems Sawyer got himself in deep with some loan sharks last year to the tune of nearly eighty grand and Monty had to bail him out. I think that's where a good portion of his savings account disappeared to. He made Sawyer promise to stop gambling and start attending Gamblers Anonymous meetings. Sawyer complied for a while, but then he managed to get himself into trouble again."

I shake my head woefully. "Wow, this family is just full of secrets."

"No kidding," Hurley agrees. He starts to say something more, but his phone rings. "Detective Hurley," he says when he answers. He listens for a moment and then says, "Yes, sir. I don't know if you've heard yet, but Monty Dixon was killed last night. I understand that you drafted a new will for him not long ago."

This tells me it must be the lawyer, Harvey Simpson, on the phone, the one who did the new will for Monty.

Hurley listens some more, then says, "Interesting. Can you send me copies?" He gives Simpson a fax number and his e-mail address, thanks him, and then disconnects the call.

"This case may not be so complicated, after all," Hurley says with a self-satisfied smile I've seen on him before when he starts closing in on a suspect. "It seems that Monty revised his will six months ago and made Sawyer his sole beneficiary. He cut Summer out completely."

"Understandable, given that he knew at that point about her and Damien."

"Yeah, but here's the good part. Monty contacted Simpson two weeks ago and told him to draft another new will. This one was supposed to cut Sawyer out completely."

"Again, understandable," I say, "given what he knows about Sawyer's gambling issues. And if he's in trouble with loan sharks . . ." I don't complete the thought; I don't have to.

"Yeah," Hurley says, nodding thoughtfully. "Except the new will was never signed, meaning the old one is still in play and Sawyer inherits everything. I'd say that's a lot of motive right there, wouldn't you?"

"It's motive, all right, assuming we can prove Sawyer knew about the new will. How can we do that?"

Hurley's smile widens. "Simpson said he sent a hard copy of the new will to Monty to review and approve. It was delivered by a courier to Monty's real estate office last week, but when Simpson called Monty a few days later to ask if he had any questions, Monty claimed he never received the thing. Simpson checked with the courier and they had a signature showing it was delivered to Monty, so he then called the courier, who actually delivered the package, and got a description of the person who signed for it."

"Let me guess," I say. "It was Sawyer."

Hurley nods, his smile big and broad now. "You got it. I think Sawyer saw a way out of his gambling debt with his inheritance. Won't he be surprised if it turns out his father really is broke."

CHAPTER 15

Our second housecleaning candidate arrives five minutes early and, once again, Hurley goes to fetch the woman while I wait in the kitchen.

Cara Solomon is a rosy-cheeked, slightly rotund woman I'd guess to be about my age—late thirties or maybe early forties—dressed in faded jeans, a tie-dyed T-shirt, and a pair of stained and worn athletic shoes, which I'm pretty sure never played a role in any sports. Her hair is brown, pulled back into a braid that reaches to the middle of her back, and her eyes are two different colors. The left one is green, the right one brown. There is a faint aroma about her, an odd mix of lemon with a hint of ammonia and a subtle under-lying whiff of bleach. But there is something else, too, something I can't quite identify.

Hurley directs her to our dining table and he and I settle into seats across from her. It's a round table, so there is little to be determined by anyone's choice of seat there, though I do note that Cara positions herself so that she has a view of the front door.

"Tell me about your cleaning business," Hurley begins.

"Sure," she says with a drowsy, drawn-out voice. "I started

it five years ago to augment our family income. My kids are all in school now, so I spend those hours cleaning houses."

"And how do you handle things in the summertime or during school breaks?" I ask.

"My mom watches them. She keeps them all summer for me, as often as I need, and she also helps out during the school breaks." She shrugs and manages a sleepy smile. "My husband, Joe, works a lot and has to travel at times, so he's not reliable for childcare."

"What does he do?" I ask.

"He's in sales," she says.

"And how old are your kids?"

She smiles and her face lights up. "Cherish—she's my oldest—is thirteen. Harmony is eleven, and Serenity is nine."

"All girls?" I say.

"Yep. We tried for a fourth, hoping for a boy, but it never happened." She shrugs and smiles again. "I guess Mother Nature is done with me. Do you have children?"

"We do," I say. "A boy, Matthew, who will be three this fall, and a girl, Emily, who is seventeen." Hurley is busy jotting notes, ironically into the same notebook he uses for all his crime notes, and there is a moment of silence. I let it ride, knowing that it will often prompt people into speaking up.

Cara does. She looks around at the kitchen, the breakfast nook, and into the living room and front foyer. "You have a lovely home," she says. "What types of services are you looking for?"

I field this one, primarily because I'm not sure Hurley knows the answer. "Mainly, we're looking for assistance with the basics, like dusting, vacuuming, cleaning up the kitchen and bathrooms, and mopping the floors that need it. I'd also like someone who is willing to do laundry and perhaps change the sheets on our beds once a week."

Cara's eyebrows rise, but nothing else in her expression changes. I'm having a hard time reading her.

"Are those things you do?" I ask.

"Of course," she says. "I'm very flexible. Are you seeing my visits as weekly then?"

I hesitate, glancing at Hurley. We've had this discussion—or, rather, this *debate,* because we haven't been able to agree—many times of late. I decide in the interest of peace to defer to Cara. "What would you recommend?"

"To be honest, I think you'll want me here at least twice a week. This is a large house, I understand you both work, and you have a toddler and a teenager living here, neither of which is known for being very neat."

I'm happy to hear her suggest this frequency, but I see a frown form on Hurley's face. "What are your fees?" I ask before Hurley can pooh-pooh her suggestion.

She cocks her head to one side, eyes narrowing, as if she is thinking. Yet I feel certain she had a figure in mind before she ever walked through the door. "How does one-twenty a week sound, with me coming twice a week, on Tuesdays and Fridays?"

Hurley looks like he just swallowed something horrible.

"We'll need to talk it over," I say to Cara. "How soon would you be able to start?"

"Tomorrow, if you want."

"On the phone, you said you would bring some references?"

"Oh, right," she says with a smile. She reaches into the purse she's been clutching the entire time and pulls out a sheet of folded paper. She unfolds it, smooths it out on the table, and then slides it over to me. There are three names on it with phone numbers listed next to them.

"Thanks," I say, taking the paper. "I don't have any other questions." I look over at Hurley. "Do you?"

He shakes his head, still looking a bit shell-shocked.

"We'll be in touch," I tell her. She gets up and I show her out. When I return to the table, I give Hurley's shoulders a light massage and kiss him on top of his head. "What's wrong?" I ask.

"Are we seriously considering paying out nearly five hundred dollars a month for someone to clean our house?"

My hands freeze on his shoulders as the tone in his voice sets me on edge. I remember our sessions with Dr. Baldwin and the things she said to me, and the big-footed praying mantis. "What would be an acceptable amount in your mind?" I ask, proud that I didn't immediately snap back with the response that first came to me: *How much is my peace of mind worth to you?*

"I don't know," he says with a sigh. "I guess I was thinking it would be a lot less than that."

"Maybe it can be," I tell him, though I know from asking around that this price isn't unreasonable. "We have some other people to consider. And it might be a moot point anyway."

"What? Why?" he asks, cranking around to look at me.

"I have a feeling about Cara," I tell him. "She gave her daughters hippie names, she was wearing a tie-dye T-shirt, and she smelled like patchouli." Hurley frowns at me. "I'm willing to bet she smokes pot."

I see enlightenment on Hurley's face. "What did she say her husband's name was?"

"Joe. I'm assuming the same last name, so Joe Solomon. Why?"

"I think I've heard that name before." He gets up and heads for the stairs. I know he's going up to his home office to get on the computer. I follow, and when I find him seated at his desk peering at the laptop screen, I walk over and peer over his shoulder.

"I knew that name sounded familiar," he says, pointing to the screen at what I quickly recognize as a rap sheet. It isn't much of a surprise to discover that Joe Solomon was arrested and convicted for a series of drug-related crimes over the past fifteen years.

"Talk about euphemisms," I scoff. "Cara said her husband travels a lot in his work. She failed to mention that his travel was to the state pen. And I think we can guess what sorts of sales he does."

"So we cross her off the list?" Hurley says.

"We do." I sigh.

"Who's next?" Hurley asks. "Maybe I should do a criminal background check now, before we get in too deep."

"Her name is Dorothy Nelson and she's in her fifties. She's a widow who works alone and started cleaning houses eight years ago when her husband died. It's something she does to help make ends meet, apparently, because her husband only had a small life insurance policy. I got her name from Jean Sheridan, the wife of one of the ER docs I used to work with. They've been using her for four years and Jean swears she's very reliable, very thorough, and reasonably priced. Rumor has it, she's also very picky about who she works for, and if she doesn't like you or doesn't like something about the work, she'll pass on the job."

"Sounds like she's going to be interviewing us rather than the other way around," Hurley says. He has entered her name into his search box, but a slew of *Dorothy Nelsons* comes back as a result. No surprise there. The surnames of Nelson and Olsen/Olson are as prevalent in these parts as cheese.

"I'll need more info on her, like a birthdate or something," Hurley says. "In the meantime, what do you say we drop in on Damien Cook and see what he's up to?"

Fifteen minutes later, we are knocking on Damien Cook's door. He doesn't look surprised when Hurley announces who we are, and he invites us into his apartment. I realize now that Summer's claim that she was at Cut the Cheese attending a cooking class was an inside joke on her part. Many of the downtown stores have living spaces on the levels above the stores, most of them apartments that are rented out by the buildings' owners, which in many cases is also the attached shop owner. Such is the case here. Damien's apartment is located above Cut the Cheese.

It isn't difficult to understand how Summer Dixon got involved with Damien. The man is stunningly handsome and has the physique of someone who works out regularly—a veritable Adonis. I place him in his mid-to-late thirties, though the gray at his temples might indicate a few more years. His facial features are sharp and chiseled, yet softened by thick, velvety-black eyelashes and hazel-colored eyes. His skin tone is dark—naturally so rather than the result of sun or tanning beds—and so is his thick, wavy hair. This, combined with his dense, muscular build, suggests a Pacific island heritage, maybe Hawaiian or Samoan.

His voice is deep and surprisingly free of any accent, though his avoidance of contractions makes me think English is a second language to him. He has a lazy, drawn-out way of speaking that is soothing and kind of sexy. During the introductions, he beams a thousand-watt smile at me, revealing perfect white teeth and deep dimples in each cheek. I feel myself flush and try to look away, but it's hard not to stare at the man. He possesses a degree of mesmerizing magnetism that draws me in and holds me prisoner.

Damien invites us to sit on his couch, a modern design with a strong Scandinavian flair. It doesn't seem to suit him, and I wonder if the apartment is rented furnished.

"May I offer you a beverage of some sort?" Damien says, beaming that smile at us.

I'm tempted to say yes, if for no other reason than just so I can watch the man move some more, but Hurley answers for us both. "No, thanks, we're fine."

Damien settles on one of the chairs in the room—a large

open area that serves as living, dining, and kitchen space—and settles back looking relaxed. Then he gets right to the point. "It is a horrible thing that happened to Mr. Dixon," he says. "He did not deserve that."

"May I ask how it is you know about what happened to Mr. Dixon?" Hurley asks.

"Summer told me."

"When?"

"She called me late last night. Around one, I believe it was. She said she was staying at a motel here in town because someone had stabbed Monty to death at the house and the police would not let her stay there. She asked if she could come here for the night, but I told her I did not think that would be wise."

"Why is that?" I ask.

He looks at me and flashes a cagey smile. I feel my face flush again. "I told her that it might be best if we kept apart until the police finish their investigation. Though that was not the only reason I told her no. I had another guest last night and it would have been . . . awkward for Summer to show up here."

"Another guest?" Hurley says. "As in another *female* guest?"

"Yes."

"Did you see Summer Dixon at all yesterday?" Hurley asks.

"Oh, yes, sir, I did. She was here for several hours yesterday evening. We fixed a dinner together, a London broil with roasted baby red potatoes and Brussels sprouts. Summer is trying to improve her cooking skills."

"Was cooking the only activity you two enjoyed?" Hurley asks.

Damien gives him a sly smile. "No, sir. Food preparation tends to make Mrs. Dixon, um, a bit randy."

"You had sex," Hurley says with a hint of irritation.

"We did."

"And when did Mrs. Dixon leave?"

"Around ten, give or take. My other guest was arriving at eleven and I had to prepare."

My mind reels as I ponder just what his preparation involved.

"And who was this other guest?" Hurley asks.

Damien's face no longer looks friendly. "I do not wish to say that," he says. "Discretion is an important thing for me. The women who take my . . . cooking classes are wealthy, important women who value their privacy. You understand?"

"Oh, I understand, all right," Hurley says. "I'm guessing that you are paid well by your guests for your, um, classes. I'm sure you are aware that there are certain activities for which getting paid is illegal. I'd be happy to call our vice detective down here to explain that to you better."

I realize that in addition to being a cook, Damien is also a gigolo who caters to a small, elite group of clientele. I can't help but wonder who his other clients are.

Damien frowns at Hurley's threat, but then drops the name of the mayor's wife. I must admit, I'm a little surprised.

"Does Summer know you . . . teach other women?" I ask.

"Of course," Damien says.

"And does Summer pay you for her, um, classes?"

"She does. In her case, it is a part of my payment for the cooking services I provide for her and Mr. Dixon."

"Really?" I say, wondering if Monty had a clue about this aspect of Summer's betrayal.

"How long have you been cooking for the Dixons?" Hurley asks.

"Just shy of two years now," he says, and then Hurley asks him to describe his typical workday. "Most days I arrive around ten in the morning and begin preparations for lunch, which Mr. Dixon likes served at twelve sharp. He is . . . was rather obsessive about his eating times. When that is done, I start on the dinner prep. Mr. Dixon liked to sit down to eat at six every day during the week. On the weekends, I only come on Saturdays. The Dixons are on their own for lunch and dinner on Sunday."

"That seems like a lot of work for you," Hurley says. Damien shrugs and flashes that thousand-watt smile. "Are the Dixons typically at home when you are there?"

"Mr. Dixon usually came home for meals only and was gone the rest of the day, including Saturdays. His line of work is not a Monday-through-Friday thing, so sometimes his hours ran well into the evening. Yet he always carved out time for his lunch at twelve and his dinner at six."

He starts to say something else, but Hurley jumps in before he can. "How do you know about his evening work hours if you weren't there?"

"Mrs. Dixon tells me."

"How long have you been providing Mrs. Dixon with your . . . um . . . cooking classes?"

"It began with real cooking classes," Damien says. "For the first few months, that is all we did. Then Mrs. Dixon started telling me how frustrated she was with her husband's lack of interest in her, and I needed some extra money. One thing led to another and that part has been going on for about a year and a half. Several of my other clients have come to me by word of mouth . . . Mrs. Dixon's mouth, though I do not know if she is aware of that. Apparently, she talks to some of her acquaintances about such things."

"And Summer knows you have other clients?" I ask, having a hard time believing this.

"She does."

"What about Mr. Dixon?" Hurley asks. "Did he know?"

Damien licks his lips and sucks in a deep breath before answering. "He does . . . did," he says, "though Mrs. Dixon did not know that. Monty approached me several months ago and asked me if I was sleeping with his wife. I denied it, of course, but then he laughed at me and said he knew because he had hired a private investigator to follow Summer. He offered to show me photos of Summer and me together, but I declined."

"Monty must have been angry," Hurley says.

Damien chuckles. "Yes, one might think so, but Mr. Dixon told me that I could continue on with Summer if I did him a favor."

"And that was . . . ?" Hurley and I both say at the same time.

"To prepare food when he entertained clients on a large scale at home. It was not all that often, and it involved hors d'oeuvres and the like for the most part. It did not take a lot of my time."

"That's all he asked of you?" Hurley says, frowning. I'm as puzzled as he is. This hardly seems like punishment enough for Damien sneaking around behind Monty's back to sleep with his wife.

"Did I mention that I had to do it for free?" Damien adds. "And buy all the ingredients?"

This makes more sense. And it gives me a little more insight into the man that was Monty Dixon, a man willing to trade off his wife's fidelity for a bit of free catering.

"You make it sound like this was something in the past," Hurley says. "Would this arrangement still be in place today if Monty was alive?"

Damien shakes his head. "A couple of weeks ago, Monty told me he was going to have to let me go. I figured it was the overdue punishment I had coming, but Monty was civil about it. He told me it had nothing to do with me and Summer, but rather with his own financial situation."

"That seems awfully understanding of him," Hurley says, skepticism rife in his voice.

"Yes, I know. I was suspicious, too, especially when Summer told me about something he did after that."

Hurley raises his eyebrows in question and Damien complies.

"She said he kept going on and on about how good some cinnamon rolls I made for him were, insisting that Summer try one. She said it was strange because he knew that she did not like sweet stuff in the morning, and despite raving about the rolls, he had only eaten one himself. He did not touch the rest of them over a period of two days."

"Meaning?" Hurley says.

Damien looks from Hurley to me and then back to Hurley again, his brow furrowed. "Well, I got to wondering if he had poisoned those rolls. If Mrs. Dixon ate a poisoned roll that was in a batch made specifically for Mr. Dixon, it would look like I had tried to poison him, and Summer ended up dead by mistake. That would have taken care of both of us quite nicely, and Mr. Dixon would have been able to cash in on Mrs. Dixon's life insurance."

Hurley narrows his eyes at Damien and says, "Do you have a reason to think Monty would do something like that?"

Damien doesn't answer right away, appearing to give the question serious consideration. "I do not know," he says eventually. "There is . . . was something about the guy, an intensity that could be unnerving, you know?"

"Did he ever threaten you? Or are you aware of him ever threatening Summer?"

Damien shakes his head. "No . . . no . . . nothing like that. It is hard to explain."

"When did you last see Mr. Dixon?" Hurley asks.

"Yesterday at lunchtime, at the house."

"Did he say anything to you?"

"No, but he almost never does. He just gives me a nod of acknowledgment and goes about his business."

"What hours were you at the house yesterday?"

"I arrived at my usual time, at ten in the morning, and I was there until around four. I fixed a salad for their dinner, along with a casserole that only had to be reheated."

"Did you see Mr. Dixon at any time other than lunch?"

"No."

"Do you know if he was out or at the house during the day?"

"I do not. I rarely venture beyond the kitchen area and Monty often shuts himself up inside his office if he is at home. He tends to come and go via the back entrance, where Sawyer's rooms are."

"Did you see Summer while you were there?"

"Yes, but all we did was discuss the meal plan. No hanky-panky. I never act anything but professional when I am on duty." He thrusts his chin out pridefully.

"Hard to believe that," I say, and Damien shoots me a wounded look.

"How about Sawyer?" Hurley asks. "Did you include him in your meal plans?"

"No. Monty told me Sawyer preferred to eat out most of the time and not to worry about him."

"Was he at the house yesterday when you were there?"

"If he was, I did not see him. But he has that private suite on the back side of the house. He can come and go as he pleases, without anyone being the wiser." He pauses and a look of dawning comes over him. "Though I did see his car in the drive when I got there yesterday morning. Apparently, there is no room for his car in the garage because it is filled up with Mr. Dixon's car, Mrs. Dixon's car, their boat, and some other toys they store there. When I left the house yesterday afternoon, Sawyer's car was not in the drive any longer. But as to when he left, I could not say."

"Tell me something," I say to Damien. "When Mrs. Dixon was with you last night, did she sustain any injuries?"

His lips curl into a half-smile. "She did have a run-in with a meat fork that was on the counter when we . . . when she . . . well, she placed her hand down quickly on the countertop and one of the tines poked her palm."

"I see," I say, afraid that I will never get that image out of my head now. Once again, I'm blushing, but for a different reason this time. I'm saved from further embarrassment by the faint buzz of Hurley's cell phone and I gratefully switch my attention to him, watching as he glances down at a text message.

"Okay, Mr. Cook, that's all we have for now," he says, tucking the phone in his pocket and standing to indicate an end to our inquiries.

I get up, too. His haste has me excited and speculating on what that text message said.

"Don't leave town unless you check with me first," Hurley says as we walk to the door.

"I would not think of it," Damien says, following us. As we are leaving, he says, "I hope you find who did it and punish them. Mr. Dixon was a nice man."

I'm tempted to come back with a snarky reply, but there is a level of sincerity in Damien's voice that makes me stay quiet.

Once we're back in Hurley's truck, I ask, "What was the text message?"

"It was Arnie. He wants me to call him right away." Hurley takes out his phone, taps in the appropriate number, and then puts it on speaker so I can hear.

"Hey, Hurley," Arnie says after half a ring.

"Hi, Arnie. I'm here with Mattie and we have you on speaker. What have you got?"

"Christopher wanted me to let you know that he and Doc Morton are doing Taylor Copeland's autopsy and they discovered a few interesting things. For one, the stomach contents contained a fair amount of drug residue, and it appears that the pills were crushed into powder."

I think about this a moment, and then realize the significance. "Why would she do that? Why not just swallow the pills? It had to have tasted awful to have ground-up pills mixed in with whiskey like that."

"Then again, there are plenty of people out there who have trouble swallowing whole pills and have to routinely grind them up," Arnie suggests. "Maybe Taylor Copeland was one of those."

It's a valid point.

"There's something else I think I should mention," Arnie goes on. "When I was looking through Copeland's kitchen, I noticed that there were three other highball glasses like the one she used in a cupboard. One of those left a wet ring on the shelf, like it had just been washed and not dried thoroughly and then put in the cupboard. I snapped a picture of it and it's on the server, if you want to look at it. It struck me as odd because the dishwasher was only a third full, and if Copeland used a different highball glass earlier for some reason and then changed to the other one, why not just toss the first one in the dishwasher?"

"Are you thinking there was someone else there who used the other glass?" I say.

"That would explain why the pills were ground up, wouldn't it?" Arnie says.

I think about this, but caution myself because Arnie is a conspiracy theorist of the first order. The man could find a nefarious plot in my son's morning bowl of Cheerios.

"And here's the best part," Arnie continues when no one answers. "I just finished analyzing the cue stick that was used to stab Montgomery Dixon. It's made from an exotic Brazilian rosewood, very elite. You don't see it often."

"Okay," I say. "How does that help us?"

"Well, I also analyzed that tiny sliver of wood that was removed from Sawyer Dixon's hair. Want to guess what kind of wood it is?"

"Exotic Brazilian rosewood?"

"You got it."

"Nice work, Arnie," Hurley says.

"And I'm still not done. Christopher said to tell you that Otto is one hundred percent certain that Taylor Copeland's time of death was between six and seven p.m. And Monty Dixon's time of death was between eight and nine."

"Copeland was killed before Monty?" Hurley says, looking surprised. "Why would she apologize for killing the man if he wasn't dead yet?"

"Because she didn't do it," I say, my eyes huge. "This case just did a one-eighty."

"And I'm still not done," Arnie says, ramping up his enthusiasm. "Junior Feller is here and wants to talk to you."

We listen as the phone gets handed off and then Junior Feller, who works as the Sorenson PD vice detective, gets on the phone.

"Hi, guys," he says, and both Hurley and I reply "hi," too. "I did a little digging into that matter you mentioned earlier, Hurley, and struck gold. There is a guy named Ringo Zimmerman, based out of The Dells, who's a known loan shark, and it seems our young Sawyer is indebted to him to the tune of nearly a hundred grand."

Hurley lets out a low whistle. "That's a lot of money."

"Yes, it is," Junior agrees, "and word has it, Ringo has been putting significant pressure on Sawyer to pay up. He sent some guys around last week to help convince Sawyer that it was in his best interests to settle the account, and Sawyer begged, pleaded, and told them he was going to be coming into a large sum of money in another week or two. Ringo told his guys to let him slide for now, but to give him a small reminder that this is serious business."

Hurley frowns and I can tell he's thinking back to earlier, the same way I am. Sawyer Dixon appeared to be fine. He wasn't sporting any bruises, he didn't limp when he walked, and he wasn't favoring either of his arms, or his ribs. So, what kind of reminder did they give him?

"There's a girl he likes who works in a bar in The Dells," Junior continues. "One Maribel Solis. Seems Sawyer gave her a promise ring recently that she was wearing on her pinky finger."

I feel a little sick as my mind makes a leap and I suss out what I suspect was Sawyer's reminder. Junior delivers the punch quickly and succinctly. "Word has it, Sawyer received the ring back in the mail a few days ago, with the finger still in it."

CHAPTER 16

I squeeze my eyes closed and swallow hard, trying not to imagine what it was like for some sweet young barmaid to get her pinky finger cut off for reasons over which she had no control.

"Have you been able to verify that?" Hurley asks.

"Not yet," Junior says. "It seems our Ms. Maribel hasn't been to work for the past three days. She called in sick every day."

"Has anyone seen the finger?" Hurley asks.

"So far, it's all talk," Junior says. "But when I came up here to see Arnie and he told me about the wood splinter, I figured I'd hang and let you know what I've dug up so far."

"Glad you did," Hurley says. "Thanks to you both."

Hurley disconnects the call and looks at me with a smile on his face. "I'm thinking Sawyer Dixon has killed not one, but two people. He made a half-assed attempt to lay the blame for his father's death on Taylor Copeland, but it didn't work. And the fact that she was killed first shows premeditation." Hurley lets out a satisfied sigh. "I'm going to go out to the Sorenson Motel and arrest him. I feel certain we have enough at this point to make the DA happy—a clear motive, no alibi, and evidence linking him to the scene and the murder weapon for his father. Plus, he knew about the situation between his father and Taylor Copeland, so he could have easily set her up as the fall guy. Want to come along?"

"Wouldn't miss it."

Hurley puts in a call to get a uniformed officer to assist us and Al Whitman shows up. Al has been with the Sorenson Police Department going on thirteen years now and has shown no interest in advancing his career. He seems quite content to work as a patrol officer forever. He and his wife have five kids, and I sometimes think he just doesn't have the time or leftover brain power for career advancement requirements after dealing with his kids. He's a mellow guy with a good reputation among the teens in town, and that is something of a rarity. For that reason alone, I think a lot of people are happy to have him as a patrol officer for eternity.

After filling Al in on what we are about to do, Hurley and I head for the Sorenson Motel in his pickup, with Al following behind us in a patrol car. Hurley pulls up to the main office and the two of us head inside to ask Joseph Wagner, the curmudgeonly owner of the motel, which room Sawyer is staying in.

Joseph is sitting behind his desk, dressed in his ubiquitous denim bib overalls and a plain and very thin white T-shirt. I've never seen Joseph dressed in anything else. His wiry gray hair, a clownish fringe that circles from ear to ear beneath his otherwise bald head, is in desperate need of a trim. There are bags beneath his eyes large enough to pack all of Marie Featherstone's groceries in, and an unlit, half-chewed cigar hangs out one side of his mouth. As soon as we walk in and Joseph sets eyes on me, he groans.

"Oh, for cripes' sake, not you again," he whines. "Nothing good ever happens when you show up out here."

"We're here to arrest someone," Hurley says. "Sawyer Dixon? I believe he rented a room from you last night?"

"What are you arresting him for?" Joseph asks, picking a bit of tobacco off his lower lip.

"Can you tell me what room he's in?" Hurley says, ignoring the question.

Joseph cocks his head to one side and narrows his eyes at Hurley. "I can tell you what room he *was* in, but he checked out about an hour ago. Hightailed it out of here like the devil himself was after him."

"Damn," Hurley mutters. "I don't suppose he said where he was going?"

"Oh, sure," Joseph says with great enthusiasm. I know immediately that he's mocking Hurley, but my husband doesn't know Joseph as well as I do, and he momentarily perks up at this response. Then Joseph continues. "Yeah, the kid wrote out his entire itinerary for the next two weeks and handed it to me right before he left."

Getting it now, Hurley glares at Joseph. The two men engage in a stare-off for what feels like an eternity, until Hurley then asks, "Have you cleaned the room yet?"

"Guy's only been gone an hour," Joseph says, looking at Hurley like he was just asked to raise the dead. "Girl hasn't gotten to it yet. We've been busy, what with the Cow Chip Tossing festival going on and all."

"I'd like to take a quick look at his room, then, please."

Joseph considers this, and for a moment, I think he's going to say no. But then he shrugs, turns around, and takes a key off a board. He hands it to Hurley. "Room eight."

"Did Mr. Dixon make any phone calls from his room phone while he was here?"

"Nope."

Hurley takes the key and starts to leave, but then he turns back. "Can you tell me what room Summer Dixon is in?"

"Room ten."

Hurley thanks Joseph, who only grunts in response. We tell

Al he can go, and then we walk down to the room Sawyer was staying in. The room is neat as a pin, except for the un-made bed, and even it is barely mussed. Hurley checks the wastebasket, but it's empty, and then he checks the bathroom trash, but it's empty as well. The shower is dry—if Sawyer used it, it must have been last night—and the notepad by the telephone reveals no indentations when I cast some oblique light on it, using the flashlight on my key chain. Sawyer has left us no clues. Hurley tries calling Sawyer's cell phone, but when he gets voice mail, he hangs up without leaving any message.

Next we head to Summer's room. She is there and, unlike Sawyer's room, Summer's is well lived in already. Her natural tendency toward slovenliness is much in evidence here. So are her spending habits, as there are several shopping bags strewn about the room and clothes with the tags still at-tached draped over the bed and chair. Apparently, Monty's credit cards are still working.

"I have no idea where Sawyer went," she says when Hur-ley asks. "It's not like he speaks to me about anything."

"When did you last see him?"

"Last night, when we were checking in here at the motel. He got a call on his cell phone that must have upset him, be-cause he was really pale and shaky-looking afterward."

"Any idea what the call was about?" Hurley asks.

Summer shakes her head. "Don't know, don't care."

Hurley thanks her, and as we are about to leave, Summer says, "Can I go back to my house yet?"

"Not yet," Hurley says. "I'll let you know as soon as we've cleared the place."

When we are back in his pickup truck, I say, "Summer doesn't appear to be letting her husband's murder slow down her spending habits any. Based on all those new clothes she had in her room, she must be setting her credit cards afire."

Hurley looks over at me and smiles. "Of course," he says. Then he sandwiches my face between his palms, leans over, and gives me a kiss on the lips. "You're so smart."

With that, he starts up the truck, while I sit in the passenger seat, utterly confused. I cave as we pull out of the motel parking lot. "Okay, I give. Why am I so brilliant?"

"Because you gave me the answer for how to find Sawyer Dixon. I just need to track his credit card expenses."

I listen as Hurley calls the station and asks for a BOLO to be issued for Sawyer, and for a uniformed officer to check the Dixon house to make sure Sawyer hasn't tried to go back there, and someone to patrol the house to make sure he doesn't try. Next he calls Laura Kingston and asks her to dig up what she can on Sawyer Dixon's credit cards and to call him with any recent charges.

I realize then that Hurley isn't driving back to the police station. I'm not sure where we are going until he pulls onto the street where my sister's house is located.

"I take it we're picking up Matthew," I say as he pulls his truck to the curb.

"It's been a long day for both of us and I can get other people working on trying to track down Sawyer Dixon, so you and I are going to get our son, head home, and enjoy a nice quiet dinner. Then we're going to get a good night's sleep so we can start fresh again in the morning. Does that sound okay?"

It sounds divine, and I tell him so. We head inside and find my sister in her usual spot: the kitchen. It's her favorite room in the house and there are times when I think she'd sleep there if she had a way to do it comfortably. Something beefy and delicious-smelling is bubbling away on the stove—homemade beef barley soup, Desi informs us—and she is rolling out dough for biscuits on the counter beside the stove. Our son is standing on a chair beside her, rolling out his own tiny piece of dough with a teeny little rolling pin.

"I'm teaching him how to make biscuits," Desi says. "He's a natural." She winks as she says this, most likely because Matthew's dough is an uneven blob and he has managed to get flour everywhere.

"You are amazing," I tell my sister, chuckling and giving her a kiss on her cheek. "Where is everyone else?" I ask, as we didn't see anyone as we walked through the living and dining rooms to get to the kitchen.

"Emily is out with some friends, Ethan is in his room, Dad is taking a nap in his room, and Lucien is in our bedroom working on some stuff."

Her easy use of the term "Dad" hits me hard. She has adapted to this new truth so easily.

"I'm going to pop in on Lucien and have a chat," Hurley says. He leaves us and I watch as my sister neatly cuts eight perfectly round biscuits out of her dough and then hands the biscuit cutter to Matthew. Having watched Desi's technique carefully, he holds the tool over his glob of dough, centering it the best he can. He only has enough to make one biscuit, but it's a doozy, a full inch thick on one side and a quarter inch on the other.

"You're welcome to stay for dinner, if you want," Desi says. "I have plenty."

"Thanks, but we have plans already. And we're both really beat and just want to go home."

Desi gives me a sympathetic look. "You poor thing. Your weekend off has been totally ruined, hasn't it?"

I nod. "It's the nature of the job," I say. "Thanks so much for stepping up to help. I don't know what I'd do without you."

"You know I'm happy to help. You can let Matthew spend the night here, if you want."

"You are sweet to offer, but I want some time with this little bundle of energy tonight." I bend over my son, kiss him on his head, and tickle his ribs. He laughs, squirms, and then spins around and throws his arms about my neck, covering my hair and shoulders with flour and bits of dough.

Desi wipes her hands on a dish towel and says, "Let me get him cleaned up for you." She grabs a dishcloth and sets about washing Matthew's hands, arms, and face the best she can.

"Looks like someone needs a bath," I say, eyeing the lingering bits of dough in Matthew's hair.

Hurley returns then and sizes up the situation quickly. "Are we ready to go?"

"We are," I say. I thank my sister again, give her a big hug, and then take Matthew by the hand as we head back out to the pickup.

An hour later, I drag a wet but clean Matthew out of the bathtub and start drying him off. I can smell the steaks Hurley is cooking on the grill and it's making my mouth water.

"I need to go and fix your dinner," I tell Matthew. "Can you go to your room and get your jammies on by yourself?"

He nods vigorously.

"Good boy. Then you can come down and help me set the table, okay?"

"Okay." He dashes out of the bathroom and down the hall to his room. I pull the plug on the tub, thinking that I'll clean it out later, and then also thinking that this is a task I'm hoping a housecleaner can tackle, assuming we ever find one.

I head down to the kitchen and start fixing Matthew's hot dogs and mac and cheese. We stopped at the grocery store on the way home and Hurley ran in to get some Cheerios, apple juice, and some more mac and cheese. Matthew and I sat in the truck and I listened to him tell me all about the "blowed up" volcano he made with his grandfather. It's clear from the light in his eyes and the lilt in his voice as he regales me with his tale that it was the highlight of his day.

I'm flashing back on that scene from earlier, trying to parse my jumbled emotions as I start fixing Matthew's dinner. I add some sugar snap peas to the menu, one of the two vegetables he will eat, the other one being corn. I've got water simmering for the macaroni and the hot dogs boiling away when it dawns on me that Matthew should have been down here by now. I go to the base of the stairs and holler up to him.

"Matthew? What are you doing?"

"Combing my hair," he says.

"Did you put your jammies on?"

"I'm all done." I hear the pitter-patter of bare feet on the floor above as my son makes his way to the stairs. I return to the kitchen and dump the macaroni into the boiling water for the mac and cheese, Hoover on the floor at my feet. The door to the backyard opens and Hurley strolls into the kitchen amidst a cloud of aroma and the sound of sizzles from the steaks he's carrying. Hoover dashes over to meet him, sniffing loudly.

"The veggies are done," Hurley says. "I just—"

"I know, I haven't set the table yet," I say, figuring that's why he paused. "I'll do it now." I grab plates from one of the overhead cabinets and turn around to set them on the table. Then I see the stunned expression on my husband's face. He is staring at Matthew.

"I can help," Matthew says, climbing onto a chair so he can help me put the plates out. I look at him and see what has my husband momentarily shocked.

"Matthew, what did you do to your hair?" I say, setting the plates down before I drop them.

"I cut it," he says proudly.

"Oh, dear." My son looks like someone gave him a haircut using a Weedwacker. In the front, he has cut off a huge chunk right at the hairline, and he has done the same on both sides above his ears and in two places on top of his head, his white scalp showing through the stubble of his black hair. "Oh, Matthew, no," I say, feeling as if I should be angry, but I'm instead torn between wanting to laugh hysterically or cry.

"Son, you can't be cutting your own hair," Hurley says. He looks at me with a stunned, disbelieving expression.

"Where did you get the scissors?" I ask. I keep a pair of nail scissors on the top shelf of the medicine cabinet in my bathroom and if Matthew climbed up to get those, we need to have a bigger discussion.

"Emily's desk," Matthew says.

"You're not supposed to go into Emily's room when she's not there," I chastise, making a mental note to have a chat with Emily and ask her to keep her scissors somewhere harder to find.

Matthew pouts. "I sorry," he says, but I get a strong sense he isn't sorry at all. He's learning how to manipulate the adults in his life.

"Don't do it again," I say in a stern tone.

"I won't."

"Looks like you're going to get a buzz cut tomorrow," I say.

"A buzz cut? Really?" Hurley says, setting down the platter of steaks.

"That's the only way we're going to be able to fix it," I say. "He looks like a chemo patient the way it is now."

Matthew, oblivious to what he's done to himself, has already moved on. "I'm hungry," he says. "Is the mackachee ready yet?"

CHAPTER 17

The rest of our evening goes surprisingly well and all of us, except for Emily, who calls to say she'll be home around eleven, are in bed sound asleep by nine-thirty. When Hurley's alarm goes off at six, we fall into our usual morning routines. Matthew, who thinks his new haircut looks "really good," surprises us by asking for scrambled eggs and toast for breakfast. Hurley fixes enough for all of us and we settle in at the breakfast nook to eat. Emily can barely stifle the hysterical laughter bubbling up inside her every time she looks at her brother.

I tell Hurley I plan to check in at the office and see if anything more was found on Monty's and Taylor's autopsies, and then I'll join him for our nine o'clock interview with Harrison Dixon. Hurley considers canceling the meeting, since we already have our suspect, but decides to go ahead with it anyway, since Harrison purportedly had some knowledge of Monty's financial situation.

I pack Matthew into my hearse at seven-fifteen and drive him to Izzy and Dom's house. The temperature outside is already in the low eighties, unusual for springtime in Wisconsin, but not unheard of. The forecast on my phone is calling for a high in the mid-nineties with plenty of humidity. This is not my favorite kind of weather. I'm not a fan of heat and humidity.

With any luck, I'll be spending most of the day in air-conditioned buildings, since it's a regularly scheduled work-day for me. This, of course, assumes there aren't a lot of death calls. I'm hoping for a slow week, since I will be work-ing office hours and be on call for the next three days, even though my time off was effectively canceled by the unusual weekend workload.

When I arrive at Dom and Izzy's, I let myself in through the garage, using a punch code for the lock, and enter the kitchen. Dom is there, fulfilling his role as the perfect house-husband by having breakfast ready for Izzy, Izzy's mother, Sylvie, and Juliana, with enough prepared to offer some to Matthew and me, if we so desire. This morning's menu in-cludes freshly baked blueberry muffins, cheese omelets made from egg whites, and freshly squeezed orange juice.

Dom greets us with a hearty "Good morning!" Then he looks at Matthew, drops the spatula he has in his hand, and claps that hand over his heart. "Oh, my goodness!" he says. He looks at me. "Did you do that?"

"Lord, no," I say, genuinely offended. "I'm no stylist, but I could cut his hair better than that. He did it to himself."

Sylvie, who is several cows short of a full herd these days, looks at my son and says, "Is this some new modern thing with the little ones?"

"No, Sylvie, it's a very old tradition of kids cutting their own hair," I say.

"You let the boy have the scissors?" She rolls her eyes and clucks her tongue at me. "*Oy vey,* they should take the kid away from you." She wags an arthritic finger at me. "Bad mother."

On this note, Izzy walks into the kitchen, coffee mug in hand. "Smells good," he says, and he starts to walk toward his mother to give her a kiss. He stops when he sees Matthew, staring at him for several seconds. Then he bursts out laughing.

Dom chuckles and little Juliana, at first looking unsure of what everyone is laughing at, decides to laugh, too, because it looks like fun. Pretty soon, the entire room is laughing, everyone, that is, except Matthew. Sensing that he is the butt of this joke, he folds his arms over his chest, sticks his lower lip out, and scowls.

"Don't worry, little guy," Dom says, walking over and scooping Matthew up in his arms. He scrutinizes the haircut and shakes his head. "I'll fix it for you this time, but it's going to take a while for your hair to grow back in. Don't ever cut your own hair again, buddy, okay?"

"Okay," Matthew says, still scowling.

"Are you sure you want to try to fix it?" I ask Dom. "I can take him to Barbara and have her do it."

"It's silly to pay someone to fix this," he says. "And you can't take him to Barbara's, um, salon." He has a point. The basement of a funeral home might not be the best place for a toddler. "He's cut right down to his scalp in some of the spots," Dom goes on, eyeing Matthew's head. "The only fix is going to be a buzz." Dom mimics running a razor over his scalp.

Matthew's eyes grow big as he watches Dom. "I don't want a buzz," he whines, though I'm pretty sure he doesn't know what a "buzz" is.

"We'll talk about it later," Dom says. "How about a muffin?"

Apparently, Dom knows the way to my son's heart, because the hair debacle is instantly forgotten. Once Dom sets Matthew down, he runs over to the kitchen table, climbs into a seat next to Sylvie, and grabs one of the muffins sitting in a basket at the center of the table.

I say "Thank you" to Dom, not only for handling my kid's

hair crisis, but for making the muffins, one of which I grab as I'm heading out the door.

Just as I'm about to shut the door behind me, I hear Sylvie say, "Your mama is doomed. Let Nana Sylvie help you."

While driving to my office, I contemplate the irony of Matthew having a Nana Sylvie, when his real grandmother, my mother, hardly has anything to do with him. This isn't because she doesn't care about him, but rather because she's afraid of the germs he carries. Her fear is somewhat justifiable, as I know from my years working in the ER that toddlers are basically just Petri dishes for every type of bacterial and viral infection that might be lurking about.

When I arrive at the office, I check in with Christopher first thing. Normally, we do a phone call transfer of duties and information on Monday mornings, but because this weekend was so crazy, Christopher texted me last night and said he was going to have to come in to catch up on paperwork and he would just update me then.

Getting an update is easy because both Christopher and I have "offices" that consist of desk space in the office library. There are no walls separating us from one another, or from anyone who might choose to use the library. Fortunately, there aren't many of us working here, so most of the time, then, the library is vacant. Christopher has beat me in and is already seated at his desk, busily typing away on his computer. I don't know if Doc Morton, or Otto, to those of us who work with him regularly, is coming in this morning or if he called and reported off to Izzy via phone.

"Good morning," I say. "Glad to see you survived the weekend. What a crazy one, eh?"

"No kidding."

"Did you get any more calls last night?"

"Nothing major, thank goodness. There were two calls from out in the county, but both were obvious natural deaths that were expected, so we were able to clear them over the phone. Let me finish typing this report and then I'll give you the lowdown."

"No problem. I'll go grab a cup of coffee and be right back." I head for the office breakroom, make a cup of coffee with the Keurig machine we have there, and just as I'm about to go back to the library, Izzy walks in.

"Good timing," I say. "Christopher is about to report off to me. Did Otto call you with his report?"

"He did. This morning, in fact. But if you don't mind, I'd like to eavesdrop on Christopher's chat with you. He often has insights that can be very useful."

"Is that what we're calling it these days, 'insights'?"

Izzy smiles and shakes his head, but says nothing. The two of us go back to the library, where Christopher is shutting down his computer, an indication that he has finally finished his report.

"Do you mind if I listen in?" Izzy says to him.

"Happy to have you," Christopher says, and he punctuates the comment with a loud issuance of gas. "Sorry," he says automatically, though we both told him long ago that it wasn't necessary to apologize every time it happened.

Christopher has a digestive disorder that causes him to produce large quantities of gas no matter what he does or doesn't eat. He has tried numerous diets and drugs to minimize the problem, none of which have worked. It has cost him one job already, and a marriage. Since he sued the employer who fired him over it—and won—we are highly motivated to tolerate the problem, which is why I suspect Izzy made no comment on my little inside joke about insights. Besides, Christopher is more than qualified for the job, does well at it, is very flexible with his schedule, and is a pleasant person. Basically, aside from the gas problem, he's the perfect employee.

"Otto said there were no surprises during Monty Dixon's autopsy," Izzy says.

"You mean other than the fact that he was killed with a cue stick?" Christopher says. "That was a first for both Otto and me."

"For me as well," I say with a smile. "I did have a guy killed with a barbecue fork once, though. This job is rarely boring."

"Can't say I've ever seen it before, either," Izzy says. "Score one for the killer for displaying some originality."

"Other than that," Christopher continues, "there were no surprises that I'm aware of, though I haven't seen all the tox screen results yet. We reviewed all of Mattie's photos and we found livor mortis in his buttocks and down the backs of his legs, which would correspond with the position she found him in."

"Good to know," I say.

"You did a great job of securing the cue stick. There are photos on the server that Otto took of the wound, and the wound track once we cut him open. Again, no surprises there. The broken end of the cue stick splintered in such a way as to create a javelin of sorts and the point of it went right into his heart. There was evidence that the stick was moved slightly after its initial piercing, maybe by the perpetrator, maybe by the victim, but it's of little relevance.

"We bagged and tagged all his clothing. Wasn't much, since he was only wearing sweatpants, a T-shirt, underwear—he's a briefs man, if anyone cares—and socks." Something about this nags at my brain again, but the significance still eludes me. "The only trace we found was a long black hair on his chest near the puncture wound. It was on top of the blood on his shirt, so it was likely dropped sometime after he died."

"Most likely his wife's," I say. "She was the one who found him, and she checked him for a pulse." Both Izzy and Christopher nod. "Although . . ." I add, thinking. "The woman

Monty was rumored to be having an affair with, Jessica Leavenworth, also has long black hair."

"Food for thought," Izzy says.

"Probably not much," I say. "Hurley is looking to arrest the son, Sawyer. He had a sliver of wood stuck in his hair that matched the rare wood in the cue stick. He clearly had motive, in that getting his father's inheritance would go a long way toward paying off the loan shark he's indebted to. It sounds like Sawyer's girlfriend, Maribel Solis, might have had a run-in with the loan shark's henchmen and they left her with a message for Sawyer." I tell them about the finger Sawyer received bearing the promise ring he gave Maribel.

"It seems Sawyer also received a draft of a new will Monty had drawn up that was supposed to be given to Monty for approval. It would have nullified the previous one, which left everything to Sawyer. The new one would have cut him off completely. Knowing that, he had a definite motive for wanting his father dead, sooner rather than later. And since he knew all about the incident with the Copeland woman, he could have easily plotted to set her up for the murder. She would have trusted him and let him into her house, and he could have slipped her the drugs that killed her. We have his fingerprints on items in the poolroom, but that's likely not going to be probative, given that he lived in the house and played pool with his father from time to time."

"Still sounds like a solid case," Izzy says.

"I don't have much else to tell you about Monty's autopsy," Christopher says. "He was a healthy man. The only medical issue we found was a mild case of psoriasis that was currently manifesting on his right knee. The cause of death was cardiac arrest following the piercing of the heart with the stakelike end of that broken cue stick. The manner, therefore, was homicide and it seems you have plenty of suspects, though it sounds like you've narrowed it down to the son."

"Now all we have to do is find him," I say. "He bolted. Hurley figures he's probably hiding out somewhere with his girlfriend, trying to avoid us and the loan shark."

"Good luck with that," Christopher says, letting out another bit of gas. "As for the autopsy on the Copeland woman, it revealed a large amount of the sleeping pill trazodone in her system, and it's known to cause heart arrhythmias, most notably torsades v-fib. Even though there was some vomit on the floor beside her body, there was no evidence of aspiration, or any injuries. Otto figured her cause of death was likely cardiac arrest brought on by the drug she took. The interesting part of her autopsy was her time of death. Based on the vitreous fluid, the level of the drug in her system, body temp, rigor mortis—basically, all the methods for determining TOD that we have—she died an hour or so before Monty Dixon. Yet I heard she left a suicide note apologizing for killing him."

"She did," I say. "It was computer generated and didn't have a signature on it, just a typed-out name, so anyone could have written it."

"Definitely an interesting case," Izzy says. "And good work by everyone involved."

"Thanks," Christopher says. "It was a hellacious weekend. I'm going to go home and catch up on my sleep. I owe you one for helping me this weekend, Mattie. Let me know if I can help you out down the road."

"I will," I say.

Once Christopher leaves, I fill Izzy in on some of the other details regarding our trip to the Dixon house, who and what we found there, and how the various interviews went.

"Quite the collection of misfits," Izzy observes when I'm done.

"They are that," I agree. "Families like that always make me feel better about my own. Maybe we aren't as much of a mess as I sometimes think we are."

"No, your family is a mess, no doubt about it," Izzy teases.

I smile back, but offer no counterargument. The odds are stacked against me. "Adding to the fun with this Dixon clan is the possibility that Monty Dixon may be broke. All these people around him are thinking they're entitled to some chunk of his estate and they are clueless to the possibility that the man *might not* have an estate." I glance at my watch and add, "Speaking of which, I'd like to head over to the station to join Hurley for his interview with the twin brother, Harrison. He's scheduled to be in at nine."

"That's fine."

"I'll have my phone with me, if anything comes up in the meantime."

Izzy cocks his head to one side and narrows his eyes at me. "You look tired," he says, a worried expression on his face.

"I am," I admit. "Hurley and I both are. He's been putting in a lot of extra hours at work and I've been handling most of the childcare and household duties. And the unexpected call this weekend . . . well, it didn't help."

"Sorry you had to do that."

I shrug. "We both know it's part of the job."

"I thought you guys were going to hire someone to help with the housecleaning stuff."

"We are. In fact, we have another interview scheduled for noon today. I'm going to run home for lunch for it, so I hope we don't get a call before then. I don't want to have to reschedule. We did two interviews yesterday, but they didn't go well." I then tell him about the incident at the grocery store and the subsequent very short interview that followed, as well as the revelations we discovered about our second candidate. When I'm done, and we've both enjoyed a good laugh over the almost instant karma with Marie Featherstone, I say, "And then there's this thing Hurley keeps doing, where he balks at the whole idea of it. At this rate, I'm afraid we'll never hire anyone."

"Didn't you agree on this weeks ago?"

"Yeah, we sorta did, but we've been doing this plan thing that Maggie Baldwin wanted us to put together, and it's kind of consumed all of our spare energy for the past couple of weeks."

"What kind of plan?"

"Basically, it's relationship homework. We're supposed to write down how we see our interactions and our relationship evolving over time, hopefully in a manner that reflects what we each envision as the ideal for our relationship." I roll my eyes. "But it also has to be realistic, so reclining all day while Hurley feeds me grapes and chocolate bonbons, in between full-body massages and occasional sessions of hot, torrid sex, is not acceptable."

"Maggie Baldwin seems to lack imagination," Izzy says with a hint of amusement. "What did Hurley put in his plan?"

"We aren't allowed to see one another's plans."

Izzy gives me a dubious look. "I doubt that stopped you."

"No, Maggie was serious," I insist. "We were given strict instructions to keep our plans private and have her be the only person who sees them. We were supposed to turn them in two weeks ago, but we were both tardy." I shrug. "At least we have that in common."

"So, what did Hurley's say?" Izzy asks again.

"We aren't even allowed to discuss them," I tell him, avoiding the question.

Izzy isn't falling for my diversion. He gives me this look. It's a look that says he knows me well enough to know when I'm bullshitting him. I try to ignore him, but he keeps staring at me that way until I finally cave, taking a moment to admire the way he broke me down without uttering another, single word.

"Yeah, okay, I peeked at Hurley's plan," I admit. "But he doesn't know that. Neither does Maggie. And neither of them ever will, right?"

Izzy gives me a smug smile. "As long as you tell me what his plan said, my lips are sealed."

"You're blackmailing me?"

"You can look at it that way, if you want, but you know you're going to tell me sooner or later."

He's right. Izzy is one of my closest confidants, ranking right up there with my sister and Hurley. I've been dying to discuss these plans with someone, because it's been weighing heavily on my mind. Clearly, I can't talk to Hurley about it, and while I could tell my sister, I don't want to. I'm not 100 percent sure I can trust her *not* to say something to Hurley, though she would only do so with the best of intentions. Her kindness and need to have everyone getting along without tension or rancor is a sweet trait, but one that sometimes makes her unreliable if I'm sharing things that I don't want to have go beyond her ears.

Sensing my lingering hesitancy, Izzy tries a different tack. "Tell me what your plan said."

I wince at him. "Mine was boring and practical and utterly lacking in romance. It was all about sharing the household duties and having more family time together, though part of that problem rests solely with me. It seems like some of the cases we've had lately have grabbed at me and refused to let go. I end up spending too much of my off time working. It's one of the things I put in my plan to try to improve. This weekend wasn't a very good start, though."

"This weekend wasn't your fault, so it doesn't count. As for the other times, at least it's something you can fix." He gives me an equivocating shrug. "Though I get it. There are times when I opt for work over family time. I'm not always sure why. Sometimes it's because a case has a hold on me, but other times it's simply because I find work more interesting."

He blushes and looks embarrassed. "I'm not proud of that, but it's how I feel."

"I get it, Izzy. I really do. I adore my son, and now that I'm committed to us having another child, I'm excited about the possibilities of creating a new little person. But the lure of motherhood has its limits for me. I'm not made to be a full-time parent, like my sister and Dom are."

"And that's okay," Izzy says. Then he winces and adds, "Isn't it?"

"I hope so. At least we have people like Desi and Dom in our lives to pick up the pieces and fill in the blanks. I just worry that Matthew and any other kid I have will grow up lacking somehow because I deprived them of my time and attention."

"But you don't deprive them. You give your time and attention to Matthew and Emily, and I'm sure you will give it to any other children you have. I'm a firm believer in the philosophy that it's the quality of the time you spend with them that matters, not the quantity."

"I hope you're right. And once we get this housekeeper hired, it will give me more time to spend with Matthew and kid anonymous."

"*Kid anonymous?*"

"That's what I'm calling any future child, until it becomes a reality and he or she becomes a real person."

"So, what did Hurley's plan include?" Izzy asks, dashing my hope that he had forgotten this line of inquiry.

I give up the pretense. "It was sweet, and thoughtful, and romantic, and all about how he wanted me and Matthew to be happy," I say, feeling the twinge of guilt that comes over me every time I think about it. "Reading his made me feel totally selfish and clinical when I compared it to mine."

"Did you redo yours after reading his?"

I give him a wry look. "You know me too well," I say. "But in the end, I threw away the revised version and stuck with my original. It was my initial impulse, and if we're going to make any headway with this counseling stuff, I figure I need to be honest and open about it all. I'm curious to see what comments, if any, Maggie will have regarding our plans and how they differ."

Izzy gets up from the chair he's been sitting in at the library table and arches his back with a little groan of pain.

"Are you okay?" I ask him, worried about his health. He had a heart attack last year that scared the daylights out of me, and I've been keeping an eagle eye on him ever since. He has cut back his hours to part-time and is currently job-sharing with Otto Morton, but lately he's been mentioning his desire to start a mentoring program here, like one we encountered in Eau Claire recently. Wisconsin is behind the times when it comes to its handling of suspicious deaths, utilizing an elected coroner system in most of the state. Some of the coroners are so unqualified for what they do as to make it laughable, and bodies are shipped from these out-of-the-way sites to either Madison or Milwaukee for the autopsies. But there is new interest in training doctors to be medical examiners, actual forensic pathologists like Izzy, and utilizing them in some of the less populated areas. Eau Claire is about to have its first official pathology-trained medical examiner start working there and Izzy is keen on starting a program like that one here in Sorenson. The only reasons we don't operate on a coroner system here in our county is because Izzy happened to live here, he was willing to do the job, and he was close friends with the state governor in office at the time. While I think it would be great to expand the coverage by forensic pathologists, I worry about Izzy ramping up his work hours again.

In response to my concerned inquiry, Izzy gives me a dismissive wave of his hand. "I'm fine," he says. "It's just my back acting up. We need a new mattress for our bed."

The mere mention of a bed makes me yawn, and after taking a big gulp of my coffee, I get up and follow Izzy out of the library. "I doubt this interview will take long, but call me if you need me," I say. I drop my coffee cup in the breakroom and then leave via the elevator that takes me to the underground garage. Though this route adds a block to my walk to the station, I welcome it, hoping the exercise will help me shake off my lethargy. But I forgot how uncharacteristically hot and humid it is outside, and by the time I arrive at the station, I'm a wet, limp noodle.

CHAPTER 18

It's eight forty-five when I arrive in Hurley's office and I find him chatting with Laura Kingston.

"I don't understand it, Detective Hurley," Laura says. "I swear there was nothing there thirty minutes ago when I accessed the account and now there's this money that seems to have appeared from nowhere. It's a puzzler, all right. I don't understand it and I can't explain it yet, but I'll figure it out and get to the bottom of it. I'll start by—"

"I don't need to know the specifics," Hurley says, cutting her off. While interrupting Laura might seem rude at first blush, it's a necessary skill one needs if one hopes to get a word in edgewise. Laura is a notorious motor mouth, or as Hurley once put it, "She spits out more crap than a honey wagon." What Laura spits out is rarely crap, however. She's an ace researcher, whip smart, and holds degrees in forensic botany, business administration, and forensic toxicology.

Laura is also aware of her verbosity and accepts the brakes others apply to her verbiage with good humor. This morning is no exception, and she clamps a hand over her mouth, smiling at me with her eyes.

"What's going on?" I say.

Before Laura has a chance to start up again, Hurley says, "Laura gained access to an investment account she found for Monty and she checked it this morning to see what the balance was. Our suspicion that the guy is broke held forth . . . for about an hour. Now there's over five hundred grand in the account."

"That doesn't make any sense," I say. "Maybe it was a glitch in the software for the online access?"

"Must have been," Laura says, lowering her hand from her mouth. "It's just weird that the account would show up at all with zero balances and then suddenly reflect all this money."

"What about Monty's other accounts, his checking and savings?" I ask. "Have you been able to access those to see if the amounts reflected in his accounting software were correct?"

"I did, and they were," Laura says.

"Why wasn't this investment account included in his computer accounting records?" I ask. "And how did you find out about it?"

"When I got access to his regular bank accounts, I went through the history and saw wire transfers in from another account that wasn't mentioned anywhere in the list of accounts on his computer. The software he uses to track his accounts provides automatic downloads and updates of the accounts if you set it up that way, and if the bank or other institution has that service available. The company holding his investment account is a small one, privately owned, and it doesn't offer automatic download service. I suppose that's why it wasn't listed with the other accounts.

"Anyway, the transfers I saw didn't name the source, but there were transaction codes attached. There's a way to track them back to their source through the bank using those numbers, but that likely would have taken time and warrants. So I started searching through Monty's internet history to see what sites he visited frequently and came across one for this small investment firm. Fortunately, like all of Monty's other programs on his computer, he let the computer save his password, so it was easy to access. I logged into it this morning at eight and it showed a zero balance. That was when your husband called, and I updated him on the status of the account and some other stuff. By the time I hung up and looked back at the investment account, the balance had changed. The money literally appeared while I was logged into the site."

"It had to have been a software glitch, or a lag in the computer," Hurley says. "At least now that we know there is some money to pass down, it strengthens Sawyer's motive."

"Any word on where he might be?" I ask.

Hurley shakes his head. "Junior thinks he and his lady friend from the bar might be holed up somewhere together, possibly to hide out from us, but more likely to hide out from the goons his loan shark uses. I've put word out to all the casinos in the area in case he shows up at one of them. Though it would be stupid of him to do so."

"I don't know," I say. "Sawyer strikes me as being a card or two short of a full deck."

Laura claps her hands and smiles. "Ooh, idioms that fit the situation. Gotta love that!"

Hurley manages a grudging smile as well, and I take a moment to bask in the glory of my linguistic coup. It doesn't last long, as the day dispatcher calls back to let Hurley know that Harrison Dixon is here.

Once again, I go to The Hole, while Hurley fetches our subject. The Hole may be an ugly eyesore of a room, but it has one thing going for it this morning. It has great air-conditioning and it's the coolest room I've been in so far today.

Harrison Dixon arrives, wearing dress slacks, a long-sleeved shirt, and a tie. In deference to the heat, perhaps, he isn't wearing a suit jacket, even though I'm betting he has one that goes with the pants.

Harrison seats himself across the table so he will be facing us, and Hurley starts up the recording equipment and states the usual introductory information. Despite the colder air in this room, Harrison is sweating, though if he just came from outside, it might take time for his body to cool down. He shifts in his chair as if he can't quite get comfortable, and scratches irritably at a spot on his right forearm.

To put him at ease, as soon as Hurley is done with the introductory stuff, I say, "You look nice this morning, Harrison."

He looks puzzled and glances down at himself. "Just my usual office wear. I have clients coming in later today, so I need to look somewhat professional."

"Clients? So soon after your brother's death?" I ask.

"The appointments are for some time-sensitive things, so I felt I needed to keep them. Besides, the distraction does me good."

It's then that it dawns on me what it was that bothered me about the clothing Monty Dixon was wearing when he was killed. In the pictures he had hanging in his game room, Monty was always dressed formally, in nice slacks, dress shirts, and ties. He sometimes had his sleeves rolled up, but that was his only real concession to informality. Yet last night he was dressed very casually in sweatpants and a T-shirt. Surely, that implied that whoever it was he was playing with was someone other than a business associate or a client . . . someone like family . . . like Sawyer. If he had met with Taylor Copeland at his house—something I doubt he would have agreed to—if he had, I get a sense that he would have dressed for the occasion in something more business oriented.

Hurley jumps in at this point. "Mr. Dixon, can you start by giving me a brief accounting of your whereabouts Saturday evening, from four o'clock up to when you arrived at your brother's house?"

"Sure," he says, frowning briefly and gazing off into space. "Let's see, at four I was at the grocery store buying something for dinner. From there, I went home, cooked, ate, and then went to my desk to do some work on my computer for about an hour. Then I settled in to watch some TV. That's what I was doing when Summer called me and told me what happened."

"Can anyone verify that?" Hurley asks.

"Afraid not," Harrison says with an apologetic smile. "I was alone."

"Can you state your address for the record?" Hurley says.

Harrison gives him an address in Black River Falls, a town a little over an hour and a half away. "My office is there as well," he adds. "In fact, it's only three blocks from my house, so I can walk to work."

"What type of law do you practice?" I ask. I recall the answer to this from before, but want to hear it again and get it on the record.

"I'm a financial and tax attorney, primarily," he says. "Though I have on occasion done some real estate work and even a divorce, here and there. Those areas tend to overlap."

"And you handled financial matters for your brother?" Hurley asks.

"Just his retirement investment," Harrison says. "Monty handled all the other stuff himself."

"Why didn't you mention that when we spoke to you at the house?"

"I didn't think it was important. I'm more of an intermediary. There's a financial manager in Brockway that I work with. He owns a small investment company and handles all the actual investment decisions. I just bring him some business and advise my clients on how to handle the tax consequences."

"What is this finance manager's name?" Hurley asks.

Harrison makes a little sucking noise with his tongue on

that space between his two front teeth. "Vic Bagman," he says.

Something about this name clicks in my brain, but I'm not sure why.

"Contact information?" Hurley asks.

Harrison takes out his cell phone and after tapping at the screen a couple of times, he gives Hurley a phone number and a PO box address.

"A PO box?" I say. "Isn't that unusual for a business of that nature?"

"Might be if he was working in a big city, but Brockway only has about two thousand souls living there, and I guess Vic prefers to use a post office box over his home address. These days, between the internet and computers, you can operate a business anywhere."

"Do you have other clients that invest with Mr. Bagman?" I ask.

"I do. Mr. Bagman is something of a wizard at reading the stock market trends and his ROI is higher than most. He averages eighteen percent."

"ROI?" Hurley says.

"Return on investment," I answer before Harrison can. Harrison bestows a smile on me like a teacher might give to a star pupil. I shrug. "When I was in nursing school, there was a time when I thought I might want to move into health care management, and to prep for that, I took some finance classes."

"You're a nurse?" Harrison says, scratching at that spot on his right forearm again. His choice of long sleeves is an odd one, given the weather, but I can see a small patch of scaly, reddish skin peeking out from beneath the cuff on his wrist and gather the man suffers from psoriasis like his twin brother.

"I am, though I don't work as one currently. But I did thirteen years at the hospital here in town before taking a job with the medical examiner's office."

"I dated a nurse once," Harrison says with a wistful smile.

Hurley clears his throat and says, "Are you married, Mr. Dixon?"

He shakes his head. "Not anymore. I was once, but we divorced after only three years. We were very young and very stupid." He sighs and looks toward the ceiling. "That was . . . twenty-one years ago. I've been single ever since. Gun shy, I guess." He shrugs.

"You live alone?" Hurley asks, and Harrison nods. "Let the record show that Mr. Dixon nodded," Hurley says for the benefit of the audio recording. Even though the room is set up to record video as well, there have been times when that part of it didn't work.

"Sorry," Harrison says.

"No problem." Hurley gives him a reassuring smile. "Were you and your brother close? Did you spend a lot of time together?"

"Well, we are . . . were twins, and that does tend to create a special type of bond. As boys, we were inseparable. As adults, we kept in touch regularly via phone calls, texts, and visits."

"Did you play pool with your brother?"

"I did," Harrison says with a fond smile. "Monty loved the game and he was always challenging anyone willing to play him. He almost always beat me." He shrugs. "I suppose that's the advantage of having a pool table in the house, where he can practice whenever he wants."

"About Monty's finances," Hurley says, shifting the topic, "it appears that he didn't have much money to speak of in any of his accounts other than this investment account. Any idea why that is?"

"Sadly, yes," Harrison says with a woeful look. "Monty

was highly successful in his real estate business and made good money. Fortunately, he had the good sense to sock a lot of it away in the early years with his investment accounts. He was doing okay with the day-to-day stuff—more than okay, truth be told—until he married Summer. Summer wanted the big fancy house, flashy expensive cars, ritzy vacations, and expensive clothes." Harrison pauses, looking hesitant. "I like Summer, and I don't want to disparage the woman, but I must say that the term 'gold digger' is an apt one in her case. Between her expensive tastes and the child support Monty was paying to his ex over the years, his bottom line took a hard hit. And I think he helped Sawyer with some things. I know he bought him a car. He paid for the thing in full, even though I recommended that he only pay part of it and let Sawyer take on the payments from there."

"Do you know of anyone who would want to cause harm to your brother?" Hurley asks.

Harrison leans back in his chair and strokes his chin a few times before answering. "I really don't."

"Did you know that your brother was drafting a new will?" Hurley asks.

Harrison shakes his head. "I didn't, but it doesn't surprise me. I think he said that Sawyer was the primary beneficiary at one point, but that was before Monty learned about Sawyer's gambling problems."

"You know about that?" Hurley says.

Harrison shrugs. "Sure. Monty confided in me about family stuff a lot. He told me he'd hired a private eye to follow both Summer and Sawyer, and I know he was unhappy with both of them recently."

"Since you and your brother shared so much information, can you tell me if he was having an affair with anyone?" I say.

Harrison hesitates just long enough to tell me the answer is yes, though he clearly doesn't want to say so. "I wouldn't want to reveal anything that would compromise Monty's position in a divorce, but I don't suppose that matters anymore. He did tell me that he and Jessica Leavenworth have been . . . um . . . you know." He wiggles his eyebrows suggestively.

"How long has that been going on?" I ask.

"A few months, I think. I'm not sure how long it might have been going on before Monty told me about it." He scratches his arm again and glances at his watch. "I have appointments this morning. Is this going to take much longer?"

Hurley thinks for a second and then says, "I think that's all I need for now. If I have any other questions, I'll be in touch." At that, Hurley stops the recording devices. "Thanks for coming in."

"Happy to help. I hope you catch whoever did this to Monty and make them pay."

CHAPTER 19

I make my way back to Hurley's office, while he escorts Harrison out, and my phone rings when I get there. It's Arnie.

"What's up, Arnie?"

"I just tried to call Hurley, but it flipped over to voice mail right away and he didn't answer at his office phone, either. I thought he might be with you."

"He probably has his cell on silent because we just finished an interview. He should be . . . ah, here he is now. I'll put you on speaker." After I've done so, I say, "Go ahead, Arnie," letting Hurley know who's on the line.

"Just wanted to let you know that I reviewed the footage from Cut the Cheese's security camera and it shows Summer Dixon going into the apartment entrance at six fifty-six p.m. and then exiting, via the same door, at ten o-two p.m. on the night of the murder. I checked, and there is no other entrance to the apartment. There is a fire escape that's accessed through a window in the back alley, which one could have used to come and go, but there is a security camera there, too, and no one used it on the night in question."

"Okay, good to know," Hurley says. "That means we can

take Summer off the list. One less alternative suspect for Lucien to put up in Sawyer's defense."

"Also," Arnie continues, "that long black hair that was found on Monty's body is a dead end—excuse the pun. There's no root attached, so it won't be useful for extracting DNA and providing any sort of definitive source."

"Too bad," Hurley says. "That means Lucien could use Monty's girlfriend as an alternative suspect. One up, one down."

"Maybe related to that," Arnie goes on, "the last thing I have for you is the review of Monty's cell phone. On the night he was killed, he only made one phone call at seven forty-five, and that was to a number identified as Linda in his contacts."

"Most likely his ex-wife," I say.

"The call only lasted thirty-two seconds, so I'm guessing he got her voice mail, and either hung up without leaving any message, or left a very short one, something like, 'It's Monty, call me.' There was also one text message he sent at seven twenty-two to a Jessica. All it said was, 'I meant it. We're done.'"

"Well, well," I say. "That puts a whole new wrinkle in the fabric of this case, doesn't it?"

"Good work, Arnie," Hurley says.

"Thanks. I'll let you know if I find anything else." With that, he disconnects the call.

"What's next?" I ask Hurley.

"I need to make some phone calls. We have another interview for a housekeeper today, right? What time again?"

"We do," I say, wondering how he could have forgotten this in the two hours since I last mentioned it at breakfast. Maybe the case has him so preoccupied that his brain can't store anything else. "At noon. I can call her and reschedule, if you want." I swear he perks up visibly at this suggestion, but then he looks at me and something in my expression must convince him to change his mind. "No, that's fine. We need to eat lunch, right? It's at the house?"

"It is. I can just meet you there then, if you want."

"Let's plan on it," he says.

I glance at my watch. "I'm going to run by the clinic to talk to Copeland's doctor. I'll get a copy of the woman's medical records to see if there are any surprises we should be aware of. Hopefully, there isn't any history of suicidal ideation in her past to complicate the picture. If there is, it's just the kind of thing Lucien would jump on."

"Even if there is, I think we have enough evidence to prove she didn't kill herself."

"I suppose I should try to get Monty's records, too, though I don't think his are all that critical right now."

Hurley chuckles. "Hard to believe there is any kind of medical condition that could impact a charge of murder for Monty. It's not like he stabbed himself with that cue stick." His cell phone rings then, and when he removes the phone from his pocket, I see it's Jonas calling. Hurley answers the call and puts it on speaker. "Hi, Jonas. I've got Mattie here with me and I have you on speaker. What's up?"

"I thought you two might be together," Jonas says. "I wanted to let you know that Arnie sent me both ends of the broken cue stick, along with a few small splinters that I collected in that poolroom, and the tiny piece we took from Sawyer Dixon's hair. I've been working on it for the past few hours and I've finished reconstructing it. There is a tiny piece of wood, a sliver about an inch long and an eighth of an inch wide, that is missing. I went back to the house and searched the room again, but couldn't find it. And I've been through all the clothing that Summer and Sawyer Dixon were wearing and there wasn't anything there, either. We haven't had access to their vehicles, so that would be the next step."

"We've ruled Summer out at this point, and my money is

on Sawyer," Hurley says. "I'm betting if we can find him, we can find his car. You might want to go back and look around the rest of the house, the grounds immediately outside, and in Sawyer's quarters, including the exit he used at the back of the house."

Jonas sighs. "Will do, but that's going to be looking for a needle in a haystack, particularly outside."

"Do what you can. Frankly, I think we have enough on Sawyer at this point without it, but it wouldn't hurt if we had it."

"Got it."

Hurley disconnects the call and then looks over at me. "Good luck with the doc," he says, and then he kisses me on the forehead. A second later, he settles in behind his desk, focused on the work at hand. I've been dismissed. It's that ability to switch gears and develop a laser focus that makes him such a good detective, but it sometimes makes me feel a tad neglected. Or underappreciated. Or something. I'm just tired.

I leave the station and walk back to the underground garage beneath our office, and then drive my hearse over to the hospital/clinic complex. The medical records department is in the basement of the clinic and I need an escort to go down there. I find the security guard, who knows me not only for my current job, but from when David and I were married, as his office is in this complex, too. The guard escorts me down to the basement level and medical records, where I once made an illegal visit on another case, and my heart speeds up with the memory.

The clerks who work down here know me well, too, as we often have to request the medical records of the people we autopsy, and the person on duty now, a woman named Catherine Knowles, is one of the nicer, more cooperative folks who work here. Some of the workers treat the medical records as if they were their own personal diamonds and they do everything they can to obstruct me and keep me from get-ting what I need, despite a law that says our office can have them.

Today my visit goes off without a hitch and I thank Cath-erine, get in the elevator, and head up to the second floor and the office of Dr. Jill Warren, the physician who prescribed the sleeping pills for Taylor Copeland.

I sit for a few minutes in the office waiting room before Dr. Warren is freed up to talk to me, and then I can feel the harsh stares of the others in the waiting area as I'm escorted back ahead of them. They don't know that I'm not a patient or the reason for my visit, but the receptionist knows me well, and when I whisper the reason behind my visit, she puts me next in line.

Dr. Warren is a tall, wiry woman with short, dark hair who reminds me of the MSNBC commentator Rachel Mad-dow. She's always been one of my favorite doctors because she's easygoing, straightforward, and doesn't have a God complex, like some doctors I know. I'm ushered into her of-fice and the receptionist closes the door behind us. Dr. War-ren waves me to a chair on one side of her desk and then takes the one beside it, rather than sitting behind her desk. "Caroline tells me that Taylor Copeland is dead?" she says, removing a pair of glasses and massaging the bridge of her nose.

"Yes, I'm afraid so."

Dr. Warren puts the glasses back on and blinks at me. "What happened?"

"Things were made to look like a suicide. You prescribed her some trazodone last week?"

"I did. Are you saying she overdosed on it?"

"Technically, she died of an overdose of trazodone, but we have reason to doubt that it was by her own hand. Can you tell me why you prescribed the drug and what her mental state was when you saw her?"

"She was upset. There were some things going on in her life that were very stressful, and she said she was having trouble sleeping and feeling depressed. Trazodone is mainly an antidepressant, but it has a common off-label use as a sleep aid and it's not particularly addictive. Her depression was situational, not chronic. In fact, her normal affect has always been very bright."

"Did she share with you what the issues were that had her upset?"

"It was work-related stuff. She didn't go into details, but she did say that she might have to look at changing careers." There is a frantic ringing sound, which I recognize from my days working at the hospital. It's a ringtone from one of the internal phones carried by docs and staffers to alert them to dire situations, such as cardiac arrests or other medical emergencies. Dr. Warren takes her phone from her lab coat pocket and looks at the display.

"Cripes, it's one of those damned Sepsis Six things." She silences the phone and then shoves it back in her pocket, giving me a look of exasperation. "I get that this new protocol for rapid identification and treatment of sepsis is saving lives, but like everything new out there, it's gotten crazy ridiculous. If you show up at the hospital with a hangnail and a hot flash, someone's calling a damned Sepsis Six."

I can't help but smile.

"Sorry for the rant," she says. "You said you had reason to doubt that her overdose was by her own hand. Are you telling me that Taylor Copeland was murdered?"

"It appears that way. Please keep this information confidential until something official comes out. We have a suspect, but we haven't apprehended him yet."

"Of course. How sad." She frowns for a moment, no doubt taking a few seconds to reflect on the tragedy. Then it's back to work. With a pleading look, she says, "Is there anything else? I have a really full schedule today."

"No. If I have any other questions, I'll call you. Could your staff give me a printout of Copeland's medical record?"

"Of course. I'll tell Caroline to send it over to your office ASAP." She gets up from her chair and I do the same. Just as she's about to open her office door, she turns back and looks at me. "I liked Taylor. She sold me my house four years ago. When you catch the bastard who killed her, I hope you string him up by his balls." With that, she opens the door and moves on to an exam room.

So much for Primum non nocere, I think, that part of the Hippocratic oath that means, "first, do no harm."

CHAPTER 20

I return to my office and settle in at my desk to tackle the endless mountain of paperwork that goes with the job. At a quarter to twelve, I check in with Izzy. "I'm headed home for lunch and my interview," I tell him. "Call me if anything comes in. I don't think the interview will take long."

"Good luck with this one."

"Thanks."

Hurley isn't there when I arrive home at two minutes before the hour and I hope he isn't planning on standing me up for the interview. I know he isn't fully behind the idea of a hired housecleaner, but if he at least has a say in whom we hire, I hope it will help mitigate some of his reservations.

Even though I don't have time to clean, I give the main kitchen–dining area a quick look to make sure there isn't anything too horrible lurking. I let our dog, Hoover, out into the backyard to do his business and shoo the cats upstairs so they won't be tempted to create any mischief. At precisely noon, a small SUV pulls up out front and I'm about to curse my husband when I hear the rumble of the garage door opening and see his blue pickup pull into the garage. I say a tiny prayer of thanks and then hurry to the front door to greet the woman and to give Hurley time to get inside.

Dorothy Nelson looks a bit like Mrs. Claus. She is short and plump with strands of white running through her pale blond hair, rosy-red cheeks, and glasses with rectangular lenses. The Mrs. Claus similarities end as soon as she speaks; she has a voice like a chain saw. She greets me with a loud, raspy, "You must be Mattie," and then pushes right past me and marches into the house on thick-soled, sensible black shoes. She is wearing pants—polyester, if I'm not mistaken— and they are a little short on her, something I find odd, given that she's short herself. Floodwater pants, as some of the kids in high school used to call them, tend to be more in the do- main of tall people like me. There is a puffiness around Dorothy's ankles that makes me think she might have some heart issues going on, but after standing at a point where she can survey nearly the entire first floor—something she does with a little *harrumph*—she follows me into the kitchen with only minimal huffing and puffing, despite the fact that she has to take two steps for every one of mine. She has a pocket- book slung over her arm the size of a small suitcase and she sets it on the table in front of her. Hurley comes in through the garage entrance just off the kitchen and I'm about to make introductions when Dorothy launches into her own clearly rehearsed colloquy as she removes a stack of papers from her purse.

"Here are my references," she explains, slapping down one piece of paper. "And here are my rates. I tend to price my work out by the task, since it seems everyone has a different list of things they want done." She pushes another piece of paper toward me. "And this is a list of the things I won't do," she says, laying down a third sheet. "I don't do windows, I won't bathe animals, I won't clean litter boxes or handle any type of animal feces, and I am not a babysitter, so please don't step out of the house and leave behind any young children if I'm here. I also don't cook, and I won't clean things outside of the house."

Hurley has joined us and he stares at the papers on the table. Dorothy isn't done yet, however. Another paper joins the assortment.

"These are the days and hours I have free," she explains, pointing to what appears to be a schedule calendar with various days and hours blocked off. "If we can fit the items you choose from the task menu into the days you want, that's great. But there may be times when I have to flex."

"We may need to flex as well," I say. "Our work hours are somewhat unpredictable and sometimes we have to sleep during the day."

"No problem," she says. "As long as you can fit any changes into my calendar." Another paper, or rather two of them stapled together, joins the stack on the table. "And this is my contract. It stipulates that you have received all the other forms here on the table, and while we may agree on a schedule, it might have to be changed from time to time. It also stipulates that if you cancel any scheduled services with less than twenty-four hours of notice, and they can't be rescheduled, I am to be paid anyway."

With that, she sits back in her chair and bestows a beaming smile on us. Hurley drops into a chair, his hands in his lap, looking a little shell-shocked. I shuffle through the papers and pick out the itemized task list and the calendar. A quick perusal of the calendar reveals that Dorothy has Tuesday and Thursday afternoons open, and every other Saturday morning. Sundays are blocked out—her one day off, apparently—and a quick perusal of the task list tells me that the items I want to have taken care of are things Dorothy will do. She isn't cheap, but I like her itemized menu, because there may be weeks when I don't need her to do some things. And if she does what I want twice a week, her fees will add up to be right around what Cara quoted us.

"Well, Dorothy, you certainly have your ducks in a row," I say. "Let me tell you the things we need help with and then we'll decide if we're a match, fair enough?"

"Yes." No editorializing. Just a straightforward answer. Despite her bullish entry, I'm liking Dorothy. She's clearly organized, knows her business, is forthright with her dealings, and reasonably priced, if my research on the matter is correct. My hopes surge as I list off the things I want her to do for us, and how often I'd like her to come.

"I would be willing to have you here every Tuesday and Thursday, and if you're willing, every other Saturday as well," I conclude. "I typically have every other weekend on call, so if you can come on the weekend when I'm scheduled to be home, that would be best. Because our schedules are kind of crazy at times, and I can't promise anyone will be here on any given day, we would provide you with a key to the front door and the code to our alarm system. Neither the key nor the code is ever to be shared."

"Of course not," Dorothy says, looking insulted by the suggestion. "If you check my references, I'm sure you'll see that I'm a very reliable person."

"We will do that," I say. "Assuming they check out, how soon would you be able to start?"

"If you want, I can start tomorrow afternoon. I would like someone to be here the first time to show me the ropes and go over exactly what you want and how you want it done. If Tuesday doesn't work, then we can plan for Thursday afternoon."

"I'll make it work," I say.

"What if you get called out?" Hurley says.

"Christopher owes me a favor for this weekend."

"What exactly is it you do?" Dorothy asks. "I know your husband here is a policeman, but all you told me about your job is that you work for the state. I confess, I asked one of my other clients if she knew you and she said you were a nurse. Is that right?"

There's a reason why I was cagey about my job. I know some people can be squeamish about it and I didn't want that to get in the way. Might as well bite the bullet, I figure.

"I am a nurse, but that's not what I do in my current job. I'm a medicolegal death investigator." I figure throwing the fancy title out there might make it sound more interesting and less disgusting than my job often is. But Dorothy is too smart for that.

"You handle dead people?"

I study her expression before answering, trying to discern if she is grossed out and will cancel the whole thing if I answer honestly. But her face gives nothing away.

"Yes, that's one of my duties."

"Well, now, there's good job security in that, isn't there? Everybody dies sooner or later. How does one o'clock tomorrow sound? Will that work for you?"

It's only when I let my breath out that I realize I was holding it. "That will work just fine, Ms. Nelson."

"Please call me Dottie. It's what everyone calls me."

"And we are Mattie and Steve," I say, reciprocating. "Our children are Emily—she's our teenage daughter—and Matthew, our toddler."

With a fleeting smile, a firm nod, and a "See you tomorrow," Dorothy . . . Dottie rises from her seat and heads for the front door so fast that Hurley and I are left behind in our chairs for a moment before we realize what's happening. I quickly get up and follow her, just in time to grab the open door as she exits. I watch her drive away, noting that her car is a late-model Honda SUV, which I take as a good sign. It should be reliable, and the newer car suggests she is doing well in her business.

"What do you think?" I say to Hurley once I return to the

kitchen. I'm excited, delighted that we might be able to get this help in place as soon as tomorrow. But I don't want to seem overeager. Hurley is still seated at the table, shuffling through the papers Dottie left behind.

"She is . . . um . . . interesting," he says.

"I like her. I'll check her references right away and, hopefully by tomorrow, we'll have ourselves a housecleaner."

"Are you sure about this?"

I nod. "Look," I say, tapping one of the papers Dottie left. "One of her references is the Davidsons. I used to work with Dr. Davidson in the ER, and I socialized with him and his wife back in the day."

"Back when you were married to David," Hurley says. It's a statement, not a question.

"Well, yes."

"And have they done anything with you or invited you to anything since the divorce?"

They haven't, and Hurley knows this. I can count on one hand the number of people who were friends with David and me when we were a couple who continued their friendships with me after the split. "It's a business reference, Hurley, not a social contract."

He pushes his chair back. "I'm going to go back to the office to get some more work done on this case," he says. "I'm way behind."

"Okay." I try to sound cheery, despite my sense that he's upset or angry about something. "Did you learn anything new since I saw you this morning?"

"Some, yes. I talked to a woman at the Wisconsin Realtors Association and to two of the other agents in Monty's office and found out what it was that got Taylor Copeland fired."

"Do tell. How about I fix us a couple of sandwiches while you talk. Roast beef on sourdough okay?"

He must be hungry because he scoots his chair back up to the table. "That sounds great."

Now that I have his focus temporarily diverted away from Dottie with the promise of food, I get busy making the sandwiches while he fills me in on Taylor's debacle. "Apparently, a house that Taylor had listed for sale was robbed when she hosted an open house. There was some jewelry missing, a video camera, and a set of rare coins. Things like this sometimes happen during open houses, which is why the agents always tell the homeowners to secure valuables or remove them from the home when it's listed for sale."

"Makes sense."

"Problem was, this wasn't the first time this had happened to one of Taylor's clients. Two other listings of hers reported items that were missing after showings or open houses. According to the other agents, this might have been just a string of bad luck, but then Monty went into Taylor's desk before she came in one morning, looking for some paperwork, and he found two of the missing items from the most recently reported robbery. Monty confronted Taylor, she swore she had no idea how the items came to be in her desk, and Monty suggested that she take some time off until the matter could be investigated. Taylor took offense at the suggestion that she did anything wrong and pointed the finger at Monty's girlfriend, Jessica Leavenworth, who had just obtained her own real estate license and who Monty wanted to bring into the firm, even though there wasn't room for her. An argument ensued, things got heated, and Monty ended up firing Taylor. He also told her that he would report the theft and the discovery of the stolen items to the Board of Realtors and they would likely take away her license. That's when things really took a turn. Monty packed up the stuff on Taylor's desk and carried it outside to the parking lot. The yelling match escalated and the police were called."

I set a sandwich down in front of Hurley and then sit across from him with my own. "Wow, that had to have been hard for Taylor," I say. "Did the other agents you spoke to think she was guilty?"

Hurley is chewing and it takes him a few seconds to answer. "That's the interesting part. No, they didn't. Both had known Taylor for years and one of them had worked with her at another firm. They said she had a stellar reputation in the community, respect from her fellow agents, and that she was very successful. Neither is a fan of Monty's new girlfriend and they supported what Taylor had said about Monty wanting to make room for her at the firm."

"I take it Sawyer was privy to all this?"

Hurley nods. "He would have known it all and he was there in the office the day Monty fired Taylor. He witnessed the whole thing. I'm guessing that in his mind that made her the perfect patsy to set up for his father's murder."

I nod, but something about that scenario bothers me. "So he kills Copeland with the intent of setting her up for his father's murder and then kills his father with a broken cue stick? That doesn't make a lot of sense, does it? The cue stick seems like a weapon of opportunity, not something that was planned."

Hurley considers this and frowns. "You're right, but maybe things got heated and whatever he had planned didn't happen because the cue stick presented itself." He shrugs. "I don't know. We can ask him, if we ever find him."

I fill him in on my meeting with Dr. Warren, including her parting comment. By the time I'm done, we have finished our lunch and he takes both our plates and puts them in the dishwasher.

"Thanks for making lunch. I guess we should get back to work," he says.

My growing sense of discomfort returns. "Hurley?"

He pauses and turns to look back at me.

"Is everything okay?"

The distance between us at this moment feels like a physical barrier and I walk over to him, rubbing a palm up and down one of his arms, looking up at him with a smile.

He rakes his hands through his hair, making it stand up in a Mohawk. "Everything is fine." He tries to smile, but I can tell it's forced.

"No, it isn't. Tell me. Is it the case?"

"That's part of it."

"What's the other part?"

He looks off to the side and I know that what he says next is something he thinks will upset me. "I'm just not very comfortable with this housecleaning arrangement," he says. "I don't like the idea of someone being inside our house, snooping around, going through all of our personal items. And then there's the cost. You've made a big dent in your divorce settlement already with this house, and the car we bought for Emily, not to mention that little gambling binge."

I wince at that. Not one of my proudest moments.

"We make good money between us, but Emily is going to need help with college, and if we're serious about having another child, I worry about what we can afford."

"Do you want me to hold off on hiring Dottie?" I offer, willing to delay the decision if it will make him more comfortable. Maybe a little more time to get used to the idea will help. I figure it's a magnanimous gesture on my part, given that the mere suggestion of postponing Dottie makes me feel like crying.

He looks at me, smiles, and reaches up to rub one thumb gently over my cheek. "No. I saw how happy you looked at the idea of having someone here."

"I'll tell Dottie that your home office is off-limits. Will that help?"

"It will help some. I guess it's just something I have to get used to." With that, he kisses me, on the lips this time, and then holds me a moment.

"You know, we have the house to ourselves," he says.

"How often does that happen?"

"Not often enough," I say. "Can I interest you in a little after-lunch dessert?"

"I believe you could," he says, his breath quickening.

I take his hand and start to lead him upstairs to our bedroom. Halfway there, his phone rings.

"Don't answer it," I plead.

He takes his phone out and glances at it, and then, with an apologetic look at me, he says, "I have to."

I stand there while he answers the call, hoping against hope that it's something that can wait. His end of the conversation gives me little in the way of clues, but I see his face light up. Then he thanks the caller and hangs up.

"Our luck may have just improved," he says, looking happy. "Sawyer Dixon is at the police station."

"He decided to turn himself in?" I say, disbelieving.

Hurley shakes his head. "Nope, his mother did. That's where he disappeared to. He went up north to her house in Bayfield and she convinced him to come back and turn himself in. And he has Maribel with him."

"Let's go get him," I say. "And then we can celebrate with dessert tonight when we get home."

"I'm going to hold you to that promise," he says, pulling me to him and giving one of my butt cheeks a squeeze. He gives me a long, hard kiss that makes me want to try to convince him that Sawyer Dixon can wait. But justice waits for no one, and minutes later, we are in our respective vehicles heading back into town.

CHAPTER 21

When we arrive at the station, we are informed by the dispatcher that Linda, Sawyer, and Maribel are all in The Hole attended by Bob Richmond. As soon as we arrive, Bob gets up and meets with us in the hallway outside the room, closing the door behind him.

"They arrived about half an hour ago," he tells us. "The girlfriend looks shell-shocked and she has one of her hands wrapped up in a bulky dressing, so I'm guessing the speculation about someone taking her pinky finger as a way of warning Sawyer is true."

I shudder at the thought. "Has she said who did it?"

Richmond shakes his head. "She's mum on the topic. I suspect she's been warned against saying anything, lest they return and take another finger. Based on her body language, I'd say she's plenty angry with Sawyer, but she's more scared than anything. I don't think she has any idea that Sawyer is the primary suspect in his father's murder."

"Have you Mirandized him?"

Richmond again shakes his head. "Nope, haven't talked to Sawyer at all. Junior took Maribel aside and tried to get her to talk, but to no avail. I left Sawyer and his mother in The Hole and turned on the recording equipment. It's been running about fifteen minutes now."

"Great. Thanks," Hurley says. Then he closes his eyes and winces. "I suppose we're going to have to let Lucien know that Sawyer is here and that we're going to arrest him," he says.

"No need. I'm here," says a familiar voice. We all turn to find my brother-in-law standing in the hallway behind us. "Sawyer already called me."

"Good for him," Hurley says with no sincerity whatsoever.

"Did I just hear you say you plan to arrest him?" Lucien asks.

"I do," Hurley says. "For the murder of his father *and* the murder of Taylor Copeland."

Lucien doesn't look rattled often, but Hurley's announcement clearly is a surprise.

"Taylor Copeland? Who is that?"

"Let's go talk to your client and you'll find out," Hurley says.

"No, it's not going to work that way," Lucien says. "I'm going to advise my client *not* to speak to you until I know the full details."

Hurley sighs. "Have it your way," he says. "But for now, I'm going to arrest him. He can spend the night in jail."

"Do what you have to do," Lucien says. "I'll have him out in the morning, once he's arraigned and his bail is set."

"I plan on asking the judge to deny bail," Hurley says. "He's accused of killing two people. And based on what his financial state seems to be, I'm guessing he won't be able to raise bail even if it's set."

Lucien looks like he's about to say something else, but Hurley doesn't give him a chance. He spins around and enters The Hole. Lucien and I follow. Bob Richmond heads into the attached observation room to watch and listen.

Sawyer is sitting across the table, and for a moment, I think that Summer is seated on his right. A closer look tells me it's not Summer but someone who looks an awful lot like her. Based on her age, I assume this is Linda Shoop, Sawyer's mother. Monty definitely had a type. To Sawyer's left is a petite, young, brown-haired woman I assume is Maribel. She looks pale, frail, and fragile enough that a hard sneeze could blow her across the room.

After checking to make sure the AV equipment is running, Hurley wastes no time getting down to business. Introductions are done and then Hurley says, "Sawyer Dixon, you are under arrest for the murders of Montgomery Dixon and Taylor Copeland. You have the right to remain silent. Anything you say can be used against you in court. You have the right to talk to a lawyer for advice before we ask you any questions. You have the right to have a lawyer with you during questioning. If you cannot afford a lawyer, one will be appointed for you before any questioning, if you wish. If you decide to answer questions now without a lawyer present, you have the right to stop answering at any time. Do you understand these rights?"

"What the hell?" he says. "The murder of Taylor Copeland? She's dead?"

"Do you understand these rights, as I've said them to you?" Hurley asks again.

"Yeah, yeah, I understand the rights. What I don't understand is the charges. You think I killed my father? And Taylor?"

Lucien says, "Sawyer, I would advise you to stop talking right now."

"But he's arresting me!" Sawyer says, looking panicked.

"For killing two people?" He switches his panicked look to his mother. Maribel starts to cry.

"Sawyer, calm down," his mother says. She puts a hand on his arm, but he shakes it off.

"Why are you arresting me? What evidence do you have?" Lucien tries again. "Sawyer, I don't advise this. Let them process you for the arrest. We'll get you arraigned in the morning and bail you out by lunchtime."

"He's not going to get bail," Hurley says. "Not when he's charged with murdering two people." Saying this now is for Sawyer's benefit, or rather to his detriment, because it's obvious the kid is panicking and people who panic tend to do one of two things: babble without thinking or clam up entirely. Sawyer is a babbler.

"You want me to spend the night in jail?" Sawyer says to Lucien.

"It will be a lot longer than the night," Hurley says.

Lucien gives Hurley an exasperated look. "Detective," he says in an admonishing tone.

Hurley responds by taking out his handcuffs.

Sawyer's eyes widen. "Tell me why you think I did this," he says to Hurley.

"Sawyer, as your lawyer, I strongly—"

"Oh, shut up!" Sawyer says to Lucien.

Lucien throws his hands up in the air and looks at Sawyer's mother. "Can you talk some sense into him?"

She smiles, at least I think it's a smile, though it more resembles a wince. "Haven't been able to do that since he was twelve."

Hurley says to Sawyer, "We can talk, if you want, but not with your mother and girlfriend in the room. Let me get an officer to see them out until we're done." Hurley turns around and leaves the room, leaving me there alone with the others.

After several long seconds of awkward silence, Lucien says to Sawyer, "At least let me be in the room while you talk to the detective and let me monitor what you say to make sure you don't say anything incriminating. Let him do most of the talking so he can lay out his case against you, okay?"

Hurley returns with Junior Feller in tow, and he ushers Sawyer's mother and Maribel out of the room. My guess is Junior will set them in an empty office, or perhaps the break-room and let them talk, taking note of anything they say.

Once they are gone, Lucien takes the seat at the head of the table and Hurley settles back into his seat.

"Okay, Sawyer, here's what we have on you so far. Your father was killed with a broken cue stick from his poolroom, and when we had you undress at the house and collected your clothes, we found a tiny splinter of wood in your hair. That splinter came from the cue stick that killed your father. Your fingerprints were also on the cue stick, and on several of the balls from the pool table. You have no alibi for the time of your father's death. Taylor Copeland was also murdered, and someone tried to make it look like a suicide. There was a note supposedly from her that apologized for what she did to your father."

"Well, there you go," Sawyer says.

"Sawyer," Lucien cautions, but Sawyer gives him an impatient glance and keeps talking. "My father fired Taylor Copeland and reported her to the Board of Realtors. She was going to lose her license. She had every reason to want my father dead. In fact, she threatened him on the day she was fired."

"And that gives me the final proof I need," Hurley says with a satisfied smile.

"I told you," Lucien says, rolling his eyes at Sawyer. Sawyer gives him a puzzled look.

Hurley continues. "You were aware of the threats Taylor

made to your father and familiar with the situation between the two of them and that's why you tried to set her up to take the fall for your father's murder."

Sawyer folds his arms over his chest. He rolls his lips in, giving a quick, annoyed shake of his head. "You're crazy," he says. "Why would I kill my father?"

"Because you need his money. Your gambling debts have gotten out of control, you owe some very bad people a lot of money, and your father wasn't going to bail you out anymore. The only way to get his money was to kill him so you could inherit. Hopefully, before your loan shark had his henchmen cut off a few more of your girlfriend's fingers."

Mention of Maribel makes Sawyer's rigid posture sag. He unfolds his arms and runs his hands over his head. It leaves him with a messy bedhead look. Between that and his obvious fright, he looks very young and very vulnerable. I almost feel sorry for him.

"We have the trifecta with you, Sawyer," Hurley says. "Motive, opportunity, and a solid connection to the murder weapon used on your father."

"How do you know Copeland didn't do it?" Sawyer asks.

"Yeah, *how do you know* that?" Lucien echoes, narrowing his eyes.

"Certain things that showed up on the autopsy," Hurley says, purposely vague.

Sawyer rubs a hand on top of his head and says, "Okay, look, I didn't tell the truth the first time I talked to you, or the second time, but it's only because I was afraid of what's happening now."

Lucien reaches over and puts a hand on Sawyer's arm. "I'd advise you not to talk until you and I have had a chance to speak in private and look at whatever evidence they have."

"And we're going to do that where?" Sawyer shoots back. "In jail?"

"You're likely going to jail either way," Lucien says. "But, hopefully, only for the night."

Sawyer gives a vigorous shake of his head and looks back at Hurley. "Okay, here's what happened. My father and I got into an argument on Saturday night when I came back from that showing. I already told you that." Hurley nods. "What I didn't tell you is that our discussion lasted longer than what I said. We started arguing, but then we calmed down and Dad invited me to play a game of pool with him. We did that. In fact, we played two games, or at least we started a second game. And during that time, we talked about my future, about the gambling, and about a career in real estate."

He pauses and sighs, his breath tremulous. "Everything was going fine. We were talking calmly, even joking from time to time. But then I told Dad that I needed some money right away because I owed it to some guys who weren't very kind about waiting." At mention of this, the color drains from Sawyer's face and he swallows hard.

"I think the amount I needed caught him by surprise, and when he found out I owed it to a loan shark, he went ballistic. We started arguing again and things got really heated. Dad went berserk. He said he wanted me to move out of the house. Then he told me he wouldn't give me the money to pay off the loan because he thought I needed to learn a lesson. He said he was going to fire me from the real estate firm and cut me out of his will. He was throwing me to the wolves!"

"You already knew about the will, though, didn't you?" Hurley says.

Sawyer bites his lower lip and color floods his face: a bright shade of red. "I did," he admits.

Lucien squeezes his eyes closed and shakes his head, but says nothing. I think he's given up on trying to keep Sawyer quiet.

"There was a copy of a revised will delivered to the office, and when I saw where the delivery was from, I took it and signed Dad's name."

"That's more of a motive," Hurley says.

Lucien mutters something under his breath. "Sawyer, please."

Sawyer ignores him. "Yeah, I knew about the will thing, but I wasn't that upset about it. I never wanted to inherit my father's money, I wanted to make my own, with his help."

"That's not what Summer said," Hurley tells him. "She said she overheard you on a phone call telling someone that you couldn't wait for your old man to die so you could inherit."

Sawyer pales again. "That was just nonsense talk to a friend. Joking around."

"You made jokes about your father's death?" Hurley says.

Sawyer has the good sense not to try to justify his behavior on this one. After a moment of awkward silence, he says, "When Dad told me he was cutting me off and firing me, it made me really angry. Something inside me snapped and I took my cue stick and whacked it hard against the pool table. It broke into two pieces, one end flying across the table and landing on the floor. I tossed the end I still had in my hand on top of the table. Then I stormed out of the house."

"After you stabbed your father?" Hurley says.

"No! He was alive when I left. I swear it. He was still yelling at me when I left. I got in my car and went driving. That part of what I told you was true. I didn't know what to do or how I was going to get out of this mess with the loan shark and I just kept driving and driving."

"And then you came back to the house," Hurley says. "Did you come back before the time when we saw you? Did you kill him then? Because you didn't seem very angry when we saw you."

"That's because I had it figured out by then."

"Because you knew you'd be inheriting money from your father."

"No!"

"Please don't put words in my client's mouth," Lucien says, massaging his left temple. "It's bad enough that he feels compelled to spit out the ones already in there."

"I wasn't mad when I came back because I'd called my mother. I told her everything that had happened. She offered to give me the money to pay off the loan shark and she told me to go home to Dad and apologize, make amends."

"Your mother offered to pay off your loan shark?" Hurley says, sounding skeptical.

"Yes," Sawyer says. "Go ask her."

"I will. How much money are we talking here?"

Sawyer looks embarrassed. "A hundred," he says so quietly I can barely hear him.

"A hundred what?" Hurley asks in a tone that tells me he knows the answer, but wants to make Sawyer say it.

"A hundred grand," Sawyer says, his head lowered. This garners a low whistle from Lucien.

"Your mother has that kind of money lying around?" Hurley asks.

Sawyer perks up at this. "I know, right?" he says with a lopsided grin. "I never thought she had that kind of money. I mean, I knew my father paid her child support for years, but our house is on the shore of Lake Superior and I know it cost a good penny. What I didn't know was how successful my mother has become at what I thought was just a hobby. She paints, mostly landscapes of areas around the lake and the Apostle Islands, and it turns out that her works sell for a lot of money. I never knew, and I think she kind of kept it under wraps anyway because she was afraid my father would find out and try to stop the payments."

Hurley stares at Sawyer for a few seconds, weighing his story. "Why didn't you tell us the truth from the get-go?"

Sawyer squinches up his face. "I should have. I see that now. But I didn't want to admit to being so angry with him . . . angry enough to break a cue stick. I didn't know then that the cue stick was used to kill him. When you told me that, I . . ." His color fades to that of oatmeal. "I knew how it would look. I knew my fingerprints would be all over that stick." He swallows hard and pins Hurley with his gaze. "I knew you'd never believe me. And I was right. You don't, do you?"

"Let's just say I'm hanging on to a healthy dose of skepticism here."

Sawyer hangs his head. "I'm screwed. You don't believe me, Maribel hates me for what happened to her, my mother is mad at me, and my father is dead. What else can possibly go wrong?"

"You will be spending some time in jail," Hurley reminds him.

"You're still going to put me in jail?"

"I am."

Sawyer looks like he's about to cry. "But I told you what happened," he argues.

"You told me the latest version. Frankly, I don't know what to believe, Sawyer. I'll talk to your mother and see what she says to support your story, but the facts remain. We have solid evidence that points to you as the killer, you have obvious motive, you knew enough about the situation with Taylor Copeland to set her up as the fall guy, and you have no alibi. I think I'll let the DA sort it all out."

Sawyer slumps in his seat, and for a moment, I think he's going to cry. Then his face flushes bright red, his eyes narrow, and he looks at Lucien with anger and disgust. "You better get me out of there tomorrow, like you said." With that, he stands abruptly, pushing his chair back against the wall, hitting it hard enough that one of the pictures crashes to the floor.

Hurley stands just as abruptly and swiftly makes his way around the table toward Sawyer, handcuffs at the ready. "That's quite the temper you have there, Sawyer," he says. "Hands behind your back."

Sawyer turns around, hands at his back, and as Hurley applies the cuffs, he mutters, "Screw you."

CHAPTER 22

Hurley hauls Sawyer off and Lucien and I sit in The Hole, just looking at one another for a full minute or more.

"I honestly don't think he did it, Mattiekins," Lucien says finally. "It doesn't make sense that he would kill the Copeland woman with the idea of framing her for his father's murder, and then go kill his father with an opportunistic weapon like a broken cue stick. It's either really poor planning, or—"

"Or perhaps whatever he had planned didn't work out the way he'd hoped?" I finish for him. "I don't know, Lucien. I agree, it does seem kind of odd." I shrug. "I suppose we'll have to wait and see where things fall out, once all of the evidence is in."

"We'll see," Lucien says, pushing back his chair and gathering his tattered briefcase. As he walks toward the door, I stop him.

"Tell me something, Lucien. Back when you were messing around with investing some of your clients' money, did you use anyone else to choose your investments or did you monitor and play the stock market on your own?"

"I did it all on my own. I thought I had a good handle for

the sorts of stocks that would make a sensible mix of risk and security, and for a while, things worked out nicely. But as you know all too well, it didn't last. I got a bit overconfident at one point when the returns were at unbelievable rates and I thought I could impress my clients by giving them a huge bang for their bucks. I took some risks, the market crashed, and I lost a lot."

"At least you paid your clients back."

"Over time, but they didn't make anything. All they got back was their original investment. In hindsight, I should have let someone with more experience advise me."

"Have you ever heard of a finance guy by the name of Vic Bagman?"

Lucien nods. "I think that's the guy that a client of mine down in Chicago uses. I tried to get him to switch over to me back when I was doing that stuff. Good thing he didn't, in hindsight. Why do you ask?"

"I've been wanting to do something more with the money I have left from my divorce settlement. It's sitting in a bank earning a paltry amount of interest and I thought I might be able to make it work better for me. A little extra money wouldn't hurt."

Lucien takes out his phone, scrolls around on the screen, and then hands it to me. "The guy's name is Doug Kincaid and he owns a tech company. I don't know how well he's done with this Bagman guy, but you can ask him. Here's his phone number."

I take his phone and enter the info on the screen into mine. "Thanks, Lucien."

"Happy to help, Mattiekins." With that, he takes his phone back and leaves the room.

I know Hurley will be tied up for a while with Sawyer, so I head back to my office, leaving out the front entrance. Once I'm back at my desk, I take out the sheet of references that Dottie gave us and start calling. The first two people use the words "reliable," "efficient," and "trustworthy," though the second one does say that Dottie can come across as abrupt and opinionated at times. That much I'd already discerned through our interview. The third person on the reference list is Dr. Davidson and his wife, and I'm kind of relieved when no one answers. I'm not keen on having an awkward conversation with one of the many people who ghosted me after my split from David. After a split second of indecision, I hang up without leaving a message or requesting a callback, figuring two good references is enough, given that I technically have a third in Dr. Sheridan's wife, who recommended Dottie in the first place.

Next I call Dottie and get her voice mail, and I leave a message with her to let her know that we are good to go and I will plan to meet her at the house tomorrow at one o'clock, assuming I'm not out on a call.

The feeling of relief I have, once it's all put in place, surprises me a little. I feel almost giddy at the idea of finally getting some help with the household stuff. I bask in my joy for a minute or two, and then start thinking about the cost. Hurley's concerns are not out of line.

I take out my cell phone, scroll to the number for Doug Kincaid that I got from Lucien, and place the call. The phone rings six times, and just as I'm certain I'm going to be sent to voice mail, a woman answers.

"Hello?" Her voice is quavery and soft.

"Hi, there. My name is Mattie Winston and I thought I was calling someone named Doug Kincaid. Do I have the right number?"

"You do," the woman says. She sucks in a ragged breath. "Are you a friend of his?"

"No, but my brother-in-law, Lucien Colter, knows him. He gave me his name and number. I was hoping to talk with him about a business reference for something I'm looking into."

"Oh," the woman says. I wait, and for several seconds, all I hear is silence. Then she says, "I'm sorry to have to tell you this, but Doug passed away."

"Oh, no. I'm so sorry. Are you his wife?"

"No, his secretary. Doug wasn't married."

Something in her tone makes me think that she was more to Doug than just his secretary. "I'm sorry for your loss," I say, the words popping out automatically. I've said that phrase so many times while on the job that it feels like part of my everyday speech. "I gather it's been quite a shock for you." I have no idea how old Doug Kincaid was, or if he had any health problems, but judging from the woman's reactions, I'm guessing his death wasn't expected.

"It has been," she says, her voice cracking. "He drove into a lake somehow and couldn't get out of his car in time. He . . . he . . ." Her breath hitches. "He drowned. It happened up in Wisconsin. He was on his way back from a business meeting with some students at the U of Dub campus in Eau Claire. They had some new tech device he was interested in."

Something about this story sounds familiar. I rack my brain to figure out why, and then it hits me. One of the deaths that Christopher and Richmond dealt with over the weekend out in the county was . . . How had Richmond put it? "Some wealthy tech CEO from Chicago."

Surely not. I express my sympathies once more to the grieving secretary and end the call. Then I log into my computer and pull up our recent case files. It doesn't take me long to find one for the guy from Chicago and, sure enough, his name is Doug Kincaid. I sit back, stunned. What are the odds? Then curiosity gets the better of me and I open his file and start looking through the details of his death.

Otto did the autopsy and found, as the woman on the phone had said, that the man had died from drowning. According to Christopher's notes, someone had seen Kincaid's car go into the water, albeit from a distance because the witness was on a boat out in the middle of the lake. The car appeared to be stopped on top of a bluff along a curved road, and then it slowly began to roll, going over the edge and down the hill, picking up speed with the descent, and then shooting out into the water. The depth of the lake where the car ended up was only about six feet, but the windows were open, and the vehicle sank rapidly. The driver made no attempt to escape from the vehicle and was found seated behind the wheel, seat belt on. There was speculation that it was a suicide, and per Otto's notes, he couldn't rule that out, but the primary reason Mr. Kincaid made no attempt to escape the sinking vehicle was because his blood alcohol level was just over four hundred, more than five times the legal limit and high enough to cause death without the accident or the drowning.

Otto's notes also indicate that Mr. Kincaid did not demonstrate any of the classic signs of a regular or hard-core drinker: no liver damage or disease, no dilated blood vessels in the esophagus, no tiny burst capillaries in his nose and face. Given that, it's a wonder that the man could function well enough to put on a seat belt and drive a car at all. He should have been passed out cold and apparently was, once he hit the water. Had he suffered some head trauma on the roll down the hill that contributed to a loss of consciousness?

I peruse the autopsy information, but don't find anything to support that theory. Mr. Kincaid must have stayed conscious just long enough to drive to the top of the hill, where he then passed out with the car in gear . . . perhaps with his foot on the brake initially? Then he passed out and the car began its fatal roll along the road, over the edge, down the hill, and into the lake.

I should let Lucien know about Kincaid's death, since he knew the man. After thinking about it for a moment, I decide to wait. Lucien has enough on his plate right now and it won't matter if he hears the news later today or even tomorrow.

Since I can't speak to Mr. Kincaid about his investment experience with Vic Bagman, I call Laura to see if she might have access to the man's financial records.

I get her voice mail and leave a message asking her to call me. Thirty seconds later, she does. "Sorry I didn't pick up your call. I was sneaking in a nap. I've been up for thirty-six hours straight."

"Crap, I'm sorry I woke you, then. I know how you feel."

I hear her try to stifle a yawn before she says, "What do you need?"

I explain to her that I'm interested in looking into this finance guru named Vic Bagman. "He's the advisor Monty Dixon used, and Lucien has heard of the name. He gave me some contact info for a friend of his who used Bagman, but when I tried to call him to see if he is still using him and happy with the results, it turns out that he's dead. Not only is he dead, he was one of Christopher's victims over the weekend, a Doug Kincaid. I don't suppose you have any information about the man's finances?"

"I don't, Mattie. Sorry. The county guys are handling most of the evidentiary stuff for that case. I think all we got was the autopsy."

"Dang," I say. "Thanks anyway, and get some rest, okay?"

"I'll try."

After hanging up, I lean back in my chair and stretch. My body feels like I've run a marathon. Or at least what I think that would feel like, since the most running I've ever done is to the bathroom. I glance at my watch and see it's time to go home. I call Hurley and he tells me he's going to be working late and that he'll grab something to eat on his own. So much for our dessert.

I turn off my computer, grab my stuff, and head for Izzy's office, but it's dark, indicating he's already gone home. After turning off a few lights, I take the elevator down to the garage and drive to Izzy and Dom's place to get Matthew. I let myself in through their garage, using the key code. The kitchen is empty, but I hear voices in the living room and make my way there. I stop in the doorway and gape at the scene before me.

Juliana is asleep on a blanket on the floor. Across the room from her is another blanket and on it are Dom and my son, working on a puzzle. Matthew's beautiful, thick black hair is gone, a shadow remnant of black peach fuzz the only thing remaining. I can see his scalp. Even more shocking is Dom's head, which is also bald, his strawberry-blond locks completely shaved off.

"Oh, my," I say, and Dom looks up at me.

Matthew looks up, too, and pushes himself off the floor. He runs toward me with a huge smile and a chant of "Mammy, Mammy, Mammy!" his combination of Mattie and mommy. He wraps his arms around my legs and hugs me. Then he grabs my hand and places it on his scalp. "Feel my head, Mammy. Feel it."

I run my hand over the stubble on his scalp. It's surprisingly soft and warm, but I still find myself fighting back tears over the loss of his hair. It's a silly reaction and I know it, but it's there, nonetheless.

"Dom?" I say, unable to get out any more words.

"There was some resistance to the fixing of the haircut," he says. "Suffice to say that Matthew was having one of his meltdowns at the prospect of the razor and I had to demonstrate how harmless it was on my own head before he'd let me use it on him."

"Has Izzy seen you?"

Dom rolls his eyes. "He has. He's upstairs in the bedroom sulking."

"It will grow back," Matthew says in a way that tells me he's mimicking what he heard someone else say. "And it feels good." He pushes my hand back and forth on his scalp.

I swallow back my tears and focus on getting Matthew gathered up and out to the car. Before I leave, and while Matthew is in the bathroom, I tell Dom, "I can't thank you enough for this. What a sacrifice. I can't believe you shaved off all your hair."

"It was no big deal," he says with a dismissive wave of his hand. "With this heat, it will be a relief to not have all that hair on my head. I almost shaved Sylvie, too. She wanted me to do it. Begged me, in fact."

"Oh, my God, really?" I say, biting back a smile. Dom nods. "I don't suppose it would have been a big difference to her, given that her hair is so thin and sparse she's practically bald already."

"True," Dom says, "but I figured Izzy would have a stroke, or another heart attack. Seeing me bald was bad enough. If his mother was shaved, too . . ." He doesn't finish. He doesn't have to. Both of us have been conspiring to keep Izzy's stress level as low as possible ever since his heart attack.

Matthew exits the bathroom, having dutifully washed his hands. Or at least we heard the water in the sink running. His hands look suspiciously dry to me, but I'm too tired to make an issue of it.

Matthew chats the entire way home, telling me about the big shaving episode and how Juliana laughed every time a big clump of hair dropped onto the floor, and how Dom gave himself half a haircut first and made Matthew laugh, and how Sylvie kept saying she should get a buzz cut, too, and how Dom also shaved the hair off of one of Juliana's dollies.

Matthew's nonstop chatter exhausts me, and given the hour, the oppressive heat, and Hurley's lack of presence, I decide to get takeout for dinner. I stop at a local spot and order chicken nuggets with a side of mac and cheese for Matthew, and salads with roasted chicken breast for Emily and myself. I haven't heard from Emily at all and have no idea if she's even home. Ever since she got a license and a car, she's been gone more than she's been home, either spending time with her boyfriend, Johnny, or gallivanting about with her girl-friends. She has a curfew and sticks to it, and she's a well-behaved kid in general, so we allow her a relatively generous amount of freedom.

I stick Emily's salad in the fridge, and Matthew and I enjoy dinner together, along with the two cats and Hoover, all three of whom circle us at the table and watch with longing, hungry stares. Fortunately, all the excitement with the haircuts has exhausted Matthew, and while we're watching TV, he falls asleep on the couch beside me at a little past eight. I carry him upstairs, get him tucked into his bed, and then head for mine. I'm out the second my head hits the pillow.

CHAPTER 23

When I awaken the next morning at a little past five, Hurley's side of the bed looks slept in, but he isn't there. I have no memory of anything since last night and I worriedly grab my phone, fearful I slept so hard I might have slept through a call. Thankfully, the call log reveals nothing that came in, and I breathe a sigh of relief. I head downstairs and find a note Hurley has left for me on the fridge white board letting me know he's gone to work already. Hoover is whining at the back door, so I let him out and grimace when I feel the lingering heat and humidity in the air.

I spend a leisurely hour enjoying my coffee and cruising the internet before going back upstairs to wake Matthew. He's in a good mood this morning, and dressing and breakfast go off without a hitch. Emily breezes through in her mad dash to get out the door and off to school, but the sight of her brother's new hairdo stops her short.

"Matthew! Love your hair!" she says, running a hand over his scalp and giving me a wide-eyed look.

"It will grow back," I say with a shrug.

"*It will grow back,*" Matthew echoes.

Emily kisses her brother on top of his head and says,

"Gotta run. I'll be home this evening for dinner." In a flash, she's gone.

I drop Matthew off with Dom, learn Izzy has already headed into work, and manage to cop a light, buttery croissant on my way out the door. When I get to the office, I find Izzy at his desk. After a brief morning greeting, I say, "So, what do you think of Dom's new hairdo?"

Izzy rolls his eyes. "It's going to take some getting used to," he says grumpily.

"I'm betting it will grow back before that happens," I say with a chuckle. "It was a big sacrifice on his part to do that for Matthew."

"I think he might have been able to find a different solution if he tried harder."

"Don't be too hard on him," I say. "It was a sweet gesture."

"Whatever," Izzy says dismissively. Clearly, he's in a bad mood for some reason. I suspect part of it is the shock of Dom's new do, but I think the oppressive heat may also be playing a role. Izzy, like me, doesn't do well in hot weather. I leave him to his mood and head for my office.

I've barely settled in and turned on my computer when there is a tap at the library door and our receptionist/secretary/file clerk, Cass, walks in. "There's someone out front who wants to talk to you," she says.

"Who?"

"She said her name is Linda Shoop and she's the mother of Sawyer Dixon."

"Ah, okay. I'll come get her in a sec."

Cass heads back up to the front office and I take out my cell and call Hurley to find out if I should talk to Linda Shoop. The call goes to voice mail, and I hang up without leaving a message. Then, on a whim, I place a call to Bob Richmond. He was hanging out at the station yesterday and

I know he went into the observation room at one point during our interview with Sawyer, so maybe he can fill me in. This time, I get lucky.

"Hey, Mattie. What's up?"

"I was wondering if you could help me out with something. Sawyer Dixon's mother is here in our front office and she wants to speak with me. I tried to call Hurley to see if he had spoken to her at all, and if so, what he learned from her. But he isn't answering. Do you know anything? Any idea why she wants to talk to me?"

"I have no idea about the last part, but I do know that Hurley spoke with her yesterday to verify what Sawyer said about the money she was going to spot him. He was telling the truth about that."

"Okay," I say. "I'm not sure if I should talk to her without Hurley. Could she be a potential suspect at all?"

"No, you're good to go there," Richmond says. "She has an alibi for the time of Monty's death. When Junior took her and Maribel out of The Hole, Shoop got to talking about her art at one point. She took out her phone and showed Junior an online picture of her at an art show up in Bayfield on Saturday night that featured some of her works."

"Okay, good to know. I guess I'll find out what she wants when I talk to her."

"Good luck."

"Thanks."

I'm about to hang up when Richmond says, "Hey, Mattie, do you have any interest these days in some gym time? I'm heading over there later to get in a workout and it always helps to keep me motivated if I have a partner. Can I interest you in coming along and doing some crunches with me?"

"Only if it's Nestlé or potato chips," I tell him. This garners me a chuckle.

At one time, Bob Richmond was more than two hundred

pounds heavier than he is now. After getting dragged out of semiretirement, he took a bullet to the gut and lost a bunch of weight while recovering. That close brush with death and the head start on the scale numbers motivated him, and today he's one of the fittest, healthiest people I know. Back when he first started his exercise regimen, I went along with him to support his efforts, and also because I needed to drop a few pounds myself. I still need to drop those pounds, and depending on the time of the month and how hungry I am when I go grocery shopping, there are yet another five to ten I need to drop. But I hated the gym, in part because a sadistic whack-job named Gunther, who claimed to be a personal trainer but who I became convinced was really one of the devil's minions disguised in too-tight Spandex because it made his junk look bigger, was trying to kill me with those exercise machines. I figured out fast that the only machine I was interested in there was for vending. Gunther even tried to get me to try weight lifting, but when I told him that the only thing I was going to bend and snap was his scrawny lit-tle neck, he finally gave up on me.

Richmond, however, has never given up on me. It's been more than three years since I last went to the gym with him, yet he still invites me every couple of months or so.

"Thanks for the invite, though," I say to him. "I appreci-ate that you haven't given up on me." As I hang up and go out to fetch Linda Shoop, I wonder if maybe I've given up on myself.

I hadn't devoted much of my attention to Sawyer's mother in The Hole yesterday, as my focus was more on Sawyer and his frail, maimed girlfriend, Maribel Solis. Apparently, Linda Shoop took back her maiden name after she divorced Monty ten years ago, and I'm guessing she hasn't looked back since. She is a tall woman with full hips, ample breasts, and large, round blue eyes framed by black hair with a few streaks of gray. She is dressed casually, yet she looks dignified and fashionable. Her hair is pulled back into a chignon and her makeup is artfully applied and flattering. She is wearing jeans and a lightweight sweater—things I vaguely noted earlier—but now I see the name on those jeans, and it tells me they likely cost more than my entire outfit. I also see that she is wearing adorable, blue, peep-toe heels, which I'm betting are expensive designer types, too. They seem far too dressy to be wearing with jeans, yet it works. Linda is an attractive woman with good taste and feet small enough to wear the kinds of shoes I never can.

She greets me with a graceful smile that belies the sad expression on her face. I steer her back to the library and point to one of the seats at the table in the center of the room. She picks one along the side of the table and I take one across from her. It's always interesting to see how people choose their seats. Those who have healthy egos and strong type A personalities tend to go with the chair at the head of the table. I offer her water or coffee, but she declines.

"What can I do for you, Linda?" I ask once we're settled.

She gives a woeful shake of her head and briefly looks hound-dog sad. "This is all such a horrible mess. Monty dead and my son in jail. It's all so wrong."

I nod, but say nothing, waiting.

"My son didn't do this," she says. "Help me prove that. You're a mom, aren't you?"

"I am."

"Then you understand. I know Sawyer. It's been just the two of us ever since the divorce, and I know him. He isn't perfect—far from it—but he's no killer, either."

"Why did Sawyer move in with his father?"

"It wasn't because of any problems on my end," Linda assures me. "I didn't want him to move out, but I knew he had to do his own thing, explore a little and figure out who he wanted to be. All baby birds leave the nest eventually, right?"

I nod, smiling, though the thought of Matthew ever leaving the nest seems far, far off in the future and somewhat incomprehensible. We do have Emily flying soon, though, and I know I'm going to miss her, partly because of the loss of a handy, ready babysitter, but mostly because we have grown quite close over the past two years. It wasn't easy getting there, but I think our relationship is all the stronger because of what we went through.

"Sawyer wanted to get to know his father better," Linda goes on, answering my question. "Boys need their fathers, you know? And Sawyer had an interest in the real estate business—though, to be honest, I suspect part of his interest stemmed from a belief that he could get rich quick with the help of his dad, and a dislike of schooling that made him averse to the idea of college."

"When did he start gambling?"

"I don't know," she says, pursing her lips into a thin line and shaking her head. "I don't think he was doing it when he was living with me, but I can't be sure. I didn't find out about it until Monty called and told me a few months back."

"How often did you and Monty talk about Sawyer?"

"Not as often as I would have liked. And it's been even less ever since Sawyer moved in with Monty. In the past, most of our discussions were based around childcare and custody, but that stopped a half-dozen years ago. And ever since Sawyer moved in with Monty, he's had less and less contact with me."

"Any chance Monty had something to do with that?"

Linda bobs her head from side to side, narrowing her eyes, apparently giving the question serious consideration. "I don't think so. Our divorce was really quite amicable. And Monty wasn't the manipulative or vengeful type. He had his faults—believe me," she says with a roll of her eyes. "But he certainly didn't deserve this. No one deserves this."

"When was the last time you saw or spoke to Monty?"

"On the night he died," she says, grimacing at the thought. "I didn't actually speak to him, but he called me. He left me a voice mail message that just said to call him back."

"And did you?"

Linda shakes her head. "I was at an art show, and by the time I got the message, I already knew he was dead."

"How?"

"Harrison called me right after Summer called him. He didn't have any details, of course, so I didn't get the full scoop until the next morning when I spoke to Sawyer. And it sounds like I didn't get all the facts even then. Is it true he was stabbed with a broken cue stick?"

"It is," I say.

"That's something I think Sawyer would have mentioned to me, had he known it. And if he was the one who killed his father, he would have known it, right?"

"And kids never lie to their parents, right?" I say, giving her a gentle smile.

She doesn't try to argue the point; she just nods her head in a woeful manner that I take to be a grudging concession to my point.

"So, when was the last time you saw Monty?" I ask again, trying to get back on track.

"I was thinking about that on the way here," she says. "I checked my cell phone to see when the last conversation with him occurred and that was back around Christmas. He e-mailed me last year to tell me he was buying Sawyer a car, no discussion, just that he was doing it. The only reason he told me was because the car Sawyer was already driving back then was in my name and he wanted to trade it in. I was fine with that. It was an old junker anyway. Monty sent me some papers and I signed the thing over to him." She pauses and looks off into space for a few seconds. "I haven't actually seen Monty in probably four years," she says.

"How often do you talk with Sawyer?"

She gives me a pained look. "Not as often as I'd like. He's been so focused on finding his way in the world, trying to establish himself in the real estate business. I think he expected Monty to hand over lots of active contacts and feed him clients right away, but Monty was firm about making Sawyer work his way up through the ranks."

"How did you feel about that?"

"Oh, I agreed with Monty's take on it one hundred percent. Sawyer's expectations were, and still are, unrealistic. Plus, he's developed this air of entitlement over the past three or four years that drives me crazy. A lot of his friends are the same way. It must be a generational thing."

I decide to change the subject and stroke her ego a little, to keep her talking. "I've heard that you are quite the talented artist."

"Oh, thank you," she says, looking a bit embarrassed. "I love painting and I've done it all my life. Less so when I was a single parent, of course, but once Sawyer became more or less independent, I went at it full blast."

"You must be very good if you've made and saved enough to be able to give Sawyer the money to pay off that loan shark."

"I've been very fortunate and have done quite well," she admits. "Though, to be honest, a good portion of the money I'm giving to Sawyer is money I set aside from the child support payments I got from Monty during Sawyer's high-school years. I was earning enough from my painting by then to be able to save that money. I put some of it into a regular savings account and invested the rest. It did extremely well, and I originally intended for Sawyer to use it as a college fund." She pauses and takes on a conspiratorial grin. "Don't let Sawyer know this, but there's three times what he needs to pay off the loan shark in that account. I'm just afraid that if he gets all that money at once, or even finds out how much is in the account, the lure of the gambling tables will be too much for him." Her expression turns to one of concern. "He really needs to get some help with that."

"Do you mind if I ask how you invested your money? I have a little bit I want to do something with, but I don't know much about it."

"I used a finance advisor by the name of Vic Bagman," she says, and I feel my heart do a little flip-flop. This man's name keeps popping up. "Monty's brother, Harrison, turned me on to him."

"I've heard of him," I say.

"I'm not surprised. He was quite the genius when it came to that stuff."

"Was?"

"I don't use him anymore. I pulled the money out two years ago and invested it in some CDs instead. Not as dramatic on the returns, but a lot safer, and I thought Sawyer would want to use the money for college. I don't dare give him free access to it now because he'd blow it all at the casino." She sighs, looking a little sad. "I've thought about investing some of it with Vic again, but these days, I'm more into buying real estate. I did recommend Vic to a couple of other people I know. They're probably still with him."

"Would you be comfortable giving me a name or two so I can contact them? I'd like to check some references before I decide to go with the guy."

"Absolutely." She takes out her cell phone and then asks me if I can give her something to write on. I fetch a pad and pen from my desk and hand them to her. She scribbles down two names, along with phone numbers, and then slides the pad and pen back to me.

"Thanks," I say.

"No problem. You can return the favor by helping me prove that my son didn't do this."

I give her a hesitant look. "I'm not sure I'm the person to do that," I tell her. "And there is an awful lot of evidence pointing to Sawyer."

"Why would he want his father dead?"

"There's the thing with the will. Monty was preparing to write Sawyer out of it. And fire him from the business. Did Monty ever talk with you about his will?"

She dismisses the question with a wave of her hand. "No, and I never asked. I make enough money on my own that I don't need to be involved with any of Monty's finances. Besides, he's remarried now, so any claim I might have had on his money is no longer valid."

"You never discussed his will with regard to Sawyer?"

Linda shrugs. "I always assumed Monty would take care of Sawyer, since he has no other children. To be honest, it never occurred to me to ask. You said he revised it recently to write Sawyer out?"

"It was revised, but never signed," I tell her. "The previous one, the one that it seems is still active, made Sawyer the sole beneficiary. Sawyer knew Monty was revising it and writing him out. He saw a draft of the new will."

Linda looks worried when I tell her this. I think she now has a better understanding of why Sawyer was arrested.

"If Sawyer did do this, he may be in for some disappointment," I tell her. "I don't think he's going to inherit much. It looks like Monty was essentially broke and heavily in debt when he died."

"Really?" Linda says, looking confused. "That doesn't make sense. Monty made a lot of money. I mean, granted, I didn't see his bank statements or his checkbook, but I've seen his cars and his house and his overall lifestyle. I've heard stories about how he entertains his clients. And he never once complained about the child support payments he sent for Sawyer. In fact, he sent extra from time to time. I figured he had to be rolling in dough."

"Maybe at one time, but not anymore."

Linda leans back in her seat and digests this news for a beat or two before speaking again. "It's hard to make money in real estate," she says finally, "especially when you're first starting out. Monty struggled a lot during his first five years and focused on building up his client base. He worked hard at it and did well, eventually getting to the point where his income grew both because of sales, and because he was doing enough in business to keep a larger part of his commissions. It's all tiered when you work for these real estate companies, and that's what he did initially. But once he got a better footing, he decided to go for his broker's license and open his own shop. He was smart about it, keeping things small, focusing on select clientele, choosing his partners and associates carefully." She pauses, looking wistful. "He was a natural, you know? Some people just are. By the time we divorced, he was raking in the money." She pauses and shakes her head in disbelief. "I can't imagine that it's all gone."

"Any idea who might have killed Monty if it wasn't Sawyer?"

Linda gives it some thought before answering. "I don't know Summer very well—she tends to avoid me at all costs. She's a little jealous, I think, afraid that Monty isn't . . . wasn't over me."

"The divorce was your idea?"

She nods. "It was. It probably didn't help that Summer looks just like me."

As does Monty's latest girlfriend, I think. Maybe he never did get over Linda. "What made you decide to divorce?"

"I grew up," Linda says with a smile. "We were so young

when we married, and I don't think I realized what I was getting into. I did love Monty, but he was so driven and dedicated to his work. I suppose that's why he was successful, but I found myself wishing I could be the focus of that dedication and devotion. It didn't take long for me to see the writing on the wall. The life I would have had with Monty wasn't what I wanted. I tried to change things, to change him, but you can guess how that went."

I nod and smile back at her.

"Anyway, like I said, I don't know Summer well, but I do know that spouses are the most likely suspects. So I suppose you should look at her." She leans forward, flashing that conspiratorial smile again. "She's having an affair, you know."

"How would you know something like that?"

"Monty told me back when we talked at Christmastime. He told me he had hired a private investigator."

I can't help but look skeptical. "Monty told you, his ex-wife, that his current wife was having an affair?"

Linda chuckles. "I know, it must seem odd, but I told you that Monty and I had an amicable breakup and we've remained friends. Despite our differences, we've always had a strong underlying friendship. I've discussed some of my dating adventures and woes with him over the years, and he occasionally shares some of his marital problems with me." She pauses and shifts in her seat. "Besides, from what I hear, Summer's affair with that cook of theirs is one of the worst-kept secrets in this town. The two of them haven't shown much in the way of discretion."

"Did Monty seem upset about the affair?"

"Not as much as you might think," Linda says. "In fact, I think he was a little relieved. Things between them had been stale for some time and he was already thinking about divorcing Summer. The affair just made it easier in his mind. Plus, Sawyer recently told me that Monty was seeing someone on the side, too, another real estate agent." Her expression turns sad again. "I don't know what his relationship with this new woman is like, and I haven't spent enough time around Summer to know if she's capable of something like this. I just know that Sawyer didn't do it."

I see frustration and hopelessness briefly flit across her face, and something else. Despair? I like Linda, and I feel bad for her situation. I can't imagine what it must be like to have your child arrested for murder . . . the murder of his own father, no less. But there aren't many reassurances I can give her.

"I do have some doubts about Sawyer's guilt," I say to her. "There are some things that don't quite add up or make sense, but there is also an overwhelming amount of evidence that points to him. The best I can promise you is that I will look into the case as thoroughly as possible and make sure the detective in charge does the same."

Linda pooh-poohs that with a skeptical exhalation. "That detective seems singularly focused on Sawyer and convinced of his guilt. I don't think anyone can dissuade him from that line of thought."

"I might have some sway there," I tell her. "I will do what I can, okay?"

She gives me a grateful smile and a nod.

"No promises," I caution her.

"I know, and I appreciate the fact that you're even willing to look at it." She gets up from her chair and says, "I've taken up enough of your time, Ms. Winston. Thank you for hearing me out."

Her use of my name raises a question. "We were never formally introduced over at the police station. How did you know who I was?"

"I didn't at first. But when I left the police station, I asked the dispatcher out front who you were. She clued me in on what you do and where to find you."

"And why did you want to talk to me specifically?"

"Because you're a mom," she says. "The dispatcher told me that. Those men can't understand what it's like, the way we moms do." She walks around to my side of the table and cocks her head to the side, studying me. "I hope you do have some sway over that detective who's on the case," she says. "He seems rather stubborn and hardheaded."

Apparently, the dispatcher didn't let all the cats out of the bag. "Oh, he has some soft spots," I tell her with a smile. "And I have his ear. Trust me on this one."

CHAPTER 24

After I see Linda out, I start back toward my office, but I get a text message from Arnie asking me to come upstairs and see him when I can. No time like the present, so I badge myself into the stairwell and head for Arnie's lab. It turns out he isn't alone. I'm pleasantly surprised to find Joey Dewhurst in the lab with Arnie.

"Joey! So good to see you!" I walk over and give him a big hug, which he returns, nearly crushing me.

Joey is one of the few men on this planet who can make me feel small. He is a hulking beast of a man, when it comes to his build, though he is a gentle and simple child, when it comes to his personality and mental capacity, which is approximately that of a ten- to twelve-year-old boy. The one exception to the latter is his savantlike ability to parse computers, everything to do with them—hardware, software, makes, models, peripherals, you name it—and he has given himself a superhero moniker: Hacker Man. It's a well-earned title, as he has helped us on several occasions to gain access to evidentiary computers.

Arnie has been a friend and supporter of Joey for years, and that's how I originally met the guy. Despite his limited mental capacity, Joey is self-supporting as a computer hardware and software troubleshooter, and he has been hired by some big-name companies. He drives a van, pays rent on his own apartment, and has a girlfriend with Down syndrome. Rumor has it, he's looking to get married, though last I heard the girl's mother was putting up some resistance.

"What brings you our way?" I ask Joey when he finally releases me.

"Arnie needs help."

"Yes, we've all known that for years," I say with a sardonic chuckle, but judging from the puzzled look he gives me, the joke goes over Joey's head. "What kind of help does Arnie need today?"

Arnie answers before Joey can. "I called him here because I wanted him to look at the Copeland woman's computer and printer. I had some suspicions, but didn't know how to prove them. I knew something was up because I couldn't find a single fingerprint on the printer anywhere, not on the outside, on the buttons, not even on the ink cartridges. That raised some red flags, and rather than send everything off to Madison, I figured I'd give Joey a holler and see if he could figure it out for me."

"And he did, right?" I say, smiling at Joey, who beams back at me.

"That, he did. Let me show you." Arnie turns to his desk and grabs two pieces of paper, both enclosed in plastic evidence bags. The first one is the suicide note that was left at Taylor Copeland's place, presumably written by her. The second one is a much longer note written to two people named Allie and Doug and dated the day she died. It congratulates them on purchasing their first home, references a bottle of something to drink to celebrate (I recall seeing a case of champagne tucked into a corner on Taylor's back porch), and it concludes with quotes—some humorous, some inspirational—from famous people throughout history regarding home ownership.

"Okay, help me here," I say, looking from one sheet to the other. "What am I looking at?"

"Based on the date, the letter to the homeowners appears to have been printed on the day Copeland died," Arnie says. "Presumably, so was the suicide note. Look at the suicide note closely. See that tiny line of void space that runs through each word near the bottom?"

I look closer and see what he's referencing. There is a minuscule line of white space that runs along the bottoms of the letters. "Okay," I say.

"Now find that same defect in the homeowner's letter," Arnie says.

I pick up the letter in question and stare at it, at one point holding it inches from my face. "I don't see it," I say finally.

"That's because it isn't there," Arnie says. "I looked at it under magnification to be sure."

"Meaning what?" I say, still not putting it together. My brain still feels muzzy from my lack of sleep.

"That tiny line of missing ink in the suicide note is an indication that the heads in the inkjet printer needed to be cleaned. The lack of it in the letter to the homeowners would seem to indicate that she did so."

It hits me with a flash, like a bolt of lightning. "Why would she bother to clean the print heads if she knew she was about to commit suicide?"

"Yes, and—"

I don't give him a chance to continue. "But it may have been an automatic, reflexive thing to clean those heads. Maybe before she died, she wanted to take care of this one last task, and she wanted it to look clean and professional." This sounds feeble to me even as I say it, particularly since the homeowner's letter never got sent. Then another idea comes to me. "Or maybe she wrote that homeowner note days ago and postdated it, knowing when the closing would be."

"Exactly!" Arnie says, looking pleased.

This isn't the reaction I'm expecting, since I thought I was shooting holes in his theories.

"It's hard to know the exact sequence of events. But that head cleaning bothered me enough that I thought I'd dig around in Copeland's computer to see if I could find out when she printed each item. Since I have a lot of other evidence to process, I hired Joey to do it for me. He can do it in half the time I can. And guess what he found?"

I have no earthly idea and I'm tiring of the guessing game. "Tell me," I say, looking at Joey.

"Not the same printer," he says.

"What do you mean?"

"Look at this," Arnie says, handing me yet another sheet of plain white paper with something printed on it.

It reads: *I'll make you pay for this. You're a dead man.* I recognize it as the anonymous letter that Monty received after firing Taylor Copeland. And when I look closely at the print, I see a fine line of missing ink running along the bottom of the letters in the same way it does in the suicide note. I hand the sheet back to Arnie, frowning.

"Let me see if I get this," I say. "You think that note we suspect Taylor sent to Monty days before he was killed and the suicide note came from the same printer, but Taylor's other printed material didn't? What about an office printer? Could she have printed the homeowner note there?"

Arnie shakes his head. "Both the suicide note and the homeowner note were written and saved on Taylor's home computer, but not her office one. I had Joey dig into the home computer registry, and it shows that the suicide note was printed from the home computer and was, in fact, the last thing to be printed from that computer, but"—he pauses, holding up a finger and widening his eyes for effect—"the suicide note was printed after the printer was changed."

"*Changed?* What do you mean by that?"

"I mean that one printer was disconnected and another one substituted for it and left there at the house. Someone took Taylor's printer and left a different one behind, the one with the dirty print heads."

"Okay," I say, still struggling to put all of this together, "but why would someone do that?"

"That is an excellent question," Arnie says, pointing a finger at me. "I asked myself the same thing, and then I had a little chat with the officer who took the threatening note from Monty. He remembers looking at it and commenting to Monty how the line of missing ink might be a way to identify the printer. My guess is that Monty mentioned it to someone, maybe several someones. Maybe he said something about it to the folks in his office, including Sawyer. Maybe Sawyer used that knowledge to set up Taylor for Monty's murder by taking whatever printer he used to create that threatening note and swapping it for the printer Taylor had in her house so it would appear that she created both the threat and the suicide note."

"Okay," I say with a nod. "Good work, you guys. Have you told Hurley about it yet?"

"Not yet," Arnie says. "But I will now."

I let Arnie make his call and while he's doing it, I chat with Joey to catch up on his life. "How are things going with Rhonda?" I ask. "Are you still thinking about getting married?"

"Maybe someday," he says with a smile. "Rhonda's mom says we aren't ready, and she doesn't like it when I kiss Rhonda. Arnie says there are a lot of fish in the sea and that means I should be patient and wait."

"Does he now?" I say, giving Arnie a look. "You should do whatever makes you happy, Joey."

"Will *you* marry me?" Joey asks. "That would make me happy."

I chuckle. "Thanks for the offer, Joey, but I'm already married, remember?"

"Oh, right," he says with a bashful grin. "To a policeman. If I tried to marry you, he would probably arrest me and put me in jail," he says, his eyes big.

"I don't think Hurley would put you in jail," I say with a laugh. "But he might give you a stern talking-to."

Joey frowns. "I don't know if I'll ever get married," he says mournfully.

"Hey, that's okay, Joey. You don't have to get married. Plenty of people don't get married and they're perfectly happy that way. And lots of people get married and then find that they aren't happy, so they get a divorce."

While Joey ponders this, Arnie disconnects his call and says, "Your hubby is busy with something right now, but said he'd drop by later to see what we've got."

"Then I guess I better return to work, too," I say. I give Joey a hug good-bye and head back downstairs.

When I settle in behind my desk, I see the note where Linda scribbled down the names and numbers of the women who utilized Vic Bagman. I want to do something to reassure Hurley that the expense of Dottie won't make us broke before the payments start going out. If I invest some of my remaining nest egg with this Bagman guy, and he's as good as he appears to be, it should help. I figure I can do it short-term, make a little on the side. Granted, the stock market can be a fickle beast and I could end up losing. Even as I think this, another part of my brain, the part I generally keep hogtied and stuffed away in a corner somewhere, questions whether my desire to invest with Bagman is simply another way for me to get a gambling fix.

I dial the first number Linda gave me. It's for a woman named Xyphonia Hunter, but I get a message informing me that the number is not in service. Had Linda written it down wrong? Cursing under my breath, I start to try the second number Linda gave me, but hesitate. Xyphonia Hunter is an unusual name, enough so that I figure an internet search for a business phone number or landline in the white pages is warranted. I strike gold when I find mention of her name as the owner of a business called Rough & Tumble. Seconds later, I have a number for the business and dial it. A woman who identifies herself as Melanie Frost answers.

"Hi, I'm looking for Xyphonia Hunter," I say.

"Why?"

I'm caught off guard by her curt, blunt response. "Why? Because I would like to speak with her about something."

"Are you a former employee?" Melanie sounds suspicious and paranoid.

"No. My name is Mattie Winston and I wanted to talk with Xyphonia about a financial advisor she uses. That's all." I say this in a much calmer voice than my current temperament calls for to try and calm the woman.

"A financial advisor? Is he one of our customers?" Melanie's voice is starting to ratchet up in both volume and hysteria. "Are you his wife?"

"What? No." At this point, I'm convinced she's a whack-a-doodle and it's probably best if I just move on. "Look, lady, I don't know what kind of company Rough & Tumble is and, frankly, I don't care. I'm not a customer. I just want to talk to Xyphonia. Can you put me through to her or not?"

"Xyphonia is dead." She drops that little tidbit out there and it lands with all the subtlety of a nuclear bomb.

"Xyphonia is dead?" I repeat.

"Yes."

"What happened?"

After a few seconds of hesitation, during which I imagine

Melanie is debating if she should just hang up or keep on talking, she says, "She was murdered."

That gets my attention. "When?"

"Last week, on Thursday." The hysteria is gone now, replaced with sadness and barely contained sobs.

"How?" I ask gently. Now that Melanie has decided to keep talking to me, I don't want to scare her off.

"She was run down by someone in a dark SUV. They hit her and just kept on going. The cops said it looked like it was intentional, like the driver was aiming for her. They think it might have been one of our clients, or the wife of a client."

Why would a client, or the wife of one, want to kill the owner of a business? "Melanie, what exactly is Rough & Tumble?"

"We're a telemarketing company that deals in franchises."

Granted, telemarketers can be downright annoying, but I don't know many people who are irritated enough by them to want to kill the business owner. "What do you market?". I ask.

She hesitates long enough that I'm about to repeat the question. Finally she says, "Sex."

It takes me a few seconds to digest that one. "Sex? As in *sex toys?*" I'm thinking of some of the late-night infomercial stuff that's out there.

"Well, our employees can sell toys if they want, and we do encourage that, but they don't have to. They can just do the phone part if they want."

The phone part. I'm starting to see the light and it's not at the end of a vibrating dildo, though it's close. "You do phone sex," I say.

"Yes."

"Xyphonia owns the business?"

"She does. She did. We did," Melanie corrects herself. "But no one knows for sure what's going to happen now. Xyphonia didn't leave a will, and she has family members who are flying in and threatening to take over the business. All of our franchisees are panicking and it's just a big mess."

"I see," I say. "What is your relationship to the company?"

"I'm . . . we . . . Xyphonia and I started the company together, but she's the one who had the capital, so everything is in her name. But we're . . . we were a couple. Xyphonia promised me that half the company would be mine. We just haven't had a chance to draw up the papers. And now Xyphonia's accountant is telling me that there is no money. Xyphonia's accounts have been wiped out, and her family thinks I did it and I'm hiding the money somewhere, and I have no idea what happened. If Xyphonia spent it, she didn't tell me. Everything she ever said led me to believe that things were doing well, great, in fact." She pauses and hiccups a sob. "I don't know what I'm going to do."

Wow. What a can of worms this turned out to be. I feel bad for Melanie and wish I could help her. "Melanie, the first thing you need to do is find yourself a good lawyer. Then let him or her fight for you so you don't have to do it yourself. Okay?"

I hear a few ragged intakes of breath before she manages an "Okay."

"Do it right away. Do it now, as soon as I hang up."

"Okay." This one comes out with a little more *oomph* behind it.

"I have to go now. Good luck."

"Okay. Thank you." There is strength—not much, but perhaps enough—behind the words. Before things can deteriorate any more, I disconnect the call.

I sit and contemplate the situation. Three people who supposedly used this Vic Bagman as a financial advisor are all dead. Recently dead. Coincidence? I don't think so. Something about it all feels wrong.

Monty's connection to Bagman was his brother, Harrison.

I look at the other name Linda gave me—Julie Olsen—and decide to give her a call. This time, I get lucky.

"Julie Olsen."

"Hi, Ms. Olsen. My name is Mattie Winston and I got your name from Linda Shoop. I'm considering making an investment with a financial advisor named Vic Bagman, and Linda said she recommended him to you a couple of years ago. I'm calling for a reference."

"Hm," she says. "I don't use Mr. Bagman anymore and haven't for a little over a year."

"Why is that?"

There is hesitation, which piques my interest. "I can't tell you, honestly. It was just a gut feeling I had about the guy. When I first went to him, he pressured me a lot to let him be the only person who could make changes to the fund. He said it was because he'd had clients in the past that had made some foolish moves and lost a lot of money as a result. His argument was that his business was a small one and being able to move money rapidly between funds was the cornerstone of his success and that decisions often had to be made in hours, not days. He said he didn't want to lose out on opportunities because he had to ask someone else's permission to move the money or hunt someone down and waste time trying to get a signature.

"I told him I wasn't comfortable not having direct access to my own money, because what if I needed some in an emergency? He assured me he would be available twenty-four hours a day, seven days a week, and would give me his private cell number. Anytime I wanted the money, all I had to do was call him and I'd have it within twenty-four hours. I insisted that I have my own access and eventually we reached an agreement that gave him the right to move the funds whenever he wanted, but also gave me the right to access them in any way I wanted. The whole thing felt . . . I don't know . . . uncomfortable." She pauses again and I get a sense she's debating what to say next. "Anyway, things continued to feel uncomfortable, so after a year with him, I decided to pull my money out and invest it elsewhere."

"Did the funds he recommended not do well?"

"On the contrary. They did remarkably well, though not at first. In the beginning, the fund was stagnant, no growth at all. After six months of that, I told Bagman I was going to invest elsewhere, and he convinced me to give it another month. Lo and behold, in those thirty days, I saw a twenty-five percent increase."

"Twenty-five? That's impressive."

"Yes, it is. It's also a little unbelievable. I'm no finance expert, but I'm not totally naïve when it comes to fund management, either. I know what sorts of returns one can typically expect. A return like that in the short term is possible, but it's not likely to be sustainable. I was curious, though, so I left the money there."

"What happened?"

"Nothing for several more months. At that point, I again told Bagman I was going to withdraw the funds, and he again encouraged me to hold off. Within a week, I saw another huge increase of nearly thirty percent this time."

"And?" I'm sensing an intriguing end to this story.

"And I found it a little too coincidental that the only time my money seemed to do well was when I threatened to pull it all out. Something smelled fishy. I waited a week and then I pulled all the money out, without telling Bagman I was doing it."

"Let me guess. He was angry with you," I say.

"*Angry* doesn't begin to describe it. He was *furious*. He called me several times a day for weeks, he sent me threatening e-mails, he even begged at one point. Eventually he stopped harassing me, but it was quite intense for a while."

"So you wouldn't recommend him, I take it?"

She lets out a hearty laugh. "No, I wouldn't. Something

doesn't feel right about the guy. Yet I can't complain about the money I made while I was with him, so I suppose it's your decision whether or not you want to gamble on him."

Gamble. The mere mention of the word "gamble" makes me feel a tiny trill of excitement. I shake it off, thank Julie for her time and honesty, and disconnect the call.

I sit at my desk for several minutes, mulling all this information over in my mind, tapping a pen against the top of my desk. And then I decide to give Vic Bagman a call.

CHAPTER 25

Just as I'm about to call Bagman, my phone rings and I see it's Hurley.

"Missed you this morning," I say when I answer.

"I thought about waking you, but you were sleeping so hard I checked to make sure you had a pulse. I figured you needed the sleep."

"I guess I did."

"I've got Monty's new girlfriend, Jessica Leavenworth, coming in for a chat in fifteen minutes. Want in on it?"

"Of course. I've got some information for you, too. Linda Shoop stopped by my office for a chat with me. She asked me to help her exonerate her son."

"Hard to do that, since he's guilty."

"Are you sure?"

"Sure enough."

"Then why are you having a chat with Ms. Leavenworth?"

"To be thorough. She's an alternative suspect that Lucien could use as a defense, so I want to determine how viable she is in that regard. Especially now that we know Monty sent her a text message claiming that their relationship was over."

"Yeah, any more insight into that?"

"Some. I'll fill you in when you get here."

"Okay, be there in ten."

I leave my office and go to find Izzy. "How's your day going?" I ask him.

"Amazingly quiet. It seems no one wants to die today."

"That's because so many of them died this past weekend. It's just the universe evening things out. It will pick back up again, I'm sure. Enjoy the lull while it lasts."

"I will. How's your day going?"

I give him a quick update on the interview with Dottie and let him know that I'm heading over to the police station and why.

"You sound happy about Dottie," he observes.

"I am. She's a bit regimental, but I think she'll do."

"Hurley is on board?"

"He is," I say, though the ambivalent sideways nod of my head says otherwise. Izzy, of course, doesn't miss this.

"But?" he asks.

"But I'd like to find a way to offset the cost some. I was thinking I could invest some of the money I have left from my divorce settlement and use any profits to help pay for Dottie's services. I think that would go a long way toward making Hurley more comfortable with the arrangement."

Izzy shrugs. "Makes sense. Where is the money now?"

"In CDs mostly, though I have some in a money market account for easy access in an emergency. But several of the CDs mature next month, and rather than just roll them over, I'm thinking I could make the money work harder for me."

Izzy nods.

"Toward that thought, let me bounce something off you. I was looking at possibly investing with the guy that Monty Dixon used because he supposedly had phenomenal returns.

Except two of the three people I tried to contact as references are dead, as in *recently dead* under potentially suspicious circumstances. And the third person I spoke to said there was something about the guy that was off."

"And is this third person still alive?"

"She was ten minutes ago. But she also pulled all her money out a year ago without telling Bagman ahead of time because she was suspicious about the fact that she only got phenomenal returns on her original investment when she threatened to pull the money out. She said he was very angry about it and harassed her for a while."

Izzy frowns. "Sounds like something the cops might want to look into."

"That's what I was thinking. Thanks." I glance at my watch. "I should get going, but I'll touch base with you before I go home. As usual, call me if anything comes in."

"Will do, but I'm hoping this respite continues."

"Hey, even the Grim Reaper has to take a holiday now and then." I leave and quickly walk over to the police station, going out the main entrance this time and letting our receptionist, Cass, know where I'm going. Jessica Leavenworth is already there, seated in the reception area when I arrive. I recognize her from the picture on her business card, but even if I hadn't seen that, I could have guessed who she was based on her resemblance to Summer and Linda. No doubt about it—Monty had a type. The dispatcher recognizes me and buzzes me through right away without saying anything. I feel Jessica's eyes on my back as I go.

My trek down the main hall is very different than yesterday's. Today the offices are all occupied and hopping, with secretaries, assistants, officers, and even a bail bondsman. *Is he here for Sawyer?* I wonder. *Has he been arraigned?*

When I get to Hurley's office, he's seated at his desk, chatting with Junior Feller. "There she is," Hurley says. "Junior was able to nab one of the henchmen that Sawyer Dixon's loan shark uses," he tells me.

"That's great," I say. "Is he talking?"

"Sadly, no," Junior says. "But the ADA might offer him a deal. We'll see how that goes."

"Has Sawyer been arraigned yet?" I ask Hurley.

"He was. No bail. He's still swearing his innocence."

"Okay, then. I saw Jessica Leavenworth out in reception. She looks just like Summer and Linda Shoop, except a lot angrier."

"Yeah," Hurley says with a chuckle. "I suppose I've let her wait long enough. Shall we?"

I nod and make my way to The Hole, while Hurley veers off toward reception. I settle into my usual seat and Hurley returns with Ms. Leavenworth a minute later. He stands behind his chair and gestures toward the other side, directing her to take a seat. Surprisingly, she opts for the chair at the head of the table. If the expression on her face is any indication, she's not too happy about being here.

Hurley sits and turns on the recording devices, and then does the usual introductory recitation. When he's done, Jessica takes the lead.

"I'm not sure why you felt it necessary for me to come in here, but can we please get it over with as soon as possible?" she says irritably, making a pointed look at her watch. "I have places to be and things to do. And while I'm sorry to hear that Monty is dead, I also heard that his son has been arrested for his murder. Why do you need me?"

I sense a bout of verbal sparring about to commence and I'm in a mood to be entertained, so I lean back and let Hurley handle this one.

"What we need are some answers," Hurley says. "Like

why you set up Taylor Copeland for those robberies when it was *you* who actually stole the stuff?"

"I don't know what you're talking about," Jessica says a little too quickly and with a scoffing laugh. "That's quite the imagination you have there, Detective."

"No imagination, just facts," Hurley says. "We have Monty's cell phone and we've gone through all the text messages in it and gained access to his voice mail. We've gone through his e-mails and computer files. And we've learned a lot of interesting facts in the process."

I see the tiniest twitch in Jessica's eye, the only indication that she might be worried at this point. But if I know my husband, that will soon change.

"Turns out one of the houses that you stole from had a nanny cam in the baby's bedroom," Hurley goes on.

Jessica's expression doesn't change, but her color pales slightly.

"On that nanny cam, there's footage of you helping yourself to a jewelry box that was stashed away in a dresser drawer in that room. The owners didn't have a good place to lock up their valuables, so they hid them at the last minute prior to the open house Taylor was holding. We know from e-mails we read and from talking to others in the office that Monty frequently recommended kid's dresser drawers as a last-minute hiding place because nosy open-house guests and potential thieves will go through adult dresser drawers all the time. However, they will rarely bother with the dresser drawers of a child. You assumed Taylor would have advised her homeowners on that, and you were correct. What you didn't know is that, as extra insurance, the homeowners made sure the nanny cam was on and aimed toward the dresser. We have you on film and the piece of jewelry you took from that house somehow ended up in Taylor Copeland's desk at the real estate office. Imagine that."

Jessica doesn't have a ready comeback for this, but to her credit, her expression and body language remain irascibly pugnacious. It takes her a couple of beats to come up with a response, but when she does, it's creative. "Yeah, so I took some jewelry one time and stashed it in Taylor's desk and then made sure Monty found it. I did it because he told me he thought Taylor was taking stuff from clients' houses, but he couldn't prove it. We both knew she was stealing. I just gave him the proof he needed."

"And then Monty discovered your little deception," Hurley says. "On the day he was murdered, he broke things off with you and told you he was firing you from the firm. That must have made you really angry. There went your meal ticket."

"That's ridiculous," Jessica says.

She stares at Hurley and he stares right back at her. This goes on for longer than I've ever seen any two people do it. It's Jessica who finally caves.

"Oh, fine, if it makes you feel better, I set up that Copeland woman to make room for myself at the office. How was I to know she'd off herself?"

Jessica is a most unpleasant person and the fact that Monty had a romantic relationship with her makes my opinion of him shift a few degrees.

"I still don't know why you need me here," Jessica goes on. "There can't be any evidence that I had anything to do with Monty's murder, and I don't think it's against the law to lie." She gives Hurley a cocky smile.

"You could be charged with murder for instigating the circumstances that led to Copeland's death," Hurley says.

I don't know if this is true, and doubt it is, but that doesn't matter. It's not only *not against* the law to lie, unless you're under oath, it's not frowned upon in police procedure. In fact, it's an oft-used tool.

Jessica chews on her lower lip, seeming to weigh the veracity of Hurley's statement. He doesn't give her much time to think about it.

"Then there's the long black hair we found stuck in a wound on Monty's body," he says. "A long black hair, just like yours."

Jessica rears back at this and gives Hurley a disbelieving look. "You're serious about this, aren't you? Am I really a suspect in Monty's murder?"

"Yes, you are."

"Then I'd like to consult my lawyer before I say anything else."

Hurley sighs. "Very well. This interview is concluded."

Jessica looks surprised. "We're done? Just like that?"

"We are," Hurley says.

Jessica's expression shifts to one of suspicion. "I can go?" she asks.

"For now. But don't leave town without checking with me first."

I'm fairly certain Hurley threw that last bit in there simply to rattle Jessica because he doesn't like her.

Hurley gets up from his seat, opens the door behind him, and holds it. Jessica gets up from her chair, eyeing him warily, as if she expects him to suddenly slam the door closed and say, "Just kidding." She walks out and Hurley falls into step behind her, directing her back to the front lobby area.

I leave the room and go to Hurley's office. When Hurley returns, he says, "Is it just me, or are people getting meaner and crazier every day?"

"She's a piece of work," I say. "But as awful as she is, I don't think she killed anyone."

Hurley drops into his desk chair with a heavy sigh. "Not yet anyway," he comments.

I kiss him on top of his head. "Guess I should get back to

work. Do you want to join me at home at one to go over things with Dottie?"

"No, I trust you to set it all up. Get her to do whatever you need help with and she's willing to do, but I would like to have my office off-limits."

"Already had that planned. I got you covered, babe."

He arches his neck back and smiles up at me. I give him another kiss—on the lips this time—and then leave feeling, at least for the moment, that everything is right in the world.

CHAPTER 26

I head back to my office and spend a couple of hours on paperwork. By twelve-thirty, I'm caught up with the documentation on both Monty's and Taylor's deaths and have uploaded all the photographs and video I took to the server in our office. I shift my focus to my pending meeting with Dottie and once again think about the cost involved. A quick internet search provides me with a business number for Vic Bagman and I dial it. I get a voice mail message, one of those generic computer-generated recordings, telling me to leave a message.

I leave my name and number with a message stating that I'm interested in investing some funds I have. After a quick check-in with Izzy, I head home so I can meet Dottie.

The weather is stifling, and I'm grateful for the powerful air-conditioning in the hearse. I let it blow on me full blast, and when I arrive at the house, I turn the thermostat down a notch to keep the house nice and cool for Dottie's efforts. Hoover greets me at the door, and I let him outside to do his business. Just as he comes back into the house, my phone rings.

"Mattie Winston."

"Hi, there," says a deep, raspy, male voice on the other end. "This is Vic Bagman. You left a message for me about some investments?"

"Yes, I did. I have some CDs that are about to mature, and I'd like to find a way to make that money work harder for me."

"How much are you looking to invest?"

"A little over a hundred grand," I tell him. "If it does well, there may be more in a few months. Any chance we could meet and talk about what you do?"

"I'd love to, but right now, I'm in New York taking care of some personal business, and it's likely to keep me here for several weeks. I have an associate you could talk to, Harrison Dixon. He has a good understanding of my business model and has referred quite a few clients to me. Would you be willing to meet with him in my stead?"

"I know Mr. Dixon, and I'm not sure now would be a good time for him. I don't know if you are aware, but Mr. Dixon's brother recently passed away."

"Yes, yes, a tragedy, to be sure." He sniffs loudly. "I can talk with Harrison and see if he thinks he's up for it."

"I would prefer to meet with you, at least initially."

"I don't see how I can do that now, but if you want to wait a few months . . ."

"*A few months?* I thought you said you would be tied up for a few weeks."

"Yes, well, it's hard to say. I assure you that Harrison is more than capable of getting things started for you."

"I'm curious, if you are in New York tied up on personal issues, how will you be able to manage your investment business?"

"Easy enough if you have a computer," he says. "Got to love the tech age, right?"

"I do enjoy modern technology," I agree, my mind whirling. "In fact, perhaps we could arrange a video call between the two of us?" I hear Bagman make a noise that sounds like a *tsk* and know he's not going to agree, but I continue anyway. "It's not as good as a face-to-face, but it would make me feel more comfortable about things. I realize the amount of money I'm talking about may not seem like a lot to you, but it's a lot to me and I need to make sure I don't lose it."

"Well, Ms. Winston, I can't promise you that. I make my money by investing in the stock market and, as I'm sure you know, it can be a fickle beast. It doesn't sound to me like you are committed to taking those kinds of risks and it might be better if you kept your money in a more conservative vehicle. Why don't you stick with your CDs?"

I'm surprised by his willingness to so quickly dismiss me as a customer, unless he's trying to play some sort of reverse psychology game with me. His entire manner is off-putting and I'm about to end this call, but some elusive nag tickles my brain and tells me not to drop it yet. Too many of his other clients have ended up dead lately under suspicious circumstances, and it strikes me as an unlikely coincidence to have that many deaths among the clients of a small-time, one-man financial advisor.

"Okay, Mr. Bagman, I'll talk with Harrison Dixon, but I'm not going to hire you as a financial manager until we have a chance to meet in person."

"Suit yourself," he says, and again I hear that *tsk* sound. "I'll have Harrison contact you." With that, he simply ends the call without so much as a "good-bye," "thank you," or "screw you."

I stare at my phone for a few seconds, replaying the conversation in my head, and I'm so focused on it that when my doorbell rings, it makes me jump. I look out the window and see Dottie's car in the drive, and I mentally switch gears.

Over the next fifteen minutes, Dottie and I finalize the contract by listing the specific tasks she will do, how often she will do them, and a final price. With that out of the way,

I give her a tour of the house: starting in the basement laundry area, then the main floor, where most of the emphasis is on the kitchen, with general dusting and vacuuming in the other areas, and, finally, the second floor. I explain that Hurley's home office needs to be off-limits and that we often keep the door to the room locked so that Matthew can't get in there and mess with anything. I start with the master bedroom and bathroom, then move on to Matthew's room. Dottie has been unnervingly quiet throughout the tour, but when she sees Matthew's latest crayon artwork on the wall of his bedroom, she clucks her tongue and says, "Busy little hands need watching all the time. I hope you don't expect me to get that off the wall."

"No, of course not," I say, feeling embarrassed. "I've become adept at removing my son's attempts to turn his bedroom into the Sistine Chapel. He's quite persistent and quick." I say this in a joking manner, but Dottie doesn't share my humor. I move us on to Emily's room, which looks like a tornado blew through it. Em is not a neat child, and there are clothes, shoes, books, and papers on nearly every available surface, and part of a dried-up peanut butter sandwich on a plate on her desk. Dottie clucks again and I can feel myself getting defensive.

"Teenagers, eh?" I say with a chuckle.

Dottie's face is a stone-hard mask of disapproval. Her attitude angers me and I come close to telling her, *Never mind, let's forget the whole thing and we'll find someone else.* But I recall how elated I felt at finally finding someone to help with this stuff and decide that a bit of old-lady judgment is a small price to pay. I decide to try a bit of flattery instead, hoping it might appeal to her ego.

"You see now why we need your help," I say. "I look forward to any suggestions you may have to offer."

Dottie continues to survey the room, her disapproval as easy to read as the top row on an eye chart. Feeling oddly guilty, I bend over and pick up a book from the floor, as if this one small gesture can somehow compensate for the disaster that is the rest of the room. I see it's one of the Harry Potter books, a series Emily has been devouring in what little spare time she's had over the past year after I told her how great the books were.

"Emily is a smart kid and she loves to read," I say in her defense. "The Harry Potter books are one of my favorites and I got Emily hooked on them."

No sooner do I say this than something clicks in my brain. Pieces of a puzzle start to fall into place, and I feel a shiver of excitement. I toss the book onto Emily's desk.

"I have to go do something," I tell Dottie. "You have the house key, and if it's okay with you, I'm going to leave you to it. Please lock up when you leave."

I spin about and practically run from the room, not giving Dottie time to respond. For all I know, she may simply pack up her stuff and leave, deciding to cancel our contract. For right now, I don't care. I've got bigger fish to fry.

I hurry out to my car, stopping long enough to let Hoover back in—I'd forgotten he was outside in this nasty heat—and drive back to my office. Once I'm at my desk, I settle in and bring up a search page on my computer. A few clicks later and I'm on a Wikipedia page for the Harry Potter books, scanning my way through a list of characters. It doesn't take me long to find what I'm looking for. It's on a page dedicated to the Ministry of Magic and the page lists the officials associated with it. The first name on the page is Ludo Bagman, also known as Ludovic Bagman, head of the Department of Magical Games and Sports.

I sit back in my chair and let my thoughts sort themselves out like they're in a Sorting Hat. The more I think about it, the more excited I get. After several minutes, I grab my phone and call Hurley.

He answers on the second ring. "What's up, Squatch?"

"We need to talk some more about the Dixon case. I have an idea about something, and it might be crazy and far-fetched, but it feels right to me."

"Okay. I learned long ago that your instincts are worth listening to. Fire away."

"First off, can you look back at your notes and tell me when all the people who were at the Dixon house on the night he was killed arrived there."

"Okay, give me a minute." I hear sounds of movement and then shuffling papers. "Summer was already at the house when I arrived," he says, "but we know she left Damien's at ten o-two that evening. Next, we have Harrison Dixon, who arrived at eleven twenty-nine, followed by Sawyer at eleven thirty-eight."

"And when did Summer place her call to 911?"

"At ten-eighteen."

"And her call to Harrison?"

"At ten thirty-five. What are you going after, Squatch?"

"What did Harrison Dixon say he was doing when Summer called him?"

I hear more rustling before Hurley answers. "He was home alone, ate dinner, did some work on his computer, and then watched TV."

"And where does he live?"

"In Black River Falls."

"So Summer calls him at ten thirty-five and he is supposedly in his home in Black River Falls, which is more than a ninety-minute drive from Monty's house. Yet he managed to arrive at Monty's house at eleven twenty-nine, less than an hour after Summer called him."

There is silence on the other end, and I know Hurley's mind is at work. "He lied," he says finally.

"And there's more. I took to heart what you said about the cost of paying for someone to help out with the housekeeping stuff and thought I'd try to find a way to make the money I have left from my divorce settlement earn enough to offset that cost. Several of the CDs I have are about to mature and I was curious about this financial consultant that Monty used, you know, the one Harrison mentioned?"

"I remember," Hurley says, sounding both wary and confused.

"His name is Vic *Bagman* and something about that name tickled my brain for some reason and I couldn't figure out why. More on that in a minute. Anyway, I thought that if the ROI he supposedly got for Monty was as good as it appeared to be, it might be a good idea for me to invest some of my divorce money with him and see what it could do."

"*Okaaay,*" Hurley says, drawing the word out.

"First, I wanted to check on some references for the guy, someone other than Monty who might have used Bagman's services. I asked Lucien if he knew the guy and he said he'd heard of him and knew someone who had used his services, a friend of his who owns a tech company in Chicago. The guy's name is Doug Kincaid, and while that name might not ring a bell with you, it will with Bob Richmond, because Mr. Kincaid was one of the deaths he got called out to the county for. The guy's car went into a lake and he drowned. But there's evidence that he might have been drugged and drunk when he went into the water, and a witness said the car was stopped on top of a hill for a minute or two and then just rolled down it."

"Sounds like a drunk-driving accident, or maybe a suicide," Hurley says.

"Maybe," I say.

Hurley chuckles because he can tell from the tone in my voice that I don't believe that's what happened. "Or maybe not," he says. "Tell me why."

"I can't, for sure," I admit. "But there's more. I spoke with

Mr. Kincaid's assistant, and during our very emotional discussion, she informed me that Mr. Kincaid's money had mysteriously disappeared."

"Then, when Linda Shoop came to see me, we started talking about money and investments and she mentioned that she used Bagman for a short time. It was a couple of years ago and she was only with him for a short while, but she gave me the names and numbers of some acquaintances of hers that she sent to Bagman. I called the first one and it turned out she had also died recently. She was the victim of a hit-and-run driver just last week. And when I talked to her business partner, who was also a romantic partner, she told me that all of this woman's money had also mysteriously disappeared. So we have Monty Dixon, who was murdered by someone—"

"By Sawyer Dixon," Hurley interjects.

"He was murdered," I say, ignoring his provocation, "and he was essentially broke when it happened. Remember that weird thing that happened to Laura when she was looking at his investment fund?"

"You mean that software glitch?"

"What if it wasn't a glitch, Hurley? What if the money wasn't there, but then someone put it back, knowing that we would be looking into Monty's financial accounts?"

"Okay," Hurley says with a heavy sigh, and even though I can't see him, I know he's raking his fingers through his hair. He always does that when he's struggling to sort through stuff. "You think all these deaths are related and somehow connected to this Bagman guy?"

"I know it seems far-fetched," I say.

"It does," Hurley agrees with a chuckle. "But I gather that hasn't stopped you from formulating a theory. Lay it on me."

"I tried to call Bagman right before I went home for lunch. I got his voice mail and left a message for him to call me."

"Why? You aren't seriously thinking of using him, are you?"

"No, but all these deaths connected to him seemed like too much of a coincidence. It piqued my curiosity. He called me back, and when I told him I had some money to invest, but wanted to meet face-to-face with him first, he had a gazillion excuses why he couldn't do that. He kept trying to pawn me off onto Harrison Dixon."

"Maybe Harrison vets clients for him," Hurley suggests.

"Or maybe," I say with great drama, "Harrison Dixon and Vic Bagman are the same person."

CHAPTER 27

M y suggestion that Bagman and Harrison are one and the same is met with a good ten seconds of silence.

"I don't follow," Hurley says finally.

"Consider what we know. Harrison told us that Bagman operates out of a PO box in some Podunk town that just happens to be a short hop from Black River Falls. We know Harrison lied to us about where he was when Summer called him. He was involved somehow in his brother's financial doings and seems to be the primary contact for the others I spoke to when I was trying to get a reference for Bagman. Granted, when I talked to Bagman on the phone today, the voice was deep and raspy, nothing like Harrison's, but I heard something that stuck with me. He made this sound a couple of times, like a *tsk*." I imitate the sound for Hurley. "When he hung up, I realized that it sounded like he was trying to pull something from between his two front teeth. Harrison Dixon has that space between his two front teeth, and when we talked to him, both at the house and in The Hole, he did the same thing."

"I remember," Hurley says, sounding more interested now.

"And it got me to thinking," I go on. "Harrison knew about the problem between Monty and Taylor Copeland. She would have let him into her house, even if she'd never met him, because she might have thought he was Monty. Harrison also knew that Monty's security cameras had been disconnected. And here's the thing that's been bugging me ever since I heard the name Vic *Bagman*. You know I loved reading the Harry Potter books and got Emily hooked on them. We discuss the books quite often. When I was showing Emily's room today to Dottie, there was one of the Potter books on the floor of her room. When I picked it up, it came to me. There's a character in the books named Ludovic Bagman. He handles money from bets that are placed on the Quidditch games."

"What games?" Hurley asks, sounding confused.

"It's a sport the author invented for the books. It doesn't matter. What does matter is that I'm willing to bet that Harrison Dixon is also a fan of the books. I'd also be willing to bet that as a kid he was likely teased a lot, based on his name alone. Harrison shortens easily to Harry and add the last name to that, and you know kids had to have been teasing him all the time about hairy dicks. A kid who went through that kind of stuff might have found solace in his later years in a character like Harry Potter—also a Harry who was teased and tormented by others as a child."

Hurley is silent for several seconds. Then he says, "Wow, that's a lot of amateur psychology there and, as far as I know, there hasn't been any indication that Harrison Dixon grew up a tortured child."

"We need to visit his house and look around, see if the Harry Potter books are there. Want to wager a little bet on it?" Even as I say this, I'm aware of the fact that I'm gambling, albeit as a friendly competition with my husband, but some part of my mind wonders if that's just a handy excuse. "And maybe we should visit the post office where Bagman gets his mail to see if anyone can tell us who rented that box and who comes to get stuff from it. Maybe someone at the post office will recognize Harrison."

"Okay, okay," Hurley says, and I can tell he's trying to slow me down so he can have time to sort through everything I'm throwing at him. "You're suggesting more than the idea that Bagman and Harrison Dixon are the same person. You think Harrison might have killed Taylor? And Monty?"

"I think it's possible, yes."

"Why?"

"One of the people I spoke to about Bagman told me that he was very insistent on having sole control over the fund management. She wasn't comfortable with that and resisted until he caved. Later, when she threatened to pull her money out of the fund because it wasn't earning, Bagman convinced her to keep it there a little longer. And within a month, she saw a huge return. Then there was another period of nothing and again she threatened to pull the money. Same thing happened. After that, she went ahead and took her money out and closed the account, without telling Bagman ahead of time. She said he was furious with her. And I don't think it's a coincidence that two of Bagman's clients recently turned up dead under suspicious circumstances and both had money invested with him that mysteriously disappeared."

"You think the guy's running a Ponzi scheme?" Hurley says.

"It would explain a lot. There was that weird episode with Monty's account where Laura saw no money one minute and then five hundred thousand the next. If Harrison had stolen his brother's money, and Monty found out, it would explain why he had to kill Monty and frame Taylor for the murder. And Harrison had to know we'd be looking at Monty's finances and eventually find that investment account. If it was empty, it would raise all kinds of questions and put a focus on Bagman, something Harrison wouldn't want if the guy is made up. So he put some money back into the account so our suspicions wouldn't be aroused."

"Okay," Hurley says. "I have to confess that it sounds a bit out there at first blush, but once you look at all the pieces, they fit." He sighs. "You've convinced me that we need to take a closer look at Harrison Dixon."

"When?" I say, feeling excited at the prospect. I always get revved up when we're doing an investigation like this and we start closing in on the truth.

"Well, I say there's no time like the present. If I drive up to Black River Falls, I can time it to make sure Harrison couldn't have made that drive in the time he claimed on the night Monty was killed. And if I drop in at his house unannounced, maybe I can get a chance to scout out the place."

"You mean *we* can make the drive and the visit, right?"

"But you're on call. You'd be too far away if a call came in."

He's right and I curse to myself. Then an idea comes to me. "I think it's time to cash in on that favor that Christopher owes me," I say. "Let me call him and then check with Izzy and I'll get right back to you."

I disconnect the call, cross my fingers, and then call Christopher. He answers after the first ring.

"What's up, Mattie?"

"I'm wondering if I might cash in on that favor for a few hours this afternoon? Hurley and I need to make a run up to Black River Falls to talk to a potential suspect in the Dixon murder."

"I thought you already had your culprit in jail."

"So did we, but new evidence has come to light and we need to check it out. I can't promise anything, but it might also be connected to one of your deaths from the weekend."

"Really? Well, I can hardly say *no* to that now, can I? Do you need me to come into the office?"

"No, if you can just be available for a call if one comes in, that should cover it. I'll let you know as soon as I'm back in the area. I figure we'll need about four hours."

"Got you covered."

"Thanks, Christopher." I hang up and head for Izzy's office to fill him in, but he's out to lunch. I send him a text message letting him know what's up, and then I call Hurley back. "I'm freed up for several hours. Want to come and pick me up?"

"Be out front in five."

Hurley is true to his word, pulling up in front of our office exactly five minutes later. The air outside hits me like the discharge from a blast furnace. Hurley has the AC going full force, and as soon as I hop into the passenger seat of his king cab, I aim the vents at my face.

"Good grief, it's hot," I say.

"And they're calling for two more days of it," Hurley says. He guns the gas and pulls out before I can get my seat belt locked into place.

"You seem eager," I say with a laugh.

"I am, though I'm not wild about the possibility that I might have got it wrong with Sawyer Dixon."

"Maybe you didn't. We don't know anything for sure."

"I don't know, the more I think about it, the more I like your theory. I'm going to drive to the Dixon house and then reset the odometer and mark the time. We'll see how long it takes to get to Harrison's place. He said his office is only a few blocks from his house, so even if he's at work, the timing and distance should be pretty close to the same."

While Hurley drives, I call Dom and let him know I might be a little late in picking up Matthew. As usual, he's more than willing to accommodate us. Dom is his happiest when he's surrounded by kids and home. By the time I finish talking with him, we have arrived at the Dixon house. The end of the driveway is taped off, though there is no one watching the place. Hurley notes the time—1:48—resets his odometer, and we're off.

"How did things go with Dottie?" he asks once we're under way.

"Okay, I guess. She seemed a little judgmental. She commented on how important it is to watch your kids closely, when she saw Matthew's latest artwork on his wall, as if we don't always do our best to keep an eye on the little bugger. I kind of abandoned her in the middle of Emily's room, which looked like a tornado had blown through it. After I picked up that Harry Potter book and had my epiphany regarding Harrison, I basically just ran out. Hopefully, she stayed and did what we discussed, but I suppose we'll find out when we get home tonight."

"Did you let her know that my office was off-limits?"

"I did, and I made sure it was locked." I reach over and give his arm a squeeze. "It will be fine, Hurley. Don't worry."

He looks like he wants to object to my reassurance, but he doesn't. We spend the bulk of our time on the drive discussing the case, though there are breaks of comfortable silence interspersed.

When we arrive on the outskirts of Black River Falls, it only takes five minutes to get to Harrison Dixon's house, but the total drive took us just over an hour and a half. Traffic was light, though admittedly not as light as it had probably been at ten o'clock at night. Hurley parks at the curb in front of the house, an older Craftsman situated on a street lined with similar old homes, most of them in desperate need of some repairs and a face-lift. Harrison's is in better shape than some, but it needs some work and the lawn is a mixture of dirt and clumps of grass desperately clinging to life.

"It looks dark and deserted," Hurley says. "He's probably in his office, but we should go and ring the bell to be sure."

Hurley turns off his truck and we both get out. I groan as

the heat wraps itself around me again, and by the time we have walked up to the front porch—a chipped and stained slab of concrete with rusted wrought iron pillars at the corners—I'm already sweating. The door is a faded wooden affair, with a spinner door ringer at its center. Hurley gives the thing a twist and we hear the bell clang from inside. We wait a minute, and when no one comes to the door, we head back to the truck.

"His office is located downtown," Hurley says, and it takes us only a minute to get there. The buildings comprising the main drag through town appear to be at least half a century old—dingy, run-down, and forlorn-looking. Harrison's office is in a brick-and-wood square building with a glass door that has HARRISON DIXON, ATTORNEY AT LAW painted in white letters on it. Hurley parks on the street right in front.

As we open the door to the office, a bell overhead tinkles, announcing our arrival. I'm expecting a respite from the sauna conditions outside, but the office is either not air-conditioned, or the thermostat is set at ninety. There is a ceiling fan overhead whirring and wobbling frantically, but it does little to dissipate the heat. There is a small desk with a computer in the front room and seated behind it is a thin, gray-haired woman who I guess to be in her fifties. A brass nameplate on the desk reads: MARGARET BASCOMB. In deference to the temperature, Margaret is wearing a lacy tank top and linen slacks. Rings of sweat stain her top beneath her arms. In contrast to her clothing, Margaret is wearing way too much makeup, with a border of foundation visible along her jawline, tiny black dots of mascara beneath her eyebrows, which look drawn on, and a too-bright shade of pink eye shadow lining her lids. While her makeup may not be artfully applied, it must be hardy stuff because it isn't melting.

"Hi, there," Margaret says with a smile. "How can I help you?"

"We're here to see Harrison Dixon," Hurley says. Behind Margaret is another room, which presumably houses Harrison, though all we can see through the open door is a wall with a trio of framed diplomas and another fan hanging from the ceiling.

"May I ask what this is in reference to?" Margaret asks, smile locked solidly in place.

Hurley takes out his badge and flashes it at her. "It's regarding his brother, Monty."

The smile vanishes, instantly replaced by a mournful expression. "Such an awful thing that happened," Margaret says, giving us the sad eyes. She then picks up her desk phone and jabs at a button. We hear a tone emanate from the room behind her and hear Harrison's slightly muffled voice say, "Yes?"

"There is a policeman here to talk to you about what happened to your brother," Margaret announces, giving Hurley a wink. There is an awkwardly long silence that follows, and Margaret gives us a nervous smile as she waits.

Finally we hear, "Send him in."

"There are two people," Margaret says into the phone, but I see the light on the button go out right before she speaks, indicating Harrison has hung up. Margaret sets her phone in the cradle, looking unsure of what to do next. I decide to make the decision for her and stride past her desk and into the back room. Hurley follows me and the two of us are standing in front of Harrison Dixon's desk before Margaret has a chance to warn him.

This portion of the office boasts two ceiling fans, though all they manage to do is circulate the hot air. Harrison is dressed in a long-sleeved white shirt, and I'm surprised that the sleeves are fully down and buttoned. The man must be severely self-conscious about his psoriasis. As if he can read my thoughts, he idly scratches at his right forearm, wincing slightly as he does so.

"Are you two always a team?" he says, forgoing any formal greeting. He does not get up from his chair, nor does he offer us a seat.

"In more ways than you might think," Hurley says.

Harrison's brow momentarily furrows at that comment, but he lets it go. "To what do I owe this unscheduled, unannounced visit?" he asks, his displeasure clear in his tone.

"We have some questions for you regarding your brother's death and your prior statements," Hurley says.

Harrison's brow furrows again and I note beads of sweat on it. The armpits of his shirt, like Margaret's, are stained with sweat. He makes that sucking noise with his tongue against his teeth.

"Toward what end?" he asks, looking genuinely puzzled.

"Just trying to firm up some of the timelines and details," Hurley tells him. "To start with, we know that Summer called you about Monty's death at ten thirty-five that night and we also know that you arrived at the house at eleven twenty-nine. In your statement to us, you claimed you were at home watching TV when Summer called you. For you to get from your house, here in Black River Falls, to Monty's house in Sorenson would have taken you ninety minutes of drive time. Yet you arrived in less than an hour. Can you explain how that's possible?"

Harrison smiles at Hurley, but it looks forced. "Did I mention that I own a DeLorean?" he says with a chuckle.

Neither of us smiles or laughs. He's stalling, trying to figure out how to answer the question.

"Not fans of *Back to the Future*, I take it?" he says, rubbing at the spot on his arm that he'd scratched earlier.

"Can you please just answer the question?" Hurley says.

Harrison's smile disappears like flash paper. "Clearly, you have some of your times wrong," he says. "Besides, what difference does it make? You have Sawyer under arrest for the crime."

"We are looking at some new evidence," Hurley says.

Despite remaining silent throughout this exchange, I see Harrison's eyes dart my way ever so briefly when Hurley says this. Hurley must have seen it, too, because he switches gears.

"Mr. Dixon, I need to meet with your business associate Vic Bagman right away."

Harrison sucks at the space between his teeth. "He's not available. He had to go to New York on some personal business."

"Then I need to speak with him. Can you please call him on the phone?"

It takes a couple of beats for Harrison to come up with a counter for this one. "He is there because his mother is very ill. She's probably dying, and I don't want to disturb him during such a personal and emotional time."

"And yet he returned a call to me earlier today," I say. "Clearly, he wasn't so pressed with his personal problems then."

"Could you call him now, on your desk phone?" Hurley asks. "And put it on speaker, please."

Harrison frowns at the two of us and picks up a handkerchief from his desk, mopping his forehead with it. When he's done, he sets it down and then does as Hurley says. We listen as the phone rings on the other end and the computer-generated voice mail comes on. I figure that if Harrison is also Bagman, he probably has a cell phone dedicated to his Bagman persona. I listen carefully during the rings on the office phone to see if I can hear the vibration or chime of a cell phone somewhere in the room, but I hear nothing.

"Do you want me to leave a message?" Harrison asks Hurley during the computer-generated voice.

"No, you can hang up."

Harrison jabs at a button and the call is ended. "May I ask

why there is this sudden urgency to talk to Mr. Bagman?" he asks.

"We have discovered several of his clients who ended up dead under mysterious circumstances over the past few days," Hurley says. "Including your brother. And it appears that they all experienced catastrophic losses of their investment money just prior to their deaths. That seems suspicious to me."

The color drains from Harrison's face. "But I just checked my brother's investment account and he has money there," he says, admitting that he has access to Monty's account. "I know it's not as much as he had at one time, but he pulled a lot of it out to help Sawyer with his gambling debts. And there are risks associated with these funds. Vic is good at predicting the stock market, but he's not perfect. He makes mistakes now and again."

"I think the man is running a Ponzi scheme of some sort," Hurley says. "Would you let us have a look at your computer?"

Harrison looks taken aback by the request. "*This* computer? Here in my office?"

Hurley nods.

"Of course not. I'm a lawyer and the information on this computer is protected by attorney-client privilege and my fiduciary obligations."

"How about a peek at your home computer, then?" Hurley says.

I know he's just messing with the guy now, trying to see how rattled he can get him.

"Same argument," Harrison says, grabbing that hankie and swiping at his forehead again. "I work from home quite often, so I have protected documents and confidential information on my home computer."

Hurley nods and falls silent for a moment. Harrison appears to relax briefly, but it doesn't last long.

Hurley says, "If I were to visit the post office in Brockway where Mr. Bagman rents a PO box and show them a picture of you, would they recognize it?"

His jump to a new topic is a tactic I've seen him use before. It's effective in keeping the people he's questioning enough off balance that it's harder for them to come up with lies quickly and convincingly.

"Are you and Mr. Bagman the same person?"

Apparently, Harrison has tired of this game. He sags in his seat and says, "Okay, look. I will admit to playing a tiny game of cat and mouse with some of my clients by pretending that Mr. Bagman is someone other than me. I did it to avoid the appearance of a conflict of interest, since some of the investment clients are also my law clients. Truth is, I do all the investing. I don't want my clients to know that, though. I have no hard background in financial management when it comes to managing funds like this, but I assure you I'm good at it. Occasionally I make mistakes, but in general my returns are excellent."

"Tell that to your dead clients," I say.

Harrison shoots me an angry look. "I have no idea what you're talking about with these deaths, but I assure you I have nothing to do with anything like that. Nor is my investment business a Ponzi scheme. I have plenty of assets to back up any catastrophic losses, enough so that I have offered some of my more reluctant clients a guarantee that, at a minimum, they will get their original investment back."

"Really?" I say. "Can you provide proof of that?"

Before Harrison can answer, Margaret pokes her head in the office and asks if he needs anything. I suspect, given the open door between the two areas, that Margaret has been eavesdropping on our conversation. I'm not sure how much she knows about her boss's dealings, but I suspect her interruption is motivated by some sort of protective instinct.

"I'm fine, Margaret," Harrison says. Then he turns back

to me. "My paperwork for that aspect of my business is at home. I don't keep any of it here."

"Then I guess we're about to visit your home," Hurley says, waving an arm toward the door. "After you."

"I don't think I want you poking around my house," Harrison says.

"Why is that?" Hurley asks. "Are you hiding something other than this alternate identity of yours?"

"I am not. Do you have a search warrant?" He asks this with a cockiness that tells me he knows we don't. "Because without one, I'm not obligated to show you anything or let you anywhere near my house. Frankly, I've gone overboard in letting you into my office."

"It's a public place of business," I say.

"And I think our business here is done," Harrison shoots back with an air of finality. "You may leave."

CHAPTER 28

Hurley and I leave Harrison's office and head for the edge of town. We don't speak for the first few miles, both of us drained from the heat and eager to let the truck's air-conditioning work its magic.

"Now what?" I ask, once I feel goose bumps form along my arms.

"Now I need to look into these other deaths you mentioned, see if I can somehow connect them to Harrison. In order to get a search warrant, I'm going to need proof of some sort that ties him to those deaths."

"Can't you get one based on his subterfuge with the investment stuff?"

"Making up a name isn't against the law. So far, I have no proof of any mismanagement of funds. And like he said, his brother's money is still in his account. I had Laura put a freeze on Monty's account right after that weird glitch she witnessed. I think you're right. Harrison put money into that account so we wouldn't get suspicious. My guess is that he took it from other clients, perhaps the ones who were recently killed, to cover the missing money in Monty's account.

And I'm betting he's going to try and take it back out after our visit."

"He can't get that money," I say, "but he might have access to other funds. We need to find a way to increase the pressure on him. We should get several of his investors to all demand their money at the same time. That might prompt him to do something stupid."

"That's not a bad idea," Hurley says. "But how do we find them?"

I think about that for a minute or two. "We could start with the two dead people that we know used Harrison's investment service. Contact their friends, family, and business associates. If Harrison was touting and eventually providing the kinds of ROI I think he was, odds are his clients would have recommended him to others. It's a lot of legwork, but it might pan out."

"Pounding the pavement is what police work is all about," Hurley says. "Even in this day and age."

"More likely you'll be pounding the phone lines," I say. "But maybe you can get Richmond to help, since it involves a death he had over the weekend. And put Laura on it, too." I pause, and then hit Hurley with, "You know, you need to ask Lucien if he knows anyone else. He not only might have a name or two, since he dabbled in that sort of thing himself a few years back, he might jump at the chance to exonerate his client."

Hurley rolls his eyes and mutters, "God, give me strength."

Hurley drops me off at my office so I can get my hearse and he heads back to the station with a plan to put my idea into motion. "I'll see you at home," he says, "but don't hold dinner for me. If I'm going to be too late, I can grab something."

I give Christopher a call while I'm in the main part of my office to let him know I'm back before heading down to the underground garage, our Superman to the bullets of cell service. Then I give Dom a call to let him know I'm on my way to get Matthew.

My son is in a talkative mood and he regales me on the way home with a recitation of a SpongeBob SquarePants cartoon he watched, telling me all about " 'kini Bottom" and the antics of its inhabitants.

When I arrive at the house, I'm so focused on Matthew and his story that I've forgotten all about Dottie until we enter the kitchen from the garage. The first thing I notice is the clean, fresh smell. I stop several feet inside the room and stare in wonder. The floors are gleaming without a muddy footprint or rolling hair ball to be seen anywhere, the countertops are polished bright and crumb-free, the stainless-steel face of the refrigerator is shimmering with nary a fingerprint to be found. Everything on the counters is clean and where it's supposed to be. And the coup de grace is a vase full of fresh flowers on the breakfast-nook table.

"Wow," I say, walking deeper into the house. When I see the living room, I find Hoover curled up in front of the fireplace, the carpet all around him hair- and stain-free.

"The house smells good," Matthew observes.

"It sure does," I agree.

"Can I have a chockit milk?"

"Sure." I grab him one from the fridge, sit him at the table, and then make a quick run upstairs to see what's been done. The floors here gleam like the ones below and there is a faint scent of lemon lingering in the air. I check the kids' bathroom first. Every surface is sparkling, spotless, and bright. There are fresh towels folded and put in the linen closet and hanging on the towel racks. The mirror and the sink are no longer speckled with toothpaste and fingerprints. The tub is scrubbed to a shine and the floor is immaculately clean.

A quick examination of the kids' rooms reveals more delights. All the bed linens have been changed. The carpets have been vacuumed. Clothing has been freshly laundered, folded, and placed at the foot of each bed. The floor of Matthew's room has been cleared and all his toys and clothes are stored in their proper spots. Emily's room, which has been a mess since the day she moved in, is barely recognizable.

Our bedroom and bathroom were relatively decent before Dottie came, but there are surprises here, too. There are clean sheets on the bed, and clean towels and washcloths in the bathroom. I note that the water spots have been removed from the glass shower walls, and our hampers are empty. Freshly laundered clothing has been folded and left at the foot of the bed. I want to leap for joy.

I hurry back downstairs, leery of leaving Matthew alone for too long, and find that Emily has come home. She is standing in the dining room, book bag slung over one shoulder, looking around at the kitchen and living room with wide-eyed wonder.

"What did you do?" she says, waving an arm about. "Go on a cleaning frenzy?"

"No, I hired a woman to come and clean a couple times a week."

Emily's eyebrows shoot up and she stares at me. "The whole house? Was she in my bedroom?"

"Yes, she was," I say with a grimace.

Emily drops her book bag and runs upstairs, and I brace myself for a teenage meltdown over this invasion of her private space. Em and I get along well, most of the time, but the condition of her bedroom has been a consistent source of conflict. I've threatened a number of times to come into her room and clean it myself if she didn't do it, but I think she always sensed that I was bluffing because I never had the time or the energy to do it. I hadn't told her about the idea of a hired housekeeper until now.

Matthew looks at me with raised eyebrows, sensing the tension. I settle in at the table with him and start mentally preparing my arguments. A few minutes later, I hear Emily come pounding down the stairs.

"Oh . . . my . . . God," she says, her eyes big. I start to launch my planned defense, but before I can utter a word, she shocks me by saying, "That is *so* ridic! I love it! How often is she going to come?"

I stare at her, confused. "You're not mad that some stranger invaded your private quarters?"

She looks at me like I just said the world is flat. "I don't have anything to hide," she says, and I believe her. Emily is a good kid, something I can't take much credit for, since she spent the first fourteen years of her life with her now-deceased mother. "I'm just glad it got cleaned. Now that it's done, I can try to maintain it. It was just so overwhelming before, trying to figure out where to start. I'm sorry I let it get that bad."

I breathe a sigh of relief and say, "Wait until you see what she did in your bathroom. And she'll be back on Thursday."

I hear the rumble of the garage door going up and my smile grows even bigger. "Your dad is home earlier than I expected," I say.

Matthew abandons his chocolate milk and runs to the garage door to greet his father, who scoops him up into his arms.

Hurley's eyes look sunken and there is a droop to his posture, probably due to a lack of sleep and heat exhaustion. He eyes Matthew's scalp, his eyebrows arched, and I realize this is the first he's seen of Matthew's new haircut. "Wow, dude, you are looking right dapper with that new haircut," he says.

"Unca Dom got one, too," Matthew says, running his palm over his head for the millionth time. This garners me a questioning look from Hurley and I nod.

"Dad," Emily says, "check out the house. A cleaning lady came today. You won't believe how good it looks."

Hurley puts Matthew down on the floor and scans the room. "It looks clean, all right," he says, though not as enthusiastically as I would have liked.

"All the beds have fresh sheets on them, all the laundry has been washed, dried, and folded, the bathrooms are cleaned, the vacuuming is done, even the floors are gleaming," I say, trying to get him to feel the same level of excitement I do.

"Even *my* room is clean," Emily says with great drama. "It's amazing!"

The general enthusiasm in the room isn't getting to Hurley, and I fear he's still having doubts about the hiring of a cleaning person.

"Can we have pizza delivered for dinner tonight?" Emily asks. "The kitchen looks too nice to mess it up by cooking."

"Fine by me," I say with a chuckle. I grab my purse and hand Emily my wallet. "Will you call and order it?"

"Consider it done."

"*Consider it done,*" Matthew echoes.

I take Hurley by the hand and lead him upstairs, ostensibly to show him the results of Dottie's ministrations, but also so we can talk in private. Once I have him in our bedroom, I say, "What's bothering you?"

"Harrison Dixon called me."

"He did? What did he say?"

"He said he wanted to apologize for what was likely an overreaction on his part. He offered to fax me papers to prove his business is legit and he has a backup fund, an escrow, as insurance."

"And did he fax the paperwork?"

Hurley nods. "It looks legit. It shows the opening of an escrow account in the name of Vic Bagman with a tax ID number and signatures from 2005. He also sent an attached statement for the account dated today that shows a balance of a mil and change. Harrison said the account has had bigger balances before, but he uses it to cover some of his clients' losses. He also sent a document signed by Monty back in 2005, when he opened his own brokerage, that gives Harrison power of attorney over his brother's finances."

"They're all legit?" I ask.

Hurley shrugs. "They look to be, on the surface. I sent them to Arnie so he can look them over, but without being able to examine a transaction history, there isn't much we can do here. I tried to verify the balance in the escrow account, but the banks are closed. I'll try again in the morning."

"They don't prove anything," I say. "And there's still the matter of the timing of his arrival at Monty's house. I don't know . . . there's something about the guy that feels wrong to me. And those other clients of his that turned up dead. Hurley, the guy could have killed several people. There has to be a way to prove that."

He nods slowly and then yawns. "This case and the heat are wearing me out," he says. "Let's sleep on it and take a fresh look in the morning."

CHAPTER 29

After eating our pizza, we spent the evening playing with Matthew and chatting with Emily, relaxed in knowing that the housework was all caught up. It was the most consistent family time we'd been able to enjoy in months. When Hurley and I went to bed, I reveled in the smell and feel of the clean sheets.

"You're more relaxed tonight than I've seen you in ages," Hurley had said. "If that's what having someone come to clean the house does for you, then I have to say it's worth every penny spent, and then some."

"Those might be some of the sexiest words I've ever heard from you," I told him, and then I kissed him . . . several times. One thing led to another and we shared some of the best sex we've had in a long time, and that's saying a lot, because it's always great with Hurley and me. Sated, relaxed, and happy, I fell into a deep, dreamless, and uninterrupted sleep. Thank goodness the Grim Reaper remained on sabbatical.

Now, as I head downstairs to get my morning cup of coffee, already showered and dressed for the day, I feel a new spring in my step. Even the coffee machine has been cleaned and I swear my morning java tastes better as a result. Hurley is looking quite chipper this morning as well, and the overall mood in our household is one of happy contentment. Even Matthew appears to be feeling it. He dresses in normal clothes, eats his breakfast without complaint, and nothing anyone says or does triggers one of his meltdowns.

Emily is the first one to leave the house as she heads off for school, and Hurley is next, stating that he wants to get an early start. I hang back and spend a little extra time with Matthew and Hoover, playing ten minutes of fetch in the backyard before we leave the house. It's already in the low eighties and this amount of play is enough that I feel like I could use another shower already.

When I drop Matthew off with Dom, Izzy is there getting ready to leave. Dom has just taken a coffee cake out of the oven, and while he's tied up in the other room with the kids, Izzy and I both eye the cake greedily. By some unspoken agreement, Izzy turns and gets two forks, two plates, and a knife out. Then he cuts and serves us each a piece of the cake. "How did your cleaning person do?" he asks, preparing to take a bite.

"Oh, it's fantastic!" I tell him around the bite I've already taken. As it is with everything Dom makes, the cake is melt-in-your-mouth delicious. "I can't believe how great the house looked, how relaxed and relieved I felt when I got home, and how happy it has made me. I know it sounds petty, but this one little thing meant a lot to me, more than I realized. Even Hurley had to admit that it was a nice change. And I thought Emily might be upset that someone had been in her room rooting through her things, but she was ecstatic, too. It may be the best decision I've made since I married Hurley."

"That's great," Izzy says with a smile and another bite of cake. "I'm happy for you."

"Thanks."

"Anything new on our cases?"

"Not really." I give him a brief rundown of our visit with Harrison Dixon yesterday. "But then Harrison faxed a bunch of paperwork to Hurley last night that seems to corroborate much of his story. I'm not fully convinced yet. I'm going to run up to Arnie's lab and look at the forms myself. Hurley and I were thinking that if we could find more of Harrison's investors, we could convince them to do a run on their funds and panic Harrison into doing something stupid, but we're not sure how to find them."

"He's a lawyer, right?"

"Yes."

"Does he work alone?"

"No, he has a receptionist, or a paralegal. I'm not sure what she is." I pause and my eyes widen. "Of course!" I say. "If we can play her somehow, maybe she'll give up the names."

"Worth a try," Izzy says.

"You are brilliant." I scrape the last bite of cake off my plate and into my mouth, and then set my dish in the sink. "I'm off to see Arnie. Let's hope the death lull continues."

When I get to the office and head upstairs to Arnie's lab area, I'm happy to see that Joey is there again.

"I was just about to call your husband," Arnie says. "I've got something on Harrison Dixon."

"Do tell."

"It was Joey who figured it out," Arnie says, making Joey blush. "Thanks to him, I can prove that the documents giving Harrison power of attorney for his brother's finances, and the paperwork establishing his supposed escrow fund, are fakes."

"How?"

Arnie bows to Joey with a flourishing gesture. "Tell her, Joey."

"The letters are wrong," he says. "They don't match the dates." He beams a smile at me.

I return it, even though I'm clueless as to what he's trying to say. Arnie puts me out of my misery.

"It's the font used on the forms. It's called Calibri and it was created by someone at Microsoft, and then released as a default font for their word processing programs." He pauses, eyebrows raised, and I know he's wanting me to prompt him. Arnie loves dramatic revelations. I oblige.

"And?"

"And it was first released for use in 2007."

I get the connection immediately. "But the forms were supposedly signed in 2005," I say excitedly.

"Yes," Arnie says. "But since they are written in the Calibri font, it's impossible for them to have been signed in 2005 because that font wasn't available then."

"That's great work, Joey!" I say. I walk over and give him a big hug, which makes him beam even more. I turn back to Arnie. "Give Hurley a call and let him know."

Arnie picks up his phone and dials Hurley's number, putting the call on speaker so we all can hear. After he explains Joey's revelation, Hurley mirrors my accolades to both Arnie and Joey. When he's done, Joey looks like he's ready to burst with pride.

"Hurley, Izzy had a good idea on how to find some of Harrison's investors," I say. "What if we tried to go through his assistant, Margaret? She might be willing to give us some names if someone pretends to be an interested investor."

"That's assuming she knows about that aspect of Harrison's business," Hurley says. "And even if she does, I can't imagine her giving us that information without checking with Harrison first, and given all that has happened, I can't see him providing that information. He's bound to be suspicious."

He's right, and I can't hide my disappointment. "But if I take this fake document information and use it to try to get a search warrant, that might help. I'll have a chat with Junior and see what we can come up with."

"That gives me another idea," I tell him. "If you can get permission to access the GPS data on the cell phones Dixon uses, his own and the one for Bagman, maybe you can tie him to the locations for some or all of the murders. We know he couldn't have been at home on the night of Monty's murder, and if we can show he was in Sorenson when Taylor Copeland died, that would help. Maybe we can even connect him to the location of Doug Kincaid's death, or Xyphonia Hunter's."

"Good thinking, Squatch. I'll see what I can do."

We bid good-bye to Hurley, and after I give Joey another hug, I head back downstairs to my office. I take out the file on Monty Dixon and peruse it again, looking for something, anything, that might help us nail Harrison. I wish he had given us a chance to see inside his house the day we went there because I'm convinced that my suspicions about his Harry Potter obsession are on the mark. I think about the psychology involved in that and, on a whim, I give Summer Dixon a call.

She answers on the first ring. "Hello? Who is this?"

"Hi, Summer, it's Mattie Winston from the medical examiner's office. I wanted to ask you some questions about Harrison."

"Harrison? What for?"

"We're trying to clear up some financial information for Monty's estate," I tell her. It's not exactly the truth, but it's not a lie, either. "Did you know that Harrison had power of attorney for Monty's finances?"

Summer scoffs. "No way. Monty would never have given that kind of power to Harrison."

"How well did the two of them get along?"

"Oh, they did okay, I suppose. Like any siblings, they had their disagreements."

"Did Monty ever talk about their childhood with you?"

"Some. He and Harrison were close when they were kids, though Harrison spent a lot of time trying to compete with Monty."

"Compete how?"

"Schoolwork and social lives. Monty had the outgoing personality and he did well in school. He loved science and math, and his mom said once that she always thought he'd grow up to be an engineer or a scientist of some sort. She was surprised when he chose to go for a business degree."

"What about Harrison?"

"School wasn't easy for him. I remember his mom mentioning that she was always getting calls from his teachers because Harrison spent so much time daydreaming and not doing his work. Monty was the more intellectual one and the more social one. Harrison has always been something of a loner, preferring to spend his evenings with his nose in a sci-fi or fantasy novel rather than socializing."

"Yet Harrison made it through law school. That couldn't have been easy."

"Yeah, Monty said Harrison struggled some, but he got through it and got his degree. He didn't attend a prestigious college or anything like that, but he did okay."

"Did the two of them argue much as adults?"

"Not really, though Monty did tell me that when they were younger, they had a big falling-out over Linda."

"Linda? You mean Monty's first wife?"

"Yeah, go figure," Summer says with a laugh. "Hard to believe that shrew could nab the interest of one man, much less two. Harrison met and dated Linda first, but when she met Monty, she tossed Harrison aside and never looked back. Linda got pregnant two months later and she and Monty got married. Harrison was livid, according to Monty. Monty told me they even had a fistfight over it. Once Monty and Linda got married, Harrison wouldn't speak to either of them. They were estranged for years. Harrison got married during that time, but Monty said it was doomed from the start because it was a rebound thing. Just Harrison trying once more to compete with his brother."

"The brothers eventually worked things out, I take it?"

"Sure. They made up around the time that Monty decided to open his own brokerage. He needed some legal advice and didn't want to fork over a lot of money to get it, so he made nice with his brother and offered to work with him. When Monty and Linda split up, Harrison helped him with the divorce."

"Do you think Harrison held a grudge?"

"Against Monty? No, I don't think so. Why? What's this got to do with Monty's estate?" she asks, her voice rising. "Did Harrison mess with Monty's money somehow? Because if he did something—"

"I can't discuss that," I tell her. "Thanks for the information. I have to go, but I'll be in touch." With that, I disconnect the call before Summer can get herself worked up into a tizzy.

CHAPTER 30

In deference to the furnace outside, I opt to stay in the office and call the local sandwich shop to get lunch delivered. Hurley calls me at three with an update.

"I was able to convince a judge to put a hold on the account Harrison sent us the information on," he says. "Turns out that statement he sent us was fake. There's only a little over fifty grand in the account. He doctored that statement. And I had Junior Feller call Harrison's office and talk to Margaret. He pretended to be someone from the Securities Exchange and said he was investigating some shady dealings with some stock trades Harrison had made and wanted the names of some of his investors. He swore her to silence and said that if she told Harrison we were looking into his activities that she could be arrested and tried as an accomplice. Margaret caved and said she would have to sneak into Harrison's office to get the information, once he left for lunch, and would call him back. We weren't sure she would, but Junior apparently scared her enough because she called back a little over an hour later and gave him the names of a dozen of Harrison's investors. We were able to reach six of them and all six agreed to call the Bagman number and demand that their funds be withdrawn immediately."

"That is brilliant," I say, smiling at the thought of Harrison's reaction when he got those messages. "Let me know what happens."

"Junior and I are going to hang here at the station this evening to see what shakes out," he says. "I'll grab dinner here."

"Okay. Keep me posted."

I do another hour's worth of work and then decide to call it a day. I check in with Izzy, who says he's going to head home himself soon, and then I brace myself for my reentry into the furnace outside. I take the elevator down to the garage and breathe a small sigh of relief. It's stifling in the garage, but the underground location and darkness have kept it a smidge cooler than the rest of the air. I sit for a minute with the windows cracked and let the air-conditioning blow out the residual heat in the interior of the hearse before pulling out into the blazing late-afternoon sun.

When I get to Dom and Izzy's place to pick up Matthew, Dom invites me to join him in the kitchen for an iced tea, while the kids play in the living room. Dom makes his own iced tea in an assortment of flavors and today's is raspberry and lemon. I slide onto a stool at their kitchen counter and take three big gulps. It's cool, delicious, and refreshing.

"Oh, wow," I say when I've swallowed. "That hit the spot. Thanks."

"You're welcome."

"I can't believe you find the time to make this, while caring for the kids and Sylvie, and doing all the household stuff on top of it." I hold my glass up to him and add, "You are who I want to be when I grow up."

He smiles, clicks my glass with his, and we both drink.

"How was Matthew today?" I ask when I've nearly drained my glass.

"Excellent. He's been in an extra good mood today."

"Glad to hear it. He was very well behaved this morning, too."

"Something he ate?" Dom asks, and even though I know he's kidding, there is something I think might have made a difference.

"You know, I had extra time to play with him last night, thanks to the wonderful ministrations of our housecleaner, Dottie. I can't help but wonder if the extra attention Matthew got last night made a difference in his temperament today. Maybe his acting-out behavior is his way of getting more attention from us. I suppose any attention, even negative, is better than none."

Dom concedes my point with a nod. "You might be onto something," he says. "He got lots of extra attention from Juliana today, too. She kept rubbing his head. She likes the feel of it."

I chuckle and lift my damp hair off my neck. "With this weather as hot as it is, I'm a little jealous of the two of you."

"I can fix you up in a flash," Dom says with a wink. "I've got the clippers in the bathroom. Snip-snip, buzz-buzz, and you, too, can be a cool cat." He makes a cutting motion with his fingers and then mimes running the razor while he says this.

"Thanks, but I'll pass. For now. But if this global-warming stuff gets any worse, I might take you up on it."

I finish my tea, thank Dom again, and then load Matthew up in the hearse. The fierce heat beating down on us helps me decide that takeout is once again called for. The idea of turning on the stove makes my fingernails sweat.

"What would you like for dinner tonight?" I ask Matthew, looking at him in the backseat via the rearview mirror.

He scrunches up his face in thought and then hollers out, "Pasketti!"

"Pasketti it is," I say, always happy to eat Italian. I drive to our favorite Italian restaurant in town, Pesto Change-o, and park out front. Since I haven't called ahead, it's going to take fifteen or twenty minutes to get our order filled, and that amount of time in a restaurant with a toddler can be challenging. So, once I've placed my order with Giorgio—restaurant owner and amateur magician—I decide to break the rules and have dessert before dinner.

Matthew and I settle in at a small table and I order bowls of ice cream for us both. This tickles Matthew no end, and he giggles and fidgets his way through his bowl, ending up with as much of the ice cream on him as in him. When our order is ready, I apologize to Giorgio for the messy condition of our table and Matthew's seat, and leave him a generous tip as recompense. Then I carry the large bag of food in one hand and grab Matthew's sticky paw with my other.

When we get to the car, I open the back door and reach over Matthew's car seat to set the food on the other side of it, and then I help Matthew climb in and get buckled up, using a container of wet wipes I keep on the floor of the backseat to clean his face and hands the best I can. When I'm done, I shut the door and head around to the driver's door. No sooner am I settled into the driver's seat when the front passenger door opens, and someone gets in the hearse.

I stare at Harrison Dixon with confusion and irritation.

"Don't look surprised and don't say a word. Start the car and drive," he says in a low, calm voice. He's holding a briefcase in his left hand and he sets it on the floor between his feet.

I give him a look of incredulity. "Get out of my car."

He thrusts his right arm in my direction, his hand low, and that's when I see the gun. Fear and anger surge through me.

"Start the car," he says again. "Or I'll use this on that little guy in the back."

That threat flips a switch in my brain. In a low but menacing voice, I say, "If you harm so much as a single hair on my kid's head, you're going to be wearing your testicles as a hat." I glance in the mirror to see if Matthew is aware of what's going on and the absurd thought that there isn't any hair on his head to harm leaps to mind.

"Drive," Harrison says, and I can tell from the look in his eyes that he means business.

I start the car, if for no other reason than to keep us from baking to death in it. I back out of my parking space, looking over my shoulder at Matthew as I do so and giving him a reassuring smile.

"Where to?" I say to Harrison.

"Head out to Monty's house."

I turn out of the parking lot and head out of town. "What are you doing, Harrison? This is crazy."

"What's crazy is that you people think you can stop me from taking what's rightfully mine."

"You mean the money you've been scamming from people?"

"I didn't scam anyone. I invested their money. They knew the risks."

"And what are you doing now? Why that?" I say, nodding toward the gun.

"I did my homework," Harrison says. "You and that cop are married."

"What makes you think that?"

"I did some digging around and found a marriage license. I'm a divorce attorney, remember? Plus, I followed you. I saw that nice house you have out in the country and watched you and your cop hubby being all cozy with the kid last night. You should get some curtains for your windows."

The thought of Harrison lurking around outside our house, watching us through the windows, sends a chill down my spine.

"Yeah, so we're married. What of it?"

"I'm guessing it was that hubby of yours that put a hold on my bank account, and I need that money. I'm thinking he'll be willing to release the hold on it and Monty's account if he thinks your lives depend on it. If he gives me enough time to wire the money to my accounts in the Caymans and then disappear, you and the kid will be fine. If not . . ." He waves the gun at me.

I have reached the turnoff to the Dixon house and pull in, driving through the police tape stretched across the entrance to the drive. When I reach the house, I pull up in front, on the circular drive by the fountain. I shift the car into park, but leave the engine running so the air will stay on.

"What's the deal with this car anyway?" he asks me, making a face. "Do you drive a hearse because you use it for work?"

"No, I drive it because it was the car I could afford at the time I bought it, and I've since grown fond of it."

"It's creepy," he says.

"Maybe to some," I observe. The feeling of security I typically have inside my reinforced hearse is negated by the fact that the madman is now in the car with me. If I can find a way to get him out of the car and keep me and Matthew inside, we might be okay. "What now?" I ask.

Harrison looks at the front door of the house, which is crisscrossed with police tape. "Now we go inside. But first give me your cell phone."

I reach into my pocket and remove my phone, handing it to him. He turns it off and shoves it into his pants pocket. I notice that he's once again wearing a long-sleeved shirt despite the heat and I see an ugly yellow stain on the sleeve of his right arm in the area where he usually scratches. Desperate to buy some time so I can think of a way out of this mess, I nod toward his arm and say, "Is your psoriasis flaring up?"

He looks at me like I asked him if he has herpes. "Psoriasis?"

I nod toward the stain on his arm and he stares at it for a second.

"It's a sore. No big deal."

"It looks like it's infected."

He stares down at the spot and prods it with a finger, wincing as he does so. "It will be fine."

"I'm hungry," Matthew says from the backseat. "I want my pasketti."

"Pretty soon, kiddo," I say with a smile.

Harrison aims the gun toward the back of his seat, which is right in front of Matthew. "Turn the car off, get out, and get the kid out. That food you have back there smells good. Grab it, too. No funny business or I pull the trigger."

I see no recourse other than to do what he said, so I get out and walk around the car to Matthew's door. I open it, lean in, and grab the bag of food first, setting it on the ground at my feet. Then I undo Matthew's straps and take him by the hand. "Come on, kiddo."

Matthew, who thankfully seems oblivious to what's going on, scrambles out of the car. "Whose house is this?" he asks.

"A friend's," I say.

Harrison gets out of the car, bringing the briefcase with him, the gun held in his other hand down by his leg. He looks like he's trying to hide the gun from Matthew, and that gives me some small modicum of hope. He gestures toward the front door and says, "Go on in."

I walk Matthew up to the door and pull down the police tape there. When I turn the knob, nothing happens. The house is, of course, locked. I turn to tell Harrison this, but he has already put down the briefcase and reached into his pocket, coming out with a key.

"You have a key to the house?" I say.

He shrugs and hands it to me. "Monty gave me one years ago."

I unlock the door and we head inside. The house has a faint, lingering odor of old blood, which makes me wrinkle my nose. I steer Matthew toward the kitchen and set the food bag on the island.

"We need to go into Monty's office," Harrison says.

I'm desperate to get Matthew as far away from this nutjob as I can. Harrison is a killer, multiple times if my theory is right, but I'm hoping he has some vestige of humanity left in him that will make him balk at hurting a child. I give him a pleading look.

"Let me set Matthew up here at the island with his dinner," I say. "He's just a kid. Let him eat." Harrison considers this and I up the ante. "If I don't feed him, he's going to have a meltdown."

"Fine. But hurry up."

I remove the spaghetti from the bag and set it up on the island. After helping Matthew up onto one of the stools, I remove the lid from the aluminum pan the food is in and give him one of the plastic forks from the bag.

"You sit here and eat, okay? I don't want you to leave this spot until I come back."

Matthew pouts at me. "Where are you going?"

"Just to another room. I won't be far away. If you need me, you just call me, okay?"

I pray that Matthew's good behavior will continue, and he'll do as he's told. If he chooses to have one of his little tantrums now, I shudder to think what might happen. I watch his facial expression as he weighs his options and silently plead with him.

"Okay," he says finally, and I let out the breath I didn't realize I was holding.

"Good boy," I say, giving him a kiss on the head. As he digs into the spaghetti, I turn and head down the two hallways leading to Monty's home office.

Harrison follows me, and once we're there, he sets down the briefcase he's been carrying and takes out what looks like a burner phone from his other pants pocket. He hands it to me and says, "Turn it on. When I tell you, I want you to call your husband and figure out a way to get him to release the hold on my account without letting him know what's going on. I need a little time to get away. Once I can transfer the funds, I'll tie you up and call your hubby to let him know where you are, once I'm safely away."

I don't believe this story for a minute, but I have no choice but to obey for now. I take the phone from him and turn it on. While it's booting up, Harrison settles into Monty's office chair and sets the gun on the desk. Then he opens the briefcase and removes a laptop. He sets it on the desk, lifts the lid, and turns it on. Once it's booted up, I watch as he connects to the house Wi-Fi—apparently, Monty gave him the password for this, as well as a key to the house.

"Your brother was a fool to trust you," I say as he launches an internet browser and navigates to the site for his bank.

"He wouldn't listen," Harrison says irritably. "I tried to explain to him that I had other accounts I needed to cover, and that the money I took from him was only gone temporarily, but he wouldn't listen. If he'd just given me a little more time, I would have been able to make it back."

"Why did you have to kill Taylor?"

He shoots me a look, but doesn't answer. I try again, with an appeal to his narcissistic personality. "That was a brilliant frame-up, by the way. One thing I couldn't figure out, though, was why you swapped printers."

Harrison frowns at that, and I guess that he didn't realize until now that we knew about that. "Monty was talking about the anonymous note he got, which I sent, by the way, and how one of the cops pointed out that there was some kind of flaw in the print that might enable them to identify the printer it came from. When I heard that, I knew that I had to use the same printer to write Taylor's suicide note so everyone would think the threatening note had come from her. But I also figured that the cops would test her printer and try to match the output to the lettering in the first note, so I swapped my printer for hers." He taps his temple with one finger and grins at me. "You got to be thinking all the time to stay ahead of the game."

"Wow, that was smart. You're really good. How did you get her to take all those pills?"

He regards me with suspicion for a moment, but his ego gets the better of him. "I told her I was there on Monty's behalf, that he'd realized he'd made a mistake in firing her and wanted to make amends somehow. She invited me in to talk and I had a bottle of champagne with me to use as a peace offering. I poured us each a glass and slipped a little GHB into hers."

"The date rape drug?"

He nods. "Once it kicked in, it was easy to fix her some more drinks and get her to down them, this time with a bunch of pills crushed up in them. She did what I told her to do without hesitation."

"How did you know she had the pills?"

"I didn't," he says with a shrug. "I brought along some narcotics I bought on the street and had planned to use those, but when I saw the bottle of pills in her bathroom, I switched plans. I'm good at thinking on my feet," he adds with self-congratulatory pride.

"Is that why you used the pool cue on your brother?"

Harrison's smug smile disappears. "That was more of a spur-of-the-moment thing. I got to the house right after Sawyer left. I saw him go tearing out of the driveway as I was coming down the road. I really didn't want to kill Monty, but he simply refused to see reason. I wanted to give him one more chance to see things my way, to trust me to make good for him. If he didn't, I was going to shoot him and hide the gun in Sawyer's suite somewhere. If Sawyer was home, I'd planned to shoot him, too, and make it look like a suicide. I knew Summer wouldn't be there. She was never home in the evenings after she started sleeping with that cook."

Some puzzle pieces fall into place in my mind. "The gun, it was Taylor's?"

"Yeah. I knew she had one. Monty told me. I figured if I used it to kill Monty, and Sawyer, if need be, that it would be traced back to her, the cops would find her dead with that suicide note, and that would be the end of it."

He pauses and sighs. "When I got here to the house, I found Monty in the poolroom practicing some shots. I saw the broken cue stick and he told me about the argument he'd had with Sawyer. Then he asked me if the money was back in his account. He expected me to put it back right away, and I tried to explain to him that I couldn't return it yet, but that I would. He wouldn't listen and then he went berserk. He started screaming at me and telling me that he was going to report me to the cops, see to it that I went to prison. We got into a bit of a tussle and he shoved me back toward the pool table. I pulled the gun and fired it, but the damned thing jammed. Monty knocked it from my hand, and it went flying. Then he came at me. I grabbed the only thing I could, that broken cue stick, and held it in front of me, hoping to make him back off, but he just kept coming, and..." He shrugs. "You know the rest. In the end, it was probably best that it happened that way. No ties to me at all, and since Sawyer fought with his father and broke the cue stick, well..." He shrugs again and goes back to what he was doing on the computer.

"Why did you take the gun? Why not leave it there? Then the cops might have assumed a scenario exactly as it happened, but with Taylor instead of you."

He looks at me like I'm an idiot. "Taylor wouldn't have left it behind, because it could have been traced back to her. I was going to put it back in her house, but I didn't want to risk going back there. Besides, I figured I might need a gun, and once I took it apart and cleaned it, it worked just fine."

He starts to turn back to the computer, and I say, "Did you

kill Xyphonia Hunter and Doug Kincaid to hide the money you lost for them?"

Clearly, Harrison wasn't expecting this question, because he spins toward me in the chair and gapes at me.

I see something shift in his face and fear I've gone too far, so I quickly shift directions. "Are you ready for me to call now?"

He stares at me for an uncomfortable amount of time before saying, "Not yet." He goes back to the computer and I use his distraction to look around the office for something, anything, I can use as a weapon. There is a pencil holder on the far side of the desk with a pair of scissors in it, and on the bookshelf behind me, I see those heavy stone bookends shaped like houses.

"Okay," Harrison says. "Time to make your call. Don't use hubby's cell phone number. Go through the main phone line at the police station. And put it on speaker."

CHAPTER 31

I dial the police station number, hit the speaker icon, and when Heidi the dispatcher answers, I ask for Hurley. Heidi greets me cheerily and then transfers my call. The phone rings four times and I fear Hurley isn't in his office, but then he finally answers.

"Detective Hurley."

"Hey, Steve," I say, using his first name, something I almost never do. I'm hoping that will get his radar up.

"Hey, Squatch. What's up?"

I see Harrison smirk when he hears the nickname Hurley uses for me.

"Listen, I've been thinking about the Dixon case and what you did with Harrison's bank account. I think you should remove the hold you placed on it and on Monty's account."

There is the briefest hesitation before he says, "Why?"

"It might make him too desperate. We know what he's capable of and I'm afraid that if we push him too far, he'll lash out and hurt someone else. Just monitor the account, and if he tries to pull the money out, you'll know he's about to run and you can arrest him."

Hurley is silent for longer this time, and I can tell he's trying to parse my request. Then he says, "We'd have to find him first. I sent Peter Carlisle up to Black River Falls last night to keep an eye on Harrison, but he hasn't been in his office or his house. He may have flown the coop already."

"Steve, I really think you need to release that hold. Harrison is a desperate man. And maybe it will help you track him if he does go after the money." I start to pace, feeling the tension in the air as I struggle to figure out a way to let Hurley know what's going on without coming right out and saying it. I don't want this situation to deteriorate to the point of Harrison bargaining with Hurley and threatening the lives of Matthew and me in the process. I know Hurley well enough to know he'll go off the deep end if that happens and things could escalate quickly. And badly. "Please?" I say in my best pleading voice.

There is another brief hesitation before Hurley answers, and I know his radar is working now. "Are you really that worried about what Harrison will do?" he says.

"I really am. So, will you do it for me? Please?" I've managed to wander over by the area of the desk where the pencil holder is, but Harrison is watching me like a hawk.

"Can I think about it?" Hurley asks.

I grimace at this and Harrison gives me a look that says: *Now or never.*

"Damn it, Steve, can't you just do this one thing for me?" I say angrily. "I don't want another death on my conscience."

"All right, fine," he shoots back. "I'll do it right now."

"Thank you," I say in a calmer voice. "And I'm sorry I snapped at you. I got your favorite dish from Pesto Change-o. What time do you think you'll be home for dinner?"

Another hesitation, but it's so brief I don't think Harrison noticed. Since Hurley already told me that he wouldn't be home for dinner, this is one more way for me to let him know that something is up. And since Harrison presumably left a vehicle at Pesto Change-o, it gives Hurley a landmark. Then I realize it's the wrong one. I need him here first. *Now.* My brain scrambles as I try to think of a way to let him know where we are. And then I hit on one.

"I can be home within the hour," Hurley says.

"Oh, good. I'll keep your food warm for you. And I got rid of those lilacs Emily put on the table yesterday. I forgot how much you hate the smell of those flowers. It's amazing how fragrant they are. I swear I can still smell them here in the house, even though I took them out to the trash this morning."

Harrison sets the gun down and starts typing on the laptop keyboard.

"Thanks for that. I'll have Junior call the bank right away and release that hold. Okay?"

"Thanks, Steve. I'll see you later." With that, I disconnect the call and watch Harrison as he tries to type on the laptop. He's favoring that right arm and having trouble manipulating the fingers of that hand on the keyboard. I eye the gun, which is across the desk from where I'm standing. By the time I could reach over and try to grab it, Harrison might beat me to it, even with his gimpy arm. The scissors, however, are directly in front of me.

Harrison is intently focused on the laptop screen, jabbing irritably at the keyboard. "Come on, come on," he mutters.

I reach down and grasp the handles on the scissors, lifting them slowly so as not to rattle the other items in the holder. My hands are sweating and I'm afraid the thing will slip from my grasp. Or that Harrison will look up suddenly and see what I'm doing. I finally manage to get the scissors free and I quickly stick them in the back waistband of my pants.

No sooner have I done this than Harrison looks up at me, his face thunderous. "He isn't releasing it," he says. He glances frantically at his watch. "He needs to do it now, before the bank closes!"

"Give it a little more time," I say. "They have to call the bank and speak to the appropriate person, and then there are a few hoops to jump through. Try it again."

I walk around to stand by his left side and peer at the computer screen. He jabs harder at the keyboard and then he pounds his left fist on the desktop. He whirls around in the chair to face me, an enraged expression on his face.

"He's not doing it!" he yells, spittle flying from his lips.

I realize it's now or never. I reach behind me, grab the scissors, and then plunge them with all my might into his right arm where the yellow stain is on his sleeve. I feel the blades hit something hard and I'm not sure if it's bone or if I've gone all the way through his arm to the desktop.

Harrison bellows like a raging bull and reels back, the chair spinning to face forward. His right arm flails back, the scissors still embedded, and I see the gun go flying off the desk and onto the floor. I reel around and take a step toward the bookcase, grabbing the heavy stone bookend with both hands. I swing it as hard as I can at Harrison's head.

Harrison sags in the chair, a moan emanating from him. The chair swivels away from me and he slumps forward, falling onto the floor. He lands on top of the gun and I waste a precious few seconds debating whether I should try to go for it. But Harrison isn't knocked out. He's moving, and that means I need to move, too.

I turn and run from the room, dashing down the hall and turning toward the kitchen. I see Matthew right where I left him—bless him—and I run up and wrap an arm around his waist, hoisting him off the stool. He gives me a startled look, and as I turn toward the door, he reaches down and grabs his container of spaghetti. I run as fast as I can, hearing my son whimper. Somewhere in my flight, he drops the spaghetti, but not before the two of us end up wearing most of it.

"We need to hide, Matthew," I say. "Hide-and-seek. Quiet now."

I get to the door, fling it open, and make a mad dash to the hearse. I open the driver's-side door and toss Matthew and his spaghetti across the bench seat toward the passenger side. Then I climb in behind the wheel and shut the door, hitting the power lock button. It's like an oven inside the car, but the keys are still in the ignition. I turn it over and the engine roars to life, along with the blessed relief of the air-conditioning.

I see motion from the corner of my eye and turn to see Harrison stagger out the front door, the gun aimed at us, blood smeared on his head, his face, his arm, his shirt. The look on his face is a murderous one. I consider shifting the car and trying to drive, but that gun is pointed right at me and I'm afraid to stay upright. What if the bulletproof glass doesn't work? I need to duck, but I don't dare set the car in motion if I can't see where I'm going, unless Matthew is secured somehow. There isn't time. Harrison is mere feet away, the gun aimed through the windshield right at my head.

"We have to hide, Matthew," I say. I grab him and pull him down on the seat and then stretch my body over his. Then I say a silent prayer that the reinforcements Hurley added to the hearse years ago are as good as he said they were.

I hear Harrison bellowing, "You bitch!" and then I hear the first bullet fire and hit the windshield. The glass shatters out in a circle on the outside of the windshield, but it doesn't penetrate to the inside. Matthew starts to cry.

"It's okay, honey," I say to him. "It's just a game of hide-

and-seek. The man is making a lot of loud noises to scare us so he can see where we're hiding. Just stay quiet and stay down and we'll win, okay?"

Another bullet hits the windshield with the same result. I hear Harrison's feet scuffling toward the passenger-side window, toward Matthew! I raise my head up just enough to see him standing right outside the window, the gun raised and ready to fire. I wrap myself over my son and wait, but nothing happens. I look up and see Harrison staring off to his left, a worried look on his face. A second later, I hear what he apparently does, and it's the sweetest sound in the world: sirens. I continue to lie on top of Matthew, supporting my weight with my elbows as the sirens draw closer. When I see the flash of blue on the dash from police lights, I finally risk sitting up and peering out the window.

Harrison is nowhere to be seen. Several police cars have pulled up, along with Hurley's blue pickup. A trio of uniformed officers have taken off on foot, running across the property toward the shed. I gather Harrison has fled that way and I tell Matthew he can sit up now.

Hurley rushes over to the car and I hit the power lock button, releasing all the doors. Hurley whips open the front passenger door, takes one look at us, and in a panicked voice says, "Oh, no! You've been hit?"

I'm puzzled by his panic and his question, until I realize that he thinks the spaghetti sauce covering us is blood. "No, we're okay. It's just spaghetti sauce."

Matthew raises his arms up toward his father and says, "We winned, Daddy! We played hide-and-seek and we winned!"

Hurley gathers his son up and gives him a huge hug, spaghetti sauce and all. "That's great, buddy," he says, his arms wrapped around Matthew's body, tears of relief in his eyes. He looks at me over Matthew's shoulder and smiles. Then he mouths, *I love you.*

I open my door, get out, and hurry over to the two of them. Hurley uses one arm to pull me in, and I wrap my arms around them both. "I love you guys," I say, and then I start to cry.

We stay that way for a long minute and then Matthew starts to squirm.

"Don't cry, Mammy," he says, one hand swiping at a tear on my cheek. "We winned!"

Yes, we did.

CHAPTER 32

It's been three months since that horrible experience.

Harrison Dixon was caught by the police officers pursuing him, but not until he'd given them a merry chase across the countryside. By the time they found him, he was sweating profusely and complaining of chest pains, so they had to take him to the hospital. There they discovered that the sore on his arm was horribly infected and caused by a wood sliver that had been driven deep into his skin. When that sliver was removed, no one was surprised to discover it was the missing piece from the cue stick that had been used to kill Monty.

Once investigators started talking to him, Harrison's narcissistic personality kicked in and he provided exquisite details in a boasting manner, ostensibly to show off his great intellect. He not only confessed to the murders of the four people we suspected him of doing—his brother, Taylor Copeland, Xyphonia Hunter, and Doug Kincaid—but two others that we knew nothing about.

We discovered his car was a black Cadillac SUV, and when it was taken in as evidence, they found damage that tied him to the hit-and-run death of Xyphonia. As for Doug Kincaid, Harrison told the cops he arranged a meeting with him, saying that he represented a student who had a great new tech device he knew Doug would love. When they got together, Harrison spiked Kincaid's drink with GHB and then continued feeding him alcohol-based drinks. He had already scoped out the hilltop spot above the lake a couple of days before and hidden a bicycle nearby. When he had Kincaid barely able to function, he drove his car out to the spot, put Kincaid in the driver's seat, buckled him in, and put the car in drive. A small push was all it took to send it down the hill, and Harrison then bicycled back home.

Much as I hate to admit it, Harrison really was extraordinarily clever in his schemes. They were well planned and creative. It's a shame his intellect was attached to such a twisted psyche. We found Taylor Copeland's printer in Harrison's house, and he hadn't bothered to wipe it down. Her fingerprints were all over it. We also discovered that Harrison's crime spree went back further than anyone suspected. He's been juggling accounts and hiding money from his investors for nearly two decades, tempering his losses and expenditures by securing enough new clients to placate the disgruntled existing ones and moving money around. But while he might have had the Midas touch in the beginning of his investment efforts, he lost it later when everything he touched went south.

It was out of desperation that he killed his first client, a wealthy, divorced woman near Milwaukee with a penchant for gambling that rivaled Sawyer's. She had already burned through most of her inheritance, so it came as no surprise to anyone that she opted to commit suicide by shooting herself in the head after she drained her investment account and apparently lost that money, too. Harrison had staged the suicide after shooting the woman, and he got lucky in that the police investigating the death assumed the victim had gambled the investment money away, since they had reports of her frequent visits to the casino.

The ability to take that money free and clear emboldened Harrison. It also carried him for a while, until he once again found himself having to placate an angry client whose account he had stripped. This one he staged as an accidental slip-and-fall down a steep set of concrete steps. Harrison had represented the man in his divorce and helped the guy hide the investment account from the soon-to-be ex-wife. Harrison also knew his client was on a blood thinner for a heart condition and one good whack on the back of his head with a rock caused bleeding in the man's brain that killed him. Since no one associated with the victim knew about the account, it was easy for Harrison to keep the money he stole from it.

Harrison spent his clients' money on things such as trips overseas, a boat, flying lessons, and he even bought himself a plane. He used the forged paperwork giving him power of attorney for his brother to sell the Caribbean island vacation home Monty had bought, and when that money ran out, he raided his brother's investment account as well. He thought he could get away with it, but when he felt us closing in on him, he tried to get back the money he'd returned to Monty's account—all that he had left—so he could flee. He planned to use the plane he bought to make his getaway, once Hurley freed the money up, and despite what he said, I'm convinced he would have killed me and Matthew if that had happened.

Rather than facing prison for life, with no chance of parole, he has accepted a plea deal in exchange for his confessions. Harrison will be eligible for parole after thirty years. If he lives that long, he will be in his seventies, and while I suppose he will be relatively harmless by then, the idea that he might one day get out of prison bothers me. Hurley has assured me that no parole board will let him out, given that he killed multiple people, but I'm not convinced.

Sawyer likely won't inherit the money that mysteriously reappeared in Monty's investment account when Harrison put it there to try to stave off curiosity, but he did inherit many of Monty's debts. If he sells off the assets to Monty's real estate business, he might break even, but he'll be left penniless. He is back living with his mother, who has forced him into rehab for his gambling addiction. Maribel has moved on to greener pastures, where thugs don't snip off people's fingers. Junior Feller tried his best to get something on Ringo Zimmerman, the loan shark that arranged for Maribel's extreme manicure, but the guy has so far proven as bulletproof as the hearse's windows. Zimmerman's associate that was caught isn't talking, no doubt because he's afraid of losing something more than a finger.

Summer was left with the house, which was mortgaged to the hilt, and she recently listed it for sale because she can't make the payments. She has since left the area for parts unknown, though I'm sure she's on the hunt for a new sugar daddy.

Damien Cook remains in town and is presumably still providing "cooking classes" to some of the ladies in the area.

Matthew has come through the ordeal at the Dixon house unscathed. To him, it was a great adventure and a unique game of hide-and-seek that he enjoyed. The hearse did not come through unscathed, but after some discussion, Hurley and I decided to invest the funds to restore it to its previous impervious state, given that it saved the lives of Matthew and me. I've developed an affection for that vehicle that's hard to explain.

I've also developed an affection for Dottie that I think makes her uncomfortable. The woman has made a huge difference in my life with her twice-weekly visits, and life in our household is calmer, happier, and much more relaxed as a result. Even Hurley has come around to the idea, after seeing what a difference Dottie's efforts have made. I found a financial advisor and have put some of my divorce money into an account that is currently earning well, helping to mitigate some of the cost for Dottie's services. And the simple task of hiring Dottie has eliminated so much of the tension Hurley and I were feeling that Maggie has approved a suspension of our counseling for now.

Today is Matthew's third birthday and we are throwing a family party for him, said family including Izzy, Dom, Sylvie, and Juliana, of course. Dom has made Matthew a birthday cake that looks like a race car. He spent hours on it and sent me a text message picture of it this morning. It looks fabulous, but he put green frosting on the car body and, these days, Matthew isn't a fan of green. I'm afraid my son will have a meltdown over it, maybe even destroy the cake if I don't keep a close eye on him.

While I got excited over the possibility that more free time for me equated to better behavior for Matthew, that brief interlude we experienced right after Dottie started didn't last. He's back to dressing in crazy outfits, having meltdowns over certain colors, and eating weird food combos. Desi assures me he'll grow out of it. I just hope he does so before his sibling arrives, which means he has another seven months.

Life is good.

ACKNOWLEDGMENTS

There are so many people in my life to whom I owe some debt of gratitude for helping me to become a writer. There were teachers in high school who both encouraged and discouraged me. (Little did some of them know that telling me I *can't* do something motivates me most of all!) There were classes in college that educated and informed me. There were online writing groups that inspired and eviscerated me. And there were dozens of places and hundreds of folks I met during my mobile childhood that made it fun and fascinating to be a people watcher, eavesdropper, and observer of life. It helped me become the vampire I am today, greedily sucking away bits of life so I can use them to sustain me.

These days, I have a kick-ass agent in Adam Chromy (though I must give a nod to Linda Hayes for getting me started in this crazy business) and I've had editors who are smart, funny, creative, and kind. I have hardworking, behind-the-scenes people at Kensington (with special mention for Larissa Ackerman) who help bring my books to life and get them out there. And I have a network of fellow writers who not only provide camaraderie, they understand how a deadline can make you go days while shut up inside your home office without showering, wearing the same pajamas the entire time, and eating meals comprised of things like coffee, cheese slices, and jelly beans.

Best of all, I have my family, my friends, and all the health-care coworkers I've known over the years: smart, dedicated, and funny people who have been willing to brainstorm with me, cheerlead for me, publicize for me, and utter witty bon mots and hilarious zingers to me (that I then steal without guilt or remorse). There are bits and pieces of most of you (physical, emotional, and, in some cases, oh so mental!) in the characters I've created over the years, so thank you for contributing, however unwittingly, to all my Frankenstein monsters. You've not only made my writing better, but my life as a whole.

Most important, there are the thousands of readers and fans out there who are the very reason I do this crazy thing in the first place. It would all be pointless without you and I can never thank you enough. Happy reading!